• Ba

The effects of the gin had quite worn off and Alice suddenly realised that she was very cold. But the shivers that shook her had little to do with the night air. It was fright and shock and shame that caused her to huddle and tremble as if in the teeth of an easterly wind. Alice felt sick, as well. Her stomach seemed to writhing within her, coiling and uncoiling like an eel.

She would have to go upstairs, now, just as she was. There was nowhere down here for her to wash or change, not even a tap in the back yard. Oh God, if Jess should see her like this ... What could Alice tell her?

She delayed a few minutes longer, then crept upstairs. She tried to pass the sitting-room door without being heard – and trod directly on the loudest creaking floorboard in the house.

'Mam?'

The door was flung open, flooding the landing with light. Framed in the doorway stood her daughter. And behind the girl appeared a hefty, coarse-featured woman. Her name was Fitch and she lived just across the road. The sight of her made Alice want to die.

'Mam?' It was scarcely more than a whisper, now.

'I'm all right, Jess. I've had a bit of an accident. It's nothing.'

This drew a soft chuckle from Mrs Fitch.

'But how did ... '

'Leave me alone, Jess. I said I'm all right.'

'Tar and feathers,' scoffed Mrs Fitch. 'Some accident.'

Elizabeth Ann Hill was born in London in 1952 but grew up in South Wales and Cornwall where she now lives. She is the author of four previous novels.

Also by Elizabeth Ann Hill

The Eve of Clancy Fair
Gypsy Hollow
The Hidden Spring
Pebbles in the Tide

· *Bad Pennies* ·

ELIZABETH ANN HILL

Mandarin

A Mandarin Paperback

BAD PENNIES

First published in Great Britain 1993
by William Heinemann Ltd
and by Mandarin Paperbacks
imprints of Reed Consumer Books Ltd
Michelin House, 81 Fulham Road, London SW3 6RB
and Auckland, Melbourne, Singapore and Toronto

A CIP catalogue record for this book
is available at the British Library

ISBN 0 7493 1577 6

Typeset by Rom-Data Corporation Ltd, Falmouth, Cornwall

Printed and bound in Great Britain by
BPCC Paperbacks Ltd
Member of BPCC Ltd

· One ·

Alice Davey was having a lovely time. Gin and compliments, both were flowing tonight, and they were what made her happy, made her feel only half of her thirty-six years. Again and again her laughter could be heard above the buzz of talk in the crowded, smoky little bar, as she flirted with a trio of admirers.

It was not the smartest of public houses at the best of times. Here, in the last weary weeks of the Great War, it was quite run-down, with fading wallpaper, cracked linoleum on the floor, and table-tops covered in ring-marks and cigarette burns. Nevertheless, there were those who deemed it too good for Alice Davey.

Hard, intolerant eyes were watching her from behind the bar. Mrs Gwennie Bonnet, landlady, would have shown her the door, but Mr Bonnet had intervened. So now Mrs Bonnet was simmering with temper, mouth clamped tight as she rubbed a sticky patch off the counter with a wet cloth. Her husband had silenced her briefly, but Gwennie could never keep her tongue in check for long. Defiantly turning to Bonnet, she said:

'If I know anything about her, she'll have all three of them before the night's out.'

It was a strong voice and she did not trouble to lower it.

'Hush, Gwen! She'll hear you.'

'I don't care. She knows what I think – what all decent people round here think of her. We keep a respectable house and you shouldn't allow her in. Let them take her somewhere down Union Street, that's where she belongs. If it were up to me, she wouldn't be served anywhere within a mile of here.'

Union Street. Words synonymous with sin. Plymouth was famous for many great sons and great adventures – and notorious for Union Street.

Joe Bonnet pursed his mouth. The same old insult. Gwennie used it nearly every time she set eyes on Alice.

'Well, it's not up to you,' he hissed, 'so hold your noise. Just pour the drinks, take the money and keep your opinions to yourself.'

The woman opened her mouth to argue, then snapped it shut again, the thrusting lower lip twitching with anger and the pale green eyes flickering furiously over her husband's face.

'For God's sake,' sighed Bonnet, 'she's doing no harm.'

This brought forth a snort and a knowing, humourless smile. 'Hmph – you, you're just like the rest of them. You'd be there like a shot if I didn't watch you.'

Bonnet flushed and gave her a sharp shove towards the kitchen door. 'Don't start that again, either. Go and see if the pies are ready, go on.'

She went, muttering. He picked up a cloth and started polishing glasses. From the corner of his eye he still observed the object of his wife's venom. A kinder soul himself, Joe Bonnet felt not scorn but sadness when he looked at the fading woman who sat at a corner table in company with three unshaven men.

She had been pretty once, so very pretty. Alice Davey, she of the bright dark eyes and honey-coloured hair. Alice, with her fine, downy skin and rounded body. He had courted her for a while when they were young. Gwen knew that, of course, and it made her doubly vicious whenever she spoke of 'the Davey woman'.

It seemed that Alice had not heard Gwennie's remarks. She was too intent on her men friends and their jokes, and too fuddled by the drinks they kept buying for her. Watching, Bonnet wondered if she really knew or cared about the way people saw her, the way they thought and spoke of her.

'The only good thing you can say is that she doesn't take money for it,' Gwennie had once sneered.

It's your sort, Gwen, who always want something in exchange, reflected Bonnet. A ring, bed and board, new curtains, a new coat ... You never give anything away, and what you barter isn't worth much. But Alice is just the reverse, too generous for her own good, too free and – easy. She always had that air of welcome and she has it still. Men sense it and gladly avail themselves, women resent it, and both alike look down on her. Poor Alice.

Widowed now, for four years, Alice Davey kept a shop selling sweets and tobacco, and so there were always plenty of men crossing her doorstep each day. She lived just a few minutes' walk from Devonport dockyard, and half an hour from the centre of Plymouth. Here were thousands of men, here was the Navy, and to Davey's little shop they came for their pipe tobacco and cigarettes.

Some of them came for Alice, too.

As Bonnet observed, they very quickly sensed her nature. She was not given to suggestive talk or glances and her style of dress was neat and quiet. Yet, there was a look about her, something receptive, trusting and ever-hopeful. Men were a weakness with Alice, the sound and the sight and the touch of men.

In truth, her sexual adventures were fewer and milder than most people chose to imagine, her nights out ending, more often than not, with just a kiss and cuddle in the doorway of her shop. What was more, the antagonism Alice Davey roused in the women of her neighbourhood had more to do with jealousy than outraged morality. She had sampled a few of their husbands and they knew it. They knew, as well, that Alice hadn't had to do the chasing. Discontented men were apt to seek her out.

One of Alice's companions stood up and came across to order more drinks. A double tot for her, he whispered, leaning and grinning across the counter, confidential, man-to-man.

Coldly, Bonnet served him.

Alice was giggling over something one of them had said. He breathed in her face, in her ear, edging his chair ever closer, venturing a hand to her leg now and then. Smiling, she reached up for her glass as the third man returned to the table and sat down. They were all around her, like dogs round a bone.

There was something about these three, something Bonnet did not like one bit. They had come off some boat or other, probably in port for just a few days. Merchant seamen, by the look of them. The youngest one struck him as being mean-tempered, and he did not care for the ceaseless grinning of the one who had bought the last round. The biggest, a man of nearly six feet four, kept glancing at the clock on the wall and whispering to the other two. Used as he was to seeing her trip off into the night with one or more strange men, the publican hoped uneasily that Alice would not leave with them.

His wife returned from the kitchen with a platter of small meat pies and set it down hard on the counter. She was galled to be rebuked in defence of such as Alice Davey and was not prepared to leave the subject alone.

'Her sort have no business raising children,' she muttered fiercely. 'I ask you, how's that girl of hers likely to turn out, after seeing her mother carrying on with every Tom, Dick and Harry? She'll go the same way, you mark my words – probably start before she's even left school.'

'For the love of God, button your lip!'

'I don't believe she's even poor old Davey's daughter,' persisted Gwennie. 'Born seven months after they married, don't forget. That Alice just used the poor old devil when she found herself in trouble, that was all.'

Bonnet declined to answer her.

Then, nudging him, Gwennie said, 'Ah, they're going. Good thing, too.'

As the landlord had feared, they were leaving together. The men were skittish, full of an odd, disturbing excitement. One of them was smacking his lips and rubbing his hands together, as if confronted with a feast.

Even Alice, Bonnet thought, should have been too fussy to mix with types like these. He supposed it was not his business to stop her, since she seemed to like them well enough, but it grieved him to see her in the company of louts.

Alice swayed a little as she stood up. She was still giggling and her hair was coming undone. Happy, as she always was when drugged with drink and what she liked to think of as admiring male company, she linked arms with two of them and tottered out into the dark streets.

It was 1918 and the month was October. In the dockyard, work had finished for the night. Muffled up in his cap, scarf and heavy coat, a night-watchman was snoozing peacefully in the light of his brazier, a half empty mug of cocoa going cold in his hand.

But suddenly he jumped, snorted, slopping the cocoa on the ground, as a piercing scream jerked him from his doze. Bobbing to his feet, he seized his lantern and held it up, swinging it this way and that, peering into the darkness.

For a moment there was silence. Then came a second wail, followed by a series of short, panic-stricken shrieks.

At first he could not tell where they were coming from, as they echoed round the great lonely spaces of the dockyard, but at last he determined that they issued from somewhere away to his right. Taking his lantern, he followed the sound, making his way between workshops and warehouses, hurrying across tramlines and skirting dry docks. All around him the towering shapes of cranes and ships loomed against the moonlit sky. Here and there his route was lit by gas lamp standards, but long stretches of gloom lay between them. The yard at night was a place of monstrous shadows and pools of dull yellow light, yet he knew it like his own back garden. The docks were his domain and he moved swiftly over ground he had patrolled for twenty years, while the screams grew louder, closer all the time. At length the watchman paused for a few seconds beside the vast dark pit of an empty dry dock, listening intently. He could hear the woman crying now, sobbing and pleading, and his ears caught the sound of men's voices too. There was jeering male laughter and he guessed there were at least two, possibly three of them.

'Who's there?' His bark brought the sniggering to an abrupt halt. 'What's doing, eh? What's going on?'

The only answer was a frantic muttering and scrambling, followed by a clatter of running footsteps which receded swiftly into the night.

The screaming had stopped. There was still weeping, though – terrified, whimpering sobs. They were coming from behind a stack of crates.

He found his way in among the packing cases and at last the glow from his lantern revealed a huddled form. She was curled up on the ground and shivering with fright, her arms thrown over her head as if to ward off blows. At first glance the watchman thought her clothes had been torn to shreds, for pale tufts of what he took for flimsy fabric hung raggedly from her body.

Drawing nearer, stooping down, he cast the light full upon her. Her dress was certainly ripped, both skirt and bodice in tatters, but those white tufts were not bits of cloth, they were feathers. And now he smelt the tar, saw that she was daubed from head to foot. Beside her lay a small drum of pitch, overturned by the men as they fled, and also a sack, from which there spilled a few last handfuls of goose down.

The watchman uttered a few strong words. Then, kneeling down, he reached out to touch her.

'Here, now ...'

She shrieked again.

'Now, now, it's all right. Are you hurt much?'

She wriggled away from him, cowering against the packing cases, her face hidden in her hands.

'I'm the night-watchman,' he said, thinking to reassure her. 'Don't be afraid. Whoever they were, they've gone.'

She still shrank away, and so he set down his lamp on the ground and tried to turn her round towards him.

'Have they injured you?' he asked again. 'Let me look at you.'

'NO!'

The scream made him recoil for an instant. Then, taking firm hold of her wrists, he pulled her hands away from her face. It was streaked with tar. Her hair was matted, tears streamed from her eyes and the stink of the pitch was mingled with the smell of gin which came with each panting sob.

'Dear Lord,' he muttered, 'made some mess of you, didn't they? There now, there, there. Can you stand up?'

She did not answer, but covered her face again, quivering in her misery.

'Who were they?' he questioned. 'And what are you doing in here anyway, and at this time of night? Are you a ... ?' He bit off the word that had come to his mind. 'Well,' he said, awkwardly, 'even if you are, you didn't deserve this. Where do you live, eh? Come on, I'll see that you get home. Or perhaps we can find a policeman – that's if you want to report this,' he finished, doubtfully. 'Local, are you? What's your name?'

'Alice,' came the numbed whisper.

'All right then, Alice ...'

'I don't want the police,' she cut in. 'And I can't go home as I am.' She hauled herself to her feet, supported by the watchman's arm. 'My girl, my daughter, she mustn't see me like this.' Still a hair's breadth from hysteria, she started to moan and hug herself, helplessly shaking her head.

'Where else do you want to go, then? Are there any friends to help you?'

She fell silent for a long moment, then said bleakly, 'I don't want to see anyone I know.'

Now that she was standing, he saw that she was quite tall. There was no sign of blood on her, but she moved stiffly, as if every joint was sore.

'Did they beat you?'

'No,' came the dull response. 'But they flung me around between them and I fell a few times.'

'Well now, there's a doctor up in Pembroke Street.

Perhaps that's where you'd best go first, just to be on the safe side.'

She shook her head vehemently. 'No. No, I can't. His wife, she knows me.' She began to cry again.

'Look ...' he was remembering his duties now, '... I can't stand here half the night with you. Where do you want to go? Make your mind up. I'm sorry for you, but it's plain to me you've been asking for trouble. You're no innocent, I'll be bound. I'll bet they didn't have to force the gin down your throat.'

For the moment Alice was too concerned with her predicament to bother defending herself.

'Is there somewhere I can wash?' she begged.

'Everywhere's locked up.' He had had enough of her now and was anxious to be rid of her. 'The doctor, he's your best bet. It's that or go home as you are.'

There was another long pause. 'Home, then,' she said, her voice scarcely audible.

'Is it far?'

'Five minutes from the dockyard gate.'

'Fair enough. I'll take you to your door.'

'P.F. DAVEY, SWEETS AND TOBACCO' said the sign, the lettering painted in gilt against a background of dark red.

The shop had one large window, divided into six panes. In the centre was a display of briar and cherrywood pipes, with a chunky meerschaum at the forefront and a row of pipe racks behind. To one side was placed an elegant hookah, surrounded by silver vesta cases, and cigars with red and gold bands. On the other stood a cluster of large glass jars containing acid drops, mint humbugs, liquorice sticks and toffees.

Alice fumbled for her key, then turned it in the lock.

'All right now?' asked the watchman.

'Yes,' she whispered, 'thank you. I'm very grateful for your kindness.'

Recalling now those disapproving words of his, she

caught him by the arm as he made to turn away. 'You know,' she said, plaintively, 'I'm not what you may think. You see, they ...'

He did not want to listen to this. He thought he had her fairly well summed up.

'It don't matter what I think, and anyway I've got to go. My job, see.'

'Oh – yes.' She nodded, quashed. 'Thank you,' she repeated, faintly.

The man hurried away, back towards the dockyard. Alice Davey went inside, quietly bolted the door top and bottom, then leaned heavily against it. Her legs felt ready to fold beneath her. Once more, hot tears squeezed from between her eyelids, and she stood for some minutes there in the dark of the shop. A rich smell of tobacco, fudge and violet cachous came to wrap itself around her as if in sympathy and welcome, but she was not comforted.

The effects of the gin had quite worn off and Alice suddenly realised that she was very cold. She had not bothered to take a coat when she went out that mild evening, for the pub was only a few minutes' walk away. But in truth, the shivers that shook her had little to do with the night air. It was fright and shock and shame that caused her to huddle and tremble as if in the teeth of an easterly wind. Alice felt more than a little sick, as well. Her stomach seemed to be writhing within her, coiling and uncoiling like an eel.

She would have to go upstairs now, just as she was. There was nowhere down here for her to wash or change, not even a tap in the back yard. Alice fervently hoped that her daughter was in bed and fast asleep. It was well past ten, but sometimes Jess sat up to wait for her. What if she should see this? What could Alice tell her? Frantically she cast about for a plausible story, but nothing came to mind.

Well, I'm not obliged to explain, she told herself, desperately. I'll just have to tell her to mind her own business. She's only a child, after all.

A very shrewd child, replied the voice of realism. One

who'll draw her own conclusions. She knows a lot about life. How could she not, with a mother like me?

Alice delayed a few minutes longer. Then, gathering her courage, she went through to the back of the shop. From there, a staircase led to the living quarters above. At the top was a landing, giving access to the kitchen, sitting room and the two bedrooms.

Her daughter had not gone to bed. Alice reached the landing without making a sound – and saw straight away the strip of light beneath the sitting-room door. From within she heard the clank and rattle of coins in a tin.

Her money box, Alice thought. She's counting her savings again.

Tensely she stood listening. There came no call of greeting. The faint, rhythmic clink of the coins went on.

She doesn't know I'm in.

Hope surged within her. Alice glanced towards the kitchen. She could slip in there quickly, push the table against the door, boil some water, undress and get washed off. Jess would hear, of course, but Alice would not let her in, not until every trace of this filth was gone. Jess would not see, that was the important thing.

I could say I fell over on the way home, thought Alice. Fell in some horse muck. Lord knows, there's plenty of it in the streets.

Eagerly she started towards the kitchen – and trod directly on the loudest creaking floorboard in the house.

From the sitting room, her daughter's voice called:

'Mam?'

Oh, damn, damn! fumed Alice.

'I'm putting the kettle on,' she said, swiftly. 'We'll have some cocoa in a while. You shouldn't be up this late. Get to bed and I'll bring it when it's ready.'

It did not save her. She made for the kitchen, but had no chance to dart inside before the sitting-room door was flung open, flooding the landing with light. Framed in the doorway stood a girl of thirteen. Curly, amber-blonde hair tumbled loosely about her face, and her eyes were large and brown, just like her mother's. Indeed, she was almost a replica of Alice at the same age.

Like a trapped rabbit, Alice stood transfixed.

'Mam?' It was scarcely more than a whisper.

And as the girl spoke, a woman of about forty appeared behind her, a beefy, coarse-featured woman whose eyes excitedly took in the spectacle that was Alice Davey. Her name was Fitch and she lived just across the road. The sight of her made Alice want to die.

A look crossed Mrs Fitch's face, a blend of contempt and malicious mirth, the joy of a scandal-monger who had found something truly exceptional to spread around.

'I came for the money, Mrs Davey,' she said, grinning.

'Money?'

Alice could not think what she meant. Her mind was filled with a dizzying apprehension of what the Fitch woman would make of this in the days to come. With this final blow there came a vague idea that even God must be against her. Why tonight, when they seldom had callers at all? Why Mrs Fitch, of all people?

'You owe my husband eight and six for putting up that new bit of guttering over your shop front. It's three weeks since he did that job for you. Still ... ,' the scratchy voice carried a note of glee, '... I can see it's a bad time to ask you, so perhaps I'd best call again, eh? Young Jess here thought she might have enough in her money box, but she's two bob short. Anyway, not to worry just now. Mustn't trouble you tonight, so I'll be off.'

Having said which, she made no move to go, but loitered to stare a little longer, hoping to hear some details.

The girl came forward, clutched her mother's arm, then stared down at the sticky mess that came off in her hand. 'What's happened, Mam?'

'I'm all right. I had an accident.'

This drew a soft chuckle from Mrs Fitch.

'But ...'

'Leave me alone, Jess. I said I'm all right.' Alice's voice rose in agitation and she pushed her away.

'Tar and feathers,' scoffed Mrs Fitch. 'Some accident.'

The child understood then. Alice saw realisation dawn on her daughter's face and she thought that Jess would cringe with the shame of being Alice Davey's girl, expected her to turn her back, run to her room and shut herself in. For what seemed an age, each one held the other's anguished gaze, while Mrs Fitch watched them avidly, enjoying every second. But then the girl's expression hardened. Her mouth compressed, her eyes glinted and she did what neither woman expected.

'Out!' She gave the bulky Mrs Fitch a shove.

'Here! Don't you lay hands on me!'

'You said you were leaving, so leave.'

'You high-handed little brute! Bloody kid like you, pushing and ordering me ...'

'This is our house and I'm telling you to take your gloating face out of it. You can call for your money tomorrow during shop hours. Go on, shift. There's nothing more for you to see or hear, so you needn't hang around.'

'Jess ... ,' protested Alice nervously, '... you mustn't ...' She had always been frightened of Mrs Fitch.

'Bad blood, that's what you've got,' snapped Mrs Fitch. 'Bossy little article – too arrogant even to feel shame like anybody normal.'

'Go!'

Mrs Fitch did not bother to argue further. She would have her own back soon enough. Oh yes, she would make a banquet of this, recounting it on doorsteps and over back fences throughout the neighbourhood. Jess knew that, of course, and Mrs Fitch smirked at her before rolling off down the stairs.

'You'd best go in the kitchen and take off your things, Mam.' The girl's tone grew level, very adult. 'I'll be there in a minute to put some water on the stove. First I have to lock up after Mrs Fitch ... ,' she raised her voice a fraction, '... and see that she doesn't pocket anything on her way through the shop.'

Halfway down the stairs, Mrs Fitch paused briefly and glared up at her, not so much insulted as piqued by the loss of an opportunity. Her husband and sons were welders at the dockyard – bringing home fat pay packets, too – and yet she was known to every local trader as a light-fingered woman who had to be watched. The girl followed her down and saw her out. Others might have tried being nice to Mrs Fitch in hopes of keeping her quiet, but Jess knew full well that nothing would stop her repeating this tale, or make the telling of it any less lurid.

When she returned to the kitchen, she found her mother hunched over the sink, forearms resting on the rim and shoulders heaving with sobs. Alice heard Jess come in and shut the door. Through the tangled strands of her hair, she turned a woeful, sidelong look upon her daughter. For a second or two neither spoke. Then:

'I've really done it this time, haven't I?' came the broken whisper. 'God in heaven, why did she have to be here tonight? As if I hadn't suffered enough.'

Alice dissolved into tears again.

The girl was silent. Pity, protectiveness and helpless anger battled within her as she contemplated her mother. Instinct prompted her to rush forward and hug Alice, tar and all. But something else restrained her – resentment that Mam, misfit that she was, had indeed 'done it this time'.

Wearily, Jess crossed to the stove and lifted down a big saucepan and a kettle from the rack above it, preparing to take charge of a mother who, in many ways, was more of a child than she was.

'Get out of those clothes, Mam, and sit at the table while I boil up the water. I'll take out the worst of the muck with turpentine and then I'll wash your hair.'

She sounded brisk, businesslike. The sympathy she felt for Alice was equalled by exasperation and she did not want to give way to either.

Half an hour later, the ruined dress and underwear were in the dustbin. Alice, in her nightshirt, sat at the kitchen table, bent over a bowl of hot water, while Jess rinsed the lather of Toxol soap from her hair. The girl had been obliged to cut some of it away, chopping out clotted clumps with her mother's dressmaking scissors. Head down, Alice watched with swollen eyes as dingy, yellow-brown water ran into the enamel pan.

They threw me around like a bundle of dirty washing, she was thinking. They jeered and they called me such awful names.

A single dry sob escaped her.

I thought they liked me. I thought ...

Suddenly, something long-suppressed came surging up from the depths of her mind. An acknowledgement of chill reality. The truth. She had kept it down there for years and years, but at last it was out and staring at her and she could not look away.

They all despise me, don't they? Even to the best of them I'm nothing but a joke. They don't really admire me, and they only spend their money on me in hopes that they'll get something back. My company? That isn't what they want, not to look at me or listen to me talk. They just hope for a favour when the evening's over. Even if they don't get one, they can still swagger and pretend, because everyone knows what Alice Davey's like. Even when I was young they must have laughed and looked down on me. God only knows how they see me now – now that I'm past my best.

It was a terrible admission for Alice, she who had been so proud of her charms in youth and refused to relinquish belief in them as time moved on. What was there in life without the admiration of men? Deprived of it, she would wilt like a plant denied water. To tell herself the truth was to give up the mainstay of her existence.

The water in the bowl had turned dark brown. As the kettle began to sing once more, Jess wrapped an old towel around her mother's head and took the pan away to refill it.

Alice had always been set apart by her looks. Even in childhood she had roused envy in other little girls and she could not remember ever having any female friends. She possessed a certain aura, too, something that said she was 'made for men', but of this she was never aware. Alice only recalled that she had been a lonely child – until the age of twelve or thirteen. That was when the boys had begun to take an interest, and she had never since been short of company. Oh yes, there had always been plenty of males – more than her fair share, the other girls had sourly agreed. Alice did not have to wink or beckon. Men simply gathered around her wherever she went. She loved being popular among the lads – and had quickly learned what pleased them best.

Another pan of water was placed before her, the towel was taken from her head and Jess began to soap her hair a third time.

'Are you a ... ?' Alice heard again the night watchman's gruff question. She knew what he had been about to say. His impression, she now supposed, was understandable. Yet she had never before imagined she might be mistaken for a street-walker, had never seen herself as a 'bad' or 'cheap' woman. She had a weakness, that was all. There were worse ones, too, in her opinion, faults of which no one could rightly accuse her. There was cruelty, dishonesty, laziness – unlike some of her 'decent' neighbours, Alice Davey kept her home immaculate and never uttered a spiteful remark about anyone. Nor would she dream of giving short weight or short change in her shop. She had, indeed, a good many kindly virtues, but they won her no respect.

They'd think better of a murderess, she told herself miserably. And that was close to being true.

Jess's voice broke in on her thoughts.

'Who were they, Mam?'

'It doesn't matter,' said Alice, quietly.

'No? I think it does.'

'They were off a ship, Jess, and they're sailing tomorrow.'

'What ship?'

'I can't remember,' said Alice, wearily. 'What do you

imagine I could do about it, anyway? Tell their captain, tell the police? How much sympathy could I expect? Should I have them up in court? What a show that would be, what a treat for the neighbours. No, I'm not injured and it's best to let things be.'

The girl scowled, breathing heavily down her nose as she rubbed at Alice's hair. 'If it weren't for the other men on board, I'd pray they get torpedoed,' she said through gritted teeth. Then, reprovingly, 'I've been afraid for a long time that you'd run into trouble sooner or later. Strangers, foreigners. You never know who or what they are.'

'They seemed all right,' said Alice, lamely, as Jess rinsed her hair yet again. 'I was out with the same three last night. Full of jokes, they were, nice as could be.' Suddenly, her eyes filled once more. 'I was so pleased when they asked to see me again. They said we'd all have such a party tonight.' Her voice cracked, catching in her throat. 'They must have been planning this, even then. They had it all ready for me, Jess, all ready and waiting in among those crates – tar and feathers, all laid on. See, they'd promised to take me over their ship, show me all around it. They said there was going to be a bit of a do on board. That's why I went into the yard with them.'

'Don't dwell on it, Mam.' Jess started towelling her mother's head. 'I know that's easier said than done, but ...'

'Then Fitch had to be here, damn her soul!' fumed Alice.

Jess took up a flannel to wipe her mother's face and hands.

'She came round just before ten,' she sighed. 'Said she'd wait because she had to have the money. Of course, you'd locked away the takings.'

'It was fate,' sniffed Alice. 'I tell you, my love, I'm ill-wished. Some people are, you know. Nothing ever goes right for them. I'm like that. I'm unlucky, Jess.'

The girl, stroking her into silence with the flannel and warm water, thought to herself: An ounce of bad luck, Mam, and a pound of foolishness, that's you.

*

Jess Davey had known no other home but these four rooms above the shop. They were comfortable, only slightly shabby, and always neat, always clean.

The kitchen was equipped with an old gas stove and a big, deep sink with a single tap. Its window overlooked a small back yard, in which were the coal bunker, the wood pile and the lavatory. Alice's bedroom lay over the shop and was quite large, with a double bed and a walnut suite of wardrobe, tallboy and dressing table. With starched cotton curtains, a blue candlewick bedspread and several rugs, it was a pretty room of which she was proud. Jess had the smaller bedroom at the back. It was narrow, with a sloping ceiling, but cheerfully decorated. In between lay the sitting room, with open fireplace, one worn but soft armchair and matching sofa, an old oak sideboard and a few odd bits of small furniture.

The ground floor below was entirely taken up by the shop and the store room behind it. Opening hours were from eight until six, every day but Sunday and early closing day.

After her ordeal, however, Alice had no heart to open up next morning. It was Saturday, but she stayed in bed, too upset to face the world.

Sitting in the kitchen, breakfasting on bread and jam, Jess did not relish the prospect either, but she would not have it said that the Daveys were afraid to open as usual. Better, she had decided, to face the neighbours down from the very start – 'brazen it out', to use one of Gwennie Bonnet's favourite phrases.

And so, at eight o'clock sharp, apprehensive but resolute, she unbolted the shop door.

The early customers were dockyard men, buying their usual cigarettes or ounce of pipe tobacco on their way to work. Few of them betrayed any awareness of what had happened the night before. Most, indeed, had not yet heard – though one made an awkward but kindly enquiry as to whether Alice was 'feeling better' that morning. Certain others said nothing, but conducted their business with knowing grins. Jess served them all with the same expressionless civility. The men, on the whole, were all right. It was their wives and mothers and sisters she did not want to see.

Like all communities great and small, Devonport had its share of the gossipy and spiteful, a sprinkling of crab-apples among a good-natured, hard-working population. And while most females merely disapproved of Alice Davey, or regarded her with pity, indifference, even mild amusement, there existed among her closer neighbours a core of the more vindictive.

It was not until mid-morning that the first of these women sidled in, making token purchases – a box of matches, a pennyworth of acid drops, a packet of pipe cleaners. They did not normally come to the Daveys' shop for anything, preferring to take their custom elsewhere, no matter how long the walk. They looked around for Alice and were disappointed to find she was not on show. Forced to content themselves with Jess, they tried to broach the subject, hoping to extract some details.

'Mrs Davey not well, dear?' This with a knowing lilt to the voice.

'Shouldn't think your mother feels like coming down today. Can't say I'm surprised.' This with a sly, sidelong glance.

'I hope you don't mind me saying so, Jess, but she does take chances, doesn't she? Something of the sort was bound to happen in the end.' This with a mixture of mock sympathy and prim reproof.

Jess refused to be drawn on the matter, always stubbornly returning to the transaction across the counter. 'Mam's well enough, thanks. Two ounces of humbugs, was it? Anything else? Three farthings, then.'

Those who persisted were met with a dogged silence and baleful stare. Some were seen off with the curt dismissal: 'I've no time for talking, I'm busy.' Frustrated, the women retreated with nothing new to report.

They're revelling in it, Jess thought, bitterly. The ones who are truly shocked won't come anywhere near us.

How well she knew the mean curiosity behind those avid eyes and singsong voices, that rapacious curiosity which longed to ferret out the most painful and personal of secrets and feast upon them.

Certain other customers were notably absent that day, something which upset her more than any of the digs and probings from the women. Almost none of the local children came in for sweets. Only three brought their coppers and ration coupons to spend at Alice Davey's shop. There were normally a score or more on Saturdays, freshly financed from their fathers' Friday pay-packets. Today they did not come. Today they had been ordered to go elsewhere, to keep away from the Davey establishment, as if the shop and the sweets were unclean. Nothing so far had hurt more than this.

· Two ·

Jess went out for a walk on Sunday afternoon. It had long been her habit, given fine weather, and this week, more than ever before, she had need of a stroll to help her collect her thoughts.

She buttoned her coat and pulled on her beret. It was a good woollen coat in a blue and black fleck. The tam was also of dark blue wool. Alice had made it for her. Sitting in the shop all day, she had much time between serving customers for knitting and hand-sewing, and so made most of her daughter's clothes. They were always in plain but good-quality fabrics with very little trimming. Jess had no need of much adornment. That hair alone, tied in the nape of her neck with a black ribbon and tumbling in a swirly tail down her back, was sufficient to make heads turn.

She left the house by the back door and the gate in the

yard. It was a cool, cloudy day and Jess had made up her mind to head for Plymouth Hoe. From the back lane her route took her first down Fore Street, with all its shops and its Hippodrome theatre. Many of those shops were looking drab for want of a fresh coat of paint, just as the few people out and about were generally shabby or sombre in appearance. As the war, with all its shortages, dragged towards its end, most were clothed in black or grey, or at least in muted shades. This town, like every other, had suffered terribly, with thousands of its young men lost at sea or on the fields of France. Battles like Jutland and the Bois des Buttes had left countless widows and grieving mothers, and overall there was a feeling of exhaustion, and fear that the fighting would just go on and on.

A couple of army lorries rumbled past. Jess gave them barely a glance. Devonport had grown used to the roar of military vehicles through its terraced streets. Facing her as she walked were the gates of the South Yard. Nineteen thousand men were employed at the dockyard now, nearly twice the number there had been before the war.

She took her usual route that day, down Tavistock Street, Cumberland Road, on across Stonehouse Bridge and along rumbustious Union Street, where all those merchant and naval seamen went to spend their leave. Bawdy, brawling Union Street, with more than a score of public houses, a music hall, a theatre, and other establishments where men who were off the leash and primed with plenty of pay could go and raise hell until their ships called them back. Known to sailors the world over, it was no place for the nervous or the puritanical.

The final stretch of her journey was all uphill, past the tall, white-fronted houses of Lockyer Street, to reach the Hoe.

All was quiet this autumn Sunday. The bandstand was empty, there were no crowded pleasure steamers plying to and fro, no pierrot shows on the Promenade Pier. There were just a few people out strolling – an elderly couple, arm-in-arm, a nanny pushing a pram, a handful of soldiers in khaki, some with girls, others alone with their thoughts and a cigarette. The air was very still and the waters of the Sound were placid. Some way out, a trio of warships lay at anchor, slivers of dark grey upon the sea, and in the distance the great curved bow of the breakwater could dimly be seen through a low-lying mist.

Jess wandered down to the Promenade Pier, with its café, slot machines and ticket kiosks. Walking to the end, she sat on a bench beside the Pavilion. Plastered on the wall were notices urging the public to 'Spend less; Save more!' and to 'Buy only War Savings Certificates'. Alongside these, a gaudy poster announced a list of forthcoming concerts and dances. They held no interest for Jess. She was dwelling on the prospect of school next morning.

She would, she knew, be made to suffer for what had happened to Mam. Briefly, Jess experienced a flaring of rage against Alice. Why did she have to be the way she was?

Men and gin, thought Jess, she can't resist either one now Dad is gone. And if the things I hear are true, she was just as bad before she married him. I'm sick to death of being sneered at and taunted because of Mam and her reputation. Why does she have to be out so many nights a week? And why can't she be more fussy about the company she keeps? It wouldn't be quite so bad if they were nicer types – gentlemen – and took her to better places.

A memory came to check her temper.

Well – there had been one or two like that. Jess's mind roved back a year or so, remembering an American officer who had bought Mam a splendid dinner at the Royal Hotel. Very well-mannered, he was, and very generous, too. Alice had come home radiant and had sat on the end of Jess's bed until after midnight, telling her all about it. But two days later his leave had ended. She never saw him again. Going back still further, there had been a man from Cambridge – a ship's surgeon, Jess seemed to recall – who had taken Mam to the Theatre Royal to see a Shakespeare play. Alice had not really understood it. All the same, she had thrilled to the plush and gilt of her surroundings. The surgeon, too, had been a gentleman, but a married one, with little time in port. Here and quickly gone again, such were most of Alice's acquaintances. She had kept the gold-embossed programme from the play, and she looked at it fondly now and again.

Poor Mam, thought Jess, her anger quelled for the moment, replaced by some degree of understanding. How thrilled she was, how flattered. She blossoms when a man is kind to her.

For a long time Jess sat staring unhappily down at the dusty boards of the pier, picturing there the reception she would get from her classmates on Monday morning.

I'll never be free of the stigma, she thought. I wouldn't be any more popular if Mam were to enter a convent tomorrow. Nobody round here is ever going to forget or see us in a better light, no matter what we do. They wouldn't want to, if the truth be told. They enjoy looking down on us. I suppose it builds them up a bit, the miserable bunch.

Her reverie was broken by the buzz of a seaplane passing overhead towards Mount Batten. A breeze had sprung up and her hands were cold. She pushed them deep into her pockets as she stood up.

I wish I had somewhere else to go, she thought, the fury welling up again. Somewhere well away from here. A place where nobody knows me, so that I could leave all this behind me, shed it and throw it away like a grubby old coat. I hate being 'Alice Davey's girl'. I'm weighed down by her, stained by her, and it's not fair, it's ...

A deluge of shame broke over her. Mam – she should not think this way about Mam, who had done her best for her child in every other respect. Kindly, soft-spoken Alice was a comfortable person with whom to live. There was seldom a harsh word from her and never a slap.

The desire to flee from Alice was pushed to the back of Jess's mind, replaced now by the old, familiar 'us against them' feelings she had harboured nearly all her life. Jess, like her mother, had always been an outsider, but had learned to cope in a different way. Unlike Alice, she had never tried to please, and was therefore said by some to be hard-bitten. They would have liked to see her meek, apologetic, and were vexed to find her otherwise. Defiance and loyalty to her own flesh and blood had carried her through most of her thirteen years. They would see her through Monday morning, too.

She knew from the moment she arrived at school next day that everyone had heard about Friday night. Coming past the railings, she saw the others huddled in whispering groups in the yard, heard the gasps and hysterical giggles.

They fell silent when they spotted her coming through the gate, turning almost as one to goggle at her. Some were grinning, others looked disdainful. A few wore worried expressions – these were the ones who had quite liked Jess but would fear even to speak to her in future. Now she would be shunned as if she carried plague. Girls would edge away uneasily if they found themselves standing beside her at assembly.

The silence as Jess walked past them and into the school lobby was breathless. She could feel their stares following her, but she did not turn to speak or even look at them. Normally a few minutes early, she had taken care today to arrive just as the bell was ready to sound, so that she could hurry straight in to lessons.

No one shared her desk this morning. It was customary to sit in pairs, but now she had the bench to herself. Even Louise, the timid little girl who usually sat with her, had thought it best to find another place. Turning in her seat, Jess looked round and caught her eye. Louise flushed and quickly glanced away.

The first lesson, being arithmetic, with the fearsome Mrs Chilcott presiding, passed in a well-ordered atmosphere of diligence. But next was 'composition' with doddery Miss Leach. She set them a subject and left them to it. After a while she fell into a doze at her desk, and now came the first direct jibe at Jess. From behind her came a gleeful whisper:

'Do I smell turpentine, Jess? Hope you're handy with hot water and a scrubbing brush. Must have taken hours to get her clean.'

She tried to ignore it.

There followed another whisper, fierce and persistent.

'My ma said there was tar enough to coat a flat roof. That right, Jess?'

It was Brenda Fitch. Stout, mousy-haired Brenda, with her thick, droopy mouth and florid skin.

Stubbornly, Jess made no answer.

'And feathers enough to stuff a bolster.'

It was too much. Brenda was leaning forward now, hissing the words straight into her ear. Mrs Fitch always dressed Brenda's hair in fat sausage curls, and a bunch of those ringlets now fell within Jess's reach. With a sudden twist round, she seized a handful and jerked them so hard that Brenda squawked and fell sideways out of her seat.

Miss Leach came to with a snort.

'What are you doing?' she quavered. 'Jessamine? Brenda? Any more of that and you'll stay in after school.'

Brenda picked herself up and slid, smouldering, back on to her bench. She waited until Miss Leach's eyes closed once more, then muttered, 'You're going to be sorry for that, and for the way you shoved my ma.'

'Your old woman's a nasty, gabby cow and you're another one like her.'

Miss Leach was drowsy, but not unconscious. 'Get on with your work,' came the weary order.

Morning break arrived and they all congregated out in the yard to hear from Brenda what had passed between her and the Davey girl. Jess loitered for a while in the classroom by herself. She was reluctant to go outside, but if she failed to make an appearance they would say she was frightened, and that was something she could not tolerate. So at last she went out, and saw that they were all in conference up in the farmost corner of the playground. Jess headed the other way, ambling down towards the gate.

But she had not gone a dozen paces before her classmates

spotted her and a shout rang out, a name she was to bear for the rest of her days in school.

'Pitchpot!' There was a shriek of laughter. 'Pitchpot, Pitchpot!' A score of voices took up the chant.

She spun round, her face flaming, wishing she could strike them all dead. Not everyone had joined in the chorus, but this was small consolation. Some were silent, but still lacked the courage to leave the main group. There were two who did at least detach themselves from it and hurry back into the school, but no one came to speak or walk with Jess. Such was Alice's shame and the fear of being contaminated by it.

The chanting frayed into laughter. Jess turned her back on them and stalked off to the lavatory. There, she slammed and bolted the door, then sat seething for ten minutes until the bell summoned her back to lessons.

The nickname stuck. Thereafter it seemed to her that no one but the teachers called her Jess any more. She was 'Pitchpot' to everyone – even those who bore her no real animosity used the name in a thoughtless, automatic way. She heard it whispered everywhere and sung behind her back. Someone carved it inside the lid of her desk, and one day she found it scrawled over her proper name on the covers of all her exercise books.

It was Brenda and a handful of her close cronies who kept this persecution going when the others would have tired of it. Reminding herself again and again that only a few months of schooling remained to her, Jess gritted her teeth and resolved to endure to the end. There was always the temptation to leave a little early, since the law was lax about such things, but she would not give the Fitch faction the pleasure of thinking they had driven her out. On the calendar at home she counted the days to her fourteenth birthday, crossing them off as they passed.

· Three ·

It was just four weeks after Alice's ordeal in the dockyard that one of history's milestones brought an unscheduled holiday from school.

Mrs Chilcott had set the class a test that morning – not because she deemed it time for one, but simply because she was in no mood to teach. It was noticed that she seemed preoccupied, not her usual vigilant self at all. Having chalked up twenty problems on the blackboard, she left them to it, too absorbed in her own thoughts to pounce on lawless pupils for cribbing, whispering or flicking paper pellets.

Jess had heard it said that negotiations were afoot, that there might be news of an end to the war, though as yet it was no more than a rumour in the press and the weary population hardly dared believe it. All the same, she guessed that this might be the reason for the teacher's mood. Mrs Chilcott's husband, as everyone knew, was a naval man. No doubt the past four years had been harrowing for her.

The clock ticked round towards mid-morning and Jess worked steadily through the questions. A problem involving compound interest was causing her some difficulty as the time approached eleven, so she did not even glance up from her paper when the first siren sounded.

From out in the harbour came a hollow, booming note.

Mrs Chilcott lifted her head, listening.

There followed two more blasts, each longer and louder than the one before it, as if with mounting elation.

Hesitantly, hopefully, Mrs Chilcott stood up. A ripple ran through the class, curiosity turning to excitement. All eyes shifted to the window, towards the dockyard and the anchorages beyond, for that first ship's hooter was now joined by a second, a third, and a fourth. The whooping voice of a warship was followed by the shrill scream of whistles from half a dozen small boats and soon every vessel with siren or bell was adding to the din.

Jess, by now, had laid down her pen and was listening to the greatest uproar she had ever heard.

'Stay in your seats and be quiet,' Mrs Chilcott ordered, as she hurried from the room.

But the instant she was gone there was a wild babble of voices and a scramble towards the window. Outside, the clamour went on and on, echoing all over the city in celebration of the message which had come over the Admiralty wireless.

Jess hovered behind the others at the window, trying to see over the tops of their heads. There was shouting now in the street. People went scurrying past in both directions and there was a rapping of door-knockers as the news was spread from house to house. Across the road, a woman flung up a bedroom window and hung a Union Jack out over the sill.

Within a few minutes, Mrs Chilcott returned, clapped her hands for silence and beamed around at them all as they turned in unison to face her. They already knew what had happened, but her words were no less thrilling for that.

'My dears,' she said, uncommonly benign, 'the news has just broken that the war is ended. Today and tomorrow will therefore be holidays. You may all go home, and God bless you.'

The war had had comparatively few ill-effects on the Daveys, who had no man to lose. Whatever people thought of Alice, her trade had flourished throughout the conflict. Indeed, with the dockyard working at full tilt, there had been a lot more customers than in peacetime, flush with bonuses and overtime pay. Yet as she walked back to the shop that morning, Jess was seized by the excitement of the moment, caught up in the tidal wave of joy and relief that rolled across the city. Everywhere the streets were filling with people as houses, shops and factories emptied. Dancing, cheering people, tearful people, and many silent, reflective women clothed in black, for whom the end, welcome though it was, would bring no homecoming men.

Outside Davey's shop, ten small boys were marching up and down, banging pots and pans. The neighbours were out on their doorsteps and Joe Bonnet's pub was crammed with men from the dockyard. All work everywhere had come to a halt.

Alice, too, had decided to close her establishment down for the day. She had a bottle of her favourite tucked away and considered this an appropriate occasion on which to open it. When Jess went in, she found her mother placidly sipping gin at the kitchen table. She was, she said, celebrating in her own private way.

Jess made an effort to coax her away from it.

'Why don't we go into town, Mam? Into Plymouth, I mean. There's sure to be a parade or two, and brass bands playing and people singing ...'

'You go if you want to, I don't mind.'

'But you've hardly been out of the house in weeks, and this is a special day. Put your best things on and ...'

'It's too much trouble to change,' said Alice, listlessly.

For a moment Jess stood sadly looking at her. Not so very long ago, Mam would have jumped at the chance of an outing. Finally, she asked, 'Are you just going to stay in and drink by yourself? While the whole city kicks up its heels?'

'I've finished with frolicking,' muttered Alice, 'and with pubs and – everything else.'

So Jess left her there alone with her gin and went out into the commotion of the streets.

Plymouth was roaring, jammed with shouting, laughing people. George Street, Bedford Street, Old Town Street, with their mellow Victorian façades and canvas awnings, were choked with surging crowds which had brought the traffic to a halt. The pubs were packed and so were the churches. Bells were peeling from St Andrew's, while from Charles Church came the swelling strains of Jess's favourite hymn, 'All people that on earth do dwell.'

Bunting fluttered everywhere, with here and there the American, Canadian and Australian flags amid the sea of Union Jacks. A great multitude blocked the broad thoroughfare outside the Theatre Royal, white and grand with its eight Ionic columns. A band was playing in front of the Guildhall, where a couple of soldiers caught Jess by her hands and danced her round and round till she was giddy. Civilians and servicemen alike were swept up in frantic jubilation, kissing and hugging total strangers, explosively happy and deafening in their display of it, with singing, thunderous cheering and hooting of car horns.

To feel part of a great event, at ease for a while among others, was truly a treat for Jess. Safely anonymous in these ecstatic crowds, she experienced a rare sense of belonging, a pleasant escape from being someone set apart. People smiled and shook her by the hand, men winked at her, women were amiable, and a naval rating gave her a ribbon rosette in red, white and blue to pin on her coat.

Jess stayed late among the celebrating crowds. The short winter afternoon soon darkened into evening, and the shops, although deserted since mid-morning, still kept all their lights blazing. Outside the library, she lingered to watch a torchlit parade down Tavistock Road, to the thump and blare of marching bands, and so it was well past eight before she thought about going home, and twenty to ten by the time she was back in her own neighbourhood.

Here, as in the city centre, rejoicing still went on, though many had quit the streets to join impromptu parties in other people's houses. Although her legs were aching now, Jess was buoyed up by a sense of well-being, and found herself pleased by the music from the public houses and the scent of chimney smoke on the cold night air. Small gatherings of people still loitered under the street lamps here and there, but they took little notice of her. One or two men clicked their tongues in approval as she passed, and someone whistled at her from the doorway of Joe Bonnet's pub. But nobody commented or catcalled – until she came within fifty yards of home.

There, in her own street, a couple of women in crossover aprons ceased their prattling to watch as Jess walked by. And then she heard a nasal voice enquire:

'What's that one doing out late by herself, I wonder?'

The answer came loudly, meant for Jess to hear. 'Probably looking for men. Most likely takes after her mother.'

And suddenly everything turned sour again. Jess pretended she had not heard and carried on at a measured pace. A reaction was what they wanted and she would not let them have it. With just a few words these doorstep hags had spoilt her day, but she would not have them know it.

Their stares followed her all the way to the shop.

'Hard as nails,' said the first woman.

'Water off a duck's back,' agreed her crony.

'All the same, that type.'

'No sensitive feelings like other women.'

'Not normal, is it? All those men.'

'Beastly, that's what it is.'

Jess went in and locked the door, then trudged upstairs swearing fluently under her breath. It seemed to her that she was not allowed a single day of being happy, free from abuse. Not even a day like this one.

Before retiring, she looked in on her mother. Alice was in bed and lightly snoring. Jess stood gazing at her for a minute, feeling the old familiar clash of love and hate. At last, sighing, she picked up the overturned glass from the rug beside the bed and then turned out the lamp and closed the door.

Whatever insult Jess had to bear, there was always worse for Alice.

One Saturday in February, she stood pondering outside the butcher's shop. In the centre of the window was a pig's head on a platter. Encircled by trotters, with an apple in its mouth, it was very pink and shiny, with sandy tufts in its ears, and pale, bristly eyelashes.

Leg of pork for Sunday lunch? Alice thought about it. Topside of beef, perhaps? That, too, could be economical, the leftovers eaten cold on Monday with pickles and boiled potatoes. But then she was suddenly seized by a mood of extravagance, for hanging up at the back of the shop she spotted a row of ducks. Roast duck was a favourite with Jess, but she did not have it often. There was never a second meal to be had from a duck. Never mind, for once, decided Alice. The takings had been good that week and her daughter deserved the occasional treat.

There was no one else in the shop when she entered. The butcher greeted her affably. A good customer, Mrs Davey, one who never quibbled or asked for credit, one who always bought a decent cut. He liked her quiet manner, too, and he did not care about her personal life, shrugging off the things he sometimes heard said of her. A genuinely nice man, Mr Holt, a proper Christian, Alice always said.

'May I have a look at those ducks?' she asked him. 'Those two on the end.'

He brought them down for her to feel the weight and test the plumpness. Alice could always pick a good duck and he smiled as he watched her choose. She had just made up her mind when the bell above the shop door tinkled and someone came in behind her. By reflex, she turned to see who it was.

The woman's name was Rogers – a friend of Gwennie Bonnet. Alice met a look of loathing and sharply turned away, hastily pointing out the bigger of the ducks. She wanted to be gone now, as quickly as she could.

'I'll have this one, Mr Holt.'

The butcher went to wrap it up, while Alice fumbled for her purse. As he did so, Mrs Rogers informed him:

'It's a duck I've come for, too.'

Mr Holt glanced at her, nodded. He did not care for Mrs Rogers. She was always apt to interrupt when he was serving other people. She also had a corncrake voice and went about in a hairnet. And now, very loudly, she added:

'But you needn't offer me that one Alice Davey's left. I won't touch anything she's pawed about.'

Alice gasped as if at the stab of a knife. She started to tremble, dropped her money. The butcher stared at Mrs Rogers. He was briefly lost for words, but she had more to say.

'You wouldn't let me bring my poor old dog in here last week. Told me it wasn't healthy, didn't you, Mr Holt? But you don't mind having this dirty bitch in your shop, or letting her handle the food.'

'Now, just a minute!' His face turned red. 'I won't have talk like that in here. I'll have you know ...'

Alice barely registered the rest of what he said – something about expecting civilised behaviour on his premises, permitting no bad language in his shop, which, incidentally, he would run as he saw fit, and so on and so forth. Mrs Rogers was talking back, saying there were other butchers, cheaper ones, too. Scrabbling to retrieve her coins, Alice could not speak for the tightness in her throat, and her brimming eyes missed half the money scattered on the floor. It did not matter. Under savage fire from one of her oldest enemies, she wanted only to escape.

She straightened up and there was Mr Holt, sympathetic, apologetic, holding out the duck in its paper wrapping. Alice grabbed it, thrust some silver into his hand and turned to flee. Before her was the Rogers woman, standing in her way. Mustering a flicker of spirit, Alice elbowed her aside. Pulling open the shop door, she heard the argument resume and then went haring homewards.

'... dirty bitch, this dirty bitch ...'

The words kept echoing in her mind, over and over and over. She had always been used to sly digs and sour looks, but it seemed that the episode in the dockyard had given them licence to come right out with what they thought, and in the nastiest words they could find.

That's why the children don't come in and buy sweets

any more, she told herself in anguish. Because their parents say to them that I'm a dirty bitch.

This was no sudden flash of insight. Deep down in her mind she had known for weeks. She was merely facing it squarely at last.

Two women were coming towards her and they stared to see her running, distraught, hugging something wrapped in paper as if it gave her comfort. Alice barged between them and sped on her way. Fuming, weeping, she was thinking:

They'll never forget, or let me forget it either. No matter what I do, I'll never live it down. It's going to follow me all my days.

That was the truth. There had been no evenings out since that awful Friday night. She found it hard enough to face the world from behind her counter. To venture out with strangers, or indeed into any pub with any man, was quite beyond her now. Cowed by her experience in the dockyard, Alice was somewhat reformed, but the neighbours had yet to realise it, and would never, in any case, forgive her past.

· Four ·

May brought Jess's fourteenth birthday and release at last from school. Her final report pronounced her achievements to be satisfactory but not outstanding, and she had no grand ambitions.

Predictably, she drifted into serving in the shop. Alice was glad of the help, and Jess was usually down by half past seven each morning, mopping the floor and stocking the shelves before she opened. She had persuaded Alice to have the front repainted royal blue and the gilt lettering retouched. Jess liked to keep the place smart. She fancied it annoyed the neighbours.

In this she was not mistaken, and one of them thought up a way to vent her feelings on the matter. However, it was quite some weeks before Jess discovered that something spiteful was going on.

At ten to eight one morning in July, she was mopping the floor of the shop when she chanced to notice Mrs Rogers coming purposefully across the road. At her side was her dog, a large and elderly mongrel bitch.

Jess had hated the woman with a passion ever since that day when Mam came running home from the butcher's and sobbed out what the old viper had said. Thereafter, Jess had loathed Mrs Rogers more than she detested Gwennie Bonnet and the whole Fitch family put together.

For a moment Jess thought she was coming in. But Mrs Rogers stopped outside, said a word or two to the dog – and then stood calmly watching while it urinated on the Daveys' doorstep. The yellow liquid pooled in the centre of the worn granite slab and some of it seeped in under the door to spread its rank odour into the shop.

This smell had greeted Jess on many previous mornings. Till now she had always put the blame on strays. But Mrs Rogers, who normally walked her dog at night, had grown bold and careless for once, making her squalid gesture in broad daylight.

Jess's mouth dropped open, rage engulfed her and she threw aside the mop. Seizing her bucket, she rushed to the door, flung it wide – and sluiced the gallon of murky water over the woman and her dog.

'There!' she spat, recalling Mrs Rogers' words to Alice. 'That's the way I deal with dirty bitches – real ones.'

The mongrel howled and slunk behind the woman's legs. Astonished, then inflamed, Mrs Rogers lifted a hard, red hand to the girl, who glared a challenge at her and followed it up with a promise.

'You'll get one back, with this.' She flourished the metal bucket.

Mrs Rogers' face was puce under trickles of grubby water. Little beads of it clung to her hairnet, glinting in the morning sun, and her wet skirts stuck to her knees. But she lowered her hand, resorting to verbal assault instead.

'You little savage,' she snarled. 'Ten to one you'll be worse than your mother ever was.'

'I'll be more of a match for the likes of you, that's certain.'

Mrs Rogers' chin thrust up and out, while her brow lowered, compressing her face like a sponge. 'Oh, you'll be a bad lot, you will. Cause more trouble than your mother ever did – and come to more grief, if there's any justice.'

'You hope,' snorted Jess.

Mrs Rogers breathed down her nose like a bull. 'Rubbish,' she growled, 'that's what you are. Done up in a pretty package, but rubbish all the same.'

'That's rich, coming from somebody who brings her dog to piss on our doorstep just for spite. That's well enough for a mean, coarse thing like you. Just the sort of half-witted trick you'd see as clever. Go on, shove off, you and your smelly animal. And if I find any more puddles on this step, it won't be a bucket of water I'll have waiting next time you pass, it'll be a chamber pot.'

With that, she went inside and slammed the door. The bucket clattered as she dropped it behind the counter, then laughter came gusting up from inside her. She sat on the stairs for ten minutes and rocked with joy.

Alice, however, was horrified to hear what Jess had done.

'Things are bad enough,' she said, 'without you antagonising somebody like her. She has a big family and most of them are nasty. We'll be lucky if they don't come round here making mischief.'

'What would you have done, then, Mam? Just quietly cleaned the step off when she'd gone?'

'Yes,' muttered Alice, 'I suppose I would. Best to avoid trouble when you can.'

'Let them ride roughshod over you,' countered Jess.

'That's what it boils down to. If you had a loud mouth and a mean disposition and gave as good as you got, they'd like you better for it. They respect that.'

'I'm just not made that way,' said Alice, feebly. 'I wish you hadn't done it, Jess.'

And it happened that on a Saturday night soon afterwards, someone put a brick through the shop window, making off with the hookah pipe and a few of the vesta cases. It could, said Jess, have been anyone – probably local drunks or ruffians off a boat. Alice did not think so, certain that this was the Rogers' revenge.

Thereafter, she would say the same each time some youngster banged on the door of an evening and ran away, or chalked something rude on the back gate. It was useless to point out to Alice that such graffiti were found all over the neighbourhood. And when, on a winter's morning, Alice went out to the lavatory and found it filled to the brim with stones and coal dust, she took it as persecution, instead of the childish prank it truly was. Hers, as it happened, had been the only back gate left unbolted the previous night, but nothing would convince her that this was not another attack by the Rogers clan.

Once, exasperated, Jess suggested that they might sell up, move elsewhere and thereby escape these tormentors. Alice's response was consternation. The prospect seemed huge and daunting to her, too much to contemplate, and all she could see in it were perils.

'We've a good trade here,' she said, by way of argument. 'It's being near the dockyard, see. What if we set up somewhere else and couldn't make a living? Anyway, your dad built up this business and I'd feel disloyal if I sold it. I must keep it going for him, Jess.'

Passive by nature, and less than bright, Alice preferred the familiar, no matter how grim.

Jess's fifteenth birthday came and went, likewise her sixteenth. Unemployment rose fast in 1921, wages fell, and the Daveys' trade took something of a downturn.

Nevertheless, they were better off now than the Fitch family and many others like them. The war years had given the Fitches a spell of prosperity, but that was over now. Mrs Fitch's husband and sons had been among the first to lose their jobs at the dockyard. The youngest man had managed, after a long time, to find himself regular work on the railway, but the other two were scraping by on odd jobs and any other labour they could find, however ill-paid, short-term or unskilled it might be.

Brenda seemed the only one with prospects. She had taken a factory job on leaving school, spending her money as fast as she earned it – mostly on her appearance. And this, it seemed, had paid off, for now it was said that Brenda had snared a successful restauranteur and was due to be married soon.

While changing the window display, Jess happened to spot her one morning, coming out of her house across the street. Ungainly in high-heeled shoes, her hair bobbed and her mouth a scarlet pout, Brenda was all dressed up in a musquash coat. The rouge and eyebrow pencil could be seen from thirty feet.

And she'd say Mam was cheap, thought Jess, sourly.

Brenda's fiancé, according to rumour, had bought her an emerald engagement ring and a lot of other jewellery besides. He took her out dancing to jazz bands, too, and they planned to go to Amsterdam for their honeymoon.

See what a man can give you.

The thought came slyly and surprised Jess, uncharacteristic as it was. Until now she had given only slight thought to marrying. She would, she supposed, just like everyone else, but the time seemed always far away, some day. Even more vague were her ideas of whom she might marry and how she might meet him. No one local, that was all she knew. No one who would keep her here for the rest of her life.

Amsterdam, she thought dryly, watching Brenda tottering off down the street. Well, she won't be out of place, painted up like a Dutch doll.

· Five ·

The cinema was Jess's weekly treat and Saturday afternoons usually found her in one of the picture houses of Plymouth city centre. The outing would always begin with a jolting ride into town on the tram, followed by an hour or two of dawdling round the shops before going in to see her chosen film.

One January morning in 1922, she arrived at her usual stop by Derry's Clock. It was nearly eleven and the pavements were teeming with people, the streets congested with cars and trundling trams. Jess crossed the road and window-shopped for a while along George Street, where most things were too expensive for a girl whose total capital amounted to seven shillings and ten. Then, rounding the corner into Bedford Street, she made for the big department stores. Her favourites were Yeo's and the giant Spooner's, and here she frittered away the hours till one. Always alone and never with much in her pocket, her pleasures were chiefly to loiter and look, and to savour all the familiar smells of the city shops – leather, calico, furniture polish, lavender sachets, soap, fresh-ground coffee ... Most beguiling of all was the coffee. It was something she never had at home, for Alice would only buy tea. Therefore, a stop at a favourite café for a large cream cake and a strawberry ice cream with a cup of coffee always accounted for the last hour before the cinema opened its doors.

As two o'clock approached, she made her way to the new Savoy in Union Street, there to join a lengthy queue for a Chaplin film.

The house was almost full by the time she went in. Of the few seats left, she chose one near the front, between a small boy and a plain young man. The latter shifted his legs and looked at her with interest as she squeezed past him and sat down.

Jess was aware of his attention, but gave no sign of it, careful not to turn her head. Settling back, she pulled from her coat pocket a bag of pear drops she had brought from home, put one in her mouth and sucked it slowly, waiting for the lights to dim.

The programme started with a newsreel, followed by various announcements. Beside her, the young man kept stealing furtive glances, surveying her profile in the flickering light, admiring the halo of curly hair around her face. Jess hoped he was not going to bother her. Now seventeen, she was used to male scrutiny in public places and from time to time she encountered the type who made a nuisance of himself in the cinema or on the tram, obliging her to find another seat in order to escape. However, the young man ventured no remark to her. After ten minutes or so his shy appraisal ceased and the film began. Jess took another pear drop and lost herself in the antics of the jerky, doe-eyed figure on the screen.

The picture was nearly finished when she dipped into the paper bag for a third sweet. She was toying with the thought of sitting through a second showing. The trick was to hide in the lavatories while the crowd filed out and stay there until the next lot came in. Casting a quick look over her shoulder to see where the toilets were, Jess twisted slightly in her seat – and the pear drops fell from her lap.

Flustered, she bent forward to pick them up, and lightly bumped heads with the young man beside her as he made a dive for them too.

'Oh – I'm sorry!' She moved back quickly.

'No matter.' He groped along the floor for the paper bag. 'I'm afraid you've lost half your sweets, though. I heard them go scattering.' His fingers closed on the bag, he brought it up, peered inside, then handed it back to her. 'Three left,' he said.

'Thank you.' Annoyed with herself, she took them, then added awkwardly, 'Would you like one?'

'Wouldn't mind.' He accepted a pear drop, then nodded towards the screen and told her, 'Charlie's my favourite.'

'Mine too.'

'I've seen all his pictures, I think.'

'Oh,' she said, mildly, hoping to end the conversation there.

'It's the Keystone Kops next week,' he informed her.

'Yes, I know.'

'Like them, do you?'

She shrugged. 'They're all right, I suppose.'

'Not that keen, eh?'

Wrinkling her nose, she shook her head and went on watching the film.

The young man said no more.

The programme ended and the house began to empty. Jess had decided not to stay and see the show again. She was hungry, and chilled too, for the place was not well heated. Standing up, she turned to her right, edging towards the aisle. The young man stood up too, following close behind her. It seemed a long time before she reached the exit, for the audience shuffled out at a snail's pace, and he was at her shoulder all the while. But at last she pushed through the big swing doors into the lobby where, with a brief smile, she swiftly bid him goodbye and hurried out into the street.

It was raining and the shower gathered into a downpour as Jess ran along the pavement towards the stop where she meant to catch the tram. She arrived there well and truly soaked – and just in time to see the tram disappearing down the road ahead of her. There would not be another for nearly half an hour.

Miserably she looked about her, hunching her shoulders against the wind and wet. Driven by violent gusts, veils of rain swept along the street, pelting the pavements with bouncing drops. Jess took shelter in a doorway. Water rushed along the gutters and had also found its way into her shoes. It ran from her hair and beret down her neck, and dripped from the hem of her coat. She wished she had stayed in the cinema after all.

Five minutes went dragging by. She wiggled her frozen toes in her sopping shoes and stockings. Pulling off her tam, she irritably wrung it out and shook her hair as an animal shakes its pelt. Just as she did so, a car drew up at the kerb and a voice called out:

'Would you like a lift?'

She looked up, frowning, and there he was – the young man from the cinema, behind the wheel of a Sunbeam. Eyebrows raised, he peered hopefully out from under the canvas roof.

Drenched though she was, Jess's instinct was to say no. It was, after all, the sort of thing that Alice used to do – going off with men she barely knew. Climbing into a car with a stranger – yes, not so very long ago, Mam would have done just that.

'Thank you, but I bought a round-trip ticket on the tram.'

'And how much was that?'

'Twopence halfpenny.'

'So you stand to waste five farthings, and you'd rather catch God knows what.'

Jess felt a sneeze coming on, but managed to suppress it. 'I don't know you,' she said, stiffly.

'I don't know you, either, but I'd hate you to catch pneumonia. Where do you live?'

'Devonport,' she said, hesitantly.

'That's not far, is it?' He jerked his head towards the passenger seat. 'Jump in, for heaven's sake.'

She wavered, her gaze running over the car. Shivering, and horribly wet, longing to get home quickly, Jess was sorely tempted. He seemed harmless enough – and she had never ridden in a motor car before.

With uncertain step she came forward. The car door swung open and after a final hesitation she slid into the seat beside him.

'Right, Devonport you say.' He pulled away from the kerb. 'That's somewhere I've never had call to go before, so you'll have to tell me the way.'

'Don't you come from Plymouth, then?' She turned towards him, taking her first good look at his face. He was unremarkable, with features that were regular but not in any way striking. His hair was brown, and his eyes were a medium blue. She judged him to be about twenty.

'No,' he said, 'I live on Dartmoor.'

'Oh – are you a farmer?'

He shook his head. 'We're timber merchants, my brother and I. My name's Robert Lawrenson.'

Ah, yes, she could hear it now, the difference in his accent. It was Devonshire speech, but not Plymouth.

He waited a moment, but she did not volunteer her name or any other information, so finally he asked.

'I'm called Jess,' she answered. 'My mother keeps a shop. We sell sweets and tobacco and we live up over.'

'Plenty of trade, I suppose, with the dockyard so close by?'

'It's not like it was when the war was on. Too many workers laid off. Still, we don't fare badly, all told.'

'I daresay. I'm no smoker, but most men are.'

He chatted on as he drove, following her directions for the most part – though twice he took a wrong turning, thereby making a somewhat lengthy and roundabout journey of it. Accustomed to the ponderous progress of the trams, Jess did not realise, either, that he drove rather slowly, spinning out the trip for as long as he could.

They were halfway there when the rain stopped, but the sky remained an ugly grey.

'I should think the winters are terrible up on the moor,' said Jess. 'I hear the snowfalls lie for weeks on end.'

'Sometimes they do. I couldn't live in the city, though. I don't like hordes of people round me all the time. Snow melts away, but neighbours don't.'

She smiled to herself at that. They seemed to have something in common.

'Which way now?' he asked, as they turned into Fore Street.

'Second left, then first left.'

The final hundred yards to the shop took them past Joe Bonnet's pub. Standing on the front step was Gwennie, together with the garrulous Mrs Fitch and a couple of other women. Gangs of children were out in the road; boys kicking a ball around, girls playing tag in the last hour of daylight. In response to a toot on the horn they cleared out of the way, retreating to the pavements. On the step of the pub, Mrs Fitch turned to look – and spotted Jess in the passenger seat.

Her mouth dropped open, she jabbed Gwennie with an elbow, then pointed at the car. All four women stared, craning their necks to try and glimpse the driver. Jess caught sight of them as she passed, seized the chance to wave in queenly fashion, and was gratified to see the words 'Cheeky little bitch' form on Gwennie's lips.

'There.' Lawrenson stopped outside the shop. 'How's that?'

'Grand, thanks very much. It was good of you to bring me all this way.'

'Tsh. My pleasure.' Glancing up at the front of the shop, he said, 'Davey – is that your name?'

'Yes.' She opened the door and hopped out. 'Goodbye, and thank you again.'

'Bye,' he said, reluctantly.

He had hoped she might ask him in.

With a farewell beep of the horn, Lawrenson pulled out into the road and started on his way. The minute he had turned the corner, a jeering chorus broke out.

'Pitchpot, Pitchpot, Pitchpot! Pitchpot, Pitchpot ...'

A handful of children had banded together to remind Jess Davey who she was. She turned her back on them and marched indoors. The chanting changed to hysterical mirth and the children went back to their games. Outside the pub, the women had their heads together, gabbling.

*

The letter arrived just three days later. Alice found it among the bills pushed under the shop door.

'What could this be?' She passed the envelope to her daughter.

Jess, too, was mystified. The writing was small and careful, and the envelope was postmarked 'Tavistock'. She tore it open and discovered a short note inside. It was from Robert Lawrenson.

Dear Miss Davey,
I hope you haven't caught cold from your drenching. Assuming you're well, I wonder if you'd like to come with me to a concert at the Pier Pavilion next Saturday evening? It's a programme of Gilbert and Sullivan favourites and said to be very good. If you agree, I'll collect you at seven o'clock. Please say you'll come. Write by return.
Yours,
Robert Lawrenson

'Fancy that,' said Jess, faintly, handing the note to her mother.

Glancing first at the signature, Alice muttered, 'Robert Lawrenson? Who's he?' Reading on, she remarked, 'My, my! How did you come to meet him?'

Jess poured some boiling water into the teapot and sat down to her breakfast.

'He was sitting beside me at the pictures on Saturday. Then, afterwards, when I missed the tram, he brought me home in his car.'

Alice frowned at her across the table. 'This Saturday just gone? You came home in a car?'

Jess was defensive. 'I wouldn't have taken the lift if I hadn't been soaked to the skin.'

'I'm just surprised you didn't mention it,' said Alice, sawing a slice of bread off the loaf. Then she asked knowingly, 'Was that when I heard those little brutes shouting after you in the street?'

Jess grunted. 'I suppose it was meant to take me down a peg.'

'Hmm,' said Alice, grimacing. She propped the note up against the jam jar, shooting thoughtful glances at it while she buttered her bread.

'What sort of man is he?'

'Young. Very ordinary,' said Jess, between sips of tea. 'He said he was a timber merchant.'

'Oh? Whereabouts?'

'Dartmoor, somewhere.'

Alice was quiet for a while, digesting all of this.

'Might be quite well off,' she observed, after a minute or two.

'He wasn't dressed up. Not even a tie.'

'He has a car, though,' pondered Alice.

She smiled, chewing on her buttered crust. His written invitation struck her as rather formal, very proper, and very different to the casual approaches she had always received. All very gentlemanly, Alice thought – not at all the way she had started out with men.

'Do you mean to go?' she asked.

Jess looked doubtful. 'It's nice of him, I know, but ...'

'But what?'

'Well, I know so little about him. Anyway, I don't like the thought of being – picked up.'

'As I so often was,' said her mother, softly.

Jess looked away, saying nothing.

'I wouldn't call this the same thing at all,' Alice went on. She paused for a moment, considering, then finally she ventured, 'And I think you're alone too much, Jess. I know there's no company for you round here, never has been, thanks to me. I suppose you're wary of the local lads in case they think you're the same way inclined?'

The girl did not deny it.

'But this Robert, he sounds as if he might be – well – a friend for you, at least.'

'You told me once that men and women are never just friends,' Jess reminded her.

'All right,' conceded Alice, 'I did say that and it's largely true. I don't want to see you lonely, though. There are a few good men about, Jess, and there ought to be more to your life than this old place and a trip to the pictures once a week.'

'You're assuming a lot, Mam, from one little note. He's asked me out for an evening. That doesn't make him a saint, or guarantee that I'll see him a second time.'

'No, but it makes a start. You have to give people a chance, Jess. Did you like him a little? He certainly seems to like you.'

A shrug. 'I wasn't with him long enough to judge him.'

'This concert would give you the opportunity. If nothing else, you'd enjoy the music.'

Jess began to weaken a little. She did like Gilbert and Sullivan – and another car ride would be nice. 'Well, there's truth in that, I suppose. But I'll have to think it over.'

In the end, she tossed a coin. Heads she would go, tails she would not. It came down heads and Jess accepted fate's decision.

At five to seven on Saturday evening, she stood before her bedroom mirror, tying back her hair with a white ribbon. She had chosen to wear her best blue woollen frock. It was very simple, its only trimming a white lace collar. Alice had bought her a new pair of shoes to go with it. They had two inches of heel and Jess felt slightly strange in them, as if she were poised to dance or run or – something else, she knew not what.

Was it just the shoes? Or was it also in her mind, this sense of being balanced on the edge of something, about to jump, and either fly or fall? Her fingers, busy with the bow, suddenly froze. Her hands dropped slowly to her sides. She stared at her reflection.

Here am I, Jess Davey, all dressed up and going out with a man, being collected from home by car and taken to a concert. Very smart.

Then she seemed to hear a jeering voice say 'Look at Pitchpot, going in style.'

She shook herself, fiddling again with the ribbon.

Miss Davey he had called her in his letter. Oh, the luxury of a little respect.

Jess took a locket from her trinket box, fastened it about her neck and – heard a rapping at the shop door. Perfectly punctual, right on seven. She did not dream that he had been sitting outside in his car for the past quarter of an hour, consulting his watch every minute or two.

Alice went down to let him in. Jess heard a murmur of greeting and then they were coming upstairs together.

He had put on a tie this evening, and his best cap and jacket too. Alice was pleased by his soft, burring speech and smiled to see his face light up at the sight of Jess in her dark blue frock. The colour always emphasised the delicate peachy shade of her skin, and Robert stumbled shyly over his words as he bid her good evening. All courtesy, he helped her on with her coat, then escorted her downstairs and out to the car.

A decent type, thought Alice. Quite stocky and not at all handsome, but very neat and civil. Peeping from her bedroom window, she heard him switch on the engine, watched the car pull away and disappear down the street. He had volunteered a promise to bring Jess home by ten. Alice had not even had to mention it, so eager was he to make a good impression and assure her that her daughter would be utterly safe with him. Alice found him touching, almost quaint. Knowing little of them, she thought perhaps it was a trait of country people.

Thrilled to have found such a lovely girl and enticed her out with him, Robert was buoyant and awkward all at once, first talking too much, then becoming tongue-tied, then rambling on again. Anxious to make a success of the evening, he couldn't relax for a moment, worrying over where to sit at the concert, pressing on Jess a bar of chocolate, a lemonade, a programme, secretly fretting lest the show should bore her.

Jess was anything but bored, delighted by the costumes and the music. There were pieces from *The Gondoliers*, *The Mikado* and *The Pirates of Penzance* and many others, all of them well performed by the local amateur operatic society. Robert kept glancing at her to see if she approved. She caught him once or twice, perceived his plight and smiled in reassurance. Robert breathed a little easier. He began to hope she might have supper with him. He even dared to think about where he could take her next time.

Yes, she said, as they left the pavilion, she had enjoyed it all very much, no, she had not felt in the least bit cold, and certainly, she would love to round off the evening with a shellfish dinner down on the Barbican.

A heady experience, this, to see a show and eat in a restaurant. The songs kept going around in her head, jolly and witty as only Gilbert and Sullivan could be. And Robert was so attentive, so respectful.

'I've never been taken out like this before,' she confided, as he drove her home. 'It was lovely, thank you very much.'

For several seconds he took his eyes from the road, looking curiously at her.

'Not once? Do you mean that? Not ever? But you must have been asked?'

She had. Hardly a morning passed in the shop without an offer from one hopeful or another.

'Oh yes, I've been asked, quite often. Never by letter, though.'

'That made a difference?' Robert sounded intrigued. 'It was simply because I live so far out of town. We haven't a telephone.'

'Nor have we. But it did seem so polite of you to write.'

He was silent for a moment, then, 'So I'm your first, uh, manfriend?'

'You are, yes.'

'A girl like you? Are you certain? There's been no one else at all?'

'Of course I'm certain. I'd hardly forget.'

'Well,' said Robert, 'I call that remarkable.' He sounded

pleased, and after a pause he asked her, 'Ever been to Newton Abbot races?'

'No.'

'Like to go next Saturday?'

'Oh!' He heard excitement in her voice. Horse-racing! That would be a novelty, sure enough. 'Oh Robert, yes! I'd love to!'

· Six ·

Robert Lawrenson had lived on Dartmoor all his life, born and brought up in a large granite house which had once been a gunpowder mill. By car it was only forty minutes' journey from the outskirts of Plymouth, yet here the city seemed remote, for this ancient wilderness, dour and unchanging, was a world unto itself.

Down in the river valleys, where streams ran under hoary stone bridges, the oak woods grew thick and shady, while up above these pretty vales were great expanses of desolate heath, and tors and baleful hills circled by buzzards and wheeling ravens. A timeworn landscape, swathed in heather and bracken and dotted in places with stunted trees, it was green and gold in sunshine, or grey with mist and granite under sullen skies. Where man had been at work, there were reservoirs and farms, peat diggings, the ruins of old mine workings, quarries and abandoned mills. Farmers there had always been, since prehistoric times, but industries had simply come and gone, leaving derelict buildings and machinery behind them. The moor had made these relics a part of itself, remaining as wild as ever, for the furze grew over everything, birds nested in the broken stonework and all was once more silent, save the wind.

Robert's home, Torvallen, lay at the lower end of a

wooded valley, just where the trees thinned out and a further stretch of open moor began. The house stood on an acre of level ground beside the river and was half encircled by woods at the rear. In front its view was broad and grand, towards a distant craggy tor. With the river at the side of it, the trees at the back of it, and the brown and purple heath in front, it was a lonely and very beautiful place.

The Lawrenson sawmill lay a mile or so further up the valley. Like the house, it had started out as something else – in this case a cornmill. It stood in a clearing on the river bank, and its water-wheel now drove a dynamo to power the mechanical saws and lathes. Around it was a spacious yard, in which were drying sheds stacked high with seasoning timber. The approach to the Lawrenson property was somewhat rough – along a narrow track – but the family had lived, traded and prospered here for over thirty years. Their lorry, purchased after the war, was now a familiar sight about the moorland roads.

The brothers employed four men, who possessed between them a variety of woodworking skills. To the local farmers they supplied gates, fencing, sheep hurdles. For builders they cut oak beams and floorboards, made window-frames and doors. Cabinet-makers came to them for supplies of elm and beech and yew, and sometimes for chair-legs made in the old-fashioned way on a pole lathe. In their time, they had turned out everything from church pews to railway sleepers.

Joel and Robert Lawrenson were generally considered to be good payers. Their mother had been dead for many years, their father for nearly three. They had made no changes to the business since his passing, taking over and carrying on with the same ways, the same workforce.

At one time the trees had surrounded Torvallen completely. The space around it had only been cleared when the gunpowder mill ceased working, and a lot of the felled timber had been used to convert the place into a comfortable dwelling. Robert did not remember it as it once was, for the work was finished before he was born. The

Torvallen he knew was a friendly house with five bedrooms, and a broad oak front door where the entrance to the old mill had been. The Lawrensons had not, as yet, troubled to provide it with electricity, relying still on oil lamps and a wood-fuelled kitchen range. At the rear of the house was a fruit and vegetable garden. There, too, in the shadow of the woods, lay a couple of outbuildings, one of which was the lavatory, the other a stable for the family's two horses. Adjacent to the back door stood a toolshed and a wash house which also served as a bathroom.

In truth, Torvallen was too large for just three people. Joel, the elder brother, was married but had no children, and the Lawrensons employed no household staff. Robert's sister-in-law, Pauline, was a very pretty woman, and he had long been restless in his single state. He felt left out and was anxious to find a suitable girl for himself. He, like Joel, should have a nice wife to help fill the house and his life.

Robert had never been as lucky with women as Joel. It had not been easy for him, as it had for his brother. No, the search had not gone well, till now. Robert had suffered awful disappointment in the past. But then, the pattern was familiar. Everything always went better for Joel.

At last, however, Robert had found a splendid girl, an outstanding girl, every bit as lovely as his brother's wife. Robert approved of Jess in every way. He would not want her fashionable, flirtatious, or a gadabout. He liked her reserve and the quiet way she dressed. Yes, she was just what he sought.

She won four shillings at Newton Abbot races. Pressed against the rails, her cheeks pink with excitement and a chilly February wind, Jess saw the horses come plunging over the last fence, her chosen runner neck and neck with a beautiful grey. She breathed in a heavy scent of horse and leather and torn-up turf as they hurtled by, and felt the vibration of their hooves go through the soles of her feet. Leaning out over the barrier when they had passed, she strained to see which one came in first at the finish.

A few moments later, the loudspeakers gave out the name of the winner.

'That's mine, he won!' Thrilled, she whirled around and her tam fell off.

Grinning, Robert picked it up. 'Let's go and collect your booty, then. I think you're due about five bob.'

'Four,' corrected Jess, who had kept better track of the changing odds.

The bookmaker bantered with her a little as he paid out her winnings. He was smarmy and took his time, grasping her hand and slyly stroking the palm with his thumb before he counted the money into it. His smile contained a big gold tooth and his eyes kept darting over her body.

And then an odd thing happened.

Suddenly he glanced up, looking over her shoulder at Robert, and the grin just dropped from his face. Abruptly he released her hand, rapidly doled out the last three sixpenny bits, and hurried off into the crowd. Jess could have sworn he seemed almost frightened. Turning, she looked at Robert.

He appeared to have noticed nothing strange. Smiling, he said, 'Want to stay for the next race, or shall we have something to eat?'

Perhaps the bookie had simply remembered something urgent. Perhaps she had just misread his look. Jess felt a spattering of rain and promptly forgot all about him. Many in the crowd were putting up umbrellas. The ground, strewn with betting slips, was already getting muddy and the shoes she wore were light.

'I've seen enough,' she said. 'I think I'd like some tea.'

They found a café in the town and went in. Robert chose the most secluded corner, a table half-hidden from other customers behind a potted plant, keeping Jess all to himself, cosily seated with her back to the wall. She had noticed from the start how very protective he was, seldom leaving her side and quickly steering her away from types like the bookie, who tried to be familiar.

He ordered tea with scones and strawberry jam. They

talked about the races and the music hall, and then about his business and his parents.

'Father's family were always Dartmoor people,' he said, 'as far back as anyone knows. Small farmers, they were, over Moretonhampstead way. Father was the first one to go in for something different. Did well from the start, I'm told.' An odd look crossed his face, something she couldn't quite fathom. 'He was one of those people who hardly ever put a foot wrong.'

'And your mother?'

A light appeared in Robert's eyes. 'She was a Plymouth girl. She had a lovely face,' he said, and he seemed to see it before him as he spoke. 'Not pretty, but there was something lovely ... Oh, I thought the world of her.' He stirred his tea and watched it swirling in the cup. 'She died of cancer when I was twelve. So unfair,' he murmured. 'So damned unfair.'

'You missed her very badly.'

'Yes. Oh yes. I still do.' He took a swig of tea, became matter-of-fact again. 'Father was in his late fifties when he went. Spanish 'flu. I remember him saying to Joel, "You're the same age I was when I started out in this business, and you already know what I took years to learn. You'll be all right without me." Of course,' added Robert, 'I knew just as much as Joel. I'd been at home and working, see, while he was in the army during the war.'

Jess nodded. 'My Dad was eighteen years older than Mam,' she said. 'They looked ill-suited, but really they were very happy with each other. He had chest trouble, though, and it finally killed him.'

'Is your mother in good health?' Robert asked.

'Fit enough, on the whole.'

He frowned. 'But isn't she a bit unwell today?'

'She's the same as usual. Why do you ask?'

'I thought she was looking pale, that's all. She's very thin, isn't she?'

'Mam never eats a lot these days.' Jess put down her cup and started buttering another scone. There was a thoughtful pause. Then, casting several glances at him from under her brows, she added bluntly, 'She drinks instead.'

Robert's blue eyes blinked. 'Oh,' he said. 'What, in particular?'

'Gin.'

'Oh,' said Robert again. 'So today she ... ?'

'Yes, a hangover.' Jess took a large mouthful of scone and ate it, her gaze fixed calmly on him. Around them was a quiet buzz of talk and the genteel clink of spoons and cups and saucers.

'Does she drink very much?'

'Mam can take it like a docker when she's in the mood.'

He stared at her.

Jess continued eating. 'She holds it very well,' she went on, lightly. 'It takes a lot to knock her out.' Delicately, with her little finger, she removed a trace of jam from the corner of her mouth.

Robert surveyed her with amazement. There she sat, in her woolly tam, exquisitely pretty with nice table manners, coolly announcing her mother was fond of the bottle.

Jess peeped at him over the rim of her teacup. 'Sometimes, when she's squiffy, she gets into bed with her clothes on. What do you think of that?'

A muscle twitched at either corner of Robert's mouth. He didn't disbelieve her, but he realised she was testing him.

'I've done the same once or twice,' he said.

Her eyebrows lifted. 'Aren't you shocked?'

'No. My brother's wife enjoys a drop, too. I've seen her merry many a time.' His brows knitted slightly. 'Why do you want to shock me, Jess? I hope you're not trying to put me off.'

'I just wondered if you were broad-minded.'

He leaned across the table and said emphatically, 'I couldn't care less if your mother drinks. It's you I'm interested in. So, when will you come out with me again? Let's talk about that.'

Jess regarded him curiously, wondering whether he would accept other revelations about Alice just as mildly.

'How about Wednesday?' prompted Robert. 'I'll take you to the Palace Theatre.'

My, she thought. He really had taken it very well. He was nice, so very nice. His tolerance put him up still further in her estimation.

'All right, yes, I'd like that very much.'

· Seven ·

It was Easter when he first took her home to meet his family. Robert had been waiting for fine weather. He wanted Jess to see Torvallen at its best.

Would she come for the weekend? he had asked. There were three spare rooms, and many things to do – and Pauline would welcome female company for a change.

'Three spare rooms!' gasped Alice, when informed. 'Must be quite a place. Lonely country out there – still, you won't mind that, will you?'

Not mind? From the moment she saw it that sunny Saturday morning, Jess was in love with Torvallen. Here was peace, here was privacy, a haven far from anywhere, nestled between the sheltering woods and the heath.

Switching off the Sunbeam's engine, Robert turned to look at Jess and saw that she was sitting almost spellbound, staring at the house. For a moment he watched her. Then:

'Well, what do you think of the place?'

She did not answer straight away. There was silence save for the rustling trees and the soft splash of the river.

'Jess? Do you like it?'

'Like it?' she repeated, absently. 'Robert, it's beautiful.'

'Yes,' he said, happily, 'it is, isn't it?' Jumping out of the car, he blew the horn to announce their arrival and the noise brought her out of her trance. As she stepped down on to the rough driveway, the front door opened and a young woman came out of the house. Very dark and elfin, with a heart-shaped face and sleek, bobbed hair, she was clothed in trousers and an old brown jersey.

'My!' she said, extending a hand in welcome. 'So this is Jess! We've heard a lot about you, but we thought Rob was exaggerating. He wasn't, though – you're lovely!'

'Thank you.' Amused, she glanced at Robert and saw him blush.

'That's right, Pauline,' he sighed, 'embarrass us both.'

'Oh, tosh!' She waved him aside. 'You go and put the car away, then bring her things in.'

He picked up Jess's bag from the back seat. 'Is Joel at the yard?' he asked, eyeing Pauline from under his brows.

'No, gone fishing. If he's lucky, we'll have baked trout tonight.'

Robert did not look entirely pleased. 'I suppose I'll have to go in for an hour or two, in that case,' he grumbled.

Pauline made no response to that. 'Come on,' she urged, ushering Jess indoors. 'You'll have to take us as you find us, mind. We don't often have a guest, and I never tidy up when we do. Gives a false impression of us. Now this,' she said, throwing open a door, 'is the sitting room.'

It was very large and full of clutter. All untidy, the Lawrensons liked their surroundings pleasantly scruffy, ill at ease with too much order in the home. There were books everywhere, lined up on wall shelves and in bookcases, piled up on tables or stuffed down beside the sofa cushions. Every surface was littered with ornaments and curious oddments brought in from the moor – an assortment of coloured pebbles in a whisky bottle on the mantelpiece, a handful of buzzard's feathers standing in a small vase, dried flowers, a case full of birds' eggs, chunks of mineral found in a quarry, a collection of ancient flint arrowheads and many other intriguing items. One corner of the room was occupied by boots and fishing rods, another by a double-barrelled shotgun. Cartridges, jars of fishing flies, weights, hooks and floats were scattered all over the sideboard. As for the rugs and furnishings, these were good but well-worn, for the Lawrensons were inclined to keep and use the things they loved until they could be used no more.

A welcoming room, with its cheerful disorder. 'Make yourself at home,' it seemed to say.

'I'm glad you're not formal,' said Jess.

'Formal!' Pauline seemed to find that very funny. 'My dear girl! I've two men to take care of and I could waste half my life picking up after them if I were silly enough. And then they'd only complain that they couldn't find anything, so I just clean around it all and leave it where it lies.'

Next door was a small dining room, noticeably dusty.

'We only use it at Christmas,' said Pauline, 'so that's the only time it gets swept and polished. I just shut the door and forget about it for the rest of the year. Now then, I'll take you upstairs.'

A bedroom had been prepared at the front of the house. It was prettily furnished in satin birch, and the white lacy curtains and bedspread were brilliant in the morning sun.

'Will this be all right?'

'Oh yes, I should say so! It's lovely!'

Jess went to the window, thrilled by the view. Before her stretched the open moor, gaunt and yet serene, with the bright ribbon of the river winding away towards the tor. She turned around, smiling, noticed the posy of wild flowers on her bedside table, and told Pauline, 'You know, I've never stayed with anyone before. This is all so nice, so kind.'

Pauline's eyes crinkled with pleasure. 'Believe me, we're delighted that you're here. Rob will be up with your bag in a minute, so I'll leave you to unpack. Come down when you're ready. You'll find me in the kitchen.'

She disappeared and moments later Robert brought up Jess's holdall, in which were packed two changes of clothing and a few other odds and ends.

'Nothing fancy,' he had told her. 'We don't dress up out there.'

'I'm sorry to run off,' he said, dropping the bag on the bed, 'but we have a big order to fill by next week. The men don't come in on Saturdays, and Joel's gone fishing, as you heard. He's like that – tomorrow's always time enough. Thinks the work will do itself, I suppose. Don't worry, I'll be back by this afternoon.'

'It's all right, I don't mind.'

'How do you find my sister-in-law?'

'Very jolly. I like her.'

'Everyone does. She'll keep you entertained till I come home.'

When he had gone she unpacked her things, then went downstairs to find Pauline.

The kitchen was rectangular, with roughly plastered walls and a flagstone floor. It was dominated by a great Welsh dresser, a large black cooking range and a central table big enough to seat ten people. The top of this table was cracked clean across, and had the bleached appearance of wood that underwent frequent scouring with a hard-bristled brush. Corn dollies and bunches of dried herbs hung from the ceiling beams, and the dresser was crowded with odd plates, coronation mugs and painted jugs.

'We'll have some tea in a while,' said Pauline. 'Like to look around a bit more first? Come out and see the horses.'

She led the way through the back door and round to the stable, where a dark brown stallion and a chestnut mare stood in neighbouring stalls. Saddles and bridles hung from the walls, and a pile of manure mixed with straw was heaped in one corner.

'Good healthy smell, eh?' chuckled Pauline. 'Don't mind it, do you? Now, this is Hector,' she said, caressing the stallion's velvety nose. 'He's getting on a bit. Nearly twenty, aren't you, old love?'

He blinked benignly at her.

'And this is Willow. She's seven or so.' She clicked her tongue to the mare, whose coat glistened ginger-brown and lustrous in a shaft of sunlight.

'She's very elegant,' said Jess.

'Sometimes I think she knows it.'

The horse swished her tail and stamped on her straw.

'Yes, we're a bit vain, aren't we?' chaffed Pauline. 'And always on the scrounge, too, always nosing into people's pockets to see if there's anything nice.'

'I expect you all ride a lot?'

'Joel and I do. Robert keeps himself too busy.' Winking Pauline added, 'But I think he'll make time to teach you, if you'd like to learn.'

Taking down a bucket from a hook on the wall, she picked up a spade and shovelled in some manure from the top of the pile. 'This goes on the garden,' she said. 'You should see my carrots and runner beans – they're beauties!'

They went outside, where she proudly showed off her vegetable patch and fruit garden.

'Potatoes, cabbages, leeks – I grow them all at various times of the year. The apple tree gives cooking apples, much too sour for eating raw, but they do make splendid jam. Those over there are gooseberry bushes ...' she swept a hand in a semi-circle, '... then I've raspberry canes, as you see, and also blackcurrants.'

Jess turned a curious look on Pauline. 'You don't sound to me like a country person. You're not from a farming family, are you?'

'No, I come from Tavistock. Dad's a schoolmaster. I've two older sisters and they're both teachers as well. But you see, I was a land girl during the war and it gave me a taste for this sort of life. That was how I met Joel, too. There I was one day, pulling up turnips in a field up by the crossroads, when an army lorry stopped and let him out. He was on leave, and carrying a great heavy kitbag. He said hello and I asked him where he was going. He still had a three mile walk down the valley to reach home, and he looked so tired, so haggard and haunted. Well, I was about to sit down for an hour and eat my sandwiches, and I asked him if he'd like to rest and share them with me before he went on. Thus I met my fate.'

'That's what it sounds like – fate,' smiled Jess. 'Was he a volunteer?'

'Lord, no!' Pauline up-ended the bucket and hurled a few spadefuls over the earth. 'Joel was conscripted in 1916. He was lucky, thank God, came out of it all in one piece. We married about six months before the end. Hadn't known each other long. Everything was very urgent in those days – no time for engagements. Of course, Robert was luckier still, just a year too young to be caught up in it. Their father was still alive when I first came here to live. He and Joel were very much alike, physically and in temperament too.'

'Is Robert different, then?'

Glancing at her, Pauline cocked an eyebrow. 'Yes, he is. Rob is more – intense – than Joel. More serious, if you prefer. He's inclined to take things to heart and he drives himself hard.'

'At work, you mean?'

'Yes, and in other ways.' They started walking back to the house. 'Robert tries to do everything specially well. Joel is less earnest about life. If you didn't know them, you'd never guess they were brothers.'

They entered the kitchen and Pauline put a whistling kettle on the stove.

'I'm pickling today,' she explained, waving a hand towards a pile of cabbage and cauliflower lying on the table. 'There's another knife in the drawer there, if you want to cut some up.'

Jess sat down and started chopping, glad to be given a task. Pauline seated herself in an old carver chair and set about shredding a cabbage.

'Rob's been so happy, you know, since he met you. I can hardly describe the difference you've made.'

'Was he lonely before?'

'Desolate, more like.'

Jess paused in what she was doing. 'Oh?'

'Utterly forlorn.'

'But why?'

'Well, because of all that business with Vanessa,' snorted

Pauline. 'She really upset him very badly. My opinion is that he had a lucky escape, but of course he didn't see it quite that way.'

Suddenly she realised that Jess was looking at her blankly.

'Oh ...' Pauline faltered, awkward now, uncertain. 'He hasn't mentioned that?'

'What?'

A brief hesitation, then a shrug. 'May as well tell you, I suppose, now that I've begun. He was, um, crossed in love, as they say.'

Her expression was wry now, and her tone cynical.

Jess thought it odd that in all their hours of talk he had never touched on this. Not a word, not a hint.

'I see,' she said, slowly. 'And her name was Vanessa? What sort of person was she?'

Pauline was dismissive. 'A bit la-di-da. She came from quite near Tavistock. In fact we went to the same school, so I knew her slightly. I never did take to her, even in those days. But Rob was mad about her, spent every minute he could with her. And then, one day, she just dropped him. Wouldn't see him any more, wouldn't answer his letters or let him in when he called. Rob was in an awful state, moping about and brooding all the time. That was eighteen months ago and we were starting to fear he would never get over it. But then he met you, thank heaven. You've certainly revived him, Jess.'

The kettle began to sing and she rose to make the tea, pulling a lacquered caddy from a cupboard crammed with tins and barrels of dried goods. For a moment, Jess was silent, mulling this over.

'Why?' she asked, at length. 'Why did she let him down?'

'Probably felt she was too grand for us. I never did think she belonged here. Her parents were landowners and had a clutch of servants. Anyway, about a year ago we read that she'd married some gentleman farmer up Okehampton way, one with a deal of money, by all accounts. Need I say more?'

'I suppose not,' murmured Jess.

Poor Rob, she thought. It sounded as though this Vanessa had merely amused herself for a while, finally discarding him in favour of someone she deemed more suitable, someone with more to offer. Jess supposed he would want to forget the whole thing. He did not wish to discuss it with her, that was plain.

The kettle was shrieking now. Pauline took it off the hob and filled a man-sized teapot.

'It's good to have another woman to talk to,' she confided. 'Rob and Joel are both good men and I love them dearly, but they can be trying sometimes.'

For Jess it was more than good, it was a rare treat to have easy conversation with a woman close to her own age, one she might venture to look on as a friend. How comfortable it was, how enjoyable, to sit at this table chopping vegetables and talking over tea with someone so companionable. The kitchen was filled with the warmth from the stove, and a Van Dyke Regulator clock hung peacefully ticking on the wall. She wondered how the girl Vanessa could have wished for anything better than this.

A short time later the front door banged and she heard the tread of a man coming down the passage.

'Sounds like Joel,' said Pauline, and it was.

In the kitchen doorway appeared a man in his middle twenties. He was wearing a dark green shirt and corduroy trousers. His body was lean, graceful in his old clothes.

'Well,' he said, when his gaze lit on Jess, 'no need to ask who you are.'

She smiled. 'Hello. You're Robert's brother?'

'Joel,' he confirmed. Coming in, he laid down half a dozen fresh brown trout on the table. 'Caught in honour of your visit, Jess. You do like trout, I hope?'

'I expect I shall. I've never tried it.'

Joel was dark and bore no resemblance to Robert. On his head was an old tweed cap, and from under the peak a pair of slate-coloured eyes were studying Jess intently. He was more assured than his brother, some would have said more impressive.

He went to the cupboard, took out a tin and helped himself to a currant bun.

'You haven't been long,' said his wife. 'Nice little catch, too.' Taking the fish, she put them in a bowl by the sink.

'Where's Rob?' he asked, taking a bite of the bun.

'Gone over to the yard to work.'

'Oh.' A look crossed Joel's face. 'There wasn't any need of it. The job's half done already and delivery's not due till Thursday.'

'He's a worrier,' shrugged Pauline.

A faint smile touched Joel's mouth, which was broad and chiselled.

'So he is.' He winked at Jess. 'We're relying on you to cure him of that.'

Robert returned at lunchtime, and in the afternoon Jess walked with him down by the river through shady green tunnels of oaks. The air was heady with the scents of spring, the woodland floor carpeted with bluebells and primroses. This had always been his world and he took it all for granted. To Jess it was a very heaven. The city had its parks and they were nice enough, but still too close to the street and all it knew.

That evening, after their dinner of trout, she played draughts with Robert till bedtime, and the only sound to disturb her that night was the squeal of some small creature in the wood and the hoot of the owl which had killed it.

Most of Sunday was spent on a drive around the moorland roads, constantly slowing for the sheep and shaggy cattle that cropped the verges and wandered heedlessly across the track. Wild ponies were everywhere, browsing among the gorse bushes and scattering nervously at the approach of the car. Now and again they saw an early foal, still shaky on its gangly legs, huddling close to a mare.

The back of beyond, some people called it, a relic of another age. So it was, and therefore precious, a tract of strange and primitive country, never ploughed and broken up into tame little toytown fields. Robert said it rained a lot, for most of the ground was high. The water could not soak away because of the granite underneath, so it pooled, creating bogs, then streams, and finally turbulent rivers that could feed a man with salmon or seize and drown him like a rat. The moor demanded knowledge and caution of those who ventured into its loneliest parts. Once away from the road, he said, it was all too easy to lose one's bearings, as some had learned to their cost. Those who perished out here usually died of exposure and exhaustion. It was no place for the careless, Robert warned.

No – but Jess had decided that it was the place for her.

It was very late before she fell asleep that Sunday night. Long after twelve she stayed awake, sitting in the bedroom window seat, her coat thrown over her nightdress. The moor was washed with silvery light, the river glistening under a full moon, and the tor stood out black against the sky like a distant ruined castle. The scene resembled a charcoal drawing, touched with something magical.

· Eight ·

Home seemed very small and shabby after Torvallen. Odd, thought Jess, to find this impression so strong after only two days away. The shop and the rooms above appeared darker than before and the tiny walled yard at the back was a cramped and depressing sight. She felt weighed down and hemmed in – and vaguely ashamed at the same time for drawing an unfair comparison. Mam and Dad had always done their best, and the Daveys' place was better by far than some.

Jess had a bath that Monday evening, sitting in an old tin tub before the parlour fire. Behind her at the sewing table, Alice was unpicking the seams of a dress she planned to alter. She worked in silence, glancing now and again at her daughter's bare back. With her hair pinned high, Jess sat absently soaping herself. She was still thinking about Torvallen, and so was her mother.

Her excited voice echoed again in Alice's mind:

'It was beautiful, Mam, and they made me so welcome. They're very free and easy, I didn't feel awkward at all. It's lovely there, and quiet, not a soul living anywhere near. I'm so looking forward to going again.'

Her face had been radiant as she spoke. Alice had never seen her look like that before, and the sight had filled her with hope and fear. This could be something wonderful opening up for Jess – an escape, a chance of happiness, and a triumph over those who ridiculed and sneered at her. And yet, the brighter the dream, the greater the pain and disappointment if things went wrong.

She's always been so down-to-earth, thought Alice. Hard-bitten, some would say. Well, that's because she's had to defend herself. I don't think Jess has ever let herself care enough about anything to be badly hurt by the loss of it, until now.

After a while, she ventured, 'I take it you'd marry Robert if he asked you?'

Jess glanced back over her shoulder, then turned her gaze to the burning coals in the grate. A blue and green flame sprang up at the back of the fire, flowing up the chimney on the draught.

'Yes,' she said, watching the wavering colours. 'Oh, of course I would!'

Alice smiled. 'A man of the right sort can make you very happy, Jess. Your father was always good to me. And he was your father, you know.'

Jess looked round a second time and met an open, level stare.

'Oh, I know what people say,' nodded Alice, 'and I don't

doubt you've heard it too. But they're wrong about that. You're Peter Davey's girl, I promise you.'

'I always felt that I was. I never did believe the whispers on that score.'

'Such a kind man, he was.' Alice's eyes grew soft with remembrance. 'Insignificant to look at, and he'd be the first to admit it, but he had a generous heart. He always forgave me everything.'

These last few words came out on a sigh. Then, 'Would you say that Robert is the same type?' she enquired, cautiously. 'He's a good man, I'm sure, and he does adore you, Jess. The way he looks at you – so proud – and the money he spends taking you around! I believe he'd do almost anything to please you.' She took a fleeting pause. 'Still, there's just one thing that troubles me ...'

Jess dipped the bath sponge in the water, smeared it with soap and pumped a lather up through the holes. 'What's that?'

'Well, I don't suppose you've told him much about me? I mean what happened to me and – all the rest of it.'

Her daughter did not turn around, but now she was motionless amid the rising steam. 'No,' she said at last. 'Do you think I ought to say something?'

Alice swallowed uncomfortably. 'It might be better than letting him find out for himself. And he's liable to do that, sooner or later. Things have a way of following us, Jess, and perhaps it's better to have it out in the open, first as last. Robert's not prudish, is he?'

The answer was hesitant. 'Not prudish, no. But he's so respectful, so protective when we're out, as if he thinks I'm delicate and sheltered. It might be a bit of a shock to him.' More confidently, she added, 'Still, all that was years ago and you're different now. Oh, and I did tell him how you like your drop of drink.'

'How did he take that?'

'Didn't turn a hair.'

'Well, it's up to you,' said Alice. 'You know him better than I do, so you're the one to judge the wisest course.

Whatever you decide, I shan't argue. But I had to mention it, Jess. I do believe the time has come for you to think this over.'

'I will, Mam, I'll make up my mind before I see him again.'

She made it up that night, lying staring at the ceiling in her room. Outside, she heard the stillness broken by singing and the crash of a dustbin being kicked down the street when the pub turned its customers out. Later, there was muffled shouting and thumping through the wall, as the couple next door commenced another fight. Noise. Day and night there was noise in the city. Hooters from the dockyard, the shouts of newsboys hawking the morning and evening papers, the metallic squeal of the trams, always some kind of uproar. She thought about the quiet of Torvallen, where the bedrooms were perfectly silent, even in the middle of the day. She heard and saw again the river and the rustling woods, the comfortable kitchen, the garden, the horses, jovial, irreverent Pauline, whose laugh was nothing short of bawdy, the men with their soft country accents. The Lawrensons, the way they lived, the house itself – she wanted it all, wanted it fiercely.

Tell him all that about Mam? Not at any price. Anyway, she assured herself, he would not care, not Robert.

Spring gave way to summer and with the warmer weather came days on the beach at Torquay, and steamer trips to places like Cawsand or the park at Mount Edgcumbe. And always Torvallen, many weekends at Torvallen. It was fast becoming her second home and Jess was received there as if she belonged, well before marriage was mentioned. It was taken for granted by all that Robert was going to ask her. His feelings were touchingly obvious and so it was simply a matter of time, a question of choosing his moment.

It came on an evening in mid-July, as they walked on the Hoe at dusk. The Sound was smooth and shining, the stars were coming out, and strains of music from the bandstand floated down on the summer air. A perfect scene for it, he thought, a lovely twilight at the end of a lovely day.

Would she be Mrs Lawrenson? he asked nervously.

Yes, of course, came the warm reply.

Then why not do it straight away? Why bother with engagements, when neither had any doubts? Robert was in a hurry. She would not have a chance to change her mind.

Jess was happy to agree to that. She would not give a toss for a church wedding. Too public, too fancy – and anyway, whom could the Daveys invite? A quick civil ceremony would suit her very well.

· Nine ·

Jess and Robert were married at the registry office just one week later, and there followed a boisterous party at Torvallen. The Lawrensons' employees were invited with their families, making it a gathering of nearly thirty people. There were gasps of admiration and approval as Robert introduced his wife to them. It was his great day as much as hers. Flushed with pride and basking in the envy of his men, he felt that for once in his life he was crowned with laurel.

An odd assortment of men, the sawmill workers. There was Eddie Pierce, swarthy, lean-featured, rather like a gypsy and full of mischief. By contrast, stout and solemn Henry Wills was full of religion. Charlie Weekes, getting on in years, with great dark eyes and wild grey hair, stared at Jess as if he had seen a vision. A bit on the silly side, old Charlie – good at his job, but otherwise silly – confided Robert. Finally, there was Peter Chivers, mild, efficient and chubby. They all had plain, strong wives and scruffy, healthy children.

Alice was looking smart, quite dignified in a pale green frock. She was much impressed with the house and full of praise for the lavish buffet lunch Pauline had provided. A succulent joint of beef, a roll of gammon glazed with honey, a leg of pork with fatty crackling, delicately flavoured lamb, vegetables, pickles and sauces galore, apple pie and cream, brandy snaps, shortcake, cheese – there was scarcely room for it all on the dining-room table. Despite all the beers and wines and spirits on offer, Alice confined herself to drinking cider, and only two glasses of that, which scarcely affected her at all. Indeed, she was nearer sober than most of the other women, including Pauline, and this was hard self-discipline, endured for Jess's sake.

It was altogether a noisy celebration and by three o'clock the newly-married couple were glad to leave. They went upstairs and changed their clothes, then came back down with cases packed. They were going to spend the next three weeks in Cornwall. Dressed in an open-necked blouse and a mauve skirt in the fashionable knee-length, Jess had tucked her hair inside a wide-brimmed hat, with a few wisps and curls pulled down around her face.

'You look a picture,' Alice told her quietly, as Robert loaded luggage into the car. 'The Lord's smiled on you, Jess, and no one deserves it more. They're a fine family, a nice, kind family, and you fit in so well with them. You'll have a good life here, you'll be respected.' She took her daughter by the shoulders, her eyes and her grip becoming fierce. 'Don't you come back to the shop too often,' she whispered. 'Do you hear? This is a fresh start and you mustn't spoil it. You keep your new life separate from your old.' A crafty look appeared on her face. 'I shan't tell anyone where you are. They'll want to know where you've gone, but I shan't tell them. You won't have to live with spite and gossip all your days. You've left all that behind you now.'

Relaxing again, she smiled, pushing back a few curls behind Jess's ears. A crease appeared on her daughter's brow, a small frown of worry. Mam would be on her own now. For a moment there was guilt at leaving Alice, a sense that she was abandoning her and fear of what might befall her. Scenes of possible disaster darted across her mind – Alice falling down the stairs and lying with broken limbs for days on end; Alice, drunk and clumsy, setting herself alight, Alice being robbed and beaten by midnight intruders, with no one to come to her aid ...

'What's the matter? Why the long face?' Alice lifted her daughter's chin.

Jess shook herself out of it, smiled. 'Nothing, Mam.' She hugged the older woman tightly. 'Except that you must promise me that you'll look after yourself. Eat properly, be careful with the gas, make sure you lock up securely at night and things like that.'

Alice was amused. Gently she said, 'You can't be my keeper any more, my dear. Now come along, your husband's waiting.'

They drove away from the house amid cheers and showers of rice. Robert delivered Alice back to the shop and she stood waving on the step until they turned the corner.

'I hope she'll be all right,' said Jess, settling in her seat. 'She's never had to live alone before.'

Robert nodded but made no comment on that. Instead he told her, 'Everyone thought she was very sweet.'

'Did they?' Jess was pleased.

'And as for you ...' He pulled her into the crook of his arm, steering with one hand. '... well, I've never seen them so impressed.'

'I liked your men. They all seem very decent.'

'They're not a bad bunch,' agreed Robert. 'We work together well enough. They're loyal and I'd swear to their honesty, every last one.'

He took his arm from her shoulders, changing gear, and she sat up straight again in her seat.

'Still,' he said, after a moment's thought, 'men are men and apt to be vulgar sometimes.' He cast a sidelong glance at her, serious now. 'I'd prefer you to stay away from the yard. The talk gets crude and the language gets rough, and

I'd rather you didn't hear it, Jess. The sawmill's no place for you.'

Thinking about them, Jess could not imagine any of those men to be really coarse. Cheeky, perhaps, on closer acquaintance, but not rank. They were anything but ruffians – she had seen some real ones in her time and knew the difference.

'Promise you won't go in there,' Robert pressed.

She thought it slightly odd that he should ask this. He was looking very earnest now, concerned, and there seemed to be no sound reason for it. Still, it was of small account to her.

She shrugged. 'All right, if that's what you want. I don't suppose I'll have much cause to go there anyway.'

Robert had booked a room at a coastal inn just a few miles from Padstow. Approached by narrow, winding lanes, it was well off the beaten track and they did not arrive until seven. The landlady had a sentimental fondness for newlyweds. She kept a special room for the freshly married, with a view over the sea towards Trevose Head. A big vase of flowers and a bowl of fruit came with the compliments of the house, not to mention a little gift of scented soap and lavender cologne for the bride. Many a couple had begun their married lives at her establishment, and she liked to feel she was 'launching' them.

It was past eight by the time they had unpacked. Neither wanted much to eat after Pauline's wedding spread, but they went downstairs for a light supper and a glass or two of wine. There, in a small dining room which overlooked the sea, they whiled away the hour and a half until the sun went down.

That night a full moon striped the floor and counterpane with silver, and the light fell full on Robert's sleeping face. Jess lay on her side for a while, her head propped on one hand, just watching him and considering the great experience, the source of all the mystery and fuss. She stretched and sighed. She had found it good. Another body, bare flesh, smooth and warm – she had known no other comfort like it, even if Robert was awkward and anxious at first and then caught up in his own urgency and relief. There was still his weight and warmth and rhythm and all these things were comfort. Feeling no longer alone in any way, and thinking back on all the solitary years, she wondered how she had borne it.

Sliding down in the bed, Jess slipped an arm over her husband and pressed against his back. In the short time she had known him, he had turned her life inside out, filled every need and granted every wish.

They were three wonderful weeks, balmy, with barely a day of rain. It seemed to Jess that almost everything was either blue or gold – sea, sky, pale fine sand, and farmlands too, for it was nearly harvest time and waving, burnished-yellow crops stood high in the wheat and barley fields.

The inn lay only half a mile from a broad and lonely beach. The couple's days were lazily spent in slow rambles across the clifftops, snoozes in among the dunes, lengthy lunches and teas at country pubs and village cafés, and trips to all the little north coast towns down as far as St Ives. Swimming and beach-combing, early nights and late breakfasts – the honeymoon slipped away without a single disappointing day to spoil it.

Although – there was just one less perfect than the others.

On the last Thursday of their holiday, the Lawrensons went across to Mevagissey, where they lunched on pasties and beer at a waterside pub and then spent an hour or so wandering around the village. Passing a jeweller's window, Robert saw a locket he wanted to buy for Jess. He thought he would make a surprise of it – purchase it without her knowledge and give it to her at dinner on the night before they went home. And so it was that, later in the day, he left her briefly by herself. Pleading a call of nature, he hurried off *en route* for the jeweller's shop.

Jess sat down on the quayside while she waited for him.

The harbour was quiet, the fishing boats tied up and most of their crews gone home to sleep till evening. Just a few of the men were still about, mending nets and cleaning up.

At first she was not aware that one of them was watching her from the deck of a lugger moored nearby. Nor did she notice him when he sauntered up the old stone steps and strolled along the quay towards her. Only when a drawling voice bid her good afternoon did she pay him any attention.

'On holiday, then?' He grinned at her.

She smiled. 'Yes, with my husband.'

'Ah.' He sounded rueful. 'Where's he to, then?'

'He had an errand. He won't be long.'

The man sat down beside her. He was roughly Robert's age, but taller and very much darker. He wore an old black jersey, and a pair of leather boots covered his trousers right up to his thighs.

'Like it here?'

'It's lovely.'

Jess was conscious of his gaze upon her, lingering, admiring. It was not offensive, nothing to cause her discomfort.

'Where you from?' he asked.

'Devonport,' she said, out of habit.

'Aw, yes? I'm often up Plymouth way, selling me catch on the Barbican.'

She asked him a question or two about the fishing and they chatted on for several minutes about one thing and another. He was eyeing her all the time and flirting a little. A harmless type, just one of those men who could never resist the chance to speak to a pretty woman.

He probably buzzes round every flower in town, she thought to herself.

Robert, however, did not take him so lightly.

Emerging from a sidestreet, he stopped in his tracks at the sight of his wife in conversation with a man. In an instant a change swept over his face. It took on a look of dismay, and that turned swiftly to anger.

The fisherman had just made a joke and Jess was still

laughing when Robert came striding up. At the sight of his scowl her laughter ceased and her smile slowly melted away.

He snapped at the other man. 'What do you want?'

The fisherman looked up, eyebrows lifting in surprise. 'Just talking,' he said, warily.

'This is my wife.'

A shrug. 'Nothing wrong in passing the time of day, is there?'

Jess tried to intervene. 'Rob, it's all ...'

But he cut across her words, still glowering at the other man. 'Making a pest of yourself, you mean.'

'Rob, he wasn't!'

'Pushing yourself on lone women.'

The dark man snorted. 'Don't talk such rubbish.'

Robert's cheeks went crimson. 'Get away from her, go on, clear off.'

'Now look, there's no need for you to act like this. I was only chatting with her, telling her about the town.'

The fisherman stood up, and so did Jess, quickly placing herself between them, afraid that one or other would lash out with a fist.

'Truly, Rob, that's right,' she told him, anxiously.

He took no notice. 'Didn't you hear me? I said go.'

The Cornishman gave him a withering head-to-toe glance and then enquired, 'Are you a bit soft in the head, or what? Carrying on about nothing, snapping and snarling like a guard dog.'

'Stop it, please, the both of you!'

The fisherman grunted, muttering, 'Yes, all right. 'Tis all too foolish to merit a fight.' To Jess, he added, 'Nice to meet you, Maid.'

And with that he was gone, strutting off in his big leather boots, all dignity and umbrage.

'Maid!' exclaimed Robert. 'Maid, he called you! Bloody nerve!'

She, by now, was angry too.

'Why? What's so very wrong with that?'

'I don't want my wife treated with familiarity.'

'Oh, for pity's sake, Robert! Talk about pompous! What on earth's come over you, to be so nasty? He wasn't doing any harm, he wasn't bothering me.'

At that, he attacked her with an accusation that left her briefly speechless.

'Which means you were enjoying it. In fact, I could see you were. Take your fancy, did he? Give him the glad eye, did you?'

There was a silence. She blinked at him, bewildered, trying to fathom this shocking change in him. When at last she found her voice, it was hesitant, subdued.

'No, Robert, I swear to you. I didn't encourage him to come and speak. Anyway, he was only being friendly – thinks he's a bit of a lad, I daresay. Dear God, we've only been married three weeks! How could you imagine I was interested in some strange man? What do you take me for?'

He faltered, then, his features relaxing, as if whatever gripped him had suddenly dropped away. He shook his head as if to shake off confusion. She saw his throat bob and then he mumbled, 'Oh, I'm sorry. I'm so sorry, Jess. God, I must have looked an awful fool.'

Weakly he tried to laugh it off, hoping she would, too. But she was staring at him still, dreadfully uneasy, jolted by this glimpse of something new and frightening in him.

'I've never known you behave like that.'

'No, well ...' Robert avoided her eyes. 'Look, there is a reason for it. Still, I should have had more sense, more self-control.'

'What reason?'

'It's not to do with you. I'll explain about it later. We'll go back now, shall we? It's nearly four.'

'Perhaps we should,' said Jess, a little stiffly.

Guilty, and embarrassed by his outburst, he was smiling now, trying very hard to restore everything to normal. They returned to the car and set off on the road towards St Austell.

Robert tried making small talk on the way, but Jess was not very responsive, so after a while he gave up. It was only when they had passed through St Austell and were moving out across the china clay country that he finally offered the promised explanation.

'That business back there,' he said suddenly. 'It was stupid, I know. You'll have to forgive me, Jess. You see, I feel a bit – unsure – from time to time. It's because I was dropped by a girl, not so very long ago. I suppose I'm still prickly on account of it.'

'Ah.' Jess turned to look at him. Now she understood. 'You mean what's-her-name? Vanessa?'

'You know about that?' He glanced at her, frowning.

'Pauline told me.'

'Oh.'

He took one hand from the steering wheel, gnawing fretfully at the thumb nail as they journeyed among the Whitemoor waste tips. On every side rose conical heaps of kaolin dust, patchy grey and green with dirt and the vegetation that was slowly growing over them. Here and there the road passed beside a quarry pit flooded with water the colour of jade.

'Vanessa had someone else all the time, you see,' he said, after a while. 'Some rich farmer up at Okehampton. She made such a clown of me, too. I was always chasing round after her, driving her here and there, even running errands. And of course I used to write her a lot of letters. She must have thought they were a huge joke. I'm ashamed to think of it now – now that I know she was just making use of me. Suddenly, one day, she turned around and shut me out completely. No apology, no hint of a reason given. I had to read in the paper that she'd got herself engaged. I can still remember how I felt and I wouldn't wish the same on anyone. Every now and then it comes back to me and I feel afraid, uncertain, because all that time she had someone else behind my back and I didn't even suspect it.'

He darted a penitent look at his wife. 'I'd no right to say those things to you, Jess. You're worth a dozen of her. It was just a reflex – a bad one – when I saw you talking to that man. You do forgive me, don't you?'

'Consider it forgotten.'

The words were warmly spoken, but Robert still felt he had not done enough to atone. Reaching into his inside breast pocket, he pulled out a little red box and placed it in her lap.

'Here, for you, to make up for words you didn't deserve. I was going to wait till Saturday, but I want you to have it now.'

She opened it, took out the locket. It was oval and set with seed pearls on the front.

'Oh, Robert!' She leaned across and kissed him. 'Thank you, it's lovely! Is that where you went when you left me? To buy this?'

She put it on straight away. The chain was quite short and the locket was held nestling in the hollow at the base of her throat. Her pleasure brought a smile to his face.

'Pearl and silver suit you,' he said, softly.

A little later, he queried, 'You don't mind about Vanessa, do you?'

'Mind what? That you used to have someone else, or didn't tell me before?'

'Any of it.' He was starting to chew at his thumb nail again.

'No, I don't mind.' She took his hand away from his mouth, lacing her fingers with his. 'I couldn't care less, my love. I'm not the jealous type.'

· Ten ·

Jess's marriage had taken the neighbourhood somewhat by surprise. She had, after all, known the young man a mere six months.

'Fast worker, wasn't she?' said Mrs Fitch to Gwennie Bonnet. 'Married before you could look around.'

'Calculating,' agreed Gwennie. 'Smarter than her mother,' she added, grudgingly. 'Alice just gave it away when she was young, but Jess was sharp enough to get a good price, by the looks of things. Crafty little monkey.'

She prodded at her dentures with her tongue, absent-mindedly dislodging the top set, poking them out, then sucking them back into place.

'The no-goods always fall on their feet.'

'Devil takes care of his own.'

They were all agog to know more about Robert, but Alice had not been very forthcoming. One day, however, they cornered her in Fore Street and set about pumping her for information. She was looking at the billboards outside the Hippodrome when a tap on her shoulder made her turn, to find herself face to face with Fitch and Bonnet.

'How's your girl getting on?' asked Mrs Fitch. 'Haven't seen her but once since she went away. Doesn't visit often, does she? Very far, is it, where she's living now?'

'Out in the country,' said Alice, nervously.

'Yes, but where?'

'Exeter way.'

'What's the name of the place?'

'It's a farmhouse,' hedged Alice, 'out on its own.'

'Oh yes? Her husband's a farmer, then?'

Alice did not correct her.

'Can't recall her married name,' probed Gwennie.

'I don't think I ever mentioned it.'

'Well, what's she called, then?'

'Jones.' Alice had long been ready with that one.

Doubting glances flitted between the women.

'My Brenda and her husband have bought a lovely villa in Mannamead,' Mrs Fitch informed her, smugly.

'That's a very nice area,' allowed Alice, glad to divert the conversation away from Jess.

'It's the best,' bristled Mrs Fitch. 'The house is a palace inside, a real palace. I go to see her every week – sometimes twice a week. I'm very proud of my Brenda.'

Alice smiled weakly. They had her hemmed in on the

theatre steps, with her back to one of the doors. She made a bid for escape.

'Excuse me, I have a lot to do today.'

But they did not move out of her way.

'Is she comfortable where she is, your Jess?' enquired Gwennie. She was staring hard into Alice's face, on the watch for signs of untruth.

'She's very happy,' came the confident reply.

'I've heard it's a hard life, farming.'

Alice just looked at her, expressionless.

'Think she'll stick it, do you?'

'Yes.'

'Can't quite see her as a country wife,' said Fitch.

'You don't know much about her,' answered Alice, tightly.

'Bad job if she starts feeling – bored.'

'Restless,' agreed Gwennie.

'She's content,' said Alice, through gritted teeth.

Fearing and hating these women, she wanted equally to run and to slap their faces.

'Is he well off, her husband?'

'Prosperous.'

'Thought he must be, to have a car. Course, my Brenda's husband has one, too. Do you get invited out there much?'

'I'm tied to the shop,' said Alice.

Another look flashed between the women. Gwennie then sought to test a theory of hers.

'Any sign of a family yet? Will Jess be a mother soon, do you think?'

Alice knew what she was getting at.

'Not soon enough to fit your notions.'

'I don't know what that's supposed to mean,' sniffed Gwennie. 'I only asked a civil question.'

'I have to go,' muttered Alice, and this time they stood aside.

'Can't believe half she says,' observed Gwennie, as Alice hurried off. 'She was sidestepping, I could tell.'

Pursing her mouth, Mrs Fitch nodded sagely.
'Jones,' she snorted. 'Hah!'

'However much you love the man, the first year is difficult,' Alice had warned.

Jess did not find it so. She settled in at Torvallen as if it had always been her proper element and she was home at last. All the world was amber that first delicious autumn, or so it seemed to Jess. Life was warm and beautiful, like the colours in the woods or the shining coat of the chestnut mare on whom, under Robert's tuition, she quickly learned to ride.

That was not all she had to learn, for Alice had never taught her to cook. Scrambled eggs, cheese on toast, bubble and squeak with a slice of grilled bacon – these were all that Jess could prepare until Pauline took her in hand. But soon she was able to bake bread and cakes, scald cream, pickle or cure all sorts of things, and make a good job of Robert's favourite meals. The Lawrenson men took a lot of feeding, and the kitchen always smelt of yeast and baking, or roasting meat, or boiling fruit and sugar.

Pauline was often ribald company, always ready to hoot and cackle over a saucy postcard or a rude joke. It was fairly obvious that she and Joel led a rumbustious love-life. She never said as much, but sometimes there were tell-tale thumps and howls of merriment in the night. As Robert had told Jess, she also liked a drop of drink, though Pauline's three or four glasses of home-made wine each day could hardly be compared to Alice's intake of spirits.

Jess had found her husband very generous with money. Not that he let her have an allowance – he did not seem to care for that idea. Yet whatever she wanted, either for herself or for the house, she had only to ask and Rob would buy it for her. He seldom questioned what she chose, rarely objected, happily paying up. It was odd, she sometimes thought, that he should be so very free with gifts and yet so unwilling to let her handle cash. Joel showed no such reluctance. He gave Pauline a sum each Monday and left her to spend it in any way she wished.

On occasion he bought her a present, too – and when he did it was a certainty that Rob would bring home something similar for Jess within the week.

'Can't have you feeling left out,' he would say with shining eyes.

She could not help but notice, though, that Robert's gift was always slightly better, more expensive.

If anyone had asked her to name a fault in her husband, Jess would have said that he vied too much with his brother. She had come to realise that his attitude to Joel was very prickly. Living with them all the time, Jess had started to notice little things which once she had missed. Or perhaps they had simply been concealed whenever she came to stay. Quite often, nowadays, she would hear a touch of sarcasm or, more frequently, a carping rebuke. It was always to do with the business, and it seemed to Jess that Robert was anxious to prove himself the more responsible, the more conscientious of the two. Joel, he often said, was too casual about his work, too undemanding of the men, and much too soft in setting prices.

'He takes it all too lightly,' he told her. 'Work comes second with Joel. If the sun's out he'll just let everything slide. He'd rather go off on his own, commune with the moor and shoot a few rabbits, than see to what needs doing. No self-discipline, that's Joel.'

It was true that Joel was inclined to down tools when the fancy took him. He kept very irregular hours. Mildly ignoring his brother's opinions, he went off to the sawmill when it suited him, and might return in one hour or ten. Often he was back and forth throughout the day.

But then again, Pauline had said, 'Joel's quick, he's strong and he's skilful. When he works he gets through as much in three or four hours as some can do in a day. He's also astute; he knows just how far he can go when he quotes for a job, he knows the most he can ask without losing the order and the least he can ask without losing a worthwhile profit. And he trusts the men. Why shouldn't he? They've been with us for years and there's not an incompetent or a shirker among them. Robert worries too much. He checks things over and over, supervises everyone else and tries to do his own work at the same time. No wonder he wears himself out.'

Jess could not say who was in the right. She noted, though, that Joel never returned Robert's criticism, peaceably letting it all wash over him. And that was just as well. Had he been at all hot-tempered, there would have been constant trouble.

Whatever the differences between the brothers, all was harmony with Robert and Jess. Proud, admiring, ardent, he behaved as if he were courting her still and could hardly believe his luck in finding such a wife. Looking back in later years, Jess would say that these were the best, the most perfect, of times. Cosy, yes, she felt cosy, tucked away from the world.

Christmas Day was specially happy that year. The whole house smelt of the evergreens nailed to the ceiling beams and over all the doors, tucked behind the pictures on the walls and twisted into garlands across the mantels. Sitka spruce and pine cones, holly and oak apples – everything came from the woods and forestry plantations of the moor. An eight-foot fir tree graced the big sitting room, hung with sweets and paper novelties.

Jess had bought her husband a green tweed jacket fine enough for a country squire. Alice had lent her the money and Jess had no idea how she was going to repay it, but none of that mattered on Christmas morning when Robert tried it on and said he was delighted.

'You look splendid, Rob' she told him, fastening the buttons and brushing back his hair. 'Truly, you look a gent!'

Robert was always so pleased when she praised him. He almost seemed to grow a little taller. He put on a tie and wore the new jacket all day.

He and Joel had bought a portable gramophone in a shiny walnut case, together with a stack of records. They played it all the morning, and the sounds of jazz and ragtime, music hall favourites, Caruso and Harry Lauder filled the house.

Robert had driven into town on Christmas Eve to fetch Alice. She was closing the shop for a week and would stay at Torvallen until New Year. She brought with her chocolates and sweets enough for a dozen people, and provided an extra pair of hands in the kitchen to make light work of the lunch.

The dining room had not been used since the wedding party. Jess went in there at twelve to make it ready, and found in the sideboard drawer the blue ribbon bow which had tied her little bouquet, and also a card decorated with tiny dried flowers and a lace horse shoe. Peter Chivers' wife had made it herself. Jess discovered as well the two little plaster figures from the top of the wedding cake. Bride and groom – rather too grand, the man in top hat and tails, the woman in a full white gown. Jess laughed to herself. In all the rush, they hadn't thought to tell the bakery it was not a church wedding.

Putting these mementoes aside, she set about laying the table. Out came the best silver, the best crockery, the best linen. It all looked very elegant when she had finished. Finally, she lit the fire and the room was gently scented with woodsmoke when the family sat down to their meal at two.

'Like to do the honours, Rob?' Joel handed his brother the carving knife and fork.

Plates of goose and stuffing were handed round, each adorned with a big baked apple, followed by dishes of potatoes, brussels sprouts and carrots.

'This bird's done to perfection, if I do say it myself,' announced Pauline, and there were nods all round.

Joel uncorked a bottle of wine. 'Alice,' he said, 'let's have your glass.'

She hesitated.

'Go on, Mam, you know you're dying to.'

Alice handed over the glass and Joel filled it to the brim.

'After all, it's only wine,' said Robert, grinning at her.

Alice blushed.

'Oh Lord!' exclaimed Pauline, suddenly, 'I forgot to buy the party hats!'

'Thank God for that,' said Robert and Joel in chorus.

'I buy funny hats every year, Alice,' Pauline told her, 'and they always grumble. Still, it's a treat to see them in agreement over something.'

The brothers looked at each other and laughed. There would be no cross words between them today.

'Hasn't been much of a party these last few years with just the three of us,' reflected Robert. He laid down his knife and fork and smiled across the table at his wife. 'This is more like it, eh? Just think, this time last year we hadn't even met.'

'Been altogether a good twelve months,' agreed Joel. 'Business has never been better, has it, Rob? We've picked up a lot of new custom and there's not a single bad debt on the books.'

'That's the truth,' said Robert, beaming. 'We're fortunate people, all of us.'

Joel's gaze strayed towards Alice, and he said, 'You know, Alice, you ought to come to lunch every Sunday. We're always glad to see you.'

'Oh, well, now and again I will,' she said, pleased. 'But Sunday's my lazy day, you know. I like to stay in bed till two.'

After a while, Robert stood up to carve again and the vegetables went round a second time.

Fifteen minutes later, Joel sat back in his chair and surveyed the ruin of the goose.

'Twelve-pound bird, that was,' he remarked, as if proud of a job well done.

'We had a struggle to fit it in the oven,' Alice said.

'Ready for the pudding, then?' Jess collected up their empty plates. 'Rob, let's have some carols for a change.'

'Silent Night', 'The First Noel' and 'Ding Dong Merrily'

played on the gramophone while they tackled the Christmas pudding. It was black and moist and it shivered on the dish as Pauline cut it.

'I don't know about you, Alice, but we never flame it,' she said. 'We don't burn off the brandy, we let it soak in.'

Leaning backwards, Robert plucked the bottle off the sideboard, baptising each portion until the plate swam with brandy. Lastly, they anointed it with clotted cream, thick and gold-crusted.

'Well,' said Joel, eyeing the wreckage a little later, 'that was some pudding.'

'Jess's work entirely,' admitted Pauline.

'Is that so? Right, then the job is hers for ever more.' He caught sight of his brother watching Jess with worshipful eyes and added, 'Any brandy left? Enough for a toast?'

There was and he charged all their glasses.

Raising his own, he said, 'May we always spend our Christmasses together, and may they always be as fine as this one.'

The five glasses clinked.

· Eleven ·

April came, bringing catkins, pussy-willows and celandines to the river valleys, and spring foals to the moors. To Jess it brought the news that she was pregnant.

She saw the doctor on a Friday, but saved her announcement until Sunday. Robert went fishing that morning and Jess tagged along for a change.

A faint haze hung just above the river that day, and the rich smell of damp earth was heavy on the air. Robert's favourite spot was a bend in the stream, where the water was smooth and slow-moving, and almost completely roofed over by the oak branches arching from both banks. There, in his wading boots, he stood in the soft-flowing current, several feet out from the bank, his face half-shadowed by the peak of his cap. Every so often he reeled in a little of his line, pulled the hook clear of the water, flicked it out into the stream at another spot, then waited again, motionless, patiently watching his float. He had brought two fishing rods, but Jess did not care to try her luck. At the water's edge she sat beneath a massive oak, content to watch him for a while before she gave out her glad tidings. Her jersey and trousers, olive green, blended so well with the moss and ivy coating the bark that she almost seemed part of the tree.

I hope it's a boy, she thought. A son – he'd love a son. I know he'll be proud, whatever it is, but a boy would please him best. Poor Rob, he'd like the chance to swagger a bit.

She frowned to herself at this last thought. She was not quite sure what had given rise to it. Why 'poor Rob'? And when had she ever seen him boastful?

The thought had come from somewhere deep down in her mind, where undercurrents were sensed and situations comprehended by instinct. After eight months of marriage she had seen and heard enough to realise that Robert's constant criticism of his brother concealed a certain envy, perhaps even a feeling of being something less than Joel.

After a time Robert turned and made his way back to the bank, winding in his line as he went. Flopping down beside her, he took off his cap, to which were pinned some fishing flies.

'Here,' he said, handing it to her, 'let's try another one. I haven't had a single bite so far. The blue one, there. Can you tie it on for me?'

Jess detached the fly and gave his cap back.

'You must be bored,' he said, watching her fumble with the tiny scrap of feather.

'No, I've plenty to think about.'

'Such as what?' Grinning, he took the fly away from her. 'No, not that way. Like this, look.' Deftly he baited the hook. Then, glancing up, he saw that she was beaming at him, bursting, as he thought, with merriment. 'What's the joke?'

'There isn't one.'

'Then you're mightily pleased about something.'

'Yes, and I think you will be, too. I'm expecting, Robert.'

'What?'

'I'm pregnant. Three months, or thereabouts.'

His mouth dropped open.

'I don't know why you're so surprised.'

Nor did he. But surprised he was – astonished – and delighted beyond all words. He leapt to his feet, pulling her up with him, hugged and whirled her round and round till he nearly lost his balance and landed them both in the river.

'A boy,' he panted, kissing her, 'it's bound to be a boy!'

Jess was gasping, laughing. 'So I hope, but I give no guarantee.'

'Of course it will!' He puffed out his chest. 'They'll all be boys! Three months, you say? So it's due in ... ?'

'October.'

'I don't think I can wait.'

'You can't chivvy nature like you do the men,' she told him, primly.

Together they sat down again, fishing forgotten now. Robert ran a hand slowly over her belly. 'No sign of anything yet.'

'Patience. I'll fill out soon enough.'

For a time they sat discussing names and all the changes a child would bring. And that was when a certain matter popped into Jess's mind, something she had been meaning to mention for quite some time.

Every fourth Monday, Pauline journeyed into Plymouth, there to buy a stock of household sundries and any foodstuffs she could not obtain from the nearest farm or the few little shops in Princetown. Jess went with her on these days in order to visit Alice, and was usually dropped at the shop by ten and collected again at some time after four. She did not, on the whole, look forward to these excursions, and the chief reason was that Pauline's driving scared her. Jess prided herself that she was not easily frightened, but the ride made a harrowing start and finish to the day, for Pauline was partial to speed. She shot along the country roads at a startling pace, roared around corners in town, revved impatiently at junctions and streaked in and out among the other traffic. Jess would not deny her skill, but was always relieved to get out at the end of the trip.

'Rob,' she said, 'I've been wanting to ask you something. I think I ought to learn to drive, don't you?'

He turned to look at her. A crease appeared between his brows.

'Drive? What for?'

'So that I can get about, of course.'

'Where on earth would you want to go on your own?'

'Well, mainly to visit Mam.'

'Pauline takes you into town, doesn't she?'

'Yes, but ...'

'And so do I, sometimes.'

'But if I could drive myself, I wouldn't have to be a bother or wait on anyone else.'

'I'm sure Pauline doesn't mind, and I know I don't.'

She pulled a strand of ivy from the tree trunk and started twisting it round her wrist. 'Robert, you may think I'm silly, but I always feel nervous in the car with Pauline. She goes so fast, and she takes awful chances at times.'

'Hmm,' he allowed, 'I can't deny that. Well, look, I'll have a word with her, tell her to take it easy, especially now that you're carrying. She'll understand.'

'But Rob, I'd still prefer to drive myself. Living out here, I need to know how.'

He started gathering together the fishing gear, the basket and the canvas satchel and the rods. 'I thought you loved it out here. You're always telling me how glad you are to be out of town.'

'And it's true, but I can't be stranded, Rob, or dependent on others to shuttle me around.'

'Stranded, is it?' The retort was stiff. 'Want to go gallivanting, then, do you?'

'Gallivanting? I'd hardly call it that! I'd like to visit Mam just a bit more often. You know I worry about her, Rob, and if I could only drive ...'

'No. I won't teach you, and that's final.'

'I'd be very careful, I promise.' She was pleading now.

'No!' Abruptly, he stood up.

She stared up at him, spread her hands. 'I'm just trying to be practical, Rob. What are you afraid of? That I'll have an accident?'

'Yes. I don't think women make good drivers. You've admitted you don't feel safe with Pauline.'

He had turned that very neatly against her. His mood had changed completely and his face was set, the jaw muscles clenched with annoyance. Picking up the basket and the canvas satchel, he slung them over his shoulder.

'Come on,' he said, tersely, 'we're wasting our time here today.'

She made a last bid to persuade him. 'When the child is old enough, he or she will have to be taken back and forth to school in Princetown. Will you want to bother with that, before and after your day's work?'

'That's years away. We'll worry about it when the time comes.'

'Nevertheless ...'

'I don't want to hear any more about this.'

With that, he was striding off along the path. Jess stared after him, mystified. All affection at the news of the baby, now suddenly all displeasure, all affront – because she had made what seemed to her a sensible suggestion.

What harm could there be? she asked herself. Why's he so put out? All I want to do is be self-reliant.

Next day, when she came across Joel tinkering with the car engine, Jess consulted him on Robert's attitude.

'What could have made him so angry, Joel? I don't want

to be helpless and a nuisance, so I thought I'd learn to drive. What's wrong with that?'

'Nothing that I can see. I suppose he's just worried about you.'

She snorted. 'I'm not stupid, Joel, I'm not careless or incapable – and the passenger seat is not a particularly safe place.'

He glanced out from the shadow of the bonnet, grinning. 'Pauline frightens you, does she?'

Jess's cheeks reddened.

'You're not alone. She's given me a few bad moments, too.'

'Leaving that aside, though, don't you think I ought to know how to drive? I can't understand his objection. After all, he taught me to ride. I could just as easily break my neck that way.'

Finished with the engine, Joel dropped the bonnet with a bang.

'No,' he said, 'doesn't make much sense, does it?' After a moment he added, 'If you're hoping I can talk him round, Jess, I'm afraid you'll be disappointed. If anything, he'd dig his heels in harder. Robert never welcomes my advice on anything, and where it's a personal matter he's apt to take umbrage. I'd just be told to mind my own business.'

She shook her head, pushing her hands in her trouser pockets. 'No, no, I'm not trying to drag you into it. I just thought you might know why he's so dead against it.' Shoulders hunched, she leaned her back against the side of the car. 'I'd assumed that when I was ready he'd be pleased to teach me. After all, it's a useful skill.'

Joel pulled a rag from his back pocket and wiped the oil from his hands.

'Tell you what,' he said slowly, 'perhaps I could give you a lesson or two on the quiet. Once you've got the hang of it, he might be made to see that it's all right.'

Excitement flared in her, and then died down again. She chewed at her bottom lip, sorely tempted and yet uneasy.

'He'd be furious with you.'

Joel shrugged. 'That's nothing new. I'm used to rows with Rob. But you're the one who's married to him, Jess. Are you prepared to risk an uproar over this?'

She pondered briefly, then: 'I think it's important, Joel. And he'll get over it, won't he, when he sees I'm able to manage a car? In the end he'll probably thank you.'

I wouldn't like to count on that, he thought.

Aloud, he said, 'All right, then, no time like the present.'

'Oh! Now?'

'Robert's seeing a customer this morning. Go on, climb in on the passenger side. We'll go out on the Postbridge road and then you can take a turn.'

It was not as easy as she had expected. Sometimes she felt she had too many hands and feet, and other times there did not seem to be enough. So many pedals and levers, so much to think about at once. Such fumbling and jerking and meandering. Joel, however, was very patient, and they chugged back and forth for an hour or more between Two Bridges and the Warren House Inn, finally pulling off the road for a break at a high and lonely spot.

'Not much fun at this stage, is it?' Joel was sympathetic.

'I didn't dream it would be so difficult.'

'It's not, just unfamiliar.' Smiling, he enquired, 'When's this baby due, then?'

'Mid-autumn, the doctor says.'

'Be nice to have a child in the house.'

An obvious question came to her mind, but she hesitated to ask it. Joel saw it in her face and volunteered an answer.

'Pauline and I just haven't – struck lucky. We don't know why. I don't think she's too upset. Truth is, it bothers me more than it does her. I'd love a child or two. Still, I don't lose sleep over it. There's always the chance we'll have one someday, and we're happy enough aside from that.'

For a while they sat in silence. A light wind ruffled the ferny slopes and the overcast sky was mottled white and grey. Suddenly, she asked him:

'Joel, could Vanessa drive?'

'Hmm? Oh, yes. Yes, she could.'

'But she didn't have a car?'

'Her family had one, certainly. I believe she used it whenever she wanted.'

Jess frowned. 'But Rob told me he was always driving her around. The way he said it, I had the impression she used him as a cab service.'

Joel looked faintly uncomfortable. 'I don't know much about what happened between those two. Vanessa didn't come to Torvallen very often. Rob says he was always at her beck and call, and that may be so.'

Jess had caught a note of doubt. 'May be?'

'Why do you want to hear about Vanessa? Don't worry, he doesn't hanker for her now. Hasn't a good word to say for her.'

'That's not why I asked. It's just that she sounds so cruel. I don't understand why Robert liked her so much, or let her treat him as she did. After all, if she had a car of her own ...'

'As I've told you, I don't know much about it. I'll say this, though – he never needed much excuse to go rushing over there to see her, and I don't remember that she often sent for him.'

There was something strange here, something wrong. She opened her mouth to ask another question, but Joel, wishing, perhaps, that he had not said so much, gave a glance at his watch and said quickly, 'Time to go back, or Rob will miss us. You drive as far as Postbridge, then I'll take over.'

She stirred herself and switched on the engine.

'All right,' he said, 'let's see you turn her round. Come on, first gear. Now, concentrate.'

The secret lessons appealed to Pauline's sense of mischief. So she took up where Joel left off, spending several hours each week out on the road with Jess. They made some extra trips to the city for practice and Jess's confidence steadily grew as the summer wore on. Robert did not dream when he saw his wife and sister-in-law depart for Plymouth that Jess was now driving most of the way in each direction. By late July she could even cope with the traffic in town and was eager to make a trip on her own.

She was not so keen to tell her husband she had disobeyed him. There would be a row involving everyone, and she kept postponing that. One day, when he was in the right mood and she knew just how to put it, she would make the confession.

But she waited so long that in the end the truth came out of its own accord.

One Monday a cabinet-maker called at the timber yard, seeking some beech for a set of kitchen chairs.

'Saw your little wife in town this morning,' he told Robert pleasantly, as they talked. 'Driving down Union Street, she was.'

Robert was not sweet-tempered that day. He had suffered a case of sunburn, thanks to working shirtless in the yard, and now it had reached the itching stage.

'You mean my sister-in-law,' he grunted, scratching at his shoulder.

'No, no. She's dark, isn't she, Joel's wife? It was the blonde one I saw. Couldn't mistake her. I remember noticing the two of you together last autumn at Tavistock fair and thinking what a lucky man you were. No, no, I know which one's which.'

Robert stared at him. 'You're certain it was her?'

'Oh, positive, positive.'

'She was on her own?'

'Yes, going Devonport way.'

'And she was driving?'

Robert's tone and expression were enough, now, to tell the man he had somehow blundered.

'Well,' he said uneasily, 'yes.'

Lawrenson's face grew thunderous. He jerked a thumb towards the other end of the sawmill, where Peter Chivers was stacking wood. 'My man down there will sort out what you want. I'm sorry, I've something pressing I must deal with.'

The cabinet-maker took no offence at being so sharply abandoned. He merely wished he had bitten his tongue with regard to Lawrenson's wife.

Robert went outside and found his brother loading up the lorry with sheep hurdles. Turning with his arms laden, Joel halted, meeting a fearsome scowl. Just for a second he eyed Robert warily, then he swung the hurdles up on to the tail-board of the lorry and shoved them back a way before asking:

'What's amiss, Rob?'

He had thought it was something to do with the business. But then:

'It seems Pauline's been teaching my wife to drive. It's against my wishes, Joel.'

'Ah.' Joel bent down and hefted another load.

'And it must have been going on for quite some time, because Jess was seen in town today, bowling along in the car by herself. Pauline must have known I'd disapprove, because she's kept damned quiet about it. Never a careless word in front of me. I didn't suspect for an instant ...'

'We've both been teaching her,' interrupted Joel. He slung the hurdles up into the lorry and then stared levelly at his brother from under the peak of his cap. 'Why shouldn't she drive, Rob? Why should you want her marooned out here?'

'Never mind my reasons! The point is, you went behind my back, all three of you, and did something I'd forbidden.'

'Forbidden,' snorted Joel. 'If I were you, I wouldn't lay down the law too much with Jess. She loves you, but she's not the sort to be bossed, and I'm certain there's no need of it, either.'

Robert jabbed a quivering finger at him. 'It's not for you or Pauline to interfere between my wife and me. Damn you, Joel, you've no right to override what I say and encourage her to disobey me. If the boot were on the other foot, I wouldn't go against you on anything concerning Pauline.'

'I don't think the question would ever come up. I'm never unreasonable with her.'

'Unreasonable? Hmph! Perhaps, for her own good, you ought to be a bit more "unreasonable", if that's what you want to call it. The rate she goes, she's likely to kill herself one of these days. Pauline is a dangerous driver, Joel, and hardly the best person to teach someone else.'

'If you feel like that, then surely it's all the more justification for Jess to drive herself – and for you to have taught her and set a better example.'

Out-manoeuvred, Robert blustered. 'I shan't forgive this in a hurry, Joel. Furthermore, it's been a waste of all your time and effort, because I will not allow Jess to use the car.'

'Don't smother her, Rob, or try to play the master. You'll do yourself no good. Haven't you learned your lesson?'

'I don't know what that's meant to signify,' said Robert, scornfully.

'Oh yes you do.' Pulling the peak of his cap down hard, Joel resumed his work. 'I recommend you think it over, give her a bit of rope.'

The force of the quarrel had spent itself. The shouting and slamming of doors was all over, the house was quiet again. Robert was feeling wretched, now, while Jess saw the chance to negotiate.

'All right, then, let's say once a week. Just once, Robert.'

'I said no, and I meant it.'

He was sitting on the edge of the bed, head bowed. Now that the rage had passed, he simply felt betrayed, disappointed in her. Edging across the quilt, Jess leaned over him, draping her arms around his neck. She was noticeably pregnant now and he felt the pressure of her rounded belly against his back.

'Look, I shan't be able to "go gallivanting", whatever that means, not with a baby to care for. But it would be nice if Mam could see her grandchild once a week. She'd love that, Rob, I know she would. I think she's very lonely since I left.'

Chin on his shoulder, she was gazing at his profile.

Robert turned and looked at her. The fair hair fell like a golden fleece around her face and down over his chest.

'You were underhand about all this,' he said, reproachfully.

'I regret that, but you didn't give me much choice.'

'Matter of opinion.'

The sunburnt skin above his waist was a deep red-brown. He reached behind him, scratching at his spine. Around his neck hung a small gold St Christopher medal. Jess had never known him take it off. Sitting back on her heels, she trailed her nails over his shoulder-blades and he wriggled with pleasure.

'Truly, I'd rather you'd been the one to teach me. You're such a good driver, Robert. You know, there are still a few things I haven't quite mastered – backing round corners, for one. I'd be so glad if you'd help me iron out problems like that. Pauline flusters me sometimes.'

'Trying flattery now?'

'Just stating facts. It was you I asked first, don't forget. I only fell back on Joel and Pauline because you refused.' Then she murmured, 'Ooh, your back is peeling.'

Her tongue crept into the corner of her mouth as she delicately scraped up a silvery tag of skin, gripped it and slowly stripped off a length of gossamer tissue, prettily punctured with pore-holes. As it tore it left loose white edges where more could be prised away. Sliding a nail underneath, she gently scaled off a ribbon a full foot long. It made a tiny ripping sound and she gave a sigh of satisfaction.

'I love doing this.'

Another tug and a long, slow, tickling tear. Robert shivered, enjoying it.

Slipping an arm round his waist, she stroked his belly, whispering:

'Once a week, Robert? Say, Thursdays?'

She was asking very little now. Robert was torn two ways, desiring to make a stand on principle, yet mindful of his brother's words as well. He hated taking Joel's advice, but perhaps this once it might be wise ...

'Say yes, and I'll peel you all over.'

'I'm not sunburnt all over.'

'You know what I mean.'

'Oh, you ...' He fought against a smile. 'You know how to get around me, don't you?' But quickly his face grew solemn again. 'Will you always defy me, Jess, when we disagree over something like this? Won't I be able to trust you?'

'I may defy you openly, but I'll never go behind your back again, I promise.' Kissing the corner of his mouth, she repeated, 'Once a week?'

Sighing, he relented. 'Thursdays.'

· Twelve ·

Five years, it would soon be five years. Five celibate, reclusive years. Nothing but home and the shop and a twice-weekly expedition to Fore Street to buy the groceries. And occasionally, very occasionally, a journey into the city centre on the tram, just to look around the stores. That was the nearest Alice ever came to excitement nowadays.

Screwing one eye shut, she peered unsteadily into her glass. Empty again. How many was that? She estimated five, or possibly six, and they had all been big ones. Half a dozen large, fragrant measures of Plymouth gin. She grasped the bottle and filled the glass once more.

It was Thursday today – early closing for most traders. Alice did not trouble to open her shop at all on Thursdays now. Thursday and Sunday were holidays, on which she could tipple to her heart's content. She and her bottle, an intimate twosome, could go to bed together, undisturbed. It was very much like being alone with a lover – the gin was something wicked, dangerous, delicious, something heady that changed the look of the world for a little while.

And why not? she thought defiantly, taking another gulp. There was nothing left to enjoy except her drop of drink. Her existence had grown as narrow as a nun's cell. Where men were concerned, Alice had lost her nerve. Not that she did not feel the occasional tug of attraction when someone personable came into the shop, not that the old yearning was utterly gone. But she was frightened now, and aghast at the risks she had taken in the past.

Self-delusion had gone as well. Her mirror spared her nothing, presenting her every morning with an image cruelly different to the one she had long preserved in her mind. For many years Alice had kept an idea of herself as she had been at twenty, dismissing the deepening lines as tricks of the light or signs of passing fatigue. She had told herself she had 'a good colour', refusing to study too closely the web of tiny veins that marred her cheeks. Confronting her reflection with honesty at last, Alice knew she was on the decline. Bored, lonely, and ill-disposed towards religion, she had only liquid solace.

Propped against her pillows, pulling at a trailing strand of hair, Alice quickly drained the glass. The clock said twenty to twelve as she moved to pour herself another one. And that was when she heard the back door slam.

Alice froze. She had locked it, she knew, and her daughter had the only spare key. But Jess was not meant to come today. Only on a Monday, once a month, was she supposed to visit. What could she be doing here this morning?

Lord! Oh, Lord!

Alice rolled over, thrusting the glass and bottle hurriedly under the bed. She had lost the cap and her shaking hand did not set the bottle down squarely on the floor. Dismayed, she heard it topple, heard the trickling of gin on the lino.

'Mam?' Jess was downstairs looking for her, in the storeroom, in the shop.

Her wits half scattered, Alice thought, I'll have to say I'm ill, that I've had a sick headache all night.

Now she heard her daughter coming up the stairs.

'Mam? Are you here? Are you all right?'

The bedroom door swung open. Jess paused, her hand on the doorknob, and Alice blurted out her lie.

'I'm not feeling too well, my love. I've such a bad head.'

Jess did not believe it for a moment. The scent of gin had reached her nostrils straight away.

'I wondered why the shop was closed,' she said, coolly, 'and now I know.'

Her gaze flicked down to the floor. A tell-tale puddle was creeping out from under the bed, pooling round one of the castors. Finally, the bottle, too, emerged, rolled gently across the floor and disappeared under the wardrobe.

'Oh, Mam.' A heavy sigh, full of exasperation.

'I wasn't expecting you today ...'

'That's obvious.'

'Why are you here? Is anything wrong?'

'Nothing. I can drive now, so Robert will let me have the car each Thursday.'

'Oh,' said Alice, without enthusiasm.

'I take it when your grandchild's born you'll be glad to see it every week?'

'Yes,' said Alice, shamefaced, 'yes, of course.'

'Meantime, I've brought you some groceries. There's a chicken and some bacon, cheese, butter, greens and a pound of haddock.'

'You're such a good girl,' said Alice, humbly.

'I'll go and put it all away.'

'No!' Alice's voice was loud with alarm and she quickly toned it down. 'No – don't you bother yourself. Pregnant like you are, you shouldn't even be carrying that bag. I'll do it later. Just sit here and talk to me.'

'After I've unpacked the food.'

'No, look, the kitchen's a bit untidy. I want to put it in order first. I'll be getting up now, I'm feeling better.'

Jess surveyed her suspiciously, wondering what it was that Alice wished to hide. Without a word she headed for the kitchen.

The scene that met her eyes was one of utter squalor.

The sink was piled high with dirty, ill-smelling pots and pans. Bits of cabbage stuck to the inside of one, congealed gravy covered the bottom of another, hardened fat lined the frying pan and something seemed to have burnt itself into the very enamel of the pie dish. Plates crusted with dried food littered the table. A jar of jam, minus its lid, contained two dead flies. A jug of milk, solid and sourly stinking, had sprouted a green, hairy mould. There were spillages everywhere; a puddle of tea and a scattering of porridge oats on the floor, a lump of rice pudding on top of the stove, packets overturned on all the shelves. The waste bin overflowed with fish and poultry bones and decaying vegetable peelings. It could not have been emptied for more than a week and had drawn a swarm of bluebottles.

A shambles. Jess had never seen the equal of it. It was never like this when she called on a Monday. The place was always in perfect order, then. This unexpected visit had caught her mother out.

Staring round her, Jess dropped her bag on a chair. Something crunched underfoot. Looking down, she saw it was a broken egg. The white and yolk were smeared across the lino.

On investigation, she found that the sitting room, too, was in chaos. It also reeked of drink. Mam had upset half a bottle of gin over the hearthrug and had simply left it to soak in. There were many empty bottles lying about.

After a while, Alice came creeping apologetically into the kitchen. She found her daughter putting on an overall.

'Jess, you mustn't concern yourself with all my muddle. It's heavy work and you're expecting. I'll be clearing up, don't worry. You just leave it to me.'

Jess ignored that. 'Is this how you live now I'm away? Do you only put it straight when you know I'm due to call, so that I shan't see?'

Alice reddened. 'It's a bit of a mess, I know.'

'It's filthy! The whole place smells. There isn't so much as a clean cup or knife to use.' Her gaze ran despairingly over Alice's figure, noting the crumpled skirt with its drooping hem, the stained cardigan with three missing buttons. 'And your clothes! You used to be so fussy, Mam.'

Alice shook her head and made a limp, dismissive gesture. 'Well, it doesn't matter quite so much now you're not here. I used to keep the place nice for you, but now I'm on my own it's too much trouble. I shouldn't leave it so long, I know. I'm always meaning to clean up, but somehow I don't get round to it very often.'

'Somehow?' queried Jess. 'That makes it sound as if you don't know the reason. But you do, Mam, we both do.'

Alice did not want to talk about that. Hurriedly taking a sponge, she started wiping the table top, manoeuvring between the dirty crockery.

'I'll give you a hand, my love, we'll soon ...'

'No,' said Jess, stiffly. Feeling waspish, she did not want her mother round her. Tossing her a cloth, she added, 'I'd rather you wiped up what's under your bed. And take the sheets off, too. God only knows when last they were changed. They've gone a very bad colour.'

But Alice stayed, hovering. 'I'm sorry, Jess ...'

Her daughter cut across the apology. 'You promised me you'd look after yourself. I shouldn't have to worry about you, Mam.' She started taking up the oats and broken eggshell with a dustpan and brush. 'It's not as if you're old and sick – though it seems to me you're doing your level best to make a wreck of yourself. I counted four bottles in the sitting room alone.'

'I haven't had any today, Jess, truly, not a drop.'

'For the love of God, I know you have! I smelt it the moment you opened your mouth. I can smell it from here! Anybody'd think you bathed in the stuff as well as drinking it.' She seized a mop and began slopping it over the lino, jerking it violently in and out of corners. 'At this time of the morning, when you ought to have the shop open! You'll lose your trade, I'm warning you, if you don't keep to regular hours. Go on down and open up, while I get on with this.'

Alice very wisely retreated and her daughter commenced a storm of scouring and sweeping and laundering which lasted a full four hours. By late afternoon the kitchen was spotless, the sitting-room rug had been sponged, the bottles and the rubbish were in the dustbin, there were fresh sheets in Alice's bed, and a load of washing was out on the line.

Alice kept out of the way until all sound from overhead had ceased. When at length she appeared again at the kitchen door, she found Jess sitting down to a cup of tea.

'You'll have to iron the laundry yourself,' she was told. 'I've done all I can for one day.'

Meekly, Alice thanked her.

Jess stood up and pressed her hands to the small of her aching back. Hours of graft and the weight of the child inside her had every muscle crying out in protest. Wearily, she said, 'I'm sorry I went for you, Mam, but it worries me to see the place, and you, in such a state. I've a husband now to look after and soon I'll have a child as well. There's a limit to what I can do for you. You must take better care of yourself, and you can't afford to neglect the business.'

'I know, I know.' Alice smiled, appeasingly. 'I promise I'll turn over a new leaf.'

A glint came into Jess's eye. 'Yes, well, as I said, I'll be calling every week in future – so I'll see that you do.'

Her mother's smile became a little sickly.

'Mind you have a good supper now, Mam.'

'Aren't you going to stay a while?'

'Not today, I've been here long enough.'

Stepping outside, Jess experienced a surge of relief. Now she could go home, back to Torvallen, back to peace and sanity. The car was parked in front of the shop. Stepping off the kerb, she went round to the driver's side.

That was when she saw the scratches – deep, ragged gouges in the paintwork, running right along the side of the car and around the back. There was also a word, a name, incised in letters about three inches high. The word would have puzzled a stranger, but was all too familiar to Jess. To cap it all, her tyres were flat. All four had been let down.

Jess supposed she was lucky they had not been cut. She was too tired and miserable to care who had done it. It was, she thought bitterly, a fitting end to the day. Resignedly, she took the footpump from the back of the car and started the long, arduous task of reinflating her tyres.

Watching through the lace curtain of her front-room window, Mrs Fitch patted her eight-year-old nephew on the head. The boy looked up at her and giggled, fingering the penknife in his pocket.

Mrs Fitch had lately had to swallow a bitter pill, for the fortunes of her own daughter had taken a downward turn. All of Brenda's hopes had been harshly swept away. Her husband had not been quite as secure as he seemed. He had a score of creditors and they had made him bankrupt. So he and Brenda were now night porter and vegetable cook at a hotel in the city centre, living in shabby staff quarters. There was little chance that they would ever be prosperous again. Small wonder, then, that the sight of Jess, nicely dressed and sitting at the wheel of a car, awakened fierce resentment in Mrs Fitch.

Something seemed to prickle at the back of Jess's neck as she laboured at the footpump. There was a brief, involuntary hunching of her shoulders, as if with the cold. She had sensed that there were gloating eyes upon her. 'Pitchpot' said the word, in clumsy, angular letters. Here, to these people, she would never be anyone other than 'Pitchpot'.

'Brats, you can bet,' snorted Robert, when he saw the damage. 'Destructive little brutes, some of them. Never mind, I'll have it painted over.' Squatting down beside the driver's door, he fingered the name scratched near the bottom. 'What does this say? Bitch-something?'

'I don't know,' lied Jess.

'Nasty little beasts,' muttered her husband.

'I'm very sorry, Rob. I didn't think of anything like this when I asked to take the car.'

'Why should you?' He stood up, smiling, and wrapped an arm around her shoulders. 'Don't worry, I'm not blaming you. Perhaps you'd better park elsewhere in future, though. Leave her in Fore Street, where it's busy.'

Jess's face brightened. She had half-feared he would use this as a reason to deny her any further use of the car. Still, he could not resist scoring a point when she told him about the tyres.

'See, it's not all pleasure, driving.'

Jess let that one pass without argument.

'See anybody you knew today?' he asked, as they went indoors.

'No one but Mam.'

'Spent the whole time with her, did you?'

'Yes.'

'Didn't go shopping in Plymouth, then?'

'No, I bought some groceries in Devonport, that's all.'

'Weather's been nice. You could have taken Alice for a drive.'

'Mam doesn't like riding in the car. She gets queasy, you know that.'

'So you stayed at her place all day?'

'I've already told you so.'

He seemed to be fishing for something, though Jess could not tell what. She did not want to let him know of the strenuous way she had spent the day, the condition in which she had found the house and Alice. Perhaps he sensed she was hiding something – no doubt she was looking tired – but his questions were searching and sometimes repeated.

'Enjoy it, out in the car on your own?'

'Yes, I did.'

'Didn't give anyone a lift, I hope?'

'Of course not.'

'Must never do that. You don't know who's about.'

'You've told me that a dozen times.'

'Yes, well, it's important.'

He kept on for a good five minutes. It was, in truth, a little tiresome, but she did not show impatience or feel disturbed by such persistent questions. For the time, she was too relieved that he was not annoyed with her about the car.

Two more months of pregnancy and Jess was at last rewarded with a son. On the second Sunday in October she gave birth to a seven-pound baby boy. They named him Colin, after Robert's father, and the christening took place at Widecombe church in the presence of all the Lawrensons' employees and their families.

Robert was bursting with pride as he showed off his son to one and all. Red-faced and squalling, the child was carried round to be admired and his father did not seem to mind the noise or the wetting of his brand new suit. All grin and broad chest, Robert felt elevated to a new dignity and status, and assured everyone that this was merely the first of the fine, healthy brood he expected to raise.

Jess stood quietly by to let him enjoy his glory. It was good to see him so buoyant, the centre of attention with the infant in his arms. She had never been sentimental about motherhood, but the very first sight of the baby had filled her with a strange new sense of female power. Her young – like a mother cat, she purred over him, suckled him and sat for long dreamy hours murmuring to him. Animal contentment lay upon her that first year of Colin's life, a soft, private enjoyment of the infant that Robert could not know. For him it was different. The boy was cause to swagger, a copy of himself, a son to be a credit to him, earning him heavy pats on the back and proving he was lusty. All very hearty, very male. What Jess felt was something quieter, more mysterious.

And when she lay wrapped together with Robert in the dark, with the child in his cot by the bed, she could now tell herself that her life was complete. Jess had everything she wanted, and the future promised only good.

· Thirteen ·

There came a morning the following May when Charlie Weekes did not turn up for work.

'He's put his back out,' Peter Chivers told Robert. 'His wife says he woke up this morning and couldn't stand straight. You know, he shifted that stack of flooring planks yesterday single-handed, loaded the lorry all on his own. He's too old for that sort of thing, Robert. I know we're very busy, but it's time for Charlie to ease off and start doing less.'

'Damn,' muttered Robert, 'I shouldn't have let him do it, I suppose. I just didn't think.'

'The way he's bent over, I reckon he'll be in bed for a good week.'

'Damn!' repeated Robert. 'All right, well look, tell him not to worry, we'll still pay him. I know he'll be back as soon as he can. And I'll keep him off that kind of slog in future.'

He went across the yard and into the sawmill to find his brother.

'Seems Charlie did himself an injury yesterday when he put that builder's order on the lorry,' he told him. 'I believe we need some extra help, Joel, somebody just for heavy work like that. Moving stuff, clearing up and so on.'

Joel switched off the lathe where he was working. 'That's not enough to occupy a man full-time.'

'No, but I think we ought to get someone in for a couple of days a week. It's that or replace Charlie with a younger, fitter man.'

'Couldn't do that,' said Joel. 'Couldn't give Charlie the push. He needs his job.'

'Of course. What's more, he's a first-rate carpenter, and

they don't grow on trees. Anyway, another pair of hands would help us all, not just Charlie.'

'Hmm.' Joel sucked thoughtfully at his teeth. 'But who can we ask?'

'There must be somebody hereabout who'd be glad of part-time work.'

'It's never been easy, finding people out here,' reflected Joel. 'It took Father years to assemble the workforce we've got. And we've had other casuals come and go. Because we're so far out of the way, they soon decided it wasn't worth the hike.'

'Yes, yes, I remember. Still, we have to try.'

'Well, ask the men if they know of anyone.'

'All right,' Robert said. 'If not, then I'll put the word about in Princetown and Postbridge. Perhaps we'll have better luck this time.'

After all, he was thinking, we're not looking for a craftsman. Anybody will do.

Three or four miles west of Torvallen, there lay a tract of dreary country where the soil was uncommonly poor and thin and the few scattered dwellings were mean.

The worst of them was an almost derelict farmhouse crouched in a hollow under a low hill. It was known as 'Liddy's Farm', though in truth it amounted to no more than a smallholding, having just eight acres of land.

The house was in a hopeless state of decay. Many of the windows were broken or boarded over and the frames were soft with rot. Most of the guttering had fallen off and what remained hung loose and creaked in the wind. There were places inside where great frills of fungus sprouted from the walls and erupted between the floorboards. The staircase could not be trusted to bear a heavy or careless tread, and one end of the roof displayed a sizeable hole, where part of the chimney stack had collapsed and fallen through at the height of a winter gale. Dark and decomposing, lined with peeling paper and flaking plaster, the house was an ugly wart on the face of the moor.

The yard outside was a quagmire in wet weather, the mud deep and sucking. There were outhouses, all dilapidated, filled with tools, troughs, feed bins and piles of sacking. Rusty sheets of corrugated iron formed a makeshift hen coop near the gate. The fields around were small, separated by tumbledown walls.

Even in summer sunshine this was a cheerless place, no longer a fit habitation for any human being. Yet here, amid the dirt and mould, there lived an individual by the name of Alec Maunder.

He had bought the smallholding just after the war, paying next to nothing, and his five years' occupation had improved it not at all. A slovenly, indolent man, he scraped a living in accord with his skimpy efforts.

Half a dozen chickens, two pigs and an old horse were the total of his livestock. Modest yields of turnips, cabbages and potatoes came from his fields, the planting and digging of which were as much cultivation as he cared to do. Having no desire for a wife or children, he considered his needs to be met as long as there was food and fuel. The moor provided both if one knew where to look. There was wood and furze to burn, there were rabbits to shoot, fish to catch, and Alec Maunder did not mind from whose land he took them.

In this way he had subsisted since 1919, eating and sleeping in the kitchen. Dried out by the warmth of the cooking stove, it was the only liveable room in the house. Shaving was a chore, so Maunder had found it convenient to let his beard grow. It covered his lower face, a wiry ginger mat, through which his teeth appeared from time to time, large and grinning, when something pleased him. His nose was blunt, his cheeks without much contour. Nature had granted him eyes that lent a little attraction to an otherwise undistinguished face, but therein lay a trap for those who took his clear green gaze as evidence of honest character. Brown hair, which he contrived to cut himself, straggled over his forehead, round his ears and down his neck.

For miles around he was known by sight, but few had

made his acquaintance. He had scant regard for hygiene and still less for grooming, and was not the sort of man who attracted social invitations from his neighbours. Women, in particular, were apt to find him disquieting and they did not want him in their homes.

The winter of 1923 had been hard for him. In January a fall of snow had trapped him for several days with hardly a scrap of food in the house, forcing him to kill two of his chickens to keep himself going. Maunder emerged from this ordeal somewhat frightened by the experience. He had been lucky and he knew it. Blizzards on Dartmoor sometimes left lonely houses cut off for weeks. Had such occurred on this occasion, he might very well have died. His clothes were wearing thin, he was short of such necessities as paraffin for his lamps and cartridges for his gun. He wanted to keep supplies in store in future, especially tinned and dried foods, and to buy himself some good strong boots and a heavy coat. However, the money that came from the sale of vegetables and moleskins was simply not enough to pay for these things. Furthermore, a string of unpaid bills ensured that no trader in Princetown would allow him any more credit.

So it was that he chanced to be seeking work that spring. Several local farmers gave him odd jobs, but not until the end of May did he happen to hear of steady employment on offer nearby. One day it came to his notice that an extra man was needed at the Lawrenson sawmill.

In the stables, Robert and Joel faced each other across the back of the chestnut mare. Brush in one hand and comb in the other, Joel was gently grooming the horse's coat and taking the knots out of her tail. He was not exactly happy about the man his brother had hired.

'Maunder?' he queried, uneasily. 'Him from Liddy's Farm?'

'That's the one. Scruffy sort of character, but strong and glad of the work. I said we could give him two days a week, occasionally three. Eight bob a day. He jumped at it.'

'Has no one else come forward for the job?'
'A couple. They wanted more money.'
His brother glanced at him from under his brows. He passed no comment, but Robert sensed dissatisfaction.
'After all, it's only donkey work, no skill involved,' he said, defensively.
'I know that. Eight bob's fair.'
Robert heard the unspoken 'But ...'
'Yes, and what's wrong with hiring Maunder?'
Laying aside the brush, Joel stood for a moment stroking the mare's nose. 'I'm not sure. I just don't like the look of him. He grins all the time. I never trust a man who smiles too much.'
'Oh, what rubbish! There's no reason not to give him a try. If he doesn't measure up, he'll be out. I told him that.'
'Hmm, all right.' The dubious note remained in Joel's voice. 'I only wish you'd discussed it with me first.'
'Look, you weren't here when he called, and I'm as good at picking men as you are.'
'You've never chosen one before,' Joel reminded him.
'Well, I have now and he starts tomorrow.'
Taking up the brush again, his brother said mildly, 'Since you've told him to come in, we'll see how he goes on.'
'It's not fair to prejudge him,' persisted Robert. 'We don't even know the man – or is that your very point?'
'Part of it,' admitted Joel. 'Up to now we've always hired on someone's recommendation.'
'We can't expect that every time. And what else is biting you? I'm allowed to make decisions, aren't I? We're equal partners, aren't we?'
'Yes,' sighed Joel. 'Yes, of course. That's why I wish you'd consulted me. I was entitled to have a say. Still, never mind now.'
'Does Maunder have the evil eye or something?'
'Something.'
'But you don't know what.' Robert scoffed. 'I thought only fanciful women talked like that.'

Joel could have made a quarrel of it, but instead he bit his tongue – as he so often did – and put an end to the argument.

'I'll be very pleased if I'm wrong, Rob, and delighted if you're right. Here's hoping he turns out well.'

'Adequate' was the word Joel subsequently used to describe the new employee's efforts at the yard. Maunder did no less and no more than he was told, unhurried in his pace of work, adept at making a given task fill the hours neatly. He did not like to fall behind for fear of being asked to stay late, but nor did he care to finish any chore too quickly, since Robert and Joel could always find him another one. The quality of his labour was such that it earned him neither compliment nor rebuke. It was tolerable, passable, giving the brothers no cause to dismiss him, but no incentive to raise his wages either. His presence was usually required at the sawmill on Wednesdays and Thursdays, an arrangement which suited him well enough, and one he was content to maintain for as long as the Lawrensons might need him.

The other men were divided in their attitudes to Alec Maunder. Peter Chivers disliked him and so did Henry Wills, while Eddie Pierce had no particular opinion. Between the brothers he was a subject of subtle contention. In the interests of peace, little was ever said, but Joel would have welcomed an excuse to fire him, while Robert, knowing this, was determined to keep the man he had hired.

So Maunder had an ally – and he also had one friend, in the shape of Charlie Weekes. Innocent and less than bright, Charlie was always friendly with everyone. He did not mind with whom he sat to eat his lunch of bread and cheese, and he talked very freely of everything and everyone he knew.

It was while they were having their midday break one day in July that the subject of the Lawrenson women came up.

'You ever seen the boys' wives?' Charlie asked.

'No,' said Maunder. 'Why?'

'Oh, lovely girls, both of them.'

A gleam of interest appeared in Maunder's eyes. He liked women, though not enough to want to support one. He hankered after females in much the way he hankered after game. If it could be poached without too much risk or effort, he found it very enticing.

'Pretty, are they?' He grinned at Charlie, his jaws working on a chunk of cold brisket. Eating with his mouth open was one of the habits Joel found most offensive in him. There were wet, mashing sounds and glimpses of churning, pulverised food.

'Pretty? Oh, I'll say! That fair one, Robert's wife, she's something special. Jessamine, she's called.' Charlie pronounced the full name with care, thinking it beautiful.

Maunder offered him a pickled onion.

'Pauline drops in here now and again, but not the other one,' continued Charlie, eating the onion whole. 'Course, she has that baby to look after, and most of the time she's tied to the house. Mind you, I believe she goes to see her mother every week, and that's a fair old trip.'

'Oh? Not a local girl, then?'

'Aw, no! She's all the way from Devonport!' exclaimed Charlie, who had rarely been off the moor in all his sixty-two years. 'Proper city girl.'

Maunder nodded affably and said no more. Charlie, however, had kindled curiosity within him. A city girl out here? He thought that strange. Something special? Was she, now? In that case, he would like to see her.

Sitting at the kitchen table, cleaning up some old silver cutlery, Jess was suddenly conscious of someone behind her. Her hands froze in motion, she half-turned her head and saw, from the corner of her eye, a long shadow cast across the floor.

Then came a brief knock and a genial, 'Hello'.

Twisting round, she saw a man framed against the light in the open back doorway.

Jess stood up and the man advanced a step or two into

the kitchen. His clothing was crumpled and none too clean, his shirt without a collar. In his hand, held by the claws, was a dead chicken.

'Good morning,' she said, wary and formal. She did not know this person and judgement of the quick, instinctive sort made her feel that she probably would not want to.

But then he said, 'You'll be Robert's wife, unless I miss my guess.'

'Yes ... ?'

'Brought you something, Mrs Lawrenson.' He held out the chicken.

'Oh. Well, thank you, Mr ... ?'

'Maunder.'

The name stirred a memory – Joel and Robert disagreeing one morning over breakfast, something to do with a new employee.

Taking the fowl, she said, 'Ah, I believe I've heard you mentioned. You work for my husband, is that right?'

'Been talked about, have I?' A chuckle, the beard splitting open to reveal the teeth.

Jess felt obliged to smile too, but it was merely polite, without warmth. 'This is very kind of you.' She put the bird down on the table. 'It's a fine chicken.'

'Well, it was good of your family to take me on. Things were a bit tight before they gave me work. I like to show appreciation.'

His eyes were fastened on her, almost unblinking, absorbing every line and curve of her face. With cunning control he did not let them stray downwards over her figure, except in moments when she glanced away. Then they would swiftly reconnoitre, slyly inspecting breasts and hips. But he did not let her catch him at it, too quick and too crafty to give her cause for offence. Always when her attention returned to him, she met that wide and seemingly respectful gaze.

'Other lady not here, then?' he asked.

'She's gone for a ride. She'll be back before long.'

'Ah.' A nod, another grin. He hovered.

Jess supposed she ought to offer him a cup of tea and a scone or something. In view of his gift, it would seem uncivil not to. She did not feel at ease with him, yet all he had done was make a friendly gesture.

'The kettle's on. Will you have a drink of tea now you're here? And some cake perhaps?'

He did not need to be pressed. 'Very nice, yes, wouldn't mind.'

Seating himself at the table, he folded his hands on the scrubbed wood, waiting, smiling.

Jess turned to the stove in response to the kettle's thin shriek. Maunder scrutinised her buttocks, round and neat beneath her plain cotton frock. Weekes had been right. She was something special. He had never seen such hair – a three-foot curtain of waves and curls. Maunder loved long hair on a woman, and that was a taste he shared with Robert. It was solely to please her husband that Jess had refrained from having it bobbed.

'You've a baby boy, I'm told,' he said, as she prepared the tea.

'Yes, nine months old. He's sleeping just now.'

'Going to have more, I daresay?'

Jess smiled faintly, cut him a piece of cherry cake and put two biscuits on the plate beside it.

'Lovely house, this,' Maunder went on. 'I looked in the sitting-room window just now before I came round the back. Lovely house. Expect it's just as nice upstairs?'

She had the feeling he was hoping she might show him round. Ignoring that, she asked him about his home instead.

'Oh, it's just a run-down old farm. Bit of a mess, to tell the truth. Being a man on my own, I'm apt to let things slide – the niceties, I mean.'

Jess set his tea down in front of him, then placed herself on the far side of the table to drink her own. Between them lay the chicken, a heap of mottled brown feathers with curled yellow claws, the dead eyes half-lidded. He had broken its neck as easily as he now snapped a biscuit in half.

'I'm sure you've a lot to do in running your own place and working for us as well.'

'That's true, that's true. I make time for a little pleasure, though.'

Jess did not ask him what kind.

'I hear you come from the city,' he said. 'Aren't you bored out here?'

'No, it suits me.'

Maunder sucked in a mouthful of tea. 'Unusual, that, 'specially in a good-looking woman like you. Very unusual, wanting to shut yourself away in the country. Town folk generally see the moor as God-forsaken – all right for a picnic, but no place to live.'

'They're wrong, it's beautiful. I have my home, husband and child here. That's enough for anyone with sense. I don't need a lot of friends and outings. I've always liked to keep myself to myself.'

The reply was crisp, even a little stiff, and Maunder was wise enough to change the subject. He went on to talk about the timber yard, the other men, his troubles of the previous winter. And all the time he stared, no matter which of them was speaking. It made him seem earnest, attentive. It was also very tiring. There was something demanding about those eyes, they did not let her relax.

Jess was glad when his cup and plate were empty and she did not offer to refill them. When at last he scraped back his chair and made to stand up, she was very quickly on her feet, ready to show him out.

'Hope the chicken goes down well,' he said, pausing at the door.

'I'm sure it will. I'll tell my husband who brought it.'

Maunder was pleased. He liked to keep in with Robert.

'I'll be off, then,' he said, and yet he loitered long enough for one more look at her before finally stepping outside. Jess watched him disappear into the woods. Then she shut the door and did something that was not her normal habit. She shot the bolt.

The back door had always stood open on fine days.

Never before had she felt unsafe – not even the time when two prisoners escaped from Princetown gaol and were known to be roaming the moor. This was the first tremor of insecurity she had ever felt at Torvallen. And in truth there seemed to be no good reason for it. One of the family's employees had brought a present and stayed for a cup of tea, that was all. Odd that she should be perturbed by that.

Jess supposed it was partly due to the way he had appeared so silently in the doorway. She wondered, now, how long he had been standing there before she became aware of him. With the door shut she began to notice, too, the smell he had left behind him. A light, damp odour, suggestive of mildew.

Next day, while they were bottling home-made wine, Pauline asked about the extra chicken in the larder.

'Oh,' said Jess, 'a man called Maunder brought it. A present, he said, to thank us for giving him work.'

'Hmm, I've heard Joel talk about him.'

'What does he say?'

'Nothing complimentary. I've never seen this Maunder. What's he like?'

Jess considered for a moment. 'Unsettling,' she said, at last. 'I didn't care for him.'

Pauline tried the rhubarb wine and smacked her lips. 'This is going to be very good,' she announced, thumping a cork down the neck of the bottle. 'It'll be just right by Christmas.'

The bottles stood in gleaming clusters on the table, waiting to be filled with parsnip, elderberry, damson and dandelion. Pauline always stored the best away for the winter. She also brewed gallons of herby beer. Now and again there were explosions, when a specially fierce brew shot its cork or even shattered the bottle.

'Odd that he came to the house,' she remarked. 'He could have taken the chicken to the yard on one of his working days and given it to Rob or Joel. He must have made a special trip to bring it over.'

Jess pursed her mouth. 'I suppose it was good of him. Still, I was very glad when he left. He had a way about him, something that set me on edge. He isn't like the other men.'

Pauline placed a funnel in the neck of another bottle and started pouring in a pale gold liquid from an earthenware flagon.

'Well,' she said, 'you're not alone in thinking so. My husband's a good judge of character, and he doesn't have much time for him.'

Joel's actual words to his wife concerning Maunder had been stronger, more blunt than that: 'A bad penny,' he had said, 'with a toady on one side and a rogue on the other, unless I miss my guess. Robert'll find him out in the end, you wait.'

The judgement was intuitive and very accurate, for Alec Maunder's history was one of petty larceny. The 'toady' side of the man, the smiling, ingratiating face, was always the most apparent. But what was underneath it was a low, pernicious nature, softly creepy like a moorland mist.

· Fourteen ·

There was going to be fog on the way home and Jess hated driving in fog. She saw it as soon as she reached the edge of the moor. The light was milky over the high ground and the mist flowed down on the hills in luminous waves, lit by the evening sun. Before very long that brightness would be gone and grey would close in on every side. Jess now wished she had not stayed for that second cup of tea with Mam. Still, it could not be helped. She knew the route too well by now to lose her way, but she switched on her headlamps and slowed her speed by half as mist crept up to the roadside verges and drifted across her path. In the back seat, the baby was sleeping in a basket cot. Robert had fitted straps to hold it firm.

Jess had three turnings to make in order to reach Torvallen. The first came at Two Bridges, and after that she carried straight on for several miles. The cloud grew thick and clammy, spreading a fine, damp haze across her windscreen. Every minute or two she gave it a flick of the wipers. The second turning came up and she made it without hesitation. Less than seven miles to go now. Jess glanced over her shoulder at the child. Deep in his blankets, Colin went on snoozing.

For five minutes more she drove on. She was down to twenty miles an hour, for her greatest fear in fog was of hitting some straying animal on the road. It was a very real danger, and sure enough, on this particular day, she had occasion to brake in a hurry – though not for the usual sheep or pony or bullock.

She was not quite sure just what it was. She only saw a shadow through the fog, dark and indistinct, standing in the road some forty feet in front of her. Jess hit the brake very hard. Some creatures were slow to respond to a horn and she had no room to steer round it, for the road was narrow and boulders littered the verges.

The jolt threw her forward, then back. She heard the basket shift on the seat behind her and whirled around to see that the child was all right. Colin whimpered but did not wake. His mother tested the straps and rebuckled them tighter, then turned around, shaken, to peer through the windscreen.

The dark shape had gone. The mist was unbroken, dirty-white. Then, as composure returned, she realised that the engine had stopped. In the panic of braking, she had stalled it.

She sighed, shook her head and pressed the starter.

Nothing happened.

Muttering, she tried again. Still there was no response, not even the groaning and whining that would prove it was making an effort. Not a sound – or so she thought at first.

After several increasingly angry and desperate attempts, Jess became aware of a faint, fluttering click which seemed to come from just behind the dashboard. She sat back, frowning. She knew how to clear a flooded engine, coax a very cold one into life, deal with wet plugs and so forth, but this she had never encountered before.

After a moment or two she got out, folded back the bonnet and squinted at the works inside. There was nothing obviously wrong, nothing broken, nothing disconnected.

'Oh, Lord,' she muttered, helpless now. 'Oh, my Lord, I could be here all night.'

But no, of course, her husband had the lorry. He would come to look for her, once she was badly overdue. All the same, she could still be stranded for hours, perhaps until after dark. The only alternative seemed to be to walk the rest of the way.

Five miles in fog and failing light? Carrying a baby? She quickly dismissed the idea. The only course was to wait in the car until Robert came to find her.

Swearing under her breath, Jess closed the bonnet again. She looked about her once more, wondering what it was she had seen in the fog. An animal? She did not think so now, pondering on its outline. It had stood too high, and its form was peculiar, humped and lopsided.

Hemmed in by cloud and wrapped in silence, she began to feel uneasy. Stories crowded into her mind, old tales of goblins, demons, cursed and misbegotten beings said to populate the moor. Things that fled from sunlight but roamed abroad in mist or darkness. Dartmoor was the devil's domain, if villagers' yarns were to be believed.

Jess, the city girl, snorted and muttered, 'Stupid,' disgusted at her fleeting lapse of sense. Yet still something troubled her, something not unfamiliar, an awareness of being observed, a feeling she knew very well. It was a sensitivity which had grown in Jess like an extra faculty, perhaps in response to being so much the focus of critical eyes since early childhood. Sometimes this watch-dog was on the alert and at other times it slept. Whatever its origins and vagaries, the feeling was certainly with her now.

To one side lay flat, empty country, completely obscured by fog, the heath and gorse bushes fading away into whiteness. On the other side the road was bordered by a rough stone wall some three feet high. The land sloped up behind it and was planted with fir trees. Vapour drifted among the tall, straight trunks, and the top branches were swallowed up in haze.

There came a sudden urgent desire to get back into the car and lock the doors, and that was what she did. Almost the instant she had secured them all, she spotted the figure again.

Something was coming down among the trees, making straight for the car. Staring, she held her breath – and then released it slowly, as she recognised the form as that of a man who was carrying something on his back. He reached the wall, swung two gangly legs over it, and dropped down on to the road. His burden turned out to be merely a sack, bulging with logs for firewood. The weight of it had bent him over, but now he slipped it from his shoulder, left it on the ground and came across to the car.

Not a ghoul or a goblin, Jess thought wryly. Still, I could wish it were somebody else.

'Having some trouble?' enquired Alec Maunder, cheerfully. 'Perhaps I can help you out.'

He was gazing through the window at her, grinning. Since it was closed, she did not hear his words but guessed the gist of them. After a brief hesitation, she opened the window a little way.

'It won't start, Mr Maunder. I don't know what's the matter.'

He squatted down. His bearded face seemed to fill the window.

'Out of petrol?' he suggested.

'No,' said Jess, 'there's plenty.'

'Battery flat, do you think?'

'Hardly. I've just driven fourteen miles.'

'Mm.' He pursed his mouth and nodded, then scratched his hairy chin, brow furrowed in thought.

'I had to pull up sharp and the engine died,' she explained. 'I'd seen something in the road. In fact, I believe it was you.'

His eyes twinkled. 'That's right, it was. Heard a car coming, heard it brake. Didn't know it was you, though. Wouldn't have walked off if I'd realised that. Lucky I chanced to retrace my steps, eh, seeing the old car's played you a trick?'

She looked at him. Chanced to retrace his steps? Jess did not believe it. She placed more faith in that instinct that so often told her when she was being watched. He had been around all the time, close by, she was almost sure of that.

Maunder glanced behind her, noticing the baby for the first time.

'Ah, got the son and heir on board, I see. My, my, well, what are we going to do, eh?'

'How much do you know about cars?'

'Fair bit,' said Maunder, brightly. 'Yes, a fair old bit. Used to maintain the staff cars and transports when I was in the army. If you move over, I'll see if I can't get her going.'

He pulled at the door handle, found it locked, looked at her expectantly. Jess made no move to open the door.

'Let me tell you the symptoms,' she said. 'I press the starter and nothing happens. All I get is a little clicking noise.'

Maunder snapped his fingers, beaming. 'I think I know what that is! Now then, when I tell you, push the starter again. Give it a good long burst, but not till I say. Got that?'

'I think so.'

He went round to the front, opened the bonnet, then picked up a stone from the roadside. Leaning over the engine, he called, 'All right, now, go on.'

She pressed the starter and as she did so Maunder delivered two hefty blows to something at the front. She heard the clank of stone on metal, and then, with a roar, the engine came alive.

Dropping the bonnet, he came back to the window. 'There,' he said, 'easy as that. Takes two, though. Not a thing you can do by yourself.'

'No. Well, thank you very much.'

The Sunbeam was chugging, ready to go, but Maunder crouched down by the window again.

'I, uh, I've been working at your place today. Thought I'd pick up a bit of wood on the way home. Lots of good wood round here.'

'Yes, I expect there is.' She smiled politely.

'Some weight, though,' said Maunder, ruefully.

Jess's heart sank, for she guessed what was coming next.

'I don't suppose you could take me part of the way, Mrs Lawrenson?' He cocked his head to one side. 'It would be a kindness to let me ride for a bit.'

Jess was reluctant, to say the least.

'I'm very late already ...' she began.

'But it won't take you out of your way. You could drop me off at the crossroads before the turning down to the valley.'

Don't give lifts, her husband had warned. But then, he had probably meant to strangers. It seemed churlish to refuse – and yet she shrank from the idea of Maunder beside her in the passenger seat.

'Might be glad to have me along,' he pressed, 'in case the old car falters again.'

Perhaps she was being silly, even unkind. A quarter of an hour ago she had actually been thinking of demons and other such bugaboos. For a while the atmosphere, the mood of the moor in mist, had affected her the way it affected simpler souls, creating fears and fancies. She felt ashamed of them now. And Maunder had helped her start her car, so she could hardly drive away and leave him to carry his load of wood for several miles. Anyway, she was his employer's wife and she guessed that he valued his job too much to misbehave.

'All right,' she said, 'there's room in the rear for your sack.'

He scurried across the road to fetch it, shut it in the back, then hurried around to the passenger side to climb in, seeming almost afraid she might change her mind. The smell of mildew came in with him and she furtively opened her window a little more.

The day he had brought the chicken, Maunder had chatted steadily on while he ate his cake and drank his tea in the kitchen. It was different now as he sat in the car. He had little to say while she drove, and the spells of silence made her nervous. Never a talkative person, Jess could sit beside Robert or Joel for an hour and happily not say a word, but in Maunder's presence she found herself rambling on about various things in order to ease her own tension. It was partly because he kept on looking at her, slyly turning his head and eyeing her intently. It felt just a little less strange and threatening if she could pretend he was simply paying attention to what she said.

Finally, and thankfully, she unloaded him at the last crossroads before Torvallen.

'There,' he said, becoming chirpy again, 'that's grand, that is. Nice when folk can help each other, eh? I'm grateful, Mrs Lawrenson, very grateful to you.'

'Not at all. Goodbye, Mr Maunder.' Jess locked the door behind him and quickly pulled away.

'Be seeing you,' he called, before the mist swallowed him up.

· Fifteen ·

There were times after that when she passed him on the road, but Jess gave Alec Maunder no more lifts, acknowledging him with just a toot of her horn as she sped past. Not until Christmas came did she meet him again.

Although Christmas Day was reserved for the family, Boxing Day lunch, tea and supper were always shared with the Lawrensons' employees, their wives and their children. It meant twelve rowdy hours of guzzling, singing, venerable jokes, and stories told for the hundredth time. The Boxing Day party was much the same each year. Charlie Weekes always had to be carried home. Eddie Pierce invariably fought with his wife, and half the children ate till they were sick and had to be dosed to settle their stomachs. Jess accepted that Alec Maunder could hardly be excluded, casual employee though he was. It was Christmas, after all, and he could not be left to spend it entirely alone – especially if the reports of his dwelling and housekeeping were true. She only wished the wretched man had somewhere else to go.

There were twenty-seven people at the Boxing Day party, including fourteen children. The house was in uproar as they charged in and out of all the ground floor rooms and up and down the stairs. Ragtime and music hall songs, cheerful and silly, crackled from the big brass horn of the gramophone. A huge lunch was demolished at one o'clock and a large tea at half past four. Great quantities of cider, ale and home-made wine were consumed. At no time did the nibbling stop; there was always a row of chestnuts roasting on the ledge of the sitting-room fire basket, the crack of Brazil and almond shells was ever in the air, while orange peel, date stones and grape pips littered the floor and the fireplace.

Henry Wills made a fool of himself by attempting the 'Turkey Trot'. Charlie Weekes spent a great deal of time on all fours, wearing out the knees of his best trousers giving the toddlers pony rides. Mrs Pierce and Mrs Wills passed happy hours in swapping complaints about their husbands. The Chivers' twins, twelve-year-old stalwarts of Widecombe Church Choir, sang 'God Rest Ye Merry Gentlemen' for the third year running. There were recitations from other children, parlour games in the afternoon and ghost stories in the early evening.

Pleasantly tipsy on rhubarb wine, Alice Davey had the care of her grandson for most of the day, since Jess and Pauline were busy in the kitchen. All the other women clustered round to admire the boy and exclaim at how much he had grown. Colin was now nearly fifteen months old, a sturdy, lively child. His brown eyes came from the Davey side and his hair was slightly darker than that of his father.

Alec Maunder had turned up just in time for lunch. He had eaten and drunk his fill, passed the time with Robert and with Charlie Weekes, and snoozed away several hours in front of the fire. Now, as suppertime drew near, he was sitting in a corner by himself, nursing a mug of ale and furtively eyeing Alice Davey.

She had had her hair cut fashionably short and the effect was flattering, youthful. Under a layer of make-up the lines and veins which marred her skin were very much less apparent. She was nicely dressed, too, in a fawn woollen frock. Everyone was in Sunday best, but the other women were stoutly built, hardy souls with plain faces and thick ankles. Maunder guessed that Alice might be forty-five or thereabouts, making her ten years older than he was. Not an unacceptable difference, he thought. Anyway, she was the only unattached woman in the room. He wished she were not so absorbed with the child and the chattering females around her.

Playful on parsnip wine, Eddie Pierce found a sprig of mistletoe and began pursuing all the women with it. Eventually he waylaid Jess on her way in from the kitchen with a fresh flagon of cider, backed her against the door-post and delivered a smacking kiss.

'Here, that's enough, Eddie Pierce!' She laughed and pushed him away. 'There's your wife over there and she'll be giving you what for!'

Eddie rolled his eyes and declared that it was worth a thick ear from old Prue. Mrs Pierce disdainfully said that Jess was welcome to him, misfit that he was. Eddie just guffawed and tossed the mistletoe to Charlie. But the old man stood somewhat in awe of Jess and his was just a respectful peck on the cheek.

Alec Maunder licked his lips and set his tankard aside. He thought he would take a turn, too. What better excuse could there be than Christmas and a sprig of mistletoe? But as he made to rise from his seat, his glance lit on Robert Lawrenson's face.

All the colour had left it and something wild was in Robert's eyes, something barely controlled.

Maunder subsided back into his chair, studying him with interest. He noted the quiver of tightening muscles at Robert's jaw, and the fist clenched tightly at his side. A little smile tugged at Alec Maunder's mouth. He was not a man who missed much and had always been good at interpreting situations.

'I've got work to do, you know!' Jess was dodging Peter Chivers now, and everybody in the room was laughing. All but her husband, who could not contain himself for another second.

Robert crossed the room in two swift strides, pushed himself between his wife and Chivers, then jerked his head towards the baby. His words were reasonable enough, but his features were taut with anger.

'Time to put the boy to bed, Jess. Take him up now, will you?'

Around them, the merriment faltered. Her face grew straight and she did not argue. The message was not lost on Chivers, either, and he made a swift retreat. Joel and Pauline exchanged a look and she quickly launched into a joke to divert attention.

Jess took Colin from Alice and went upstairs to settle him down for the night.

Robert followed her. He stopped her on the landing and hissed, 'Don't you ever let anyone do that again! How could you let them be so familiar? Remember you're my wife and have a bit of dignity!'

She stared at him. 'I can't be haughty with them, Rob. You wouldn't want that, would you?'

'Chatting and joking is one thing. That's all right. But not to let them slobber over you.'

'Look, it's Christmas and they're tipsy. They didn't mean any harm.'

Uneasily she stroked the child, who was already snoozing on her shoulder.

'They took a liberty and you allowed it.'

'Well, I'm sorry, I'm sure.' Irritation crept into her voice. 'I thought I was just being sociable and joining in the fun.'

Turning, she swept off towards the baby's room. Robert scurried after her and caught her once again.

'Listen,' he whispered, fiercely, 'I know Eddie Pierce. He's always been one for the women. He'd have his hands all over you, given the chance.'

'In front of his wife and children? In front of you? Don't be silly, Rob.'

'What I'm saying is, you could easily give him the wrong idea.'

'Oh rubbish! To hear you, anyone would think I started all that nonsense with the mistletoe. As for the others – well, is poor old Charlie a satyr, then? He must be well past sixty. What about Peter Chivers? A Lothario, I suppose?'

Robert started to stammer a little, realising now that he might have made too much of it.

'Jess, I only ... I just want ...'

She gazed at him coolly, waiting. The child was sound asleep in her arms, untroubled by the fuss.

He struggled for a moment more. 'I'm sorry, Jess. You see, there was another party once – Vanessa's birthday party. There she was, like you, being kissed by all the men. The memory came back to me downstairs just now. It rattled me, I suppose.'

Her gaze wavered. Vanessa again.

'Is it fair to go for me every time something reminds you of her?'

'No,' muttered Robert. 'Still,' he added, defensively, 'it's true what I say about Eddie Pierce.'

'I'll bear it in mind,' she said, quietly. Then: 'You know, it's lucky I'm not a jealous woman, Robert. You just can't forget Vanessa, can you?'

Downstairs, the women sitting with Alice finally drifted away in search of their offspring, so Alec Maunder quickly took his chance. Sidling across the room, he seated himself beside her on the sofa.

'Mrs Davey, isn't it?'

She looked at him and was greeted by the ever-ready grin.

'Yes ... ?'

She smiled uncertainly, making swift appraisal of his features, his clothes. In honour of the occasion, he had put on a clean blue shirt and a brown checked jacket he had not worn for years. These, together with his workaday trousers, made an assembly of odd garments such as Alice had never seen. She did not need to be told that he had no woman to look after him.

'Is that what I must call you? Mrs Davey?'

'Well, no. Alice will do.'

'Alice. That's pretty.' The teeth flared. 'So are you. Thought you must be a sister to Mrs Lawrenson till Charlie told me otherwise.'

Alice knew it was blarney. Still, it pleased her a little. Maunder saw that her glass was nearly empty.

'Shall I fetch you some more? What would you like?'

'Elderberry, please.'

He went to the sideboard, filled the glass to the brim and hurried back.

'Been staying here all Christmas, have you?'

'Yes, I'm going home tomorrow.'

'To Devonport, I understand.' Maunder looked thoughtful. 'Charlie tells me you're a widow. Live all by yourself? It's a wonder to me you don't move out here to be with your girl and the baby.'

'I've a shop to run.'

'Oh?' The green eyes grew even more alert. 'What sort?'

'Tobacconist.' Alice swallowed a gulp of wine. 'I've always lived in town. I don't belong in the country – don't feel right, if you know what I mean.'

Maunder nodded. He could see she was faintly fuddled by the wine, and noted that she drank uncommonly fast, but he did not guess that she could not bear to live anywhere outside walking distance of an off-licence.

'I've been thinking I might take up pipe-smoking,' he said. 'Sell pipes, do you?'

'Yes, oh yes, I do.'

'Perhaps I'll drop in on you, then, one day when I'm in town. Give me a discount, would you?'

'Perhaps,' said Alice, lightly, 'seeing you're a friend of the family.'

'I could tell you were a decent sort.' Maunder's tone became a little plaintive. 'It's a treat for me to talk with a nice woman like you. I've been alone for such a long time.' He nudged her, a chuckle rising in his throat. 'Mind, I bet you could guess that just by looking at me. Picture of neglect, eh?' There came a second chuckle. It sounded like a blockage clearing from a drain.

The words were disarming, though, and they had their intended effect. Alice felt a little sorry for him. He urged her to finish up her wine and she let him fetch her yet another glass. Before very long, she was laughing aloud at his jokes and giving him directions to the shop. Giggling, drinking ever faster, she felt exhuberant, as if her young days had briefly returned.

Maunder was wondering if she had much money. He thought it would be very nice to have a friendly, self-supporting widow on whom he could call when he felt the need. Alice struck him as the type who might prove generous in many ways.

· Sixteen ·

'Shop!'

In the store room, Alice had just broken open a carton of cigarettes. She pulled out a dozen packets and took a box of pipe cleaners down from a shelf.

From beyond the door, the call came again and louder. 'Shop!'

Alice hurried out to serve – and then stopped short at the sight of her customer.

'Hello,' said Alec Maunder, genially. 'Bet you thought I wasn't coming.'

She had. It was now mid-March, ten weeks since the Christmas party.

'Weather's been foul,' he explained, 'else I'd have been here before.'

Yes, January and February had been bad months, wet and freezing.

'What's the matter? Forgotten me, is that it?'

'Uh – no.' Turning from him, she started lining up the cigarette packets on the shelf behind the counter. 'I remember you, of course.'

Yes, but somewhat differently. Maunder had taken no trouble to groom himself today. Furthermore, Alice was sober this morning. On Boxing Day she had seen him through a happy haze. Now, with a clearer mind, she did not like him so well. There was something offensively cocky in his manner and her nostrils picked up his curious mouldy odour. He had not been half so grubby at the party.

Maunder beamed. 'You know what I've come for, then.'

Shooting a sidelong look at him, Alice muttered, 'A pipe, wasn't it?'

'And all that goes with it.' He came and leaned his forearms on the counter, head thrust forward, grin enormous. 'Baccy, and pipe cleaners, and anything else you think I need.'

'I'll fetch some out for you to see.' Alice unlocked the little display cabinet that stood on one side of the counter and laid out in front of him a small selection of pipes.

'This one's cherrywood and here's a briar. This has a nice tortoiseshell stem, or you might prefer this very plain one.'

'How much is that?' He pointed out a handsome pipe on the middle shelf of the cabinet. The wood was golden, with a band of ebony inlaid around the bowl.

'That's a dear one, nearly a guinea.'

Alice tried to hide the inflection which added: You can't afford it, I'm sure.

'Let's have a look, then.'

Somewhat reluctantly, she handed it over.

'I like this.'

He turned it this way and that and she saw that his fingernails had not been cut for weeks. Then, before she had any chance to object, he stuck the pipe in his mouth and manoeuvred it from one corner to the other, then back again.

'How do I look?' he asked, sucking wetly on the stem.

Annoyance flickered in Alice. 'I don't like customers to do that until they've firmly decided to buy.'

'Oh – oh yes. Sorry about that.' He removed the pipe, having slobbered into it. 'Well, then, I suppose I'd better take it. I'll have two ounces of your best tobacco as well, and a good leather pouch to keep it in. Oh, and some matches, of course.'

'You'll have no change from thirty shillings,' warned Alice.

Maunder winked at her. 'I seem to recall we talked about discount.'

Alice could not remember exactly what she had said.

'I'd had a few drinks, as you know, Mr Maunder. You

can't hold me to any silly promise I made when I was tipsy. I'm not well off and I can't let things go cheap.'

'Mr Maunder?' He stepped back, eyes popping with feigned surprise. 'It's Alec, remember? I thought we were friends.'

'No, look, I'm sorry if I misled you. You'll have to pay full price for anything you have. I can't afford ...'

'Nor can I. Only got six shillings.'

'In that case,' said Alice, 'you'd better give me back the pipe.'

She would wash it off in hot water, that was what she would do. And probably a bit of disinfectant, too.

Maunder's stare was unnerving. 'I said I liked it. How about giving me credit?'

A sign on the counter right in front of him stated that such was not available. Alice pointed to it. Her finger shook and she snatched it back, folding both hands tightly together.

'Not so sociable now, then?' His bantering tone had disappeared. 'Climbed up on your high horse a bit.' The green eyes had changed, the pupils narrowing. 'I didn't come just for this, you know.' He flourished the pipe – then put it in his pocket. 'I came to visit you.'

'That's very nice. I do appreciate it ...'

'More'n twenty miles, I've come. Took an hour and a half on the old bus from Princetown – and that's a four mile walk from where I live.'

'I'm sorry you've gone to such trouble, but I didn't ask you to make the trip, and I haven't time for socialising. I'm, uh ... ,' She racked her brains. 'I'm stock-taking, see, and that's a big job.'

'Oh yes, you're very different now.' His face and voice had grown hard. 'Just a bit of seasonal stooping, was it? The boss's mother-in-law mixing with the lowly?'

'No!' exclaimed Alice, shaking her head a little too earnestly. 'That's not fair. I'm not being hoity-toity, I just have a living to make.'

Maunder went on as if he had not heard. 'You don't look

the same, either. Not so good in daylight, without a bit of powder.'

Feeling her eyes fill, she blinked to beat back tears.

'Still ...' He started moving towards the end of the counter. '... I don't mind all that much.' Lifting the flap, he slid in behind. 'And I expect you're lonely, being a widow and past your youth.' Smiling again, he was almost playful now. 'There's more to trade than cash, eh, Alice? I'm sure you could let me have the pipe for, say, five bob? And I could help you out with any, you know, personal needs, anything that's lacking in your life.'

Alice was appalled. 'Get out! Oh God, go away! Go away!'

He pointed behind her. 'I hear what you say, and yet you're backing towards the stairs.'

Cornered, she had nowhere else to go.

'I believe you're putting on a show, as women do,' chuckled Maunder, wagging a finger at her. 'I know, you have to pretend a bit at first. It's part of the game.'

'Get out of my shop!' ordered Alice, being as brave as she could. 'I mean precisely what I say, there's no pretence about it. Don't make me lose my patience.'

Maunder knew bluff when he heard it. He could see she had no fight in her.

'Come on, Alice, I still like you, even if you have been a bit chilly this morning. We all get our moods, I understand that.'

She dissolved. 'Please, leave me alone. You can have the pipe. Just take it. I don't even want the five shillings.'

Maunder paused in his advance. He considered, then he pursed his mouth and frowned. 'No – no, I wouldn't feel right doing that. That would be taking advantage. A generous gesture, though, and I truly thank you for it. But I insist on doing you some kindness in return. Be honest now, Alice, you do like me, don't you? No need to be embarrassed, I'm a bit lonely too.'

She had reached the foot of the stairs, but the last thing she wanted to do was go up. There was nothing left to do but shriek for help, and she would if he came any closer.

'I think you're a tease, that's all it is,' said Alec Maunder, winking.

Her mind kept flicking back to those men who had lured her into the dockyard, the way they had joked, half-threatening, just before they started pulling her about. Maunder, in his fashion, was every bit as sinister and insulting. He would 'help her out' he said. She wished she had the courage to claw his face, kick him between the legs, beat his face to mince with the two-pound weight off the scales. But she could not even summon spit or wind enough to scream.

Help had come a little late that night six years ago. Today, however, Alice was more fortunate. The shop door suddenly opened – luckily, Maunder had not thought to bolt it – and Alice had never been more thankful to see an old customer. A decent man by the name of Banks, one of the few she trusted now, he was a stevedore at the dockyard and he had the muscles to prove it.

He paused in the doorway, taking in the scene. He saw the plea in Alice's eyes.

'All right, Mrs Davey?' His gaze was on Maunder, who quickly summed him up and began retreating towards the counter flap.

'I don't think you've got what I want after all,' he said to Alice. 'Never mind, it was worth a try.' He smiled at the man Banks, who received it stony-faced. Maunder thought it might be wise to return the pipe before Alice mentioned it. Digging in his pocket, he laid it on the counter.

'Nice of you to offer, but I can't accept.'

'Alice?' queried Banks. 'Anything wrong? You've only to say.'

She swallowed, composing herself. 'I'd just be glad if you'd show this man out. He's come to the wrong shop.'

Maunder gave a very soft snort of laughter. Silently, Banks pushed wide the door and stood aside for him to leave. Maunder went cautiously past him, without a backward glance at the woman he had terrified. Banks shoved the door shut before he was quite clear of it, and Maunder stumbled out over the step.

'Not likely to come back, is he, Alice? Want me to see him off properly?'

'It's all right, thank you, Mr Banks.' Her smile was weak and trembling. 'When you're gone I'll be closing up for the rest of the day.'

It would take half a bottle to calm her after this.

Outside on the pavement, Maunder spat and then muttered something profane. He had gone to a lot of trouble to call on Alice Davey. The way she had played up to him at the party, he had thought the journey would be well worthwhile. Two bob, it had cost him. Two bob and a long walk – a trek he would have to repeat in the dark on his way home. Nothing to show for all that effort and expense. The cold shoulder, that was what she had given him. She was nothing much, either, on close inspection. Still, he would have availed himself, given the chance, after travelling all this way.

Feeling savage, he set off down the street. He had hours to wait before the bus went back and the day was very chilly. Hunching his shoulders against the wind, he plodded on a few yards more. And then he spotted the pub on the corner.

Joe Bonnet's establishment was empty that morning, save for one old man lingering over a pint of mild and bitter. Behind the bar was Gwennie, wiping out the drip-trays.

'Light ale,' grunted Maunder, without any greeting.

Gwennie looked him up and down, took him for a rough type off a boat, and dourly poured him a pint. He put down a sixpenny bit on the counter and she handed him twopence change. Maunder sucked the froth off the top, then gulped down the rest of the beer in a matter of seconds. Pushing another four pennies towards her, he had his glass refilled. When this one, too, had gone down, a mood of jagged humour began to steal over him. Sipping at his third pint of ale, he eyed Gwennie Bonnet over the rim of his glass, and his cheeks twitched with the spreading of a grin. She put him in mind of something he had seen on a fishmonger's slab, something baleful and pugnacious-looking. He thought it was called a John Dory.

Gwennie mistook the grin for geniality. She thought he was going to spend a good bit, too, so she made herself agreeable.

'In port for long, then, are you?'

'What? Oh ...' he shook his head, '... I'm not a seaman. Farmer, that's what I am.'

Her eyebrows lifted. 'Brought in stuff to sell, have you?'

'Been visiting a friend.' Maunder's mouth was half-submerged in his beer and Gwennie did not catch the sardonic tone of the words.

'Someone round here? Who would that be? I know everybody hereabouts. What's the name?'

'Davey,' grunted Maunder.

'Alice Davey?' Now he had Gwennie's rapt attention.

'That's the one.'

'Close friend, is she?'

'No, I wouldn't say that.'

'You've, uh, just come from there, have you, Mr ... ?'

'Maunder. Yes, I have.'

She wondered if that meant he had spent the night.

'How'd you come to meet Alice, if I might ask?'

'Christmas get-together. I do a bit of work for her son-in-law.'

'Aah!' The sound was quiet, long-drawn-out. 'Yes, of course. You'll know young Jess, then? Pretty girl, isn't she? Nice place, is it, where she's living? I see her now and again, all dressed up and driving that smart car. Done well for herself, hasn't she? Taken a step up.'

He made a grimace, sourly finishing off his ale.

'I'm afraid, though, it's likely to go to her head,' ventured Gwennie. 'I always found Jess a bit cool – you know, lofty, very distant.' Her tongue crept into her cheek. 'Not like her mother, eh?'

Maunder said nothing. He was not about to tell this woman he had been rebuffed.

'Another?' Gwennie reached for his glass. 'Now, Alice

is just the other way about, isn't she? Very – forthcoming – as it were. Too sociable for her own good, if the truth be told.' She turned off the beer tap and placed his brimming glass on the counter, her gaze lifting slyly to meet his.

Having found Alice anything but sociable that morning, Maunder was mystified by this remark.

'How do you mean?'

Gwennie made a small pretence of reluctance to speak, edging daintily round the subject. 'Well, she has no caution, she's not – discriminating. Makes friends too easily, too quickly. It led her into trouble once, poor soul. Shocking thing. I've always thought it a wonder she recovered so well.' Maunder worked hard to suppress a grin. He was nothing if not perceptive and he judged this woman no friend of Alice Davey. She had something unpleasant she was bursting to relate.

'Something happened to her? What?'

'Not the sort of thing she'd want to advertise,' said Gwennie, primly. 'It was a great scandal at the time.'

'Surely not?' He leaned closer. 'None of this sounds like the Alice I know. I find her very proper, very reserved.'

'Reserved! Proper!'

Mirth and derision combined in Gwennie's exclamation. Who was he trying to fool? Or was Alice fooling him? Perhaps she was out to catch a husband and therefore playing coy. If so, Gwennie felt it her duty to warn the poor man.

'You couldn't be more wrong, Mr Maunder. Now, I'm not fond of spreading tales, but I may as well tell you this, for by and by you're bound to hear what's only common knowledge.'

Pushing her face close to his, she explained:

'Anything in trousers. She'd have anybody, Alice Davey. Out every night of the week when she was younger, always with different men – locals, navy men, foreigners off the boats, boys half her age. Everybody knew it.'

Maunder stared at her. His face was blank, but excitement and a certain indignation stirred within him. He wondered if this knowledge might be put to use. He was also doubly nettled now to think she had refused him. After a moment, he pressed:

'But you said something happened?'

'So it did. One night she got more than she bargained for.' Gwennie took up her cloth again, whisking it busily round the little trays. 'Just near the end of the war, it was. She'd picked up three of them and been drinking in here all evening. Seems that on the way home she went into the dockyard with them.'

'And?'

She stalled for a few seconds more, relishing his suspense, then confided in a hiss, 'They tarred and feathered her, Mr Maunder. Oh, she wasn't hurt much, I don't think – but it's the degradation, isn't it? Friend of mine happened to be at the Daveys' place when Alice got home that night. Said she was an awful sight, covered in pitch and poultry feathers, clothes all torn.'

He released a long, ragged breath, wondering whether Robert knew of this. If so, it was a family secret, for never had he heard it mentioned by any man at the sawmill, not even the talkative Charlie Weekes.

'That was why the children gave Jess her nickname,' Gwennie went on.

Maunder's attention snapped back to her. 'Nickname?'

'They used to call her Pitchpot. Little devils.' Her titter suggested she thought them very clever little devils. 'Well, you know what children are. Of course, it was hard that the girl should have to bear the stigma of her mother's carryings-on,' allowed Gwennie. 'But she wasn't a likeable child. Tough and defiant, never any sign of shame. And stuck-up, too, as I said before, always stiff and frosty. God knows, there wasn't a girl in the street with less reason to be haughty.'

She paused suddenly. Maunder was smiling. Indeed, he did not seem the least bit shocked or upset. Gwennie felt a little disappointed.

'I hope I haven't said too much. I do go on a bit, I know. Last thing I want is to cause trouble. But the truth is the truth, after all.'

'So it is, and I thank you for telling me.'

A coy smirk disturbed Gwennie's hard face. 'Well, I felt it the right thing to do, Mr Maunder. I can see you're a decent man.'

Alec Maunder's grin was fierce. 'And I can see what you are, too.'

He was gone before she could summon any retort, his walk so bouncy he was almost dancing.

· Seventeen ·

'Mr Lawrenson!'

Robert paused, looked behind him. There was Alec Maunder, hurrying along the woodland path. Robert was on his way home for his tea, but he waited.

Maunder reached him, puffing a little. 'Been wanting to have a word with you in private,' he said. 'Haven't had a chance till now.'

Robert began to walk on. 'What about?'

'Well, uh, money, I'm sorry to say.'

'Oh?' Lawrenson stopped again, facing him squarely.

'I'm finding it hard to get by these days. Price of everything goes up all the time.'

Like a farmer at market, Robert kept a blank face.

'And since I've been with you best part of a year now, and done the job to your satisfaction, I was thinking you might be ready to put my wages up a bit.'

Confronted with this, Robert echoed his brother's words, which he knew to be true ones.

'We pay you enough, Alec. You're not worth more than

the eight bob a day you get already. I've never known you put yourself out or do a stroke extra.'

Maunder's smile vanished. 'An extra four shillings a week, that's all I'm asking. You can afford that – and you need me at the yard, I know you do.'

'You need the job,' countered Robert. 'We'll leave things as they stand.'

A cunning glint appeared in Alec Maunder's eyes. He scratched the scalp beneath his greasy locks. 'Never took you for such a hard man,' he remarked. 'Thought you were more reasonable than your brother. Or is it that he has the final say in everything? He don't like me, I know that.'

Shrewd and manipulating, he had quickly perceived the rivalry between the Lawrenson brothers and he thought he could make use of it. This time, however, he had miscalculated. Robert was not going to fall for that.

'If Joel had his way, you wouldn't be here at all. It's me you have to thank for your job, and I say eight bob's ample.'

'Two shillings increase a day won't break you.'

'I don't pay out what hasn't been earned.'

Robert's blue eyes were calm and unwavering under the peak of his grey checked cap. He was shorter than Maunder, but hardly seemed so, his bearing more dignified than that of the other man. For a moment there was silent deadlock. Around them, the rowans and the aged oaks seemed almost to listen and breathe their own opinions as a fitful wind stirred the branches.

'Course, you don't know what it is to be poor,' said Maunder, softly.

'I'm not a rich man.'

'You don't go short, though. I mean to say, you've got that lovely house and a nice car.'

'That's what hard work brings, providing you use your head as well.'

Maunder ignored that. 'You don't have to pinch and scrape, or think twice before buying some little treat. Me, I can't afford anything.' A look came into his eyes, like that of a man about to play a good card. 'For instance, this Monday just gone, I couldn't even find the money to buy a decent tobacco pipe.'

Robert was unmoved.

Maunder sighed and rubbed his chin. 'Your mother-in-law's as tough as you are,' he said ruefully, 'asking a guinea for the one I wanted. I came away without it in the end, but I would've thought ...'

'You went to Alice's shop?'

'I like to trade with people I know. Still, turned out we couldn't do business, so I had a wasted trip. Funny sort of woman, isn't she? Changeable, if you know what I mean.' He shook his head, as if lamenting something. 'Might be on account of what happened to her, I suppose. Thing like that's enough to unbalance a female.'

He peeped slyly at Robert, saw his brow pucker, saw a question forming on his lips, and quickly carried on: 'Course, it was a long time ago, wasn't it, but I daresay it's left its mark. Must have been terrified, poor soul. I'm not denying that she asked for trouble, mind. Any woman who's a bit loose is liable to run into some bad characters sooner or later. Still, tar and feathers – that was wicked.'

He paused, gazing with elaborate innocence at Rob. Lawrenson seemed dumbfounded.

'What ... ? Where did you ... ?' His voice trailed away, but his mouth and throat were working, robbed of spit.

'Hear about it?' finished Maunder, cheerfully. 'Why, I happened to drop in the local pub, got talking to someone who knows her well. I must say, I admire your wife for standing by her mother like she does. Visits every week, without fail. Very loyal, I call it. After all, she could have abandoned her, couldn't she? Must have been a big relief for your Jess to move out here, away from all those pointing fingers.'

A pallor was spreading over Robert's face. His eyes were piercingly cold and his mouth had drawn down at the corners.

'Oh, now don't you worry,' Maunder reassured him. 'I'll keep it to myself. Wouldn't dream of telling anybody hereabouts. Not that it's any reflection on you or Mrs Lawrenson. I don't mean that. What I'm saying is, there's no sense bringing bad talk here where your poor little wife's found refuge.'

Robert had turned an awful colour. Maunder scrutinised his face and suddenly his glee knew no bounds. No, Lawrenson had not known.

'Here,' he breathed, moving back a pace or two, 'don't tell me this is news to you? I mean, I took it for granted she'd have told you – your wife, that is. Well, what can I say? Put my foot right in it, haven't I?'

'Get away from me!' snarled Robert. 'Get out of my sight, before I lay you out!'

Maunder held up the palms of his hands, as if to pacify.

'I understand, I truly do. You've had a shock and it's all my fault. Me and my mouth! I'm awful sorry, Mr Lawrenson. Still, don't you fret now – like I said, I shan't tell a soul.' He began to move away. But then, turning, he said quietly, 'You'll think again about my rise, though, won't you? Those few bob would come in very handy. How about making it eight and six? I'd really appreciate that.'

Robert barely resisted the urge to punch him. Maunder had thrown him off balance, but Lawrenson managed to summon his wits and his self-control.

'There will be no pay rise,' he said through gritted teeth. 'And if any talk is spread around there will be no job for you at all. Is that understood?'

His bluff called, Maunder regarded him sullenly. He had always considered Robert a weaker, more vulnerable character than Joel, for whom he felt a wary respect. Unpleasantly surprised, he nodded sourly and slouched away.

In her nightdress, Jess was sitting on the edge of the bed. Her back was turned to her husband and her unpinned hair fell down about her face. She had known all evening that something was wrong. Being a little late back from Devonport, she had taken that to be the cause of his sulky mood. He had waited until bedtime to confront her with the real reason.

'Why didn't you tell me?'

'It wasn't something I was proud of, but I wasn't greatly ashamed, either, and I didn't see any call to make a confession. It happened to Mam, not to me.'

'You couldn't confide in the man you were going to marry?'

'I've just told you, I didn't see any need. It wasn't important.'

'Surely you knew it was bound to come out sooner or later?'

It was bound to come out.

The phrase jarred her. Oh, the disgrace of it all! she thought, bitterly. My terrible secret! The awful stigma!

'I'm a stain on the family, then, am I?'

'Don't be so silly, I didn't say that.'

'Sullied? Impure?'

'I haven't suggested any such thing.'

'Then why am I being taken to task?'

That was an awkward question to answer. Robert was no puritan, but he could not stand to be laughed at. He had always yearned to be envied, admired. His threat to Maunder, intended to prevent any whispering and sniggering among the men at the yard, had been a shield for himself as much as for Jess. Something else chafed him, too. Robert had felt that in marrying her he had gone one better than his brother for a change. He had loved her, of course – but she had been a prize as well, a triumph for him. Now he had discovered a blemish in her background, like a worm inside a golden apple. He would not like Joel to know of it – Joel, who had always been first in everything. It was Robert's fancy that life always gave him second best. It was something that had gnawed at him since childhood, yet he knew how petty and groundless it would sound to Jess.

'You weren't exactly honest with me, were you? I had to hear it from Maunder.'

He took off his shirt and sat down to pull off his boots. 'If I had told you when we were courting, would it have made a difference?'

The question was tense and it hung in the air for many agonising seconds.

Robert had an uneasy feeling that it might indeed have put him off. The knowledge that Alice drank had never bothered him, but this was another matter. This had to do with doubts and worries altogether closer to the quick. Yet, he was always a man inclined to fall hard for a woman, and he had been besotted with Jess in those early days. One might pardon all sorts of things in a beloved fiancée that were not so lightly dismissed in a wife who had grown familiar. Their marriage was now in its third year, and when romance wore off, a lot of tolerance went with it. Robert decided it was useless to speculate on what he might have done, had she come clean at the start. He only knew how he felt now, but he gave her the answer she wanted.

'Of course not, it wouldn't have mattered a jot.'

'Well, I wasn't certain of that, and so I didn't tell you. I loved you and I didn't want to lose you. I'd never had friends. I was always alone till you came along. Not many people aside from Mam and Dad were ever nice to me like you were. It was lovely, I was happy. Everything was suddenly different, bright and hopeful, thanks to you.'

'Now you contradict yourself. You said a few minutes ago that it didn't seem important. Now you admit you felt it was, you thought it over and chose to hide it from me.'

'All right, yes! But you can understand that, surely? It was all so ugly, Rob, what happened to Mam and the way we were treated afterwards. I wanted to forget it. Not that I can,' she ended, wearily. 'Whenever I go to see her, I feel it all press down on me again, and now it's followed me here.'

'Look,' he said clumsily, 'I'm sorry if I'm being unkind. But can't you imagine what a fool I felt, standing there and hearing that from a hired man? I didn't know what to say. He enjoyed it, too, the sod.'

'I can well believe that. I think he's a horrible man. Joel doesn't like him, does he? Never did, I understand.'

She had said the wrong thing. Robert grunted, scowled.

'And good old Joel is always right. He doesn't make mistakes like I do.'

Cursing herself for that little blunder, Jess slid into bed. Irritably yanking open his trouser buttons, Robert finished undressing and dragged his pyjamas on.

Turning, he looked at his wife sitting up in the bed, and suddenly an awful picture came into his mind – Jess with matted hair and torn clothing, smeared with pitch from head to foot. She was so very much like Alice, just like Alice must have been when she was twenty.

'Did she bring them home with her?' he asked, abruptly.

'What?'

'Her men friends. Did she bring them to the house?'

'No one ever came upstairs,' said Jess, stiffly.

Some prurient side of him wanted squalid details. He hated his own curiosity, thinking it vulgar, unworthy of him, but finding it hard to quell.

'Where, then? Where did she go with them? Shop doorways? Alleys? Their lodgings? The park at night?'

'Damn you, I don't know!' Her face flamed. 'She didn't often stray when Dad was alive and I was growing up. After he was gone she took to going out a lot, but most of the time she said nothing about it and I didn't ask her, either, even though I was old enough by then to understand. There were one or two occasions when she'd been somewhere special and she told me all about that – but nothing else, Robert. I knew what went on, of course I did. Everybody shoved her reputation down my throat. I didn't need to hear exactly how or when or where. But she was a good mother to me in every other way and she didn't deserve what was done to her.'

Jess kept her voice down low and yet it was fierce. Had it not been for Joel and Pauline across the passage, she would have shouted at him.

'I won't pretend I didn't have mixed feelings. Sometimes

I thought I hated her – after they'd been calling me names in school, or someone said something snide to me in the street. I used to dream about going away, so I'd never have to see her again. Even now, she tries my patience with her drinking. But when all's said and done, she is my Mam and I have to stick by her. She hasn't anyone else. No matter how much she angers me, I won't hear you running her down, even though you are my husband, and I won't answer dirty, prying questions about her, either!'

Robert received all this in total silence. When she had finished, he released a long, uneven breath, fidgeting from foot to foot, avoiding her snapping eyes. Finally, without a word, he climbed into bed and lay down.

Jess let her temper subside, then said quietly, 'I'm sorry if it's going to be embarrassing for you at work. Maunder will spread it around, I suppose.'

Robert turned on his side, away from her. 'No, he won't say anything. I threatened him with the sack. And you're not to mention it to Joel or Pauline.' He rolled over for a moment, fixing her with a stare across his shoulder. 'I want your word on that.'

She looked down at him, frowning slightly. 'I wouldn't care if they knew, Rob. I'm sure they wouldn't give a toss.'

'Well, I care very much. Promise me, Jess.'

Coldly, she turned out the lamp. 'All right, Robert,' she said to the darkness. 'I shan't let you down in front of your brother.'

Things were never the same after that, not for either one of them. Turning the matter over in his head, Robert began to suffer certain doubts concerning Jess's character and motives. He kept remembering Maunder's suggestion that she had wanted a refuge, an escape from 'all those pointing fingers,' and found it here. It raised a question in Robert's mind.

Was it me she wanted, or Torvallen?

Women could be quite cold-blooded about such things. Vanessa had taught him that, deserting him for a wealthier man. He picked at the memory, ripping off the scab and digging at the sore place underneath. Was there ever a female born who was totally straightforward? Limited though his experience was, Robert decided probably not. He had thought he knew all there was to know about Jess and was shaken to find himself wrong. Three years and she had never let slip a single word about this. How secretive she had been, how careful all that time. What else might there be that she had kept from him? Robert felt no certainty about her any more.

Why had she married him? He wondered constantly, recalling her very own words.

'I wanted to forget it ... and now it's followed me here.'

Perhaps she had not really wanted him at all. Perhaps it was this house and the haven it represented which meant the most to Jess.

Another question plagued him, too, one even more disturbing. Could she be entirely free from Alice Davey's inclinations? Might it not run in the blood? Robert's thoughts kept turning back to his wedding night. Jess had not been at all reluctant, had she? Not frightened, not shy. Oh yes, he had noted a small red stain on the bottom sheet next morning, proof enough that he had been the first. Still, with hindsight, he felt that she had taken to it with more than normal enthusiasm. In their marriage she had never been slow to tell him when she wanted him. Could that be a touch of Alice Davey showing through? And could it be that as Jess grew older more of it would surface?

'All women become like their mothers.' That was a saying Robert had heard somewhere. He did not like the sound of it.

So far, of course, she had been a good, contented wife on the whole. But if ever she grew restless, bored, all that could change. Jess was certainly capable of deceit – she had proved it by the way she learned to drive. True, she had been satisfied to use the car on Thursdays only, as they had agreed. Still, it was a thing she had done behind his back, and that little breach of faith had occurred before their marriage was even one year old.

Doubts were always with him nowadays. Suspicions were always popping up like pimples. Sometimes Robert felt ashamed, not just for thinking ill of his wife, but also because he recognised sheer foolishness in his fears. What mischief could a woman find in a lonely place like this? A woman with a child of eighteen months to mind? It was silly, he supposed, and yet he was seldom entirely at ease when Jess was out of his sight. It roused in him a consuming need to know just how she spent her time.

It took a while for Jess to realise that her husband was keeping track of everything she did and everywhere she went. At first she was conscious only of what appeared to be Robert's interest in her day. Each evening he would ask her how she had spent it, listening, smiling, while she recounted all the domestic chores and upsets which had filled her hours while he was at work. No, to begin with, she was not aware of being slyly interrogated.

As time went on, however, Robert began to want more and more detail of what she did with her days. On occasion, too, he contradicted her answers, objecting, querying, as if he were trying to catch her out in a lie. There was always something bothering him. Why had she pinned up her hair in that way, when she knew that he liked it left loose? Why did she so often take the same route when out for a ride by herself? A farmer had told of seeing her pass by his house three times in a single week, heading for Beardown Tors. What was the great attraction of that particular place, when the moor had so many lovely spots to offer? Why had she bought some postage stamps? To whom was she writing? And from whom had she caught a cold in the head, when no one at Torvallen had a cold? And so on and so on and so on.

When at last the penny dropped, Jess was overcome with dismay to think her husband did not trust her any more. Although – when she thought back – there had been other instances of cross-examination, milder perhaps, but similar in nature. For example, whenever she used the car. Yes, always, right from the very first time, he had held a little inquest as soon as she returned. The inquiries were more intense these days, more frequent and wide-ranging, but the pattern was not entirely new. Something was coming out in him. Something, of which she had only seen buds and shoots before, was bursting into full, suffocating growth, like a dark, constricting vine.

Yet she found it hard to tackle him on the matter. For the most part the questioning was crafty, oblique. They were casual, conversational enquiries, never aggressive, never obviously accusing. His approach was such that she could not object to his endless prying without appearing as if she had something to hide. On days when she felt too tired to humour him, she did grow somewhat snappish – and then he would fancy that he must have touched on some secret guilt. He would go away and brood about it for a while, and later return to the subject again, dissecting it more persistently than ever, so that in the end she wished she had held her temper.

Even if nothing was said, Jess could always tell when something was fretting him, for he bit his fingernails down to the quick. She came to recognise it as an infallible sign. Slumped in his chair of an evening, Robert would pick at nailsprings and chew them off, gnawing away at the skin regardless of pain, till raw red patches surrounded the cuticles. The state of his mind and the state of his fingers were normally much in accord.

To make things worse, there was confrontation when Jess found out how Maunder had terrified her mother.

'Sack him, for God's sake!' she yelled at Robert. 'I don't care what tales he tells, just fire the brute!'

Her husband, however, was not about to do that. He felt confident of Maunder's silence only as long as the wretched man remained in his employ.

'Are you that ashamed of us, Robert?' demanded Jess. 'Don't you care how I feel, or how he upset Mam?'

'You'll feel a damned sight worse if he opens his mouth

and makes that business known round here,' came the heated retort. 'I'm only protecting you.'

'Come off it, Rob, it's not my face you want to save, it's yours.'

'All right, and what's so wrong with that? Yes, I need the respect of those with whom I work and trade. I don't want people sniggering behind my back. Men will talk as much as women, Jess. You promised me you'd keep quiet, now don't go making trouble. After all, it's you who've brought me this embarrassment.'

She thought it cowardly of him, disloyal. Jess had believed that her husband was her champion, first and foremost. Now she found that his fear of ridicule was stronger than any concern for her feelings. In all, Robert had shown himself less noble than she once imagined. He was not, after all, so understanding or broad-minded. He who had laughed off Alice's drinking was repelled by her sexual adventures. Jess allowed that it must have been hard for him to learn that his lovely flower had been grown in what he saw as unwholesome soil. All the same, she had not thought his love could be quite so easily undermined.

In the interests of peace, Jess gave way in the end and said no more about sacking Alec Maunder. But she felt aggrieved, and just as disappointed in Robert as he had been in her. All the remaining lustre of romance had been stripped away from both of them, and now that they saw each other plain they were sadly disillusioned.

· Eighteen ·

On one of the last days of summer that year, Jess took the chestnut mare and went up into the higher parts of the moor. Low cloud covered the sky, but towards the west the sun broke through it, the rays spreading out like the spokes of a wheel. The day was balmy, the heath firm and dry beneath the horse's hooves.

The high moor was an eerie, wistful place. There were relics here of lives played out long, long, before the time of Christ. Rows and rings of stones, standing where human hands had set them thousands of years ago, burial mounds and chambered tombs, and remains of huts, their circular foundations sunk down into the ground. Little homes, where people had cooked and slept and given birth and huddled away from the wind and rain and all the horrors they imagined in the dark.

Jess had a special fondness for one particular settlement. It lay beneath a rocky outcrop and must have comprised about a dozen dwellings in its day. Here there was a ceaseless wind that hissed through the heather and whined among the boulders. Overlooking miles of lower country, it seemed to Jess the loneliest place on earth and the very age of it helped to put her worries in perspective.

That day, climbing down from her horse, she went to sit for a while on the edge of a round, shallow pit that had once formed the floor of a hut. Her eyes followed the changing patterns of the clouds and the shadows they threw on the hills, but her mind was on her husband.

She had tried to make allowances, battening down her temper, hoping this trouble would pass. She had tried and she was trying still, but over the months a distance had grown between her and Robert. Nothing had outwardly changed in their lives, but they were no longer close in the way they had been before. Resentment, disenchantment, had taken away the warmth.

Plucking a tall stem of grass, Jess put it in her mouth and chewed the end.

She was not including sex as part of Robert's cooling off. Something else had happened in that respect. When first they were married, sex and love had been one and the same, but that was no longer so. Robert had lately been very zealous in bed, often coupling twice nightly with fierce energy and much attention to her pleasure. And yet she sensed little affection in it, just a drive to prove that he was a lusty man. Once or twice an uneasy suspicion had crossed her mind that he feared she might find him lacking and seek to fill her needs elsewhere. The notion was insulting and she did not care to dwell on it too much.

It was more pleasant to think that he simply wanted another child and was working hard to make one. Robert had always said that he wanted four sons. Colin was nearly two years old and there was as yet no sign of another baby.

Jess smiled as she thought about her boy. He was running about quite steadily now, and full of babbling talk. She had left him with Pauline for the afternoon, as she always did when she went for a ride. Colin loved his Auntie 'Paulie' and his Uncle Joel. A stranger seeing the three of them together could be forgiven for thinking they were his parents. Lately, the boy's hair had grown very dark, resembling theirs.

'I daresay that comes from my father,' Joel had said. 'His hair was nearly black.'

I hope I fall pregnant soon, thought Jess. Perhaps it'll bring Robert round a bit. Lord, I'd do anything I could to make him his old self again.

After a time she consulted her watch. It was almost four o'clock and she had five miles to ride home. Tossing away the stem of grass, Jess stood up and turned around.

She had left the mare tethered to a bush in the shadow of the crag. The horse still stood there, patiently waiting, but she was no longer tethered. Someone was holding her reins.

Jess's stomach jumped with shock, then loathing rose to quell her nerves.

'My,' said Alec Maunder, smiling, 'you've been deep in thought, I must say. Sitting there, just like a statue, staring into space ...'

Her gaze was baleful. She cut across his words.

'How long have you been here?'

'Minute or two, no more. Didn't like to interrupt you, seeing you were so absorbed.'

She noticed, then, the shotgun propped among the rocks, and the two dead rabbits laid beside it.

'I see.' She walked across and held out her hand for the reins. Maunder passed them over.

'Been out and potted me supper,' he said. 'Like rabbit, do you?'

'No, I can't say I do.'

'Pity. You could have had one of these here.' He grinned to see her lip curl in disdain. His green eyes fairly danced. 'How's your ma?' he asked, softly.

'A lot worse for your visit,' snapped Jess.

'Oh? Well, she invited me.'

The answer was a snort.

'Then gave me short shrift when I took her up on it. I call that uncivil.'

She rounded on him, teeth bared. 'So you frightened the life out of her. You reptile! You vile, dirty oaf of a man! She told me all you said and did – and would have done, given the chance.'

'Aw, now that was just her wishful thinking!' A rich chuckle erupted from his throat. Her abuse seemed to bounce off him, deflected by a barrier of maddening good humour. She wished she carried a riding crop. She would have striped his face with it.

'It would be about your level, scaring women. You're the type.'

He spread his hands. 'Not scaring you, am I? What have I done here today but hold your horse and offer you a rabbit? Soon as you set eyes on me I get the sharp edge of your tongue, and what have I done to deserve it? I was led to believe I'd be welcome if I went to see your ma. Of course, I understand now why she's odd – unbalanced – but it had me baffled at the time. Needled me a bit, I must admit.'

'My mother is not unbalanced!'

'All right, then, nervy, put it that way.' His eyes grew round with innocence. 'If I'd known about her little – upset – I wouldn't have been so brash with her. Still, no real harm done, was there?'

No harm? No harm! She suspected he had some inkling of the trouble his tattling had caused between her and Robert. Maunder's next words confirmed it.

'Mind, I'm sorry I let the cat out of the bag when I spoke to your husband. Didn't dream I was giving a secret away. Haven't set off any strife, I hope? Didn't mean to do that.'

'Not much, you didn't.'

'I was making conversation, that was all.'

A mirthless smile went flitting across her face, then sharply disappeared.

'Oh, you're insidious, aren't you, Maunder? I've met many a woman like it, but never a man before. Poisonous, that's what you are.'

'There you go again! What did I say wrong?'

'Oh, get away from me!'

She went around to the other side of the mare to mount, but Maunder quickly followed her.

'Help you up, shall I?'

'No.'

He came closer, intimately lowering his voice. 'By the way, what are you doing out here today? Why come to a lonely spot like this? Hoping to meet someone, were you? Let you down, has he?'

'I enjoy it here, that's all, not that it's any business of yours.'

'I know, you like the view,' said Maunder, playfully.

'That's precisely right,' came the curt reply.

He moved still closer, backing her up against the mare.

'Sure you don't feel fidgety sometimes?' he queried, softly. 'Don't feel the need for a bit of diversion now and again?'

'Quite certain.' The words came out staccato, but she was trembling, too, detecting an unmistakable jutting in his trousers.

'Your ma took a lot of amusing, I hear, when she was young. You the same, by any chance?'

'I'm different in a lot of ways,' snarled Jess. 'For a start I'm not so easily frightened. Now move aside!'

But she was afraid, and a sparkle of insolence in his eyes told her that he knew it.

'Oh, well ...' He stepped back. '... as long as you're happy. Can't bear to see a nice lady unhappy.'

She spun round, put her foot in the stirrup, seized the pommel – but had no chance to heave herself up before Maunder grasped her waist and propelled her into the saddle with one effortless push.

'Light as air,' he said, and she fancied it was less a compliment than a statement of his own strength. Gripping the bridle, he persisted, 'So you're content, then, are you?'

'Let go of my horse,' growled Jess.

He took no notice. 'Just as well,' he went on. 'I believe he's a jealous man, your husband. A terrible jealous man. Then, who's to blame him, eh, with a lovely wife like you?' His gaze became reproachful. 'Should have been honest with him, shouldn't you, Jess? Might have saved a lot of awkwardness. Sooner or later he'd have heard it somewhere, so don't be too hard on me for letting it slip. You should have told him yourself.'

It was all she could do not to kick at his face. 'I don't need advice from a thing like you,' she spat. Turning the mare's head sharply, she wrenched the bridle from his grasp and saw him shake his fingers as if the leather had cut them.

Brushing him aside, she urged the mare into a trot. Maunder called a jaunty farewell after her. He used her Christian name again, a small familiarity he knew she would not like.

'Goodbye now, Jess.'

The smirk remained on his face until she was well down the hill. Then it snapped off. He looked down at the graze across his fingers and licked it sullenly. She had called him some ugly names. He would have loved to pull her off that horse and put her in her place. Were she not who she was, were it not for Robert Lawrenson ...

Alec Maunder's smile returned. Never mind, he had worked some mischief there, he could tell.

'A jealous man,' he repeated to himself, as he bent to retrieve his rabbits and his gun. 'I'll bet it's no picnic living with him. A terrible jealous man.'

· Nineteen ·

October passed, dead leaves fell ankle-deep along the woodland tracks, and the air began to smell of winter.

The Lawrensons always spent Bonfire Night at Ottery St Mary, where, on November 5th, the people observed a tradition older than any gunpowder plot. It was more than an hour's drive from Torvallen, but Robert and Joel enjoyed the spectacle of the blazing barrels being carried through the streets and they went to see it almost every year. A dangerous, often unruly event, it was supposed to bring good luck and those who took part were almost exclusively natives of the town. The custom had survived a few official attempts to stop it, and local men still proved their nerve and strength this way.

Jess had only seen it once, in the first year of her marriage. She thought it no place to take an infant and had stayed at home with Colin twice thereafter. This year, however, Pauline had offered to mind the child if Jess would care to go.

There was a very great crowd in Ottery that night. The streets were lined with jostling people and the way left clear was narrow. The men cut hellish figures charging through the mob, dark forms with head and shoulders haloed in flames, bent forward under the barrels of burning tar they hoisted on their backs. With nothing but wet sackcloth mittens to shield their hands, they held them like yokes for as long as they could, till the fire was consuming the wood too fast and the barrel had to be dropped. Sometimes they smashed as they hit the ground, flying apart in a hail of sparks and burning chips. Sometimes they stayed intact and were kicked on down the road by yelling youths. Cheering, the crowd surged back and forth, clapping and urging the runners on, braving showers of cinders and drops of hot tar. There had, on rare occasions, been bad accidents, with barrels falling into the thick of the crowd, but the night more often passed with no casualty more serious than a singeing.

Jess and Joel and Robert, at the forefront of the crowd, had felt the blast of heat from many a passing barrel. It was coming on for nine o'clock and they were thinking of finding a pub in which to have a drink before going home, when a small mishap occurred.

Racing towards them came a very large man. The top of the barrel he bore was a mass of flames and the onlookers screamed to him to let it drop. People shrank back out of the way, but he stubbornly ran on for another twenty yards before stumbling forward and heaving the barrel over his head. It crashed into the road and disintegrated, spewing fire in all directions. Robert seized his wife, pulling her out of the way as bits of burning wood went flying round her feet. He bent down quickly, brushing and patting at her legs, her ankles, the hem of her coat, to put out any live sparks.

The big man straightened up, panting, laughing, hands on hips. People were applauding him now and he was pleased with himself. Wiping sweat from his face and neck, he looked around and his gaze fell on Jess.

He swaggered over. 'All right, are you, Maid? Scorch you, did I? Sorry for that.'

'There's no harm done,' she said.

He grinned at Robert. 'Lovely girl,' he remarked. His eyes lingered on her, playful, shining. He was dark, with a bush of curly hair.

'You held on too long,' Robert told him, coolly.

'Yes, I did, a bit. Still, no one's hurt.'

'Only by sheer luck.'

The man peeled off the mittens, charred to rags, and handed them to Jess.

'Souvenir,' he said.

'More guts than sense,' observed Joel, as they watched him strut away. 'Bit of a show-off. Still, I admire his nerve.'

Robert took the mittens from Jess's hand and tossed them into the gutter.

'You don't want those. Come on, we've seen enough.'

They found a cosy public house and went inside. Joel ordered beer for himself and his brother, and a glass of barley wine for Jess. Lucky enough to find a table, they sat for half an hour, during which time Robert had two more drinks.

The place was packed and very noisy, with more and more customers pressing in. The Lawrensons did not notice when the big man entered, nor did he see them as he made his way to the counter and bought a pint of stout. A group of his friends clustered round him, praising and chaffing him for his daring.

Not until she rose from her seat and went in search of the lavatory did he spot Jess. He watched her go out the back door. Then he said a word or two to his companions and left them, threading his way across the crowded room. When Jess returned a few minutes later, he was waiting just inside the door.

'Hello again.'

She turned and there he was, stout in hand, beaming down at her.

'Oh.' She half-smiled. 'It's you.'

'Enjoy it tonight, then, did you?'

'Yes, very exciting.' She made to move past him, but he placed himself squarely in her way.

'Who are they?' He jerked his head towards the table where Robert and Joel sat.

'My husband and my brother-in-law.'

'Oh,' he said, deflated. 'Married, eh?'

'Yes. Excuse me ...'

'Some pretty, aren't you?'

'Thank you. Now please ...'

'Could I buy you a glass of cider or something, seeing I gave you a scare?'

He smelt of fire and smoke, and she noticed now that one of his hands was bandaged, while traces of ointment showed around his ears and neck.

'No. I've one back there I haven't finished.'

'You're not local, are you?' he asked. 'I'd remember if I'd seen you before. Where do you come from, then, eh?'

'Over Princetown way.'

'Oh, I know some people over there ...'

He mentioned names. She did not know them. And as her gaze flicked uneasily across the room, she saw her husband twist round in his seat, saw him look straight at her and then at the big dark man. It was a hard, intent look, summing up the situation.

'I can't talk any longer,' she said, sharply. 'Do please let me pass.'

Her tone was stern enough to make him stand aside. She hurried back to the table and sat down. Robert said nothing, but he eyed her from under his brows and she knew that he was angry. Joel plainly did not realise that anything was wrong. Jess was glad of his presence, for Robert would not start his tiresome questions in front of his brother. Later there was bound to be the usual inquiry. She held out no hope of escaping it, but better at home than here and now.

A few minutes later, Robert left the table, saying he was heading for the lavatory himself.

'Like a second one?' asked Joel, as she drained her glass.

'Yes, I wouldn't mind.'

'What about something to eat? Scotch egg? Meat pie?' Pausing, he studied her keenly. 'You look unhappy, Jess. Is anything amiss?'

'No.' She summoned a smile. 'I'm tired, that's all. I'm not hungry.'

'One more drink and then we'll go. Home by eleven, all right?'

'Are you going to drive?'

'Yes, Rob's had a couple too many.' He nodded at the half-empty glass by Robert's chair. 'That's his fifth. He's drinking fast tonight.'

There were many milling around the bar and it was quite a while before Joel was served. Waiting, Jess kept glancing round for her husband. He was taking a very long time. She noticed, too, that the curly-haired man had disappeared. She supposed he must have moved on to another pub.

Joel finally brought her barley wine and a second glass of ale for himself. He had taken only a sip when a sudden babble of voices broke out. Across the room, men were gathering round the back door, peering out into the yard. There were shouts and guffaws, then someone cried:

'There's a fight!'

'Oh, my God,' breathed Jess, suspecting at once. 'Don't tell me ...'

'What?' Joel stared at her. Then: 'Here, why's Rob so long out there?'

In a trice he was out of his seat and across the room, elbowing his way to the back door.

Outside, among the dustbins, two dark figures were exchanging punches. The smaller one was knocked to the ground but sprang straight up again. There were thumps and grunts and cracking sounds amid the crash and rumble of the bins. Grappling and scuffling, they fell and then regained their feet, elbows pumping in and out as they landed their blows.

Joel saw at once that his brother was having the worst of it, for the other was by far the bigger man. For all Robert's strength, he was outmatched now by someone heavier than himself and just as muscular.

Striding into the fray, Joel pulled them apart. Robert was down on his back once more and taking awful punishment. Hauling the other man upright, Joel had to dodge a punch himself.

'Enough!' he bawled, shaking him by his shirt lapels. 'Enough! You've won, all right? Now let it be.'

'No, he hasn't bloody won,' gasped Robert, struggling to his feet. 'And I don't need any help from you!'

'Shut up!' roared Joel.

His brother tottered, and grabbed at the open lavatory door for support. In truth, he could not take any more.

To the big man, Joel repeated fiercely,'It's over now, finished, calm down.'

'I didn't start it! I didn't look for this!' The other flung a gesture towards Robert. 'He came out here after me and picked a fight. Just because I passed a few words with his wife. Civil words, what's more.'

Joel did not disbelieve him. He knew his brother too well. He glanced up and his eyes took in the gawking mob at the back door. There at the forefront was Jess, and she hurried forward now to tend her husband.

'Look,' muttered Joel, too quietly for the rest to hear, 'he's had a drop too much to drink. Let's not argue the whys and wherefores. She's upset already. Don't embarrass her any more. You had the best of it, so leave it at that.'

The man prodded gingerly at his jaw, as if he feared it might be out of joint. Deciding it was not, he grunted, 'Ah, all right.' Then he hissed, 'But all I did was chat for a minute or so. At first I couldn't believe it when he came out here, taking me to task, pushing his fist in my face. If he's like that the whole time, I don't know how she stands him. I'll bet he makes enemies right, left and centre.'

'It's just the drink,' said Joel, loyally.

With one last killing look at Robert, the man slouched off. In a minute or so the audience dispersed and the three in the courtyard were left alone.

Robert was hunched over, leaning on Jess and clutching his stomach. She was trying, with her best silk scarf, to staunch the flow of blood from his nose.

'You great fool,' growled Joel. 'What a way to end the evening! Oh, come on, let's go home.'

He was silent all the way back to Torvallen. He knew it did no good to remonstrate with his brother, and Robert had paid for his belligerence already. It was just a crying shame, thought Joel, that the outing was completely spoilt for Jess.

Robert sat in the rear seat, his head thrown back, his eyes closed and his nose still dripping blood, while Jess tried to clean the cuts on his face and knuckles with a wet handkerchief.

'Robert,' she sighed in exasperation, as she dabbed at his swollen left eye, 'why did you have to go and do this? There was no call for it, no good reason at all.'

He pretended not to hear her. Humiliated and sore all over, he knew that she was right. And the worst of it, the very worst, was the fact that Joel had stepped in and rescued him. He had lost in front of everyone, and his brother had probably saved him from a spell in hospital. Robert had never felt so small.

He was off work the following day. Jess fetched the doctor early in the morning, just to make sure no bones were broken. The physician said not, but told him to stay in bed for twenty-four hours. Jess took up his meals on a tray. Tight-lipped, she annointed him with liniment and salve. Robert could not look her in the eye.

Late that night, she tackled him about it. It was time, she felt, that certain matters had an airing.

'What were you afraid of, Rob?' she asked, as she undressed. 'That I'd arranged a secret meeting with the man? Is that why you took him on?'

His gaze went wavering everywhere. The flesh around his left eye was plum-purple and his lip was split in two places.

'No, of course not! No such thought ever entered my head! I saw him annoying you, Jess.'

'I'd already dealt with it, hadn't I, made my own escape? What harm was done? None, till you went looking for trouble. Had to make an issue of it, didn't you, Robert? Had to make something out of nothing?'

'I'm your husband. It was my business to ...'

'Every move I make is your business, isn't it?'

'What do you mean by that?'

Jess slipped off her frock and tossed it over the bedroom chair, then took her nightgown from under her pillow.

'There's hardly a man I dare speak to in front of you. However innocent it is, however casual, you don't like it. And you constantly question me, don't you, Robert? You expect me to account for every minute of my day. Sometimes you ask me the same thing three times over in three different ways, as if you're trying to catch me out in a lie. And you imagine I can't see what you're about! Why don't you come straight out and say that you don't trust me any more – if you ever did? I think it's just as well that I receive no letters, or you'd be steaming them open in case they came from a lover.'

'That's ridiculous,' spluttered Robert, appalled that she had seen through his manoeuvres, his delicate probing for information and covert attempts to trip her up. He had thought himself quite subtle, like a clever barrister in court, but plainly she had not been fooled. Indeed, she had been humouring him. Still, he could not bring himself to admit it.

'Jess, you're imagining things.'

'Oh no ...' She slipped into bed, '... I leave that to you.'

'I'm only interested in what you do with yourself! I like to hear about your day, that's all! Some men don't bother to talk to their wives, do you know that? A dozen words and a grunt, that's all some women get.'

'You don't talk to me,' said Jess, calmly, 'you interrogate me. And after that performance last night I don't think I shall want to go out anywhere with you again, unless you come to your senses. If a trivial thing like that could end in so much trouble ...'

'Look,' flared Robert, 'if I'm a bit touchy sometimes, you know the reason very well.'

Ah yes, Vanessa, always Vanessa. It was like a reflex to blame Vanessa whenever he was challenged about his moods, his behaviour.

'The same thing happens to thousands of men,' said Jess,

'and women, too, come to that. Most people just put it down to experience. That was years ago, Robert. The excuse is getting very stale. I'm tired of being made to suffer for – whatever she did.'

Robert flashed her a look that was almost shifty. He had heard a note of doubt in that last phrase.

'And for what Mam did, too. That's more to the point, isn't it? That's what's really gnawing you. From the day you learned of that, you changed towards me, Robert.'

'Look, we're not newly-wed any more. The gilt wears off the gingerbread, that's all it is. Women! You always want romance for ever.'

'No.' She slowly shook her head, her eyes wide and sorrowful now. 'There's more to it than that. Please, Rob, don't doubt me all the time. Don't make me feel I'm on trial. You and Colin, you're all I want. I don't look for anything else.'

'I haven't said you do. And I hardly ever mention Alice. When did I last accuse you of anything, eh?'

'You don't need to accuse me in so many words.'

'Oh, I've no patience for this!'

'I'm the one who's had to be patient, Robert. But how much longer must I ... ?'

All of a sudden he rolled over, pressing her down in the bed so hard that it robbed her of breath for a moment.

'Do I mistreat you, Jess?' he enquired. 'I certainly don't neglect you, do I? Especially not this way. Don't I give you all you need, even when I'm bone tired? Most men only please themselves, you know.'

She had seen him wince with pain as he moved, and yet he was willing to perform in spite of it. He was able to, all right, she could feel that. It would doubtless hurt him, but still he would do it, in a dutiful, mechanical way. He would do it to send her off to sleep and end this discussion he did not like. He would do it to underline that she was his and display his power, but not to apologise, or comfort or reassure her. In his face she saw no fondness, just an anxious wish to shut her up.

'Thank you, Robert,' she said, quietly, 'but I don't think I want to be serviced tonight. You're excused.'

· Twenty ·

Thereafter, Jess found herself thinking a lot about Vanessa Crane. For most of her married life she had accepted Robert's claim that Vanessa had made him the way he was, especially as Pauline's comments seemed to back him up. Lately, however, Jess had begun to wonder if she had been seeing the situation back to front. After all, she had never heard Vanessa's version of events. She had been presented as grasping, heartless, a bitch who had wounded Robert deeply. Yet Joel, who freely voiced opinions on everyone else, was strangely silent concerning Vanessa. His only remarks about her had been guarded, non-committal, as if he feared his views might stir up strife if he expressed them. Jess began to wish that she could meet the 'villainous' Vanessa.

Early in the New Year, fate obliged her with an opportunity.

There were few things Pauline loved more than the January sales. Joel always gave her money for Christmas, knowing she would spend the lot in Plymouth on the day the sales began. Sure enough, the second Monday of the month found her joining the scramble at Spooner's department store. Jess was tagging along that day, having left Colin with Alice. There was little she wanted to buy for herself, but they planned to have lunch in Spooner's restaurant and go to the cinema later, provided Pauline had finished her shopping in time.

The store was packed to bursting with people and goods. Everywhere there were racks crammed with cut-price clothing, and tables piled high with bargains. Hordes of women picked over heaps of woollen jumpers, socks, vests. Grabbing frocks off hangers, trying and discarding hats, stretching out bloomers to test the elastic, searching for the shoe or glove to match an odd one, they shoved and weaved their way round every floor, noisy, determined, and often ferocious.

The first two hours after opening were frenzied. Stacks of table- and bed-linen disappeared, and shelves were stripped of kitchen-ware. Winter coats were much in demand, along with children's clothing. The shop assistants were harassed, and canisters of money and receipts hurtled constantly back and forth across the overhead change rail. A ceaseless babble and murmur filled the air, a rushing hither and thither, with endless swooping and seizing.

Joel would have called it undignified, but the sales brought out in Pauline the same joyous aggression that characterised her driving. Jess kept out of the scrum, preferring to stand back and guard the spoils while Pauline rummaged for more. By mid-morning, she had purchased a set of saucepans, an eiderdown, a blazer and a silk blouse. Life at Torvallen offered little opportunity for dressing up, but every year at sale time Pauline treated herself to a few smart clothes, some lacy underwear and scent.

The time rolled around to twelve o'clock. While Pauline sorted lovingly through evening frocks she would never have any occasion to wear, Jess began to think about lunch. She was not especially hungry, but her feet and legs had started to ache.

'Look at this!' Pauline pulled out a flimsy affair in turquoise. The bodice was skimpy, the shoulder straps little more than strings, while the skirt was cut to whirl and flutter as the wearer danced. 'Isn't it pretty! Or this!' She held up an amber satin shift with a dark gold fringe around the hem. 'Oh, I'd like this!'

'Oh yes, lovely,' agreed Jess. 'You might even wear it once. Next Christmas, say. Then it'll end its days at the back of the wardrobe.'

'Killjoy,' sighed Pauline, hooking it back on the rail. 'I still have two guineas for something special, but I don't know what to buy.' She looked around her as she spoke, eyeing a dozen different racks.

Jess grasped her chance. 'Let's go and eat while you think about it. Come on, there's plenty left to choose from. It won't all vanish in the next hour; the rush is over now.'

Up on the second floor was a large and rather plain dining room, furnished with dozens of identical square tables, each with four chairs. A no-nonsense restaurant, this, devoid of frills – everything neat, clean, serviceable, with a menu offering nothing fanciful or foreign. Some fifteen or sixteen tables were occupied, mainly by women lingering over morning coffee and cakes. Most were with a friend or two, so anyone sitting alone was apt to be conspicuous. That was why, on glancing round the room, Pauline quickly spotted somebody she knew.

She had given her order and the waitress was now attending to Jess. While Jess considered the menu, Pauline's eyes kept darting towards a young woman seated close to the window. As soon as the waitress departed, she leaned across and whispered:

'Look, over there! Sitting alone – the one in the brown coat. Guess who that is.'

Jess stole a glance. She could see the woman only in profile. Intent on her meal, she seemed unaware that anyone was watching her.

'I don't know. Who is she?'

'That's Vanessa.' Pauline mouthed the words.

'Oh!' Jess took another, longer look. Her forehead creased. 'Are you sure?'

'Of course I'm sure!'

'But she's, well ...'

'What?'

Jess was at a loss. 'Just not what I expected. I thought she'd be smarter, I suppose. She doesn't look especially well-off.'

'Don't let the scruffy clothes fool you,' said Pauline,

softly. 'She was never very interested in fashion, always plainly dressed. She prefers to spend her money on horses, paintings, things like that. Goes around looking quite shabby, but when she opens her mouth and you hear the strangled vowels, you know straight away she's a county type.'

As if some sense of their attention had finally reached her, Vanessa suddenly looked round. Her gaze fell first on Pauline, who pointedly turned away, unwilling to acknowledge her. Vanessa gave no sign of surprise or discomfort. Then, for a few seconds, her eyes turned calmly on Jess.

She had what some would call a 'good' face – good in the sense that it was sculptured, striking, with a full mouth, straight nose and high, taut cheeks. Her hair was the lightest of browns – the colour of weak tea – and very sleek. Fine, shiny hair with no hint of a curl, it was bobbed exactly like Pauline's. Her eyes had a slightly sleepy look that could easily give an impression of arrogance.

Jess returned the stare, studying this woman who, by his account, had made Robert the difficult man he was. Pauline had declared her a snob and she did indeed have a lofty air. If asked to make a quick judgement, Jess would have said that Vanessa was proud and probably humourless, traits guaranteed to antagonise the boisterous Pauline. But whether she was the type to play games with the feelings of others, Jess was not so sure. There was something very forthright in her gaze. She looked as if she would not stoop to toying with a man's affections.

Vanessa turned away and went placidly on with her meal.

'I don't suppose she knows who you are,' Pauline murmured. 'I'll bet she hasn't given poor old Rob a thought in all these years. Of course, they weren't suited, as I've said before, and it's all turned out for the best. But she led him a merry dance at the time, and the way she dropped him was very cruel.'

'How do you know what happened between them?' Jess asked, slowly. 'I mean, did you often see them together and hear what went on?'

‘Well, no. She came to the house a few times, but mostly she used to summon him over to her place.’

‘Summon him? Did she?’

‘Every time he came home he would tell us she’d asked him to call again on such and such a day to take her somewhere. She obviously thought it fun to have him shuttling back and forth. I don’t believe she liked Torvallen at all, or else she’d have visited more often, nor do I think she had any care for Rob. It’s my guess that Vanessa was simply flattered that a young man would drive twenty miles to have tea with her or run an errand, and she kept him on a string for as long as it amused her.’

Ah, your guess, reflected Jess. And perhaps that’s all it is. All you know is what he told you, about a girl you already disliked. You’re willing to credit the worst – which is only human, but may be warping the picture. I suppose I’d be the same. I’d believe almost any evil I heard of Brenda Fitch.

The waitress brought their soup, and as she put it down in front of them, Vanessa rose from her table.

‘She’s leaving,’ Pauline said, and pulled a face.

Breaking apart her bread, Jess paused to watch her go. Had it not been for Pauline, she would have run after her.

With Vanessa gone, Pauline’s interest returned to the subject of clothes, and they ate their meal discussing styles and items she meant to try. Afterwards they returned to the dress department, where she spent a happy half-hour flitting in and out of the changing rooms with different frocks and suits. None of them pleased her enough to buy, until she lit on a knitted jumper suit with a red pleated skirt and a loose cream top trimmed in red at the neck and cuffs. Excited, she rushed off yet again to try it on, leaving Jess to mooch around by herself for another ten minutes.

It was then that she spotted Vanessa once more. At the farmost end of the store, among the rails of overcoats, Vanessa was browsing and looking at price tickets.

Just for a moment, Jess was undecided. Conscience said she was being disloyal to Robert, but in the end she was driven harder by the need to satisfy doubt. When Vanessa disappeared among the coat racks, Jess went hurrying after her.

'Excuse me.'

Vanessa turned, and seemed a little taken aback at the sight of Pauline Lawrenson's companion.

'Yes?'

'You're Vanessa Crane, I understand?'

'I was. Lambert is my married name.'

'Oh, yes, of course.'

'And you, evidently, are a friend of Pauline's. What is it you want with me?'

Her speech was light and crisp, not as supercilious as Jess had been led to expect.

'I'm Robert's wife, Jess Lawrenson.'

'Ah.' The sound was slightly wary. 'I see. I didn't know he had married. Of course, it's been a good many years, so I ought not to be surprised.'

Her gaze ran over Jess, taking in the Dolly Varden hat and the curly blonde hair which showed beneath it, then the mulberry coat and the neat suede shoes.

'You're very pretty,' she said. 'Have you any children?'

'One, a boy.'

'That's nice. I'm sure Robert's proud of you both.'

She did not smile, but her words had the ring of sincerity.

'Thank you.'

Neither felt comfortable, and now that she was face to face with her, Jess did not know how to broach the subject. But then Vanessa prompted:

'If there's something you want to say to me, please come straight out with it. I assume it's to do with Robert, though I can't think why you should want to discuss him with me. I daresay you have the full Lawrenson version of what happened between us and it can't have flattered me one bit.'

'That's just it,' said Jess, stoutly, 'it didn't. But I'd like to hear your side of it, too.'

Vanessa considered her thoughtfully, a flicker of puzzlement crossing her face. 'May I ask why?'

'I, uh, like to be fair to people.'

'But surely you'll believe your husband, rather than a stranger? And why should it matter to you anyway? As long as you're happy together, what difference can it make?'

'Please, Mrs Lambert, I'd like to know why you left him.'

'Left him?' queried Vanessa. 'I really wouldn't put it that way. We were never attached, so how could I have "left him"?'

'Threw him aside, then.'

'That's not appropriate, either.'

'Tell me what is.'

'I would rather not. I don't like to fuel trouble, Mrs Lawrenson, and I doubt I can tell you anything much about Robert you don't already know.'

'Then you can't cause any harm, can you? Are you aware of what the family say about you, Mrs Lambert?'

'I'm sure I can guess.' Vanessa's tone suggested that she did not greatly care. 'Pauline believes me a snob, I know. Oh, and mercenary, too. She's certain I married my husband for his money, having toyed with poor Robert and then discarded him.'

'That's more or less right.'

'And Robert, of course, has told you how callous I am, how devious and treacherous. He called me all those things last time I saw him. And ungrateful into the bargain, after all the time and money he'd spent on me.'

Jess nodded her agreement. 'Is it true?'

Vanessa sighed. 'Remember, Mrs Lawrenson, you started this conversation. You insist on hearing my side of it. Very well. To begin with, I'll say that Robert is a good man in very many ways. He's industrious and utterly reliable. He'll never be a philanderer, he'll never lose money in foolhardy ventures. He'll never be neglectful, either – quite the reverse, in fact. But therein lies a problem for any woman who likes to call her soul her own.'

Something showed on Jess's face and Vanessa did not miss it.

'I see I've struck a chord,' she said, quietly. 'Now, I must make one thing clear from the outset. Robert was merely one of my many friends, and certainly not the closest. Tell me, do you still have that chestnut horse at Torvallen?'

'The mare? Yes.'

'He and Joel bought it from my father, and that was how we met. I liked Robert in a casual way, but there was never more to it than that – except in his mind. He decided that we were a pair, a couple, and things became very trying for me after that. Not only did he pursue me quite relentlessly, but he also behaved as if he owned me. Of course, he was only about nineteen at the time – I'm four years older than he is – and at first I made allowances. I thought it was just a silly crush and sure to wear off soon. Unfortunately, I was wrong, and he simply became unbearable. I've always had a lot of friends, but Robert would have cut me off from everyone. Whenever I spoke to another man, however casually, he would sulk and demand to know what was said. He was always on the doorstep, too, always calling round at the most inconvenient times. And I was supposed to be there waiting whenever he arrived. He was always very aggrieved if he turned up and found I was out.'

She made a helpless gesture, spreading her hands.

'I don't think I ever misled Robert, and I certainly didn't make him any promises. He just assumed too much – and God knows, he couldn't take a hint. After about six months, he even started to talk about becoming engaged! Marry Robert? Dear God, the very idea! All marriages involve constraint, of course, but he would have kept me on a choke chain! As I said at the start, Robert has many good points, but I never felt any affection for him, and all the presents and flowers he bought me, all the letters he wrote, just made me feel obligated, cornered. I stood it as long as I could, and I did try at first to let him down gently, but he wouldn't accept it and so, in the end, I had to be brutal.'

She saw Jess moisten her lips and she nodded wisely.

'You understand all too well, I think. Truly, Mrs Lawrenson, I'm not the villain he'd have you believe. You loved him enough to marry him, but if, as I suspect, you are experiencing that same stifling devotion and senseless jealousy, then you have my sympathy. It can't be easy, living with a gaoler.'

'Well,' muttered Jess, 'I was never a sociable person like you. Torvallen is a lonely place and that was what I wanted.'

'Then there should be no difficulty, surely?'

'There should be none,' sighed Jess, 'and yet there is.'

'Has it helped to talk to me?'

'You've clarified a thing or two. I can't say you've made me feel better.'

'I feared not. I'm very sorry for you, Mrs Lawrenson. I do hope you'll find a means to resolve your trouble. I don't suppose Robert is happy, either. Pain is pain, even when it's self-inflicted. How sad for you both.'

Then, glancing across the shop, she said, 'I see Pauline is searching for you. She appears to have bought something. You have my good wishes, Mrs Lawrenson. I'd ask you to give my regards to Robert, too, but I don't think they'd be well-received.'

Bidding her goodbye, Jess went back to join Pauline.

'Where on earth have you been?' asked Pauline, though she did not wait for an answer. 'I bought the suit,' she went on gaily, 'and a nice cloche hat to go with it. I hope we've enough money left for the pictures. To tell you the truth, I forgot about that.'

'It doesn't matter,' said Jess. 'I don't feel like going after all.'

Pauline peered at her. 'Are you all right? You look washed out. God, I'm thoughtless, aren't I, dragging you around all morning?'

'It's just the crowds, all the gabble and shoving, they've given me a bad head. Could we go straight home?'

'By all means. I wonder if you're sickening for something. It is that time of year. Or perhaps it was the lunch.'

I've had a dose of undiluted truth, thought Jess. That's what's disagreed with me.

· Twenty-one ·

While Jess's ship had entered choppy waters, Alice had long been marooned, alone and going nowhere. Seven years without a man, withdrawn from life like a hermit on a little isle.

Then one spring morning the tides of fate washed up a treasure on her shore.

Men in shabby working clothes or service uniforms were all she usually saw, so her surprise was great indeed when a colourful, dapper little figure appeared in her shop that day. He was short and round and balding, and brown as a hazelnut. The thinning hair was curly, and so were the lashes round his soft dark eyes. They were smiling eyes in a smiling face. Nature had given his mouth an upward tilt, so that he always seemed on the verge of laughter. He wore a smart tobacco-coloured jacket, a mustard-yellow waist-coat and a pair of fawn checked trousers. A gold pin glinted in the centre of his deep red tie. In one hand he held a valise, and in the other a violin case.

He wished Alice good morning, calling her 'dear lady', and purchased a tin of cheroots. He also bought some chocolates, confessing to a weakness for strawberry creams. Alice thought his accent very pleasant and was moved to ask him where he came from.

'Buckinghamshire, dear lady.'

'My, that's a long way,' said Alice, who had never been further afield than Exeter. 'Are you visiting friends here-abouts?'

'Why, no, in fact I'm taking up a post in this fine city. I'm to join the orchestra at the Alhambra Theatre.'

'Oh, you're a professional musician?'

'Skilled enough to earn my living,' beamed the little man.

'I expect you enjoy your work,' said Alice, smiling.

'I do, I do. Indeed I do!' The laughter bubbled up again. 'And that makes me a lucky man, don't you agree?'

'I should say you are.'

He looked around him. 'What a nice shop this is, dear lady. All the sweets so pretty in their jars, all the cigar boxes with their handsome gold crests, and such a fragrance in the air!'

She had never thought of it like that. To her it was just the business, just humdrum.

'Well, thank you,' she said.

'I take pleasure in things like that, you know. The loveliness of ordinary things. People sometimes think me strange, but I firmly believe it's the secret of happiness. One should notice and savour the little everyday delights.'

'I daresay you're right,' said Alice, politely.

These artistic types, she thought. Well, they are a bit odd, aren't they?

'How I ramble on!' he exclaimed. 'I must be on my way.'

His gaze travelled over her tired face, and the brown eyes showed a flash of kindly curiosity. He was a gentle soul and he sensed that she was, too. The difference was that he enjoyed his life, exuding bounce, while Alice had an air of sadness and defeat. Traces of her prettiness still remained and he briefly wondered what sort of trouble had befallen her. But of course it was not his place to ask. Instead, he enquired:

'Would you know of any boarding houses hereabouts, dear lady? The theatre recommended several places where I might find lodgings, but either they were full or else I found them uncongenial. Hotels, I fear, are a shade too expensive for me.'

Alice thought, then pulled a regretful face. 'None of my neighbours take in lodgers. Most people round here have big families and no room to spare. There are boarding houses, certainly, but I think they'd be a bit rough for you. They're just for seamen who come and go every few days, not for a working gentleman who needs a permanent place. If I were you, I'd buy the local paper and look in there.'

'A sensible idea,' he said. 'My thanks to you, dear lady.'

'Good luck,' said Alice.

Another radiant smile and a nod of his head, then out he went. Alice watched him cross the road. His valise looked very heavy and he seemed a little lost, undecided which way he should go. A strange sort of waif, thought Alice, all life and cheer and yet all on his own. She hoped he would find a nice room before nightfall.

The day went by and after four it started to rain. The dockyard hooter sounded, bringing the usual flurry of customers as the men came off shift. By six o'clock all was quiet again. Alice emptied the till and locked the money away upstairs, then went down once more to bar the shop door.

And there he was again, with his luggage and his violin. He was wet, his curls plastered down by the rain. Water dripped from his clothes and formed a puddle round his feet. His smile was just a little strained.

'I have not been fortunate, dear lady.'

'Oh,' said Alice, 'I'm very sorry to hear it.'

Lord! she thought. Why's he come back here?

'It occurred to me,' said the little man, 'to ask if you could accommodate me for tonight. If so, I would gladly pay you for a room and a bath and a meal. You see, I travelled all last night by train and today I have walked many miles. I'm quite exhausted and loath to go any further this evening.' The brown eyes were hopeful, beseeching now. 'Do you have a spare room, dear lady? Would you consider putting me up? Would I be imposing too much?'

He's a stranger, thought Alice. I can't possibly!

Consternation showed on her face. She shook her head. 'Oh, no. I'm afraid I can't help you. No, and I'm closing now.'

He did not press the matter, too much of a gentleman.

'I'm sorry. I shouldn't have presumed. It was just an idea.'

Turning around, he made for the door. His shoes squelched and he cut a forlorn figure now, his brightness extinguished by cold and fatigue. Outside it was raining hard.

Alice let him go.

Then she argued with herself.

Finally, her soft heart got the best of her. Running to the door, she called him back.

'There's only my daughter's old room. It's small but comfortable. I suppose you could use it just for tonight.'

His smile was eager, grateful.

'I could make some steak and kidney pie,' offered Alice.

'Oh, splendid, splendid! Would five shillings be enough?'

'Quite enough,' she assured him, though she really had little idea of what a guest house would charge.

'How kind, how very kind!' He was much relieved and his spirits revived like magic. 'Do I take it you're Mrs Davey, as it says on the sign?'

'That's right.'

He held out a chubby hand. 'My name is Kenneth Honey.'

What am I doing? she thought, as she showed him upstairs.

It was strange to have a man in the house again. Alice had been a widow for nearly twelve years, and something of a recluse for seven of them.

At first she was sorely unsettled, sharing her home with Mr Honey. She wanted to drink but felt that she could not while he was there. Nor could she undress and sit about in her underwear as she was often wont to do when alone. Instead she had to cook a meal, and stay in the kitchen while he had his bath by the sitting room fire. Alice was altogether discommoded, her habits disturbed, her home invaded.

After his bath, he sat down to dinner wearing a dressing gown of dark green satin. Underneath it, Alice caught a glimpse of crimson silk pyjamas.

'I love strong colours,' he explained, when he saw her looking. 'I must admit, I spend too much on clothes. I can't resist dressing up.'

Alice smiled faintly, picking at her own small portion of pie. 'It's a harmless pleasure, I suppose.'

'Quite so, and therefore I indulge. Life is short and ought to be as merry as we can make it, don't you think?' Wreathed in smiles, he tapped his knife against his plate. 'You know, you are a very good cook, Mrs Davey.'

She gave him baked egg custard for dessert. When he had finished eating, he pulled from his valise a bottle of brandy.

'Shall we have a couple, Mrs Davey? I do enjoy a drop, don't you?' He twinkled at her. 'Where do you keep the glasses?'

Alice was not about to say no. In the end they each had three, and while they drank he told her a few entertaining stories about his experiences in the theatre. Warming to him, Alice wondered why he was alone and living such a footloose life. He was somewhere in his forties and she would have expected such a man to have a wife and children. At last she ventured to ask, and learned that Mr Honey was a widower.

He bid her goodnight as the clock struck ten, thanking her effusively for all her hospitality. Relaxed by the drink, and feeling benevolent, she made him a hot water bottle to take to bed.

He left next morning after breakfast. He was gone for the whole of the day. But then, once more near closing time ...

'I begin to despair, Mrs Davey. What am I to do? I don't suppose you'd consider putting me up for a week? I could pay you two guineas if you would provide me with full board. My situation is becoming awkward. Tomorrow I must take up my appointment at the theatre. I'm expected there for rehearsals and shan't have time to seek out accommodation. You see my plight, I'm sure.'

A week? Oh Lord! To have him around, in her house, for a week, however nice he was ...

Alice wondered if he had really searched so very hard for lodgings, or if he had simply taken a fancy to her home and cooking. Whatever the truth, she thought it safest to refuse.

'Oh, well, that's rather different. I mean to say, I'm not in the business of taking boarders.'

'Of course, of course. But it's only temporary, I assure you.'

Upon the counter stood a small scales. She began fiddling nervously with the weights, stacking them up, then laying them out in a row, then building them up again.

'No, I don't think it's a good idea.'

'Perhaps I could manage two pounds ten shillings.'

'It isn't the money,' said Alice, quickly.

'The intrusion?'

'Partly. And people hereabouts are apt to talk.'

'Ah.' He nodded solemnly. 'I didn't think of that. I'm insensitive to gossip, but that makes me the exception, I daresay. Naturally I would not wish to embarrass you, dear lady, or be the cause of any stain on your character.'

Alice nearly laughed out loud at that. As if he could darken what was black already. She had not the gall to pretend there was any good reputation to protect. It hardly seemed fair to use that as an argument.

'Don't worry, Mr Honey, you couldn't damage it at all,' she said, dryly. Quickly she returned to the theme of intrusion. 'But you see, I'm used to living alone. It's not my habit to cook three meals a day, or ...'

'Cold cuts, boiled eggs and so on are often enough,' said Mr Honey. This time he was not about to give up easily.

'Well, I don't know ...'

Her fingers roved fretfully among the weights, sorting, arranging and rearranging them. So reasonable, so undemanding, he was talking her into a corner.

Mr Honey saw that she was wavering. 'I'd be out a great deal,' he coaxed. 'We do a matinée, you see, as well as the evening performance. I wouldn't be under your feet all the time.'

Alice hesitated, still thinking about her neighbours.

'People', she had vaguely said. There always seemed to be a horde of them, a critical horde with countless eyes and ears. And yet, on reflection, she could only name half a dozen real persecutors. Still, she was loath to give them ammunition.

'Only a week,' came the plaintive reminder.

They'd soon realise, she thought, when they saw him coming and going. The way he dresses, he'd stand out like a sore thumb. There isn't the slightest hope that he'd go unnoticed.

'I'm very tidy,' offered Mr Honey. 'I have my own towels and all my washing can go to the laundry.'

Alice looked helplessly at him. What have I to lose? she wondered. They talk about me anyway. How could this make things much worse? My life is almost blameless now, yet I'm sneered at just the same.

'By the way, I'll be getting you a complimentary ticket to the show,' said Mr Honey. 'To thank you for putting me up last night, I mean.' He would, too. She felt certain he would, even if she refused to accommodate him any longer. It was generosity, not a bribe. When had she last received a kind gesture like that? Alice could not remember.

He's a good sort, she decided. And I suppose it would be nice to have the extra money.

'You won't be bringing any friends here? Or making any noise?'

'I have no friends as yet, Mrs Davey. You forget that I'm new in town. As for noise, I shall only play my violin if and when you want to hear it. I do know some splendid tunes.'

'No screeching,' specified Alice, warily.

'Tunes, dear lady, as I said. A few of your favourites among them, I daresay.'

'You mean you'll play requests?' Alice began to laugh. 'All right, Mr Honey, you may stay for a week – or until you find somewhere permanent.'

But he never did find anywhere else. Mr Honey moved in that day and became a fixture. A week, a fortnight, a month, then two – somehow the time just rolled away and the understanding quietly grew that he did not want to go and was not expected to. He was lodged with Alice, sure enough, snug as a chestnut in its pod. He fitted, he was comfortable, he would stay as long as he was welcome.

Alice had soon lost any desire to winkle him out. Privacy came to seem less important than cheerful company each day. Like a steadily strengthening tonic, he buoyed her up with his optimism and his kindness, filling her drab, lonely existence with colour and humour. Life, in short, began to seem worthwhile to Alice Davey. It was good to have someone again to look after – she had never been one to look after herself, but the instinct to care for the needs of someone else was strong in her. She had reason now to cook and clean and lay the table nicely and put up pretty curtains. She tended her house with pleasure instead of resignation, doing it not because Jess would nag when she called on Thursdays, but because Mr Honey would praise her efforts every single day.

They called each other Kenneth and Alice. She purchased and prepared all his favourite foods, while he, to her surprise, turned out to be quite handy at odd jobs, mending broken hinges and handles, nailing down loose floorboards and so on. Two or three times a week he would bring her a bunch of flowers, and sometimes a bottle of cologne or a box of scented soap.

Sometimes, when he was out, she went to the cupboard in the little bedroom, and looked in wonderment at all his natty clothes, stroking the fabrics and searching for buttons that needed sewing or trousers that would benefit from pressing. He had striped blazers, white trousers, numerous shirts and coloured waistcoats, suits light, dark and medium in fine-textured fabrics or knobbly tweeds. There were plus-fours and chequered jerseys, ties and bow ties, diamond-patterned socks, a boater, a trilby, a panama, and seven pairs of shoes. He was altogether a dandy and never wore the same outfit two days running.

Alice did his washing now. She knew just how to starch

his collars and cuffs the way he liked them. She said they charged too much at the laundry and she could not possibly let him pay it.

Late at night they giggled together over their brandy and gin. He always had new jokes to tell, and she liked to have him play some jolly Hungarian music on his violin. Now and again he took her out to supper, and sometimes they went shopping together – for as he had said, he could not resist buying clothes. Every week there was something new and it was not long before Alice started making room in her wardrobe for some of his things.

After a time, inevitably, she made room in her bed for him.

Alice Davey blossomed like a rose. Happiness took years off her and she started to dress a little more smartly. After all, she had to look nice beside Kenneth, spruce and stylish as he was. She had her hair waved once a week and took to wearing lipstick. Despite middle age and gallons of gin, her good looks were not entirely gone. They were wonderfully revived by a few cosmetics and some genuine affection from a man.

All along the street, the tom-toms had been beating from the day Mrs Fitch first saw the situation. The neighbours were appalled, or so they claimed. They said Alice was 'back to her old ways with a vengeance, keeping a fancy man in the house'. She was 'living the high life', they said. And they didn't like the look of 'him', done up like a hambone all the time. They liked a plain man, they did, a man with a proper job and a flat cap and boots and no nonsense about him. They didn't think much of men who wore buttonholes and dickie-bows. They preferred a man who was out of the house at half past seven each morning, back at six for his food, down the pub all evening out of their way, and too tired to bother them in bed. Mr Honey, bouncy, chirpy, tipping his hat as he bid them 'Good-day', looked as if he did not know what weariness was. They felt sure that he and Alice were up to all sorts of things at night.

Mr Honey did not seem to mind their black looks and

mutterings. He was always utterly charming to women, no matter how awful they were. As for Alice, she had long ceased to care what they said. She was walking on air and not even jibes in the street could bring her to earth for long. There was only one opinion that concerned her. She badly wanted her daughter to approve of Mr Honey.

Jess reserved judgement for several months, but finally she admitted:

'Yes, I like him very much. I'm glad he's here. I must confess I was taken aback when first I met him. Apart from anything else, he's a bit, well, startling. Even for a theatre type, he's flamboyant. Of course, he's very winning, but I don't mind telling you now, I was worried for a while. There are men, you know, who prey on solitary women. You always were a bit of a soft touch and if he could persuade you to take him in, I was afraid he might also talk you out of some money or something like that.'

'He's never borrowed so much as a penny, Jess. He pays his rent each Friday on the dot and never complains about anything.'

Alice was sitting in front of her bedroom mirror and plucking her eyebrows. It was mid-September now. As usual, Mr Honey was playing a matinée this Thursday afternoon.

'Still pays his rent, eh? Despite the fact he's more than a lodger?'

Alice glanced at her. Jess was perched on the edge of the bed and she knowingly patted the quilt.

'He doesn't use my room any more, does he, Mam?'

'Do you mind that, Jess?' Slowly, Alice put down the tweezers.

'No, not as long as you're happy.'

Glowing, dewy, Alice sighed. 'Kenneth is such a dear man. I doubt he's ever said or done anything hurtful to anyone. I don't think he's capable of it.' She met Jess's gaze, reflected in the mirror. 'I believe it's because he enjoys life so much. He sees everything and everyone in the best possible light, so he isn't bitter or envious or spiteful.'

'A rare bird,' observed Jess.

'More's the pity.' Alice leaned close to the mirror and deftly whipped out a couple of straggling hairs. 'If only everyone could be like that.'

'His job at the Alhambra – is it permanent?'

'Oh yes, he's a member of the resident theatre orchestra.'

'I'm glad of that. I thought it might be just for the summer season.'

'No,' said Alice, confidently. 'He likes the area, too. He's here to stay.'

'I hope so,' said Jess. 'You don't drink as much these days, do you?'

'Oh, we always have a drop before we go to bed.'

'But you don't drink alone any more?'

'No.' Alice smiled at her daughter in the mirror. 'I can't remember when I last did that.'

'For which I'm very grateful to Mr Honey.'

Alice chuckled and took up her powder puff. 'Do you think I could do with some rouge?' she asked.

'You've colour enough. You look healthy, Mam. It pleases me so much.'

'It's all because of him,' said Alice, radiant.

Yes, all because of him. Jess watched while her mother prinked like a young girl. The shabby, scruffy, hopeless woman of six months past had disappeared entirely, and all on account of a man. The house was shipshape and so was Alice. As Jess had said, there was much for which to thank Mr Honey. All the same, it troubled her a little that a male had been the cause of this transformation, no matter how engaging he was. Jess doubted that Alice would ever have rallied this way by herself. She had always been apt to crumple without a man. Jess therefore prayed that Alice was right, that he was indeed there to stay. For if Mam's well-being depended on him, Jess did not care to dwell on what might happen if she lost him.

He seems so perfect, she thought. But there are no perfect men.

She recalled the illusions of her courting days. Robert, the answer to everything. He had seemed to lay a new life at her feet, an ideal life, all for the taking, without a snag and free of cost. Happy ever after? Jess knew better now.

She had never mentioned to Robert her talk with Vanessa Lambert. She did not intend to, either, knowing it would only cause a row and increase his distrust. There would be denials, counter-accusations, Vanessa would be called a liar and Jess a traitor for listening to her. How, he would indignantly demand, could Jess believe her, even for a moment?

But she did believe her, completely. The only comfort she could draw from what she had learned was the knowledge that any woman, regardless of her background, would suffer the same cross-questioning, the same suspicious surveillance she had been enduring.

'Will you fasten my necklace?' asked Alice.

Jess slid off the bed and came to stand behind her, hooking together the bolt and ring clasp of a strand of coral beads.

Alice patted her hair and glanced at the clock. 'Kenneth will be home in a minute,' she said.

Jess nodded, smiling again. Perhaps she was being too cynical. Perhaps Mam would have better luck with Mr Honey. Perhaps he was all that he appeared to be and perhaps he would marry her. Neither ventured to voice the possibility, but Jess knew that was what Alice was hoping.

A moment later they heard him come in downstairs. Alice's face lit up and she hurriedly patted some cologne about her throat.

Whatever the future, she's happy now, thought Jess. Just as Joel and Pauline are happy. Everyone's content, it seems, except for Rob and me.

· Twenty-two ·

'I must go, I'm very late. I promised I'd be there by one.'

Pauline rummaged in her bag, searching for her purse, then slipped a coat on over her red and cream suit. A year had passed and the outfit was no longer new, but still it was one of her favourites. Today was her father's sixtieth birthday and all his daughters were taking him out for a big lunch at a country hotel.

'You're looking very smart,' said Jess, who was curled up on the sitting-room sofa, knitting Robert a Fair Isle jumper. At her feet, Colin had his clockwork train set laid out on the floor and the engine went racing round and round with a loud, metallic whirr. Carriages, goods wagons, signal box, level crossing and station – his doting father had bought him all the accessories.

Pauline was wearing silk stockings and court shoes, and her dark hair shone. A change of clothes was all it took to make an elegant figure of Joel's wife. She moved across the room to pick up her hat and gloves. Hurrying, she caught the toe of her shoe in Colin's railway line and the engine jumped from the track, landing on its side with the wheels still frantically spinning.

'Oh, aren't I clumsy!' Bending down, she lightly tweaked the boy's nose and set his train going again. 'I really should have left at twelve,' she said, straightening up.

'Will you be back for dinner?' asked Jess.

'Probably not.' Pauline pushed her face close to the mirror over the mantelpiece, stroking on some bright red lipstick. 'Dad likes to have a game of chess with me back home, and it always lasts for hours. There, I think I'm presentable now. See you later.'

'Enjoy yourself. And do take care – don't drive too fast.'
'Fusspot,' said Pauline.

And with that she was gone, pulling on her hat as she went. Her footsteps receded down the hall, the front door slammed behind her, and a moment later Jess heard the car start up. Glancing through the window, she saw it move down to the gate and out into the lane. Returning her attention to her knitting, she found she had dropped a stitch.

Once on the main road, Pauline put her foot down hard. The car snarled across the moor, flashing along straight stretches, braking late into the bends and shooting out of them with engine roaring, sometimes cutting across them on the wrong side in order to save a second or two.

She hated being late for anything. The table was reserved for one-fifteen. She and her sisters had planned to start Dad off with a drink or two before ordering. As it was, Pauline would be lucky not to miss the first course.

She bobbed like a cork as the Sunbeam bounced over a hump-backed bridge, then swayed from side to side, throwing the wheel from left to right and back again as it swung through a double bend.

Pauline had bought her father a book for his birthday, an illustrated history of Plymouth, learned and highly detailed, quite magnificent with all its maps and colour plates and green leather binding. Within its pages was contained the city's whole vibrant story of war and siege, piracy and exploration, from the days of the first medieval settlement right up to November of 1918. Here were the press gangs and the epidemics, here were Drake and Captain Cook, Sir Walter Raleigh, the Pilgrim Fathers and the Spanish Armada. Pauline was sure he would like it. Local history had always been his passion.

Her foot shifted quickly to the brake as the next turn loomed ahead. Her actions were automatic, allowing her thoughts to range here and there. Before her eyes was the road, the road unfolding and flying away beneath the wheels. But other images hovered there too, wavering mental pictures of her father, in his study, in the garden among his shrubs, or pondering over the chessboard.

As she mused, her speed crept up still further. She knew the road well and in ten years of driving she had never had any but trifling accidents – all of which had been in town. Little dents when parking, one or two minor collisions at busy junctions, silly things like that. Out here it was different. Out here there was almost no one on the road. Now and again she would pass a cart, slowing to a crawl for the sake of the horse, but encounters with other motor vehicles were few. There was just the occasional bus or delivery van, almost never another car. The road was hers and she tore along it, a tiny, buzzing projectile in the great emptiness of the moor.

The sun came out as she went through Princetown, pale winter sunshine filtering through thin cloud. A few short miles to Yelverton and then she would be off the moor. Perhaps she would not be very late after all. Pauline took a hand from the wheel, shaking back her sleeve to glance at her watch. She was cresting the brow of a hill, emerging from a belt of trees on to high, open ground.

Only twenty to one? Pauline wondered if her watch had stopped. She looked at it again. Yes, she decided, the watch had stopped.

Her eyes flicked back to the road – and then flared wide in fear. She had peered at the dial for an instant too long, an instant she could not afford at such speed. A gasp of shock filled her lungs with air and terror held it in. Straggling across her path were half a dozen ponies. Two had reached the other side and were galloping away across the heath. The others were starting to scatter in panic, but not quite fast enough to clear the way.

For one split second she could not think what to do. Then came a raucous, grinding squeal as she went for the brakes. The frightened horses hardly knew which way to run, any more than Pauline could decide which way to steer. She realised now it was no use to brake, for she could not stop in time and the back wheels were pulling sideways, taking her into a spin. And so she released the brake and veered to the right, narrowly missing a dappled mare. The Sunbeam careered off the road and on to the heath. The offside wheels rode up on a big granite boulder, the vehicle tilted, then flipped right over and came to a halt upside down. The canvas roof was flattened under the weight and broken glass sprayed outwards over the ground as the windscreen shattered. Finally, all was silence and stillness, except for the spinning of a front wheel.

Pauline's life had been cut off so swiftly and cleanly that she had not had time to register pain, only a sickening jolt and heave when the car turned over. Then a snap, a flutter, and nothing more, like the breaking of a film that could never be spliced again.

Twenty-five minutes later the post van came along, on its way back from the moorland round. The driver pulled up, jumped out and hurried across to the wreck.

He tugged at the door on the driver's side and found it would not budge. So he tried the passenger door instead, kneeling and pulling with all his might until at last it gave a little, inching outwards over the wiry grass. He managed to move it about a foot and then he peered inside.

Dead eyes stared blankly back at him. Reaching in, he touched his fingers to the livid mark where Pauline's temple had struck the door handle. There was something grotesque about the angle of her head and he did not need a doctor to tell him her neck was broken.

He knew Pauline Lawrenson slightly, just as he knew all the moorland people – enough to exchange a few minutes' chat whenever he made a delivery. And many a time she had passed him on the road, hurtling by with a toot of her horn. He had always thought she drove too fast.

'All dressed up,' he murmured, sadly. 'Going somewhere special, I suppose. Well, my dear, I'm afraid you've kept a different appointment today to the one you expected.'

Misery, sickness and loneliness descended on Torvallen like a pall. Although the weather was fairly mild, Jess would always remember this as the grimmest of winters. Joel was inconsolable and for many weeks after the funeral he seemed like a man half-dead himself. Grey-faced and hollow-eyed, he hardly ate or slept, nor did he try to lose himself in work. Instead he went out on the moors each day, regardless of rain or mist or easterly wind. Often he came back soaked to the skin, and would have let the clothes dry on him if Jess had not badgered him to change them. He no longer troubled to shave or to comb his hair. Untrimmed, it grew down over his brow and collar, and the muscle melted off him till his shoulder-blades were sharply visible through his shirt.

'He's lost without her,' said Jess one evening when Joel had just gone up to bed. 'And he'll never find another one like her. What can we do for him, Rob?'

Without Pauline to give her a hand of euchre or gin rummy, she was now reduced to playing patience. Tapping the Jack of Spades against her bottom lip, she was racking her brains for ways to help.

Her husband threw another log on the fire. 'Nothing I can think of,' he said. 'It's going to take time, that's all there is to it.'

'It's my opinion he ought to go back to work. I'm sure it would do him more good than wandering about by himself, remembering and brooding. Until he has something else to occupy his mind, he'll keep on going downhill.'

Robert made no reply to that. He liked having sole charge at the sawmill. He would not really care if Joel did not return to work for the rest of the year. In his brother's absence, Robert had seized the opportunity to effect a change or two in the working practices and make a couple of major purchases. He had already bought a new car, a Humber, to replace the Sunbeam. He had bought a second lorry, too, without consulting Joel. Robert had told himself it was not fair to bother him with matters like that just yet. He guessed that Joel would not be interested, and in that he was correct. Robert did not mind. For as long as it lasted, he meant to use his unchallenged authority.

'If only they'd had a child or two,' murmured Jess. 'At least he'd have something left of Pauline. It's going to be so hard for him, living with you and me and Colin, now he has no one himself.'

'I don't doubt he'll marry again, eventually. He's never had trouble attracting women.' Robert sat back in his armchair, crossing his feet on the fender. 'Pauline would want it that way.'

'I know she would. But Robert, where will he find a wife out here? I don't know of anyone suitable, and he's certainly not the type to go socialising in town. Truly, I don't know what he'll do. He's going to be very lonely.'

Robert slid a glance in her direction. She thought she saw a gleam of displeasure in it.

'Don't concern yourself too much. I trust the Lord will provide.'

Jess laid down the Jack on the Queen of Diamonds. 'I miss Pauline terribly,' she said. 'My days are so solitary now, while you're at work. I used to be content on my own before I came here and grew accustomed to having her for company.'

'You have the boy,' said Robert.

'Of course, but it's not the same. Pauline was my friend.'

Yes, and if the truth were told, Pauline had been half the life and cheer of Torvallen. She was a bitter loss, with her chat and her bawdy chuckle.

'Anyway,' added Jess, 'Colin will be starting school next year.'

Giving up the game, she swept the cards into a pile and gathered them up to begin again.

Joel fell ill near the end of March. The weather had been cold and wet, and when the first mild symptoms of fever appeared in him, Jess feared that it might be pneumonia and made him take to his bed. But within a few days the ailment had declared its true identity. A string of blisters surfaced on his skin, running in a semi-circle from his spine around his side and halfway across his stomach.

'Shingles,' said the doctor, at a glance. 'I should think it's shock that's caused it. Grief can bring it on. I'll prescribe some ointment, but it's mostly a case of letting it run its course, I'm afraid. You'd better feed him up, as well. Look at his ribs, he's far too thin.'

'He just won't eat,' said Jess, as they left the room. 'And he goes out traipsing around on the moor in all winds and weathers. He's had me so worried.'

'He won't be going anywhere while he has this,' the doctor said, as they went downstairs. 'It's a bad attack and he won't be able to stand his clothes on for a fortnight, so you have him captive, my dear.'

He was right. Smarting and burning, the blisters would not tolerate even Joel's pyjama jacket. The lightest touch could set them stinging and he therefore spent the days that followed sitting up in a chair before the bedroom fire, bare from the waist up. At night he managed fitful sleep on his unaffected side. But he could not bear the weight of the bedclothes and every so often was woken by cold when the fire died down, or by an unconscious movement that turned him over on to the blisters, jerking him awake with a gasp of pain.

Having him in custody, Jess made the most of her chance to feed him. She cut his hair as well, and coaxed him to shave off what was fast becoming a great black beard. Always up and down the stairs with trays of food, cups of tea, and logs for the fire, she seldom left him unattended for more than a couple of hours. And sometimes, while she treated his blisters with the ointment the doctor had left, they would talk a little about Pauline.

Absorbed with the household chores and nursing, Jess was not aware at first of a new unease in her husband. There was little Robert could say, since his brother was bereaved and sick and had to be tended. But it troubled him to know that Jess spent so many hours alone with Joel. He did not like to think of her dabbing calamine on his brother's back and stomach, touching him so much, seeing him half-naked. There was, he realised now, an unfortunate side to his extra responsibilities at work. The more hours he had to put in at the yard, the less able he was to keep a close eye on his wife.

Still, he tried his best to do both. Robert began to shuttle back and forth between the sawmill and the house, often several times a day. It had always been his habit to return for a midday meal, but now he was apt to appear at any moment with some excuse or other. He had come to fetch a bill, or a warmer jumper, or his pocket watch. He was peckish, or he had a stomach pain requiring a dose of medicine. There was something he wanted to tell Jess, or to ask her – usually something quite trivial, as it turned out. He had a score of explanations, but only one true reason for his constant comings and goings.

He wished to satisfy himself that nothing untoward was going on, and Jess soon realised that. She was used to his distrust, but it angered her that he could harbour such suspicions of his brother – as if Joel's grief for Pauline were a shallow thing, as if he would want another woman with his dead wife barely two months in the ground. Of course, there were men a-plenty who could and would take comfort in that way, but Joel was not one of them, as she knew very well.

One day she walked into his bedroom and found him leafing through a photograph album. He jumped slightly when she tapped and opened the door, looked around before he could stop himself, then quickly turned away with the typical reluctance of a man to be seen crying.

'I'm sorry.' She set down the bowl of soup she had brought for his lunch. 'I'll go away if you like.'

He shook his head, wiping the wetness from his eyes and face. 'You've never seen these, have you?' His voice was hoarse and he cleared his throat.

She seated herself beside him on the edge of the bed and he laid the album across her knees.

'These are your wedding pictures, are they?'

'Some of them.' He flipped back to the early pages. 'These were taken just after we met.'

He pointed out one of Pauline, standing on the deck of a ferry boat. She was laughing, her hair whipped in all directions by the wind.

'We were on our way to Mount Edgcumbe for the day,' said Joel, fondly. 'She took this one of me on the quay when we landed.'

The picture showed him in uniform, with cap and gaiters and wide leather belt.

'1918, that was,' he said, reflectively. 'There were only six months left of the war, but we couldn't know how long we had. I'd already made up my mind to propose. In fact, I asked her that evening. After all, we'd known each other the best part of a week.'

He reached for his soup and began to eat as Jess turned over the pages. The next one showed him with Pauline on the Barbican, sharing a jar of cockles. In yet another they were arm-in-arm outside Torvallen. There was one of Pauline and her father, standing at their garden gate in Tavistock, and then the wedding photographs began. Joel in khaki, grinning at the camera from under the peak of his army cap, Pauline smiling up at him. Bride and groom posing with, and then without, their friends and relations, kissing, cutting the cake, and finally leaving to spend the remaining two days of Joel's leave in a little hotel near Westward Ho! Happy from the start, despite the war, happy to the end. Nothing had ever gone wrong between them.

'Nine good years,' murmured Jess.

'Yes, they were.' He swallowed a spoonful of soup. 'And it would have carried on that way. We were well-matched, we were lucky.'

Suddenly a catch came into his voice. He put down the bowl and a sob came up from his chest.

'I never really thought she'd come to grief, never believed that anything could happen to her. Fortune had been so kind to us before. The way we met each other, the way I came out of the war in one piece, the way we got on together afterwards. Everything always went so well for us.

If we'd had children it would have been perfect. I suppose I thought our lives were charmed.' He was shaking now and his eyes were brimming. 'She always loved to speed and she never would take warning, but somehow I always felt she'd – get away with it – because we were such lucky people.'

Jess took his hands in her own and squeezed them gently. There was nothing she could say to console him, but her silent sympathy was welcome. A quiet, soothing presence, she was always there when he wanted to talk, but never tried to force it if he did not.

Indeed, had it not been for Jess, he would have received no comfort at all. Once, when Robert asked why she had been so long upstairs, she rounded on him, saying:

'How much time have you spent listening to him, Rob? He's seen damned little of you since he fell ill. You don't bother with him, do you?'

'I've been doubly busy, you know that.'

'You could spare an hour a day to look in and see how he is, but you rarely do. I'm sure he'd appreciate it.'

'There's nothing I can say to make him feel better. And perhaps he doesn't really want you around him so much. Perhaps you're making a nuisance of yourself.'

'The only one I'm annoying, Rob, is you.'

· Twenty-three ·

For everyone's sake, she was glad when Joel at last went back to work. There were plenty of orders to fill that spring, and the season passed quickly, gobbled up by labour that left the brothers spent at the end of each day. Sheer fatigue sent Joel swiftly to sleep at night, leaving him no time to lament the empty space beside him in the bed. Dull acceptance came to replace the anger and the agony, and he lived from day to day without giving thought to the future. No desire for remarriage had entered his head, no thought of women at all. It was far too early for that. His life had been blasted and for now he just dwelt in the wreckage, without any plans to rebuild.

What little spare time he had he filled with pastimes that needed concentration – detective stories, crossword puzzles – things to engage his mind. And something for his skilful hands as well – all through April he passed many hours in the toolshed by the stable, with a bar across the door and a piece of sacking pinned over the window. Sounds of sawing and hammering sometimes drifted out, followed by lengthy silences. Some mysterious project was under way, but Joel would not be drawn on what it was and a padlock secured the toolshed door when he left it. Robert was disdainful of his brother's secrecy, and rather unkindly suggested that Joel might be turning a little bit odd.

But then one Sunday morning the mystery ended when Joel presented his nephew with a most magnificent Noah's Ark, fully four feet long and crowded with carven beasts and birds. There were elephants, horses, giraffes and leopards, llamas, vultures, cattle and bears, monkeys, doves, wolves and tigers, all of them beautifully formed and detailed, their stripes and spots and distinctive colourings carefully painted on. The deck of the ark could be lifted off, revealing the animal pens and stalls and perches inside. A venerable Noah with long white beard and flowing robes presided over all.

'Colin, look!' gasped Jess, as her brother-in-law set it down on the sitting-room floor. She knelt beside the child to admire it. 'Isn't that splendid! Aren't you lucky?' Beaming up at Joel, she said, 'It's wonderful. What work you've put into it, Joel!'

The boy was nearly beside himself with excitement, trotting round and round the ark, pulling out the animals, then marching them back through the door in the side.

'What do you say?' prompted Jess.

The child looked up at his uncle and stretched up his arms. Smiling, Joel squatted down, receiving a hug in thanks.

'That'll keep you quiet for a bit, won't it?' He tickled the boy until he shrieked. 'Give your poor mother a bit of peace, eh?'

A shadow fell across them and both of the adults looked up. Robert stared at the Noah's Ark, and then at his son, who was on all fours, lining up the creatures two by two. For a moment he was lost for words. The craftsman in him paid tribute to a fine piece of work. But the husband, father, competitive brother was stung to see Jess and Colin so impressed.

Jess knew what was going through his mind. She stood up quickly, linking her arm with his. 'Now we know what Joel's been doing in the toolshed all this time.'

Robert managed to smile. 'It's ... Well, it's a grand job, Joel. I didn't know you could do such things.'

'Nor did I. It's turned out better than I hoped.'

'You've, uh, got everything nicely to scale. It's very well finished, too.'

'Can't leave splinters and nail points and rough edges. A child's sure to find them.'

'Yes. Oh yes, you've done him proud, I must say. Used a few offcuts from the yard, I suppose?'

'That's right. All I had to buy were the paints.'

Robert had never thought of making something for his son. He had spent a small fortune on toys from the shops, but never had it crossed his mind to fashion anything himself. Watching him, he fancied that Colin had never been so excited about the expensive playthings brought from town. In a way, Robert supposed, they were inferior gifts in spite of their price, for they had not cost him the effort Joel had given.

Trust Joel to think of doing this. He would.

'You're clever with your hands, Rob. Why don't you have a go? Make him a fort and soldiers or something like that?'

Robert smiled weakly at his wife. He knew what she was trying to do. He knew she sensed his feelings. But in his mind lay a little fear that he might not be able to produce anything as good as the ark. What if he made the attempt and the end result compared badly?

Carelessly, he said, 'I daresay I could. I'll give it some thought. Depends, though, whether I have time.'

Jess knew it meant he would not try.

Glancing at his brother, Robert said, 'It's not his birthday, you know, for another five months. Mustn't spoil him, Joel.'

'I needed something to occupy me, that was all.'

'I know. Still, if you're thinking of starting on anything else ...'

The smile faded from Joel's face. He stood up. 'Yes?'

'Well, there are plenty of children less fortunate than Colin.'

A pause. Then, 'So there are,' agreed Joel, quietly. In Robert's eyes he read a clear message.

Remember he's my son, not yours. I'll provide his toys.

'I take your point, Rob. It's a – charitable – idea.'

Robert smiled.

Jess looked down at Colin and the ark. She could have slapped her husband.

It was just a few days afterwards that Robert came home for lunch and said to his son, 'Like to go down to the yard with me this afternoon, so everyone can see how big you've grown?'

Colin nodded, eagerly. He liked to watch the men at work, to see great tree trunks sliced into planks and slabs and blocks by the circular saw, splitting apart to reveal the clean, pale wood inside with its pattern of rings and whorls. He loved to see the sawdust fly, spurting in a plume from the edge of the blade. He even enjoyed the screeching noise, bathing in it and laughing up at his father.

'All right, then,' said Robert, 'just for an hour.'

They went by way of the footpath along the river bank.

The woods were a tender new green and the day was very mellow. They were halfway there when Robert abruptly stopped, catching Colin by the shoulder. Puzzled, the boy looked up him. Robert pressed a finger to his lips and pointed across to the opposite bank. Colin looked and saw a bouncing, loping movement in the grass. Then a whiskery face poked through it, followed by a sleek brown body.

'That's an otter,' Robert whispered. 'Quiet now, or else you'll scare him away. And look, another one! They're a pair, see, that's his mate.'

The second otter emerged from the water, scrambling up the bank with something trailing from its mouth.

'She's caught an eel,' said Robert, squatting down.

The boy watched, delighted, as they romped about and tossed the eel around.

'We're lucky to see them,' Robert said. 'Like to stay a while?'

'Oh, yes.'

They sat for fifteen minutes while the otters held a tug-of-war with the eel and then devoured it. Robert made some little boats from twigs and leaves and the river swiftly carried them away.

'Like animals, don't you, boy?' he asked, ruffling Colin's hair. 'What about the ones your Uncle Joel made? What do you think of those, eh? Good, aren't they? Which do you like the best?'

The child considered carefully. 'The tigers,' he said at last. 'And the monkeys.'

'Nice of Uncle Joel, wasn't it?'

'Mammy said it took him hours and hours.'

'Yes, I'm sure it did.' Tentatively, Robert went on, 'I, um, don't have much time for things like that. Otherwise ...'

He faltered, because the child's eyes had turned on him with a strange intentness, as if Colin sensed his anxiety. Very large and brown, they were Jess's eyes, and yet they had a look in them which hers had never held. A benevolent look unusual in a child. Had he ever troubled to study his mother-in-law, Robert would have realised that it came from Alice.

'I don't mind,' said Colin.

'Not at all?'

The boy shook his head. 'I like everything you've bought me,' he said. Then his gaze returned to the otters.

It was unnerving, almost as if he understood. For a moment, Robert stared at him. Was he so transparent, even to a child?

'Look!' the boy exclaimed, as a streak of blue and orange, followed by a splash, marked the dive of a kingfisher. A second later it broke the surface, rising up in a sparkling shower with a tiny fish in its beak.

'Did you see him, Dad?'

'Yes,' said Robert, absently. 'Yes, I saw him.' Glancing at his watch, he added, 'Come on, we'd better go now.'

Some of the men were still taking their midday break, eating outside in the spring sunshine, when Robert and his son arrived at the timber yard. And it happened that a customer called in about that time, a builder seeking a price for roof trusses. The order, if terms were agreed, would be a large one. Robert always liked to be involved in any bargaining, so he left Colin in the care of Charlie Weekes while he and Joel went inside to haggle with the builder.

'Want some bread and cheese, boy?' offered Charlie. 'Or a split and some blackberry jam?'

Perched beside him on a log, Colin accepted the split and jam. He was very much enjoying it, until a throaty voice from behind him remarked:

'Hope they weren't October blackberries, lad, because they belong to the devil.'

Alec Maunder sat down beside him.

'He spits on them, see, every October eleventh, and they're bad luck after that.'

'My old dear picked this lot well before Michaelmas last year,' Charlie told him. Nudging the boy, he winked to reassure him. 'The jam's all right, son, you just carry on.'

'Long as you're certain,' Maunder said. He leaned down, whispering to Colin, 'Never pays to trifle with Old Nick, eh, boy? 'Specially round these parts, where he lives.'

Colin slowly put down the split, his hunger forgotten. He usually knew when he was being teased, but this time he was not so sure.

'You do know who I'm talking about, don't you? Old Dewer himself.'

The child had never heard these names before. The Lawrensons did not care for religion or folklore.

'Why, Charlie, I do believe they've never warned the boy.' Maunder sounded shocked. 'Someone ought to tell him, don't you think?' He glanced behind him, over both shoulders, as if afraid some dreadful thing would hear. Then he confided: 'Lot of folk have seen him hereabouts, mostly on stormy nights or when it's dark of the moon. He goes around stealing children from the cottages and hunting down sinners who stay out late. Oh, and he's terrible to see! Out he rides with the Wild Hunt, a black figure on a black horse, with a pack of red-eyed hounds. Horns, he's got, and hooves like a goat, talons on his fingers, curved and sharp and shiny.' Maunder's green eyes threatened to pop right out. 'Blood, that's what he likes, hot and fresh and red as the pit where he comes from. If you hear howling at night, well, that's his dogs, running down some poor traveller who's strayed from the road. Happens all the time, don't it, Charlie?'

Charlie looked uncomfortable, for he did not disbelieve the tales.

'Fire streams from his horse's hooves at the gallop, and the sound of it is like the booming of a great bass drum. Don't you ever go out on the moors at night, boy, and mind you keep your bedroom window shut so he can't reach in. He'd love to catch one like you.'

Maunder wagged a finger at Colin, who by now was blinking with fright.

'Alec, you're scaring him. That's enough now,' Charlie said. 'Don't go telling him no more.'

Maunder surveyed him maliciously, knowing Charlie Weekes to be superstitious and nearly as easily frightened as a child. Charlie believed in pixies, and witches and curses and birds of ill-omen.

'I'm only putting him wise, that's all. There now, boy, you mark what I say. He's out there, all right, up on the high moors, up round the tors where the ravens fly. Only, now and again, he comes down prowling through the valleys and the villages, or even drops into Princetown or somewhere for a drink. Why, just last month he was out at the Warren House Inn one evening, having a pint of homebrew. Wearing a hood, he was, a black hood hiding half his face. But oh, his voice! A hiss like a red-hot wheel rim going in a water trough! That's what the landlord said.'

Colin's mouth was dry and his heart was thudding, for what he understood of Maunder's talk had terrified him. Fire and darkness, snapping dogs, and a hideous, wicked man in black – these were the pictures Maunder conjured up for a four-year-old.

'Know what?' continued Maunder. 'When he took a sip of his ale, the rest of it boiled in the tankard. And when he set it down for a minute, it burnt the varnish off the bar! That's gospel truth, that is. There's a ring-mark there to prove it. Oh, it was him, all right. I wouldn't ...'

'What the hell are you telling that boy? Damn you, Maunder, shut your mouth!'

Joel's quiet approach had caught him unawares. Maunder eyed him shiftily.

'Only trying to amuse him, Mr Lawrenson. Children enjoy a story, don't they?'

'Not that sort,' snapped Joel. 'Not the kind that keeps them from sleeping at night.'

'Well, I'm sorry ...'

'Filling his head with daft ideas, telling him things to give him nightmares. You bloody misfit, you.'

Maunder fell silent and glanced across the yard to the sawmill door, where Robert stood concluding his deal with the builder. He had plainly seen that something was up, for he kept looking over, frowning slightly at the sound of raised voices.

'Come on, Colin.' Joel picked up his nephew and carried him off.

Robert exchanged a few parting words with the customer, shook his hand, then came across the yard, stopping Joel on the way.

'What's the matter?'

'Oh, Maunder's been spinning him yarns about Old Nick. Fine way to entertain a child.'

Robert grunted. 'Ah, he's just a fool.'

Colin was clinging to Joel like a limpet to a rock, his face buried in his uncle's shirt.

'He's upset,' said Joel. 'He wants his mam. I haven't eaten yet, I'm going up to the house. I'll take him with me, shall I?'

'You don't really want to go home, do you, boy?' Robert asked.

Colin did not look round, but nodded against Joel's chest.

'Come on, you're braver than that. You're not worried by some silly old story, are you?'

'I want Mam,' confirmed Colin.

'Oh, all right, then.'

The boy half-turned his head, regarding his father with one great dark eye. His dad sounded impatient, even slightly irritable now.

Robert sighed. 'Go on,' he said, more gently.

As soon as Joel had gone, Maunder came sauntering over.

'Didn't mean no harm, you know. Wouldn't distress the lad for the world. Bit of local fable, that was all it was.'

Robert eyed him coldly. 'Not exactly fitting for a small child.'

'All right,' allowed Maunder, 'perhaps that's so. I just didn't think. Don't have much to do with youngsters, see, so I might have done wrong, I admit. I apologise, Mr Lawrenson. I can't do more than that. Won't hold it against me, will you? I daresay the boy'll forget it soon enough.'

'I damn well hope so.'

Maunder had a sudden inspiration. He saw an opportunity for mischief and could not resist the temptation to use it. A 'bloody misfit' was he? He recalled the contempt on Joel's face and it rankled.

'I don't believe you need worry, sir. Nothing soft about that boy of yours. Handsome little chap. Intelligent, too, and big for his age. He'll grow to be taller than you, unless I miss my guess. Very dark, I notice. Take after a grandparent, does he?'

'My father, I should think.'

'Ah.' Maunder nodded, smiling a little. 'Well, as I say, he don't strike me as the nervous kind. Your brother said I'd give him nightmares. Load of nonsense, that is. Went for me something ferocious, he did. Wasn't no call for that, Mr Lawrenson. The way he tore into me, anybody'd think the boy was his!'

Something flickered in Robert's eyes. Maunder's smile grew broader. How easy it was to plant a tiny seed.

'Any excuse, I suppose, seeing he don't like me. I'll go and have my dinner now, if that's all right with you. Glad we cleared this up. Wouldn't want to cause any ill-feeling.'

For a few seconds Robert seemed ruffled, but then he collected himself and said, 'You've ten minutes, no more.' And with that he turned and headed towards the sawmill.

Maunder grimaced at his back, thinking his bolt had missed its mark after all. It had not, but the armour of common sense was strong enough, as yet, to turn it aside. Briefly, Robert thought about the Noah's Ark. All that care and effort for a nephew. Would he have gone to so much trouble for his brother's child? He was certain he would not. But then, it was only natural, surely, for Joel to be extra fond of Colin, because he had no children of his own? Robert pushed away the poisonous thought called forth by

Maunder's remark. It was just too ugly, too absurd, and he would not give it credence.

Colin's forehead grew clammy as he slept in his bed that night. From time to time he twitched and whimpered, rolling from side to side. All was peaceful in his room, but baying and hoofbeats filled his dreams.

From out of the east, in headlong flight from the coming of day, the hunt was bearing down on him in a moorland landscape vast and empty, lit by a crimson glare on the skyline unlike any dawn he had ever seen. He was anchored in the heather, for it seemed to be tangled and twined around his feet and ankles. Behind him was a precipice, but not so much as a rock or stunted tree on either side. There was nothing to hide him, he could not run, and the dogs were coming very fast, with the terrible huntsman racing before them.

The clock on the mantel was ticking softly, slowly, but the breathing of the child was becoming frantic. His muscles grew taut, as if he were struggling to move but something restrained him.

The nightmare coils of heather suddenly shrivelled and fell away. The gold of sunlight flashed up in the east and he fled, but the rider and hungry pack were at his very heels. They would catch him or run him off the cliff, and the devil's horse was breathing down his neck as the edge drew near.

The boy gave out a piteous wail, and in the room next door his mother stirred.

Now he was on the brink, and over it, shrieking like a banshee as he fell. Above him he saw the hunt launch itself outwards over the edge and vanish into the dark of the western sky, while he continued falling, down and down and down.

Screaming tore through Robert's sleep and he shook himself awake, unable for a second or two to identify the sound. It was shrill and strained, almost a whistle, pitched as high as Colin's voice would go. By the time Robert realised what it was, Jess was already out of bed, rummaging round for the matches, then rushing for the door. Robert hurried after her, cursing as he stubbed his toe on something in the dark.

Colin was sitting up in bed when his mother burst into the room, sitting there bolt upright, shrieking, still in the grip of his terror, not even properly aware that he was now awake. Striking a match, she lit his lamp and the glow revealed a wild-eyed, tear-drenched face. He was gasping with fright, staring this way and that, and gabbling about the Man and the Big Black Dogs. Pulling him into the folds of her dressing gown, she wrapped it around them both as Robert appeared in the doorway.

'What is it? What's wrong with him?' He came inside and shut the door.

'He's had a nightmare, Robert. Dear Lord, his nightshirt's soaked in sweat!' She stroked and whispered to her son, 'It's all right, Colin, Mam's here now and so is Dad. There's nothing for you to fear.'

Robert sat down beside her. 'What's the matter, boy?' He felt Colin's forehead and found it cold and damp. 'What did you eat for supper, eh, to make you have bad dreams?'

There was no reply. Sobbing, the child huddled closer to Jess, hiding his face and trembling.

'It wasn't anything he ate,' she said testily. 'I know what sparked this off. That cursed Maunder.'

'Oh,' said Robert, awkwardly.

'Yes. Joel told me all about it. Spinning yarns about the Yeth Hounds and such stuff!'

'That might not be the reason ...'

'Of course it is! Colin's never been any trouble at night before.' A wrathful colour spread across her cheeks and her eyes acquired an angry glitter. Robert knew what was coming next.

'I told you to fire him, didn't I?' she hissed. 'Damn him, now look what he's done! You should have dismissed him today.'

'He had his knuckles rapped. There wasn't any call to sack the man.'

'It would have been sufficient reason for me.'

'Look, the boy's upset enough. This is no time to argue. Why don't you go and make him some cocoa, nice and milky and sweet, the way he likes it. And bring him up a piece of cake. We'll take him into bed with us for the rest of the night.'

For a moment Jess was silent, simmering. Then she kissed the top of Colin's head and passed him to his father.

Pausing at the door, she repeated tersely, 'You should have sent Maunder packing long ago. It's cowardly not to, Robert.'

His head jerked up. Cowardly – that hurt, and Jess saw him wince.

She went downstairs to make the cocoa and Robert sat rocking the boy on his lap. Jess was right and he knew it. And yet he knew as well the story Maunder could spread, not only among the men at the sawmill, but in the pubs of Princetown, too, and he could not stand the thought of it. He, who was so much admired and envied for his wife. Robert dreaded ridicule as much as he craved respect. Nothing had ever brought him more pride and more congratulations than his lovely wife and his son.

His boy, his very own.

Maunder's laughing remark came back to tweak him again.

'... anybody'd think the boy was his!'

Of course, it was ridiculous, and just an unfortunate choice of phrase, signifying nothing at all. Robert glanced down at his child, who was quiet now, pacified by his father's presence. The lamplight cast a sheen on Colin's hair, and Robert took a strand of it between his fingers, letting it gently fall away again. Very dark. Yes, the boy was very dark, just like his grandfather.

The parting, though, the way it grew – Robert noticed that was not the same. His father's hair, just like his own, had always parted in the centre, no matter how much he tried to comb it other ways. Colin's was different, spreading out from a whorl far back on the crown, shaping itself to his head like a well-fitting cap. In that respect it was much like Joel's.

As he waited for Jess to bring the cocoa, Robert looked down long and thoughtfully on Colin's head, reflecting on family traits and the strange ways they sometimes came out.

· Twenty-four ·

There were many more nightmares to follow.

Colin was a child with a strong imagination. Once fed on Maunder's grisly fare, it became a torment to the boy and a bane to both his parents. Bad dreams were soon a regular trial, occurring as often as three or four times a week. Colin came to dread bedtime and was usually exhausted in the morning for lack of sleep, so that he had to take naps in the day instead. Worst of all, he began to wet the bed. So on top of fear there was shame as well, and as the summer wore on he grew to be a very unhappy little boy.

Patience had never been one of Robert's major virtues. The change in his son dismayed and perplexed and defeated him, and after about a couple of months he found himself growing annoyed with Colin. When he told him, over and over again, that there was no wicked huntsman out on the moor, he expected the boy to believe him. Frustration set in when he could not convince him. Colin, after all, would take his word on anything else. To all the normal childlike questions about the world around him, he had always accepted Robert's answers as gospel truth. If his dad said such and such a thing, then it surely had to be right. Only on the subject of his nightmares did he ever doubt his father, refusing to be reassured no matter what Dad might say.

Robert had explained to him that Mr Maunder was a liar, that even adults made up silly stories, that Dad, who was twenty-six years old and had lived on the moor all his life, had never seen or heard any terrible rider and hounds, and if he did he would certainly go out and shoot them. He had pointed out that there could not possibly be any dogs or demons lurking in the house. Every night before bed, they conducted a search, did they not, inspecting Torvallen from top to bottom, locking all the windows and the doors?

None of it made any difference. Colin still wet the bed at night and the bad dreams carried on. Jess was constantly washing his sheets and nightclothes and Robert reflected that Colin had not been half as much trouble when he was a baby, not even when cutting his teeth.

Jess had taken him to see the doctor twice, but it had not helped. Robert could not think what more to do and he harboured a growing fear that the son he prized so much might at best be turning into a sissy, or at worst be in some way unbalanced. Neither he nor Joel had ever suffered such nocturnal frights. He did not know of any other child who did. He had asked among his employees and learned that their offspring slept soundly, no trouble at all.

Robert tried to be understanding, but every time the screaming began, exasperation flared in him. If the truth were told, he was starting to feel just a little ashamed of Colin. He wanted his son to be a bold, rumbustious lad, not a ...

More than once, the phrase 'snivelling Mama's boy' had crossed his mind. He knew it was harsh and cruel and he pushed it away. Yet it stubbornly returned each time his wife turned out of bed at night and flew to Colin's room.

Eventually, it occurred to him that Jess might be too indulgent. One night in July they almost came to blows when he told her so.

It was two in the morning and Colin was wide awake. On top of his wardrobe crouched a big black dog. He could see the shape of its head and ears, darker than the darkness in his room, and he knew it was ready to spring. He dared not move or even breathe too loudly, and he prayed it could not hear his thudding heart. What was worse, he sensed there was a second one under his bed, waiting to bite off any incautious foot he might set to the floor. An hour had passed since he first awoke from a doze and became aware of the dogs, and in that time he had barely twitched a muscle. Even to cover his head with the sheet would be too much of a risk, so he lay there aching with fright and listening intently.

He fancied he could hear them breathe.

The looming shape on the wardrobe had two cold, glinting eyes, but he knew that the other beneath the bed had caverns that burned and glowed between slitted lids. There they would be, mere inches from his face, if he leaned down over the mattress to look.

Colin, of course, was not about to do that. Any little movement would bring the horrors down on him. He would have to lie motionless till daybreak, come thirst or cramp or the need to pass water. The dogs would creep away as the sun came up, they always did.

He would try not to wet the bed tonight and make his dad angry again. Robert said it was a dirty thing to do and made a lot of work for poor Mam. Colin had told him about the dogs, but his dad didn't seem to believe him. Afterwards he had heard his parents arguing about it, which made him feel worse than ever. Tonight he was determined not to make a mess – yet his very fear was filling his bladder and already the pressure was giving him great discomfort. The summer nights were short, but dawn seemed very far away.

Ten minutes dragged by, then half an hour, and his nerves were drawn out like elastic, further and thinner and tighter, until they could take no more strain. And then came a shock to snap them entirely.

Out in the woods he heard a scream – hideous, agonised, as if some creature were being torn apart. Close by, almost beneath his window, something screeched like a soul in torment.

The boy jumped, gasped, and echoed the sound with a wail of his own. It was out before he could stop it and he knew the dogs would come for him now, so he gave himself up to his terror and screamed with all his might.

Next door, Robert groaned and flopped over on to his back.

'Oh God, not again.'

Tired out after a hard day's toil, he opened groggy eyes and worked the dryness from his mouth. Oh, he was so sick of this performance, so fed up with it all, so resentful of having his rest disturbed.

Beside her husband, Jess was moving, lighting the lamp, getting up as usual in response to Colin's cries. She never hesitated, never seemed to mind. As soon as she heard the boy she would run to the rescue, and sit with him half the night if needful.

Yes, that's part of the trouble, Robert thought. His mother's too quick, too willing to go when he calls. He gets hot milk and biscuits and cuddles, a lot of fuss and attention.

His hand shot out and seized Jess by the wrist.

'Don't,' he said tersely.

'What?'

'Don't go to him, Jess. I think it's making him worse.'

'Robert, listen to him!'

'I know, it's awful and it makes me cringe to hear it, but pandering hasn't done him any good.'

'Are you saying I should leave him to it? Let him scream all night?'

'He'll wear himself out and fall asleep. It might be the very way to break him of this.'

'Break him of it!' exclaimed Jess, furiously. 'He isn't a mule!'

She twisted her arm from his grasp, started for the door and pulled it open.

Robert bounded out of bed and shoved it shut again.

'You'll make a mother's boy out of him,' he whispered, angrily. 'I want my son to grow up with plenty of backbone.

He's the only one I have and I don't want it said that I produced a milksop.'

Jess was outraged. 'Oh my, yes! That's more important than his feelings, isn't it? You must be able to hold up your head and strut!'

The screaming was desperate now, distracted. Across the passage, Joel was getting up, searching for pyjama trousers, for he always slept naked in hot weather.

'I'm not being callous,' snapped Robert. 'I'm being cruel to be kind, that's all.'

'One of those handy phrases that excuse all sorts of things.' She tried again to open the door, but he held it shut. 'Let me go to him, Robert,' she growled. 'I shan't forgive you if you don't.'

'I'm his father and your husband and you will do as I say.'

'I will do as I see fit!' yelled Jess. 'In a way this is all your fault. If it weren't for that rodent Maunder, whom you hired and still won't fire ...'

'Don't start that again!'

Her lips drew back over her teeth in something close to a snarl. 'Get out of my way.' Each word, precise and separate, sounded like a curse. In a second she would hit him. Her hand was rising as if of its own accord, and her riotous hair stood out around her face like the ruff of an angry cat.

Robert was fighting the very same impulse. He had never slapped her before, but he was ready to do it now.

Then suddenly a door slammed. They heard Joel crossing the landing, heard him go into Colin's room. In a short time the wailing ceased. Robert caught his brother's voice, soothing, comforting the boy. Jess, who was instantly calmer, was looking at him now, expectantly. He stepped back, allowed her to open the door. She went through, then paused and asked him stiffly:

'Well, are you coming?'

He turned away, exasperated. She shook her head and hurried to the boy's room.

'Only a fox,' Joel was saying. 'That was what you heard, a vixen. Make a fearsome racket, don't they? Still, it's nothing to be afraid of. She's calling to other foxes, see. They hear her a long way off.'

The child was sitting on his lap, head against his shoulder. He looked up when his mother entered, but made no bid to go to her.

'Now, about these dogs,' said Joel. 'Where were they?' His voice was soft, amused, consoling.

Timidly, the boy pointed up at the wardrobe. On the top was a crumpled knapsack with two shiny metal press studs on the front to fasten the flap. In the gloom, to a child, it could well resemble the head of a dog. Jess reached up and pulled it down.

'Damn,' she said. 'I tossed it up there yesterday after cleaning out some cupboards.'

'So there, it was only a canvas dog,' said Joel, rocking the boy. 'And what about the other one, eh?'

'Under the bed,' mumbled Colin. 'Like always.'

Jess sat down, gently rubbing her son's back.

'Yes, there's always one beneath the bed,' she told her brother-in-law, sighing. 'The other's usually over there in the corner under the table.' She made a helpless gesture. 'What can I do, Joel? I'd like to have him sleep in our room until he grows out of all this, but Robert won't allow it. And I'm afraid to leave a light in here, in case Colin knocks it over and starts a fire.'

Robert appeared in the doorway and Colin's eyes lifted to rest on his father. There was reproach in them and after a moment he looked away, huddling closer to Joel. Why had his dad not come before? Why had it been Uncle Joel?

Taking in the scene before him, Robert suddenly felt excluded, and he wished he had not tried to make a stand. The last thing he wanted was for the boy to turn to his brother. They looked disturbingly natural together, Joel and Colin, and Jess.

'I, um, think we'd better have him in with us, Jess, after all,' he muttered. 'Just for tonight.'

'Hmm,' she said, coolly.
'I only want to do the best thing for him.'
'Yes,' she relented, 'I know.'
Robert took his son from Joel and started back to his room. Nervously, the boy informed him:
'Dad, I didn't wee, but I'm going to.'

It was not long afterwards that Colin committed a cardinal sin. He let his father down in front of an acquaintance.

One morning they went to Widecombe to have the old stallion shod. The sky was a deep, hot blue and along the lanes the hedges were brilliant with foxgloves and ragged robin. The horse clopped on at an idle pace and the boy rode in front of his father, secured by Robert's arm around his waist. Lawrenson had little else to do that day. The weather was balmy and he did not try to hurry the elderly Hector. Robert's shirt was open, his sleeves rolled up and his cap pulled down low to shade his eyes. Every so often the boy looked round and up at him and smiled, pointing out something he'd seen in the hedge or a field beyond. He wanted to impress Robert by observing things and naming them, telling what he knew of different birds and plants and animals. Gratified, Robert laughed and nodded and Colin was happy because his dad approved. He felt that it helped make up a little for the broken nights and the bed-wetting. Colin knew that Dad took a dim view of it all. He was not as tolerant as Uncle Joel. It was not so much what Robert said, but the way he sometimes looked at Colin that told the boy how he felt. Baffled. Disappointed. Colin was very sorry to displease him. At the same time, though, he wished his dad were more sympathetic, more like Uncle Joel.

They reached the blacksmith's forge at just after twelve. The village was very quiet. Most people were either working out on the land or sitting down to their midday meal. The few little shops had closed for an hour. The child looked around him with interest as they passed through. He had never been here before.

Nor had he ever been to a blacksmith's shop.

When Robert brought the horse to a halt, the boy saw before him a very large wooden door with brown paint flaking off it. Fully open it would let a hay-cart pass inside, but for now it was standing ajar and beyond it there appeared to be a vault of fire-shot darkness.

Colin stared at it. He felt his innards tighten. From within the forge there came a rhythmic clanging. He glimpsed a shower of sparks and heard a sizzling sound.

Robert jumped down from the horse, leaving his son in the saddle. He had not noticed the look on Colin's face or the way the boy gripped at the pommel. Lawrenson slipped inside to find the smith and the old horse stood placidly waiting. Seconds later, Robert returned. He lifted down his son and held him by the hand. And then the door swung back.

Colin's mouth went dry. His heart and stomach turned a cartwheel.

Before him lay a cavern of gloom, lit only by a small, grimy window – and a great big bed of glowing coals. Like a living thing, it changed all the time from dull red to orange to yellow-white and back again in concert with the hollow gasp and sigh of the bellows. There was smoke in the air, and around the walls hung chains and files and hammers and pincers. Everything looked burnt and a smell of singed hair came wafting out.

'Come on, Mr Budley's waiting.' Robert took the horse's reins and started to lead him in. The animal went willingly, but the child did not. Colin pulled back, trying to work his hand free of his father's grasp.

'What's the matter?' Robert turned and frowned at him.

Colin shook his head, eyes pleading.

'Don't be silly, we're only going to get new shoes for Hector. Look, he doesn't mind.'

Still the boy hung back, tugging fiercely to escape Robert's grip. He was not going in there, not at any price. He was going to stay out here in the sun, sit on the grass there, under that tree, and wait until it was over.

'Will you stop this and do as you're told!'

Robert's tone grew sharp and a glint came into his eyes. He would not have Colin play him up in front of other people.

'Do you want Mr Budley to think you're a baby?'

Colin did not give a toss what some strange man might think. It was Dad who cared about that.

'Won't!' he exclaimed, really struggling now. 'No, I won't, I won't!'

The commotion brought Mr Budley out, and the sight of him was the final straw. A big, balding man in a leather apron, he had heavy black eyebrows and a large, fleshy nose. Shirtless, he displayed a muscular chest and arms, and a snake was tattooed on his shoulder. He carried long-handled tongs and on his feet were hob-nailed boots.

Mr Budley liked children. He had three of his own. He smiled at Colin.

Colin screamed.

Mr Budley looked puzzled.

'For God's sake, what's the matter with you?' snapped Robert.

The child was writhing to escape. Tears spilt down his face and his nose was running.

'Colin, behave or I'll give you a hiding!'

Robert bent over and smacked Colin's legs.

'Aw, now don't do that.' Mr Budley came forward a pace or two. 'Is it the fire, son, is that what you're afraid of?'

Colin did not take in what he said, only the fact that this huge, alarming man was bearing down on him. There was a scorched smell about Mr Budley, and hair grew out of his nostrils. He was stretching out a great thick paw and smiling his most reassuring smile. Colin felt he would faint if Budley touched him. He cringed away and the smith had the sense to stand back. Still the boy whimpered and squealed, fighting his father, wanting to run.

Robert's face was crimson with fury and embarrassment. Cuffing Colin across the head, he hissed, 'There's nothing in there to hurt you. Anyway, I'm here, aren't I?'

'I don't care!'

'I've had just about enough of you and your hysterics. Calm down and say you're sorry to Mr Budley.'

'No need, no need. Look, why don't you wait out here with him, Robert, while I get the old horse shod? Don't force the child if it's going to upset him. A forge must look a frightening place to a little lad. I know others in the village who won't come in, though I must say I've never seen one panic like this.'

'I'm not giving in to him. His mother does, but I won't.'

Mr Budley had an idea. Fishing in a back pocket, he drew out a shiny new penny and held it out to Colin.

'Tell you what, boy, why don't you and your dad come and work the bellows while I make Hector's shoes? See, I'll pay you to do it. My lad'll be going off for his lunch in a minute. How would you like to help me while he's gone?'

Colin would not like it one bit. The smith was coming close again, too, trying to tempt him with the coin, so the boy took desperate action. He kicked Mr Budley, and then he kicked his father.

The long leather apron protected the smith, but Robert was not so lucky. Colin's shoe caught him hard on the shin. He let out a yell and a curse, and just for a second he loosened his grip on his son. It was all the boy needed. Jerking his hand free, he went scooting off up the road.

Mr Budley shook his head as Robert set off in pursuit. 'Don't be too hard on him, now,' he called. Taking Hector's reins, he led him into the forge.

Round the corner and up the lane, Robert caught up with his son in the churchyard, where Colin tried to hide behind a gravestone. His father soon spotted and dragged him out. There among the long grass and the dandelions, he knelt and shook him madly, panting and scolding all the while.

'You little misfit, you! Whining and cowering, humiliating me, being rude to a nice, kind man! And then kicking him! You're going home in disgrace, my lad. Creating such a fuss, making a fool of yourself and me! Making me ashamed of you! I'll never take you anywhere again. I have enough of your nonsense at night. Is it going to start in broad daylight now, as well? Eh? Is it? I've told you and told you there's nothing to fear. Don't you trust me? Don't you think I'm telling you the truth? What an exhibition that was back there! Blubbering like a little coward! My son! I want to be proud of you, Colin, but by God you're making it hard these days!'

The shaking ceased, but he still held the boy by his shoulders. Colin was gasping, his eyes wet and glassy. He tried to say something, but his voice dissolved into sobs at the first attempt. Robert, even though he was squatting down, seemed to loom above him, not his dad for the moment, just an angry presence offering not a jot of comfort, only condemnation. Behind him, the grey church tower soared high in the blue summer sky, making the boy feel even more tiny and helpless. He badly wanted his mother.

'You're nasty,' he sobbed. 'You hurt me!'

Robert's face was a mask of glaring eyes and clenched teeth, but as the fury ebbed a dazed expression came over it.

'What?'

He let go of Colin's shoulders. For some seconds his hands hovered either side of the boy, as if the lightest touch would break him in pieces. Then, gingerly, he drew him forward, hugging him and stroking his back.

'No, I didn't hurt you, did I? Where? I didn't mean to, son, I'm sorry.'

The child had grown still and was whimpering. 'Squashed my hand,' came the muffled reply.

Robert lifted Colin's right hand in his own and saw the faint beginnings of a bruise across the back of it. He moistened his lips and swallowed. His insides felt quaky.

'You shouldn't have squirmed and pulled like that,' he muttered in his own defence. 'And I had to smack you, see, because you were in a frenzy.'

'I don't like that place! I won't go back!'

Robert fought down another flash of vexation. 'All

right,' he said, 'all right. You can wait outside while I fetch Hector.'

Colin looked suspicious. 'Promise?'

'Word of honour,' grumbled Robert.

The boy still eyed him dubiously.

'Trust me?' sighed his father.

After a lengthy pause, there came a somewhat uncertain, 'Yes.'

Together they stood up. For a moment they looked at each other and no smile passed between them. Robert felt guilty, now, yet still disappointed in him. The boy had made him feel so small in front of Mr Budley. Colin was gazing reproachfully back at him. Robert held out his hand. His son, rather slowly, took it. Then they walked down the path between the graves towards the gate.

· Twenty-five ·

'Well, what do you suggest?'

'Go to the root of the trouble. Take him out on the moor one night and show him there's nothing to fear. Make an adventure of it.'

'Adventure? Hah!' Robert thought it a ludicrous idea. If Colin did not feel safe in bed, how could he face passing the dark hours out there where his terrors lived? 'That's a joke, that is! He'd never go.'

He jerked the two-handed saw blade towards him. The wood was green and tough and the blade kept jamming.

'He might. Try asking him.'

Joel hauled the blade back again. It was August and the weather was scorching. Winter seemed a long way away, but the brothers were already laying in a store of fuel for the months ahead, sawing up a fallen tree in the woods.

They would chop the trunk and larger branches into logs for Torvallen's fires. The wood would dry out nicely by the time the coldest days arrived.

'Even if I coaxed him out there, he'd only panic as night came on,' said Robert. 'You should have seen him at Budley's forge. He went half-mad, I couldn't do anything with him.'

Bracing a foot against the tree trunk, he dragged the saw through the wood once more.

'Damn,' he muttered. 'Where's the grease?'

Lifting it clear, he paused to smear the length of the blade with lard. They set to work again and for a minute or so no more was said as they pulled it back and forth, arm and shoulder muscles bunching and relaxing in steady rhythm.

'You lost your temper with him, that was the trouble,' Joel remarked, at last. 'You shouldn't have tried to force him to go into Budley's.'

'I'm his father and he should obey me.'

'Didn't, though, did he?' Joel stopped for a moment, pulled off his cap and wiped his brow. 'Didn't work, did it, being heavy-handed?'

'Nothing works, it seems to me. I can see this going on for years. Take him out on the moor?' Robert scoffed. 'Talk about a daft idea! He'd die of fright.'

Thoughtfully, Joel inspected his palms, brushing his thumbs across the tender patches that would soon be blisters.

'Perhaps he'd come with me,' he said.

'With you? And why would he do that?' Robert was indignant, hands on hips. 'What's the difference which of us it is?'

'I wouldn't bully him, Rob, and he knows it.' Joel flipped his cap back on.

'Oh, you're so righteous, so cocksure. Always have all the answers, don't you? Always know best.' Robert's voice was low and mocking.

'I didn't say that.'

'You're saying you know better than I do how to handle Colin.'

'Ordinarily, no. I just think you're tackling this one problem badly.'

Robert snorted. 'It's easy to hand out wiseacre advice, but I'd like to see you put it into practice. You wouldn't feel so clever afterwards.'

'Well, I'm willing to risk being put in my place. I shan't be wounded if it turns out I'm wrong. How about it, Rob? I promise I'd look after him.'

'I know. I'm not worried on that score.'

'Any other objection, then? Afraid I might be right?'

Robert's answering grin was wry. He was tempted to let him try it. It would do Joel good to find himself as helpless as anyone else in the face of Colin's hysterics. And Robert doubted that the boy would thank him for it. He might not think so much of his Uncle Joel after a frightening expedition out on the moors at night.

'I'll think it over,' he said, dryly. 'And we'll see what Jess has to say.'

'If you approach him the right way, Rob, the boy might be willing to go with you.'

Robert's brows shot up. 'Oh, now what's this? Backing out?'

'No, but he is your son.'

Robert was not even going to ask him, knowing Colin would shrink away. He would not go anywhere with his dad any more, not after the scene at Budley's forge, not unless he was carried kicking and screaming. The child was wary of his father now, conscious of his scorn and fearful of his impatience.

But Joel? Well, yes, the boy might venture out with Joel, though Robert expected no successful result if he did. Perhaps Joel had realised that and was having second thoughts.

'Changed your mind?' taunted Robert. 'So much for you and your bright ideas.'

'I'll gladly take him,' said Joel, calmly, 'if he's prepared to come.'

Robert's smile was half a sneer. 'We'll see, then. For once, my know-all brother, I think you'll find you've bitten off more than you can chew.'

On a fence-post by the roadside sat a buzzard. It shifted from foot to foot, stretched and then refolded its wings and settled down again, only mildly disturbed by the approach of a man and boy on horseback.

They had ridden six miles from Torvallen and soon they would turn off this rough, pitted track and travel some way further over the heath. The man had a knapsack on his back, and the child sat in front of him, quiet and apprehensive. It had been another sultry day in a heatwave which had lasted nearly a month. Grass and bracken and heather were growing brown and dry, and the winds that blew across the moor were hot, giving no relief to man or beast. In open country the few thorny little trees afforded virtually no shelter from the sun, and creatures far from forest land just stood or lay wretchedly sweltering. Along the roadside verges, sheep huddled in little hollows in the ground, while long-haired cattle gathered dejectedly round every bush or stood in the streams to cool off. The emptiness that made the moor such a bitter place in winter could expose it just as surely to merciless summer heat. Even in the wooded vales the days were too sticky for comfort and only the nights were pleasant.

At the sight of the buzzard, Colin turned nervously to Joel and pointed it out. They had come within several yards of it and he did not like the look of this big speckled bird with its hooked beak. It stuck out its neck, inspected him with fierce black eyes, and did another little shuffling dance on top of the post.

'It's all right,' said Joel, 'it'll fly off in a minute.'

The boy looked dubiously at him, then once again at the bird.

'What does it eat?' he asked.

'Oh, little scuttling things – mice, voles, rabbits, lizards. Don't worry, he won't bother you.'

On they went. The bird lifted into the air, skimming across the track in front of them and cruising away over the moor. A few minutes later, Joel left the road, turning northward over the heath towards high country. The evening was gently warm and the air was sweet with the smell of grass and gorse. They followed the course of a brook with a spiky green edging of reeds. The water was shallow and very clear, and the bed of the stream was brown and strewn with pebbles. Ahead of them lay two tors, aloof and brooding. One was almost cone-shaped, and granite rubble littered its sides from the summit to halfway down. The second was a brutal crag, surmounting a hill that rose amid a thick growth of gorse. Very lonely, very stern, they stood like a pair of sentinels in the last glare of sunshine at the end of this burning day. Around them the land stretched away in still and eerie emptiness. No one lived out here, not a soul for many miles.

Colin, though, had yet to be convinced of that. He had come because he wanted to be brave, and because he trusted his Uncle Joel and reckoned him a match for anyone, even Old Nick and all his hounds. So here they were, in the heart of Dewer's domain, if Alec Maunder spoke the truth, and prepared to spend all the dark hours on watch. A very great and courageous adventure, this was. The boy was full of awe and dread, but moved by an odd excitement too. There was a peculiar thrill in the prospect of facing his horror – as long as Uncle Joel was there to see him off.

After half an hour the upward climb became steeper and soon the crag was looming near. By now, long shadows were slinking across the hills as the sun dipped low. Eventually they came to the source of the stream, a patch of mire which lay in a wide, shallow basin of land. It had shrunk to half its normal size after weeks of dry weather. Cotton grass and bright green moss marked out the extent of this quivering bog, which gurgled and squashed underfoot like a dirty sponge. It smelt of decay and every so often it bubbled, emitting a puff of gas.

Joel skirted round the marsh, then suggested they stop for a while.

'Time enough to rest,' he said, 'and still reach the top of the tor before dark. Keep an eye on the mire,' he told the boy. 'When the light fades you might see a will o' the wisp.'

Colin was not much interested in that. Now, with the approach of night, there were other things on his mind. He kept glancing up at the rocky outcrop, expecting to see Old Nick astride his horse. He very much wished he was somewhere else. And yet, if Joel had offered then and there to take him back, he would have steeled himself to stay, having ventured this far. Clasping his hands together between his knees, he released a huge, pent sigh, scanning the desolate country around him and thinking that in a minute he would have to go and wee.

Watching him, Joel smiled. This was no picnic for Colin, but he was bearing up. Joel admired that very much. Once, when he lost his patience, Robert had used the word 'spineless' to his child. Joel did not think much of his brother for that. Robert underestimated Colin, the boy was anything but craven. Joel would have given a lot for such a son.

The evening grew dim and all of a sudden a pale blue flame flickered in among the rushes. Joel nudged the boy and pointed. For a good many seconds it danced in the dusk and then it was gone. Colin was intrigued, forgetting his fears for a moment.

'There, that's a will o' the wisp. Some people call it a pixie lantern – nothing to do with pixies really. It's only gas thrown up by the marsh. On a warm night like this it'll often catch light. If we stayed for a while we'd see some more, but I think we ought to go, don't you? We have to get to the top.'

Joel raised a questioning eyebrow. Colin nodded stoically. The sky was streaked with red behind the tor. The last place he wanted to spend the night was up there among those rocks. But he was going to be brave, no matter what. He knew his dad didn't think he was. Colin couldn't bear it if Uncle Joel reached the same conclusion.

They tethered the mare at the foot of the crag and began to climb. The final stretch was not as hard as it looked. Joel knew an easy way up among the boulders and finally they found a niche where they could sit and light a fire and see for miles around. The twilight deepened and took away all the colours of the moor, turning it into a wasteland of grey. Then the moon rose, flooding it all with a spectral radiance, and pin-points of starlight stippled the sky. Joel spread out blankets, then laid a fire of sticks and furze and put a match to it. On the way he had gathered fuel enough to last for several hours, and the short summer night would be warm in any case.

'Now then, we'll have some supper.' He winked at the boy in the glow of the flames and rummaged in his pack for the food Jess had provided. There were two large potatoes to bake in the fire, hard-boiled eggs, fresh brown splits, lardy cakes, wortleberry tart – and a half pound block of chocolate. She had also put in a bottle of milk and another of ginger beer.

Colin looked warily about him while they waited for the potatoes to cook. With his back to the rocks he felt fairly confident that nothing could creep up on him from behind. Now and again he heard a flutter in the air around him, and once or twice a small dark shape went gliding past, just on the border of the firelight.

'Bats,' said Joel. 'They don't do any harm.'

He poked a potato out of the fire with a stick, cut it open and put it aside on a stone. 'Let it cool for a minute or two, or else you'll burn your mouth.' Thoughtfully, he added, 'Would you like to have a pet when you're a bit older, Colin?'

The boy nodded eagerly. Then, growing grave, he said anxiously, 'Not a dog.'

'No, all right, you don't like dogs. There are plenty of other things. I'm sure your mam and dad won't mind.'

The child was pleased at the idea, and set to work on his potato with good appetite.

'I used to keep all sorts of creatures when I was a boy,'

continued Joel. 'Birds, fish, insects. And I knew every fox's den and badger's sett for miles around. I used to go out on moonlit nights like this one and watch for them, especially when they had young. I liked to see the cubs. Perhaps in a few years' time you'll be able to do the same.'

'Didn't Dad have any pets?'

Joel thought back and his forehead puckered. 'No,' he said, musingly, 'funny thing, but he never took much interest.'

Between them they finished up most of the food and by midnight Colin was very drowsy. So far, Old Nick had not turned up. He had kept an eye out for him, constantly scanning the land below and listening for the thud of hooves or distant howling. But nothing moved on the face of the moor and all was silent save for the rustle of wings now and then, or the tiny sound of a mouse or a lizard scampering among the rocks. Colin tried to stay awake, but the journey and all that supper were making it very hard to fend off sleep.

Joel wrapped a blanket round him, and soon the child had nodded off. He woke up twice in the night. Once at two o'clock, when Joel threw the last of the wood on the fire, and again at half past three. The hour before dawn was very dark. The moon had gone down, the fire was a few feeble embers amid a pile of white ash, and Joel had gone to sleep. Staring out into blackness, the child reminded himself where he was, the heartland of his awful dreams. He thought he ought to be afraid. Yet he was not, and suddenly he knew with overwhelming certainty that the huntsman was not going to come, not this or any other night. There was nothing here but the heath and the rocks and the sky. He sensed no horrors abroad in the dark, no presence of any sort. There was nothing in the air but peace. Closing his eyes, he settled down and slept another hour.

When Joel awoke at sunrise, he found the boy gone from his side. Alarmed for a moment, he looked around – then saw him sitting on a boulder by himself, watching the day break in the east. A few wispy clouds had come over, pink and gold in the dawn.

Stiffly, Joel rose to his feet. A night on granite had left him all aches and pains, but he guessed it had been worthwhile.

'Well,' he said, softly, 'no sign of him, eh?'

The child answered that with a sheepish grin.

'We could sit here every night for a year and still we'd never see him. Because it's just a story, lad. It isn't true, it isn't real. Do you believe that now?'

'Yes,' said Colin, 'now I do.'

'Certain sure? All right, then. Nothing like seeing for yourself, is there? Come on, let's go home for breakfast.'

Colin thought it strange the way his dad reacted after his night out on the tor. The nightmares stopped, the bedwetting too, and Robert was of course glad about that. Yet, he was not entirely pleased about it all. His praise was a little grudging. And he looked at Colin in an almost wounded way, as if the boy had somehow betrayed him. He said an odd thing, too, about Uncle Joel.

'Does he never fail at anything?'

Robert muttered the words to himself, but Colin heard them just the same.

And one time his mam remarked, 'That's two weeks now without a broken night. We can't thank you enough, Joel.'

Whereupon, his dad snapped at her, 'Yes, yes, he's performed a miracle. Don't keep on about it.'

Colin saw Uncle Joel shoot Dad a hard look from under his brows.

'Anybody'd think you'd lost a bet,' he said.

Colin puzzled a lot over that, but he couldn't make sense of it.

· Twenty-six ·

The winter months went by. The weather did not turn really cold until January had passed and then it did so with a vengeance.,

One February morning, the matter of an unpaid bill took Robert into Plymouth. He had an appointment to see the Lawrensons' solicitor at ten, and he left Torvallen at just after nine on a day that was bitter. A vicious wind hit him full in the face as he came out of the house, a wind that made his ears and temples ache. Then he had trouble starting the car, and he cursed the man who made this errand necessary – a builder who owed the family more than two hundred pounds. Joel had been inclined to give the debtor, an old customer, one more month before taking action, but Robert had never been a patient man and scornfully said that his brother was too easygoing.

After much persuasion, the engine finally responded. Robert set off with his mind on nothing but money. Towards the north-east the sky was a gun-metal grey behind the tor.

In the kitchen, Jess was ironing. On the floor was a basket piled high with bed- and table-linen, underwear and shirts, all crumpled from the wash. A faint scent of scorching rose as she worked, the smell of hot, clean cotton. Her two irons were the old-fashioned kind, heated on top of the cooking range, and the scrubbed pine table gave her ample space to spread out large items like sheets. This was one of the biggest chores of the week and she laboured steadily through it that day without even pausing for a cup of tea. On a chair beside her, the pile of smooth and neatly folded linen grew higher, while the basket gradually emptied. She did not mind the ironing, never had. She found it satisfying, oddly soothing.

Joel had gone down to the sawmill, and Colin was in the sitting room with all his toys around him. That strong imagination had its beneficial side. Never bored on his own, the boy could amuse himself quietly for hours. The house was all but silent.

The snow came silently too. Jess had her back to the window and she did not see the first flakes flutter down. By the time her son rushed into the kitchen to tell her, it was already falling thickly and settling on the ground. She put down her iron, setting it on its heel, then picked up the boy and stood to watch for a minute or two. The wind had dropped and the crystals were coming straight down, floating peacefully to earth. The trees at the back of the house were half screened from sight, as if by a moving net curtain. A layer an inch or so thick had collected on the roofs of the stable and other outbuildings, and the vegetable garden was fast disappearing under a cloak of white.

Colin exclaimed and laughed, delighted. His mother smiled at him, but then she glanced at the kitchen clock and thought uneasily about her husband. It was twenty to eleven. She supposed he was safely in town by now. She very much hoped he was.

The snowfall grew heavier still, loading every branch and twig in the woods, blotting out the green and brown that mottled the moor, and camouflaging its contours too, as hollows filled and drifts began to build up.

Some time later, Joel came in. His cap and jacket and boots were encrusted with white. He had sent his men home an hour before.

'I think we're in for a big blizzard,' he said, rubbing his hands together at the stove. 'Sky's an evil colour over Exeter way.'

'Joel, what about Robert? What if he's been caught in this?'

'Shouldn't think so. It didn't start till after ten. He must have reached town by that time.'

'But he may not be able to get back.'

'I'm quite sure he won't. Don't worry, he wouldn't be rash enough to try. He'll just have to stay in the city until the roads are clear.'

'Lord,' said Jess, 'that might be days.'

Joel knew it could be weeks, if the worst should come to the worst, but decided not to say so.

'Mam would put him up, of course,' she murmured. 'Although I don't know that he'd want to ...' Her voice trailed worriedly off.

'What?' Joel glanced at her over his shoulder. 'Wouldn't want to what?'

'Uh, well, he might feel he was imposing on her, especially now, with Mr Honey there.'

There was something in the way she spoke, something evasive, guarded.

'Are you thinking he'd be embarrassed? Or that they would?'

'I'm sure they'd make him very welcome. But Rob – well, he just wouldn't like it.'

'He isn't narrow-minded, Jess.'

'Not in a general sense,' she muttered, taking up her iron again. 'Oh, he can laugh about outsiders and their little weaknesses. He isn't quite so tolerant when scandal comes too close to home.'

Joel frowned. Alice had brought Mr Honey to the last Boxing Day party and everyone had liked him very much – including Robert.

'Scandal? Has he called it that?'

'No, he hasn't spoken of it much at all. I know, though, what he thinks about Mam these days.'

If that was Robert's attitude, Joel considered it very stupid of him.

'Damn fool shouldn't have gone out today,' he said, sitting down and bending over to pull off his boots. 'Couldn't wait to start proceedings. I know we're owed a fair bit of money, but we won't go under for the lack of it.'

Outside, the wind returned and now it was shrilling round the house, spinning flurries of flakes against the windows, driving them into wild, reeling dances. A few came drifting down the chimney, each expiring with a tiny hiss when it hit the stove. The woods were just a shadow, now, seen through veils of white, and the moor and sky were a single swirling plain.

'At times like this I wish we had a telephone,' said Jess, 'so that he could ring and let me know he's all right.'

'Stop worrying. He's probably taken a hotel room already, if he really doesn't care to stay with Alice.'

The blizzard carried on till half past three, and then it suddenly stopped.

Colin wanted to go outside, so they put on coats and boots and woollen hats, and when Joel opened the front door a three-foot pile of snow fell in on the mat. The sky had lightened now and the world was gleaming. The air was very sharp and once again still. The trees seemed dressed in lace and caster sugar, and the pristine snow on the ground looked almost plump, like a vast, fresh pillow.

Colin plunged into it with a yell, ploughing through it, gathering up armfuls and throwing them over his head. Jess had knitted him a red hat with a bobble on top, and a pair of matching gloves. His hair was glossy black beneath it, his cheeks very pink and his brown eyes very bright. Joel picked up a handful of snow and threw it at him. Colin hurled some back and then they pelted each other, chasing to and fro, ducking and weaving and falling over, while Jess stood clapping, booing and whistling in the porch.

After all these years, her favourite headgear was still a woolly tam. At twenty-three she looked little different to the girl she had been at thirteen. Very slightly taller, a bit more full in the bosom, that was all. Even her hair was much the same, still long, tied back with a ribbon, defiantly out of style and very beautiful.

Joel hoisted the boy on his shoulders and charged around and around till all the snow was trampled and he was out of breath. Panting, he caught sight of Jess and called, 'Think you're keeping out of it, eh? We'll see about that, won't we, boy?'

He put Colin down and they started showering her. Jess took cover behind the water butt, lobbing snowballs over the top as fast as she could make them.

'Let's throw Mother in the river,' shouted Joel, when she scored a bullseye which knocked his hat off. And he lunged at her, scooped her up and rushed her, screaming, down to the water's edge.

'Shall I?' he called to Colin, swinging her outwards a little.

Colin couldn't decide. He put a forefinger in his mouth and pondered, dark eyes sparkling.

'Come on,' pressed Joel, 'it's up to you.'

He winked very slyly at Jess.

The boy made up his mind and shook his head.

'Aw,' said Joel, 'where's your sense of fun? Go on, say the word and I'll drop her in.'

'Put me down,' she told him, quietly. 'He might start thinking you mean it.'

Joel looked at her and grinned. Then something new crossed his face for a moment, something intent, a yearning, a confusion. Slowly, and reluctantly, he lowered her to the ground. He smiled and it was awkward, which was not like Joel at all.

This was the first time he had ever held his brother's wife. Even like this, in play, the contact and his own reaction shocked him. He had always thought she was lovely, but he had never truly wanted her before.

It was due to being lonely, he supposed. Pauline had been gone just a year and ten days, but it somehow seemed more, a long and empty, dragging time.

Jess had read his feelings clearly, Joel knew she had. She had seen the desire, the embarrassment, the guilt. But now she pretended she had not, and put a quick end to the situation.

'Tea,' she said, briskly, 'and muffins and cake, that's

what we all need next. It'll soon be growing dark, in any case. Come on, let's go indoors.'

It started to snow again in the evening and carried on relentlessly. In the sitting room, Jess and Joel sat before the fire long after Colin had been put to bed.

For some time neither had spoken. Joel was reading and Jess was worrying. She kept imagining Robert, trapped in his car in a snowdrift because he had tried to come home and the Humber had broken down, run out of fuel or simply become stuck. She pictured him losing control on ice, or leaving the car to try walking back, losing his way and stumbling off into the trackless wastes of the moor, there to die, exhausted. Twisting her wedding ring round and round on her finger, she stared at the burning logs in the grate and every so often heaved a great sigh.

'Stop fretting,' Joel ordered, at last, laying aside his book. 'He's all right, I'm sure, and anyway there's nothing to be done until the snow clears. We're well and truly cut off, so you might as well settle down.'

'I know, I know.' She went and fetched the last Sunday paper and tried to concentrate on the crossword puzzle. But after a while she tossed it aside.

'Just his luck,' she murmured, 'to be caught out like this.'

Joel turned down a page and closed his book.

'Funny,' he said, reflectively, 'Rob always was unlucky, always falling foul of sod's law, even as a child.'

'In what way?'

'They were little things, mostly – but so many of them. For instance, he'd come down with measles on his birthday, or break his arm at the start of the summer holiday. It was always Rob's toys that accidentally got smashed, or his fish that slipped off the hook. He could never win anything at the fair. He could never make any mischief without being caught. It was always Rob who was stung by a wasp on the beach, and if there was a bit of broken glass in the sand, he'd be the one to tread on it and cut his foot. If a slot machine was going to jam, it would choose the moment he put his coin in. Things had a way of going wrong for him, as they never did for me, and I know he resented it. I think he reckoned he was somehow singled out for misfortune. Mother and Father used to try and joke him out of it, but Rob can't shrug or laugh things off. He takes mischance like a slap in the face. Mind you, sometimes he brought misery on himself. That's been especially true of him as an adult.'

She guessed what he was thinking about, and ventured to pursue it.

'Joel,' she said, quietly, 'what was your opinion of Vanessa Crane?'

'Why do you ask?'

'I met her in town one day when I went shopping with Pauline.'

A blink of mild surprise. 'And?'

'I – quite liked her.'

'Yes, so did I. She's not a bad sort. Pauline always called Vanessa spoilt, maintained she had too much of everything, but I'd say she was wrong about that. I only met Vanessa two or three times, but I had the feeling she'd been strictly raised, with firm ideas of right and wrong. Call it a code, if you wish. I don't believe she was ever the kind to lead a man on for the fun of it.'

'I thought you might say that. She, um, told me certain things about Rob – that he chased her, made a pest of himself. Did you know?'

'I guessed at something of the sort, but I never said anything to him. He idolised Vanessa and I didn't dare interfere. You know how he is towards me.'

'Why is that, Joel? Why does he pit himself against you in everything?'

'No good reason I know of. Mother and Father treated us both alike. He was never made to wear my old clothes or disciplined more than I was. I did better in school, I think, but that made no real difference to his life or mine. We knew we were both going into the business with Father. Yet I've always had to – what's the phrase – walk on eggshells, just to keep the peace. I hoped he might change when he married you. Oh, he was proud of you!' said Joel, smiling. 'Nothing so good had ever happened to him before, and he did improve at first, for a while.' The smile went away. 'But it didn't last. If anything, he's worse than ever now.'

She cast a glance at him, then turned it back to the crackling flames in the grate. Her profile was very pale and clear-cut in the lamplight.

'Yes, well I'm not as perfect as he thought,' she said, dryly. 'I tumbled off my pedestal a good two years ago.'

Joel's eyebrows drew together. 'What in the name of God could he find wrong with you?'

She looked at him again. Sensible, uncomplicated Joel, so easygoing. She wanted very much to tell him all of it. She longed for someone understanding with whom to talk about Alice. Joel was such a person. But then, she had promised Robert ...

'Is Robert disappointed that there haven't been more children?'

'Yes,' she said, 'but it isn't that so much. There's something else.' From the corner of her eye she surveyed him, then went a little further. 'It's largely because of Mam, because of something he found out.' Wryly, she added, 'He made me promise I would never tell you.'

A slow smile lifted his mouth. 'Something shocking, eh?'

'Most people would say so, yes.'

'Hmm,' mused Joel. 'Has she been to gaol?'

'Good heavens, no!'

'Spied for the Germans during the war?'

'Oh please, be serious.'

He thought for a moment, then suggested shrewdly, 'Perhaps there's been more than one Mr Honey?'

It was just as if a door were inching open. Now he was on the right track and her face told him so.

'Yes,' he said. 'I see. Very many, Jess?'

She stalled for ten seconds longer, then nodded. 'A lot

of men, though none of them was anything like him. He's a dear little man, a kind man, as good as a husband to her. Most of the others were – ships in the night.'

'You don't mean she made money at it, do you?'

'No! Oh no! She just ...'

'... liked men,' finished Joel. He considered a moment, then nodded. 'I'm not altogether surprised. Alice always did strike me as being, well, childlike, defenceless – the generous sort who might fall easy prey. And that's what's biting Robert? Nothing more?'

There seemed no point now in holding anything back. The details all came tumbling out – Alice's experience in the dockyard, the sniping and jeering, the persecution, the nickname. And finally Maunder's tattling and the change it had wrought in Robert.

'I suppose he saw me as tarnished after that,' she ended, glumly. 'For certain, he hasn't trusted me since. It might be in the blood, you see,' she explained, bitterly. 'Mind you, from what Vanessa told me, he'd behave in a similar way to any woman. It's all a matter of degree. He's ten times worse with me because of Mam.'

For a short time Joel was silent, digesting all this. At last he said, 'Poor Jess. Poor Alice, too.'

She pulled at a trailing strand of hair and gave a helpless shrug.

'Well, Robert's only human, after all. Perhaps he's entitled to feel disenchanted.'

'Rubbish. He's a prize fool to let a thing like that come between you. I'll be very pleased to tell him so, if you want.'

'You mustn't, Joel. As I said, he didn't want you to know. You won't let on I've told you? It'll only make things worse.'

'Oh, all right, if that's your wish.'

'He dreads the thought of people round here finding out. That's why he wants that beastly Maunder man kept on in spite of everything.'

'Mmph!' Joel leaned forward, stretching out his hands before the blaze. After a second or two he looked up and lively shadows flickered on his face. 'Well now, there is something I can do about him. Just say the word and I'll sack him.'

'Robert wouldn't stand for it.'

'I don't plan to consult Robert. Would you like me to get rid of Maunder, Jess? I'll see to it there isn't any talk.'

'How?' she asked, dubiously.

He grinned, took a poker and rummaged under the logs, shaking down the ash. 'Mr Maunder is afraid of me, I fancy.'

Sitting back on the sofa, Jess pulled up her feet and tucked them under her. 'What are you thinking of doing to him? Please be careful, Joel.'

'Nothing fatal, but I'm sure a scare's in order.'

The beginnings of a smile touched her mouth.

'Agree?' he pressed.

A chuckle escaped her. 'Yes. Oh yes!'

'Good. I'll deal with it as soon as the snow clears.'

Jess grew sombre again. 'He brought that nastiness out here like a rat carrying plague. Oh Lord, I believed I'd left all the woe behind me. Torvallen was so peaceful, so far from the street and the neighbours. I imagined I'd be safe from gossip here. I suppose I was too optimistic. And I didn't know Rob very well. I only thought I did.'

'Courting means best behaviour,' observed Joel, 'and marriage means true colours. Anyway, the country's no refuge, Jess. Everything gets magnified in isolated places – love, hate, and jealousy. There's as much idle talk in a village as in the city, probably more. I know of at least one woman who moved into town to escape! Being different is hard wherever you are. It's perilous, breaking the rules and not being one of the mob. They'll always make you pay for it, little or much. Either they'll condemn you or they'll pity you. Not very pleasant, whichever it is.'

Jess twisted her mouth as if she were chewing on something tough and sour.

'Mam never did fit in with the herd and nor did I.'

'To my mind, that's a recommendation.'

'Robert cares so much what other people think of him.

You don't give a fig, though, do you?'

'The only answer is not to care. Anyway,' he sniffed, 'half the people I know aren't equipped to think.'

'Oh Joel ...' Her laughter was buoyant now, '... it's always a pleasure to talk with you.'

A light burned late in Joel's room that night. He had tried but he could not sleep, too aware of Jess across the landing on her own. A little fantasy played in his mind, of going over there and being welcomed.

Joel could not help but wonder how his brother treated her in bed. She had carefully said nothing about it, but it might be that Jess had been deprived of good love for a long time now. In that way she could be lonely, just as he was ...

A wave of shame engulfed him. His brother's wife. How dirty to speculate about them. How dishonourable to covet Jess, how disloyal to Pauline after only a year. Yet the fantasy repeated itself a second time, and a third. Then he varied it so that she came to him, imagining how he would hear her door opening, and then a quiet tap at his own. He would not feel much guilt if it happened that way.

After a while he snuffed the lamp and turned on his side, curling up in a ball. His thoughts ranged over the things she had told him of Alice. Joel was neither shocked nor repelled. All he felt was sympathy for a silly, vulnerable woman, more innocent in heart than those who persecuted her. He understood now the toughness he had always perceived in Jess. Joel admired her for it. She had her soft side, too, but unlike her mother, she was not weak.

No, nor faithless, either. In telling him all those things about Alice, Jess had gone as far as she meant to go. Whatever the trouble between them, she would not betray Robert. She would not come to Joel's room. The fantasy was just that, nothing more.

Joel rolled on to his back and trained his mind on Alec Maunder instead. He would deal with him, all right. He was looking forward to it.

*

Twenty miles away, in a city hotel room, Robert, too, was thinking of Jess. The idea of staying with Alice had not appealed to him – which had little or nothing to do with Mr Honey. Robert simply could not look at Alice without recalling how she once was and what had befallen her, nor could he quite forgive her for it. To accept her hospitality would make him feel shabby, two-faced.

He had tried to drive home, but the weather had forced him to turn back. So here he was, marooned for he knew not how long. Under his window the snow in the road was furrowed with wheel tracks. It shone beneath the street lamps and all was very quiet. His room was warm and clean, albeit plainly furnished, and cost seven shillings a night. Every so often he heard a car go crawling by and the glow of its headlights would sweep across the wall that faced the bed. He had eaten a good dinner before retiring, and was easy in his mind concerning the stock of supplies at Torvallen. Plenty of food and plenty of fuel. The larder and woodshed were crammed. No need to worry on that score.

His thoughts concerning his wife were less reassuring. She was out there with Joel tonight. She was going to be alone with him for several days to come. Undisturbed, sealed off from the rest of the world. No one else there but the boy. The boy, who was so very fond of his Uncle Joel.

Rancour stirred afresh in Robert's soul when he thought back to the summer and his son's night out on the tor. Joel had a way with Colin, he could manage him where Robert could not.

'Anybody'd think the boy was his.'

Robert's right hand clenched at the coverlet as the echo of Maunder's remark jabbed at him like a bee sting. He flung himself on to his side and then his stomach. A child should have more affinity with his father than his uncle. By all that was natural, surely that was so?

Well, Joel had a way with everyone. He had always been liked by all – the customers, the men at work, and women. Without the slightest effort, Joel attracted people of all kinds, but especially females. How they had gathered round him at fairs and fêtes and markets when he was still as young as sixteen!

Images formed in Robert's head – of Jess and his brother, eating together, talking and laughing together, going upstairs together, whispering on the landing so as not to wake the child, softly debating whose bed to use.

Robert sat up against his pillows and started nibbling at his thumbnail in the dark. In his mind's eye it was Joel's fingers he could see, long, slim fingers, graceful for a man. They were casually undoing Jess's blouse. Button by button, taking his time. Then the hands were slipping inside to cup the breasts.

Robert gasped as he tore the nail down to the quick, but he kept on gnawing at it.

Skirt, stockings, underwear. He could picture it all coming off. And then his brother's clothing. Oh, Joel was finely built. Robert was shorter, so much plainer. He did not compare at all well. Jess must always have noticed that.

The sound of voices coming down the corridor broke into Robert's imaginings. He heard a man and woman go by, she with a ripple of husky female laughter, he with a murmur about a morning call. A key went into a lock, a door banged shut and silence fell once more.

Returning to Torvallen, Robert found Jess and Joel between the sheets. Dark head and fair together, bodies fused and limbs entangled, going on and on in plunging motion.

Earthy, that was Joel. Many a morning Robert had noticed the looks he exchanged with Pauline at breakfast, looks that told of a bout or two of plain, uncomplicated lust the previous night.

He'd be good, thought Robert. Damn him, he'd be good.

He ripped back the bedclothes, jumped out of bed and went to the window. The snow glittered up at him. Robert pressed his forehead to the glass, closed his eyes, tried to quiet his busy mind and persuade it all was well.

Jess would not betray him. No, she would not. She was Alice's girl, but not Alice. And his brother was an honourable man. Robert had to admit that Joel had never done anything base in his life.

He went to the wash-basin, filled the tooth-mug with water and drank, then returned to bed and tried to forget that Jess and Joel were under the same roof, free to follow any desire they had for one another, and there was nothing he could do about it.

On the moor, the snow lay heavy for days. Farmers took out what forage they could for their cattle, while the ponies fended mostly for themselves. Men dug in snowdrifts for buried sheep, rejoicing when they pulled one out alive. Every morning the snow outside Torvallen was pitted with animal tracks, for foxes, rabbits, stoats and weasels nosed around the house at night in search of scraps. An owl moved into the stable, taking up residence in the rafters. Small birds of every kind, feathers fluffed out till they looked like pom-poms, loitered in the bushes outside the back door, ready to swoop on whatever was offered. Jess put out food several times a day – bread and dripping and stale cake, over-ripe fruit and leavings from the table.

Joel spent a morning making a toboggan, then he took his nephew up on a nearby slope to try it out. Thereafter, they spent a couple of hours each day trudging to the top and careering down again with whoops and yells, sometimes head first, sometimes feet first, always falling off at the bottom.

Thus the days went by, whiled away in silly games, with no work to do except keep the fires going and cook. A happy time for all of them, imprisoned though they were by the snow. In the evenings Jess and Joel played draughts, or read or simply talked of one thing and another. But nothing very personal again. Little more was said about Robert or Alice. Feelings were once more safely stowed away in private.

For Robert, it was not a holiday. As the time dragged by, his fears grew greater and nearly drove him to distraction.

Frustrated, he paced about his hotel room, or sometimes he went out and paced about the town. Piles of slush, mottled grey and brown, had been shovelled into the gutters to clear the roads and pavements so the life of the city could carry on. But snow still lay a foot thick on the rooftops, and reports on the hotel wireless assured him that country roads were still impassable in remote areas.

He hated being trapped here. He had work to do at home. And the longer Jess and Joel were left alone, the more temptation there would be. A night or two might not be enough to try their self-control. But a third, a fourth, a fifth? Fidelity might waver, restraint might ebb away. They were both so very attractive, a natural match for each other. Robert knew he was not on their level, not really the sort of man to hold on to a pretty wife when faced with such a rival.

Tormenting himself, he watched the sky each day and yearned for rain. In the afternoons he sat in the hotel lounge beside the radio, morosely drinking tea, so grumpy and preoccupied that other guests and staff alike all wondered what was wrong with him. The receptionist remarked to the porter that she had noticed how Mr Lawrenson's thumbs were bitten raw, the cuticles red and bloody. They agreed that he must have some dreadful weight on his mind.

· Twenty-seven ·

The snow had lain for five days when the thaw began. At Torvallen, the icicles round the eaves began to drip, the crust of ice on the water butt melted and every so often a thump was heard as another load of snow slid off the roof. On the sixth day it was melting fast, and exactly a week had passed since the blizzard when Joel once more went down to the yard to work.

On that same morning, his brother left the hotel to make his way home. The journey took him over an hour and a half, for the moorland roads were still treacherous. He reached Torvallen at ten to ten, but he did not drive in through the gate. Robert parked in the lane instead, skirted through the trees at the rear of the house and entered, very quietly, by the back door.

There was no one in the kitchen and the house was very quiet. The remains of breakfast lay on the table. Three plates, three mugs.

Well, it seemed he would not catch them still in bed.

Robert padded out into the passage and thence across to the sitting room, where he found his wife and son. Cross-legged on the floor, she was cutting out pictures of cowboys and indians from a comic, and the child was sticking them into a scrapbook with flour-and-water paste. Both were so intent on this that Robert stood in the doorway for fully a minute before they realised he was there. Unsmiling, he looked down on Jess's fair head as she bent it over her task. It was only when she raised it to pass a cut-out to the boy that she became aware of a silent, watchful figure at the door.

She jumped, gasped, thinking instantly of Alec Maunder. Relief broke out all over her face when she saw that it was her husband.

'Robert! Oh, you gave me such a fright!' Pushing the tattered comic from her knees, she sprang to her feet. 'Look, Colin, here's your dad!'

Brush in hand, the boy smiled up at his father, but he did not seem especially excited to see him and went on daubing busily with the paste.

Robert took note of that, and his face remained dour as his wife greeted him with a thankful squeeze.

'I didn't hear you drive up,' she exclaimed. 'I've been so worried. Thank heaven you're safe. I had visions of you freezing to death in a snowdrift.'

They say the wish is father to the thought, reflected Robert.

He looked down at her. Jess saw something hard and remote in his eyes.

'Where ... ? Did you go to stay with Mam?' she asked, hesitantly.

'No, I took a room at a hotel.'

He was gazing round him, surveying the room as if he were searching for something. Jess could not imagine what, and in truth he did not know either. Clues, he vaguely supposed. Something tell-tale. Evidence of mischief. But this, of course, was not the place to look. In a moment he would go upstairs, inspect the bedrooms.

'I'll make you some breakfast, shall I?' she asked, uncertainly. 'A nice big plate of bacon, eggs and sausage? Or scrambled eggs on toast, if you'd prefer.'

'I've already had my breakfast. I was up very early this morning. Thought I'd better get home quickly. I knew how much you'd miss me.'

Jess took her husband's hands between her own and found them very cold. Rubbing them, she said uneasily, 'Of course we missed you. I was so afraid the snow might last for weeks.'

'Oh, I'm sure you would have found plenty to do while I was away. Where's Joel?' he asked, abruptly.

'Gone to work.'

'Hmm. Been home for most of the week, though, I daresay?'

'Well, yes.'

'I expect you had a jolly time while I was stuck in town?'

'How do you mean?'

'Fun and games,' said Robert, silkily.

'We took the boy out to enjoy the snow, if that's what you're talking about. Joel did a splendid job of keeping Colin amused.'

Robert nodded, and then he half-smiled. It was not a smile she liked.

'And what about you? Did he manage to keep you amused?'

Jess experienced not a second's doubt of what it meant.

Oh God, she thought. Oh God, not this. Not all this again.

'He plays a good game of draughts.' She knew her laughter sounded false, a little desperate. 'Not so clever at cards, though. Thank the Lord we both had plenty to read.'

'Ah,' said Robert, 'I see.' He took off his coat and cap, tossing them on to a chair. 'Had a few early nights, I expect? Each of you with a good book.'

'Yes.' There was an edge to her voice this time.

'Isn't that nice,' he said, wryly. 'Very wholesome.'

She tried to turn the tables on him. 'I might equally ask what you've been up to in town. And Robert, where is the car? Why did you come creeping in here that way?'

'To surprise you, of course,' he replied, as he made for the door.

'Where are you going?'

'Upstairs, if that's all right with you. I have to change for work.'

'You'll find clean clothes all ready,' Jess said, tightly.

'Everything in order, eh? Everything just as it should be?'

'Nothing changed because you were away.'

Robert went upstairs. She heard him moving overhead, and with sinking heart she guessed what he was doing.

First he went into Joel's room and discovered the bed neatly made. Any evidence of boisterous action had been smoothed out. Robert peeled back the covers and looked under the pillows. His eyes darted here and there in search of tiny giveaways – a hairpin, perhaps, or a long golden hair. He sniffed the pillowcases, too, for a trace of the jasmine perfume he had given Jess at Christmas. Next he rifled through the cupboards and drawers, then got down on his knees and peered beneath the bed to see if there might be some small, forgotten item of her clothing.

Nothing at all. No trace of any misdemeanour here.

All the spare bedrooms were in immaculate order, so Robert finally turned to his own. Here he looked for signs of Joel's presence, but again there was nothing to see. Except ...

There were fresh sheets on the bed. They had not been slept in even once, they bore not a single crease.

Robert hurried out to the cupboard on the landing, looked in the laundry basket and found it empty. Thundering downstairs, he strode out to the wash house, where, sure enough, he discovered them in a tin bath of water. Jess already had them in to soak.

Returning to the sitting room, he stated tersely, 'I notice you've changed the bed-linen.'

She was kneeling, gathering up some chippings of paper her son had upset on the hearthrug. Rising to her feet, she said, 'I thought it would be nice for you. I had a feeling you might be home today, seeing the thaw was well under way.'

His glance fluttered over her, bleak with distrust. 'So you were ready for me. Dealt with the laundry quickly, didn't you?'

'I only put it in to soak,' came the wary reply.

'Very efficient, all the same.'

'You married a good housekeeper.'

What else did I marry? he asked himself. Why are you so nervous, eh? You must have been up to something, Jess. You're flushed, you're agitated. Didn't you think I'd guess?

'I do know how to pick a woman, don't I?' A grim sort of bantering coloured his tone. His mouth smiled, but his eyes did not.

She wanted to scream at him in protest: Nothing happened between your brother and me, nothing whatsoever. I'm too loyal and he's too decent. We wouldn't do such a thing!

But she clamped down her indignation and held her tongue. It would be a great mistake to give vent like that. Jess knew her husband too well by now to make such an error. Robert had his methods, his ways of trying to provoke her into defending herself before she was even accused. He was very good at that. He had not, in so many words, suggested she had slept with Joel. Nothing would make her sound more guilty than hotly denying a charge he had not actually voiced.

'I'm going to put the meat to boil,' she muttered. 'We're having stew today.'

'Joel's favourite.'

'You like it too. Still, if you'd rather, I'll make something else.'

'Oh no,' said Robert, dryly, 'I mustn't be too much of a nuisance.'

After he had gone to work, Jess sank down at the kitchen table and took a powder to ease her head. Fear had truly set in now. For Robert to be jealous of strangers, outsiders, was one thing. But how would it be if the man he most distrusted lived in the very same house? His brother, his deeply envied brother. Her home would become a battlefield if Robert continued like this.

That evening, Robert volunteered to put his son to bed. It was not a task he normally undertook, but for once he seemed uncommonly keen. Wise as she was to his ways, not even Jess suspected his motive. After all, he had not seen the child for nearly a week.

Upstairs in Colin's little bedroom, buttoning up the boy's pyjamas, Robert slyly set about questioning him.

'Was it nice playing out in the snow with Uncle Joel?' he asked, lightly.

Colin assured him it was.

'Did your mam join in sometimes?'

The child said yes.

'What did Mam and Uncle Joel do the rest of the time?'

Colin's replies contained nothing disturbing. All very innocent, all very proper.

A thoughtful pause. Then, elaborately casual, 'Did you ever hear Uncle Joel in your mam's room at night?'

The child was positive that he had not.

'Did they ever go upstairs together during the day?'

Colin did not think so.

'Or go off anywhere by themselves and leave you alone?'

Again, no.

Robert tucked him into bed and the boy lay gazing up

at him with puzzled, uneasy eyes. The questions seemed pointless to him, but his dad appeared to think them important. He was very persistent, and instinct told the child that this was something not very nice, not good for Mam and Uncle Joel. He wished his father would stop it.

Robert kissed him goodnight and Colin hoped the quiz was over. But then his father asked, 'Have you ever seen Mam kiss Uncle Joel the way she kisses me?'

'No,' came the firm reply.

'Never, not even once?'

Another emphatic shake of the head.

'What did they say about me being away?'

'Mam was afraid you'd be froze.'

'That's all? There must have been other things.'

Yawning, the boy said, 'Can't remember.'

Robert sighed. There was obviously nothing to be learned from Colin.

'All right, if you're certain,' he said.

Turning out the lamp, he left the room. He had gleaned no scrap of evidence, but his mind had not been set at ease. Perhaps they had simply been careful in front of the child.

Stepping out on to the landing, he suddenly halted. There outside the door stood Joel. His back was against the wall and his arms were folded. He had heard and he was waiting for his brother.

'Shut the door.' He mouthed the words so Colin should not hear.

Robert closed it firmly. For a moment they glared at each other. Then:

'I thought you knew me better, Rob,' said Joel, softly, 'even though there's no love lost between us.'

'I'll tell you what I know – that you've been out here alone with my wife for nearly a week. That she was jumpy when I came home this morning ...'

'She's been worried sick about you!'

'But you were a comfort to her, I'm sure. Kept her entertained, playing cards and board games? Oh, and I hear you each had a few early nights,' mocked Robert, 'with nothing but a book for company.'

'You bloody idiot,' Joel growled. 'She'd never let you down.'

'Oh, she might. You've always had a way with women, Joel.'

'I'm no seducer!'

'You're a healthy man, and she's a big temptation, isn't she? Must be hard for you without Pauline.'

'Yes,' spat Joel, 'that's true, it's hard, but I've never tried anything on with Jess.'

'Saintly of you,' Robert said. He was staring keenly into Joel's eyes and trying to read him. He had seen something there, a softening, a momentary wistful light when he had spoken of Jess as a big temptation. 'Because you do want her, don't you, Joel?' he whispered, fiercely. 'I saw it just then. It was plain on your face. You can't hide something like that from me.'

He saw his brother swallow hard.

'I haven't laid a hand on Jess,' hissed Joel. 'Try not to be a bigger fool than God made you. She's loyal to you, Robert, but the way you act, you don't deserve it. Nobody could blame her if she did turn elsewhere. And as for pumping the child that way – do you think he doesn't understand that there's something nasty behind it? He's bright, he's sensitive, and he's not to be used as a spy!'

'I'm tired of hearing you tell me how to treat my son! Do you covet him as well, Joel? I often have the feeling that you do. Would you like to win him away from me?'

Joel's gaze became a little pitying and then he shook his head. 'I've never tried to take anything from you, Rob, not when we were children or at any time since. But you were always very good at losing, breaking and spoiling what you had. And brother, you're on course to do it again.'

· Twenty-eight ·

On the first Tuesday after the thaw, Joel took a horse and rode over to Liddy's Farm. He went without his brother's knowledge of what he meant to do. No longer willing to indulge him over Maunder, he did not care in the slightest how Robert would take it.

The ground was hard with frost, and stubborn patches of snow still clung to the hills and lay by the roadside. He cantered up over the rise above the hollow and saw the roof of Liddy's Farm below. A wisp of smoke trailed out of one chimney, but nothing else moved. The mare trotted on, down the slope and through the gate into the yard. Joel looked around him with contempt. A better man would have made the place a bit decent, repaired it, cleaned it up. The squalor of his dwelling said much about Alec Maunder. It was, after all, his own property, and he was young and fit.

Joel tethered the horse to the rusty gate, went up to the door and thumped upon it, hard. He had to rap again twice before Maunder answered. He came to the door half-dressed, and Joel correctly assumed he had woken him up. It was twenty past eleven. The hairy face blinked dazedly out, peered first to one side of him, then to the other and enquired:

'What's up, then? What you doing here? I haven't had my breakfast yet. I can't come down your place today ...'

'You don't have to,' said Joel, gruffly, 'not this day or any other. That's what I'm here about.'

'Eh?'

Lawrenson shoved the door back and stalked inside. The stench of dry rot was overwhelming. Beetles and spiders fled away into dark corners as he tramped down the passage.

'Best go in the kitchen,' Maunder said. 'It's where I live.'

Passing the parlour, Joel saw that a huge flap of plaster hung from the ceiling, ready to fall at any time. The room was crammed with Maunder's rubbish – decaying newspapers, empty tins and jars and cardboard boxes. He used it as a dustbin.

The kitchen had a different smell. Cooking fat and cabbage. Boiled turnip and cold, congealed gravy. A rotten, greasy odour, it went down Joel's throat and made his stomach lurch. The room was warm – too hot if the truth were told – but Maunder seemed to like the heat, for his bed lay alongside the stove. It sagged in the middle and the blankets were moth-eaten.

Turning to face him, Joel said, 'I'll come straight to the point. I'm here to do what I've wanted to do for a long time. As of now, your job with us is finished.'

'Eh?' said Maunder, again.

'You heard.'

'Are you saying I'm not needed any more?'

'I'm saying you're not wanted, and that's a different thing.'

'You're saying,' repeated Maunder, indignantly. 'But what about your brother, eh?'

'We'll both be glad to see the back of you.'

Maunder slumped down at the table, glowering at him. Joel stood in the middle of the room. He was the only clean thing in it, and looked out of place with his neat, plain coat and brown tweed cap. Sullenly, Maunder dug some dirt from under one fingernail, using another. He pondered briefly, then he sneered, 'I'll wager Robert knows nothing of this. That's why you've come up here to tell me.'

'Would you rather I fired you in front of the other men?'

'Oh, you're not trying to spare my dignity, don't give me that. You're doing this behind his back, that's what it is. Because he likes me, Robert does. He knows I'm a good worker, and he won't thank you for this. I'll be seeing him about it, mark my words. I'll be down tomorrow and we'll hear what he has to say.'

'Likes you? Robert despises you as much as I do. You know that and you know why. There's only one difference between us where you're concerned. He's afraid of your nasty mouth, but I'm not.'

'Ah.' Maunder sat back in his chair and his look was calculating. 'How long have you known about that, then?' he asked, at length.

'Not long. It explains a lot.'

'Jess confided in you, did she? I can't see Robert telling you.' A grin, a snigger. 'He wanted that kept very quiet.'

'So do I,' said Joel. 'For her sake, no one else's.'

'Why should you care so much about her?' Maunder gave a titter. 'Perhaps you've a hankering for her, Joel? Is it mutual, then? Is that why she told you her secret, I wonder? I take it you don't mind what her mother is? No, you're not the sort to care. Now Robert, he's like some prissy old matron, scared of what people will say ...'

In a movement that was purposeful but calm, Joel took one stride forward and seized him by his braces and his filthy flannel combinations, lifting him clean out of his chair and slamming him up against the kitchen dresser. The crockery rattled and crashed. Joel balled one hand into a fist and pushed it under the squirming man's nose.

'Watch your tongue, Alec.' His voice was strangely soft and all the more frightening for it. 'Now then, understand this. You are dismissed from our employ. Your face is not to be seen henceforth on any Lawrenson property. You will never work at our place again, because I will not allow it. I will physically throw you off the premises, so there's no point appealing to my brother. All clear so far?'

Maunder indicated that it was.

'As to the other matter, if I should develop the slightest suspicion that you've been shooting your mouth off, if I hear so much as a whisper or a hint about Alice Davey, I'll know the source of it and I'll be up here after you.' His eyes were very close to Maunder's, grey and glittering. 'By the time I've finished, you'll need a dozen splints and a pair of crutches.'

'All right, all right! I didn't say I was going to blab!'

'Good, then see that you don't.'

Slowly, Joel released him. Quick and shallow, Maunder's breath came out in little panicky puffs. He was pale with fright and his Adam's apple kept bobbing. Shorter by a head than the dark man standing over him, round-shouldered by comparison, he had never looked more like the runt he was.

His point effectively made, Joel turned away and crossed to the door. He was stopped on the threshold, however, by a question.

'She asked you to do this, didn't she?'

Joel looked at him over his shoulder. Maunder was shaking still, but an ugly scowl had come to his face.

'I've always wanted to sack you, and you know it.'

'But you didn't do it – till now. This is to please her, isn't it? You don't care any more how your brother feels about it. Jess is the important one and you don't mind falling out with him as long as you make her happy.'

'Don't provoke me any further, Alec.'

Maunder had the sense to drop the subject. But then, as Joel was leaving, he astounded him with a final piece of cheek.

'How about ten bob in lieu of notice? You owe me that.'

He had followed Lawrenson to the front door. Joel stared at him in disbelief.

'When hell freezes,' he said.

'Six?' revised Maunder.

Joel almost admired his effrontery, but his face did not betray it. Shaking his head, he crossed the frozen mud-ruts of the yard and untethered the mare.

'Four,' called Maunder piteously. 'Have a heart! My old rooster died last week.'

Lawrenson set off. Maunder mouthed the foulest words he knew. Then he spat copiously on the ground, went inside and slammed the door with all his might. Another piece of guttering fell from the eaves.

Not until he had covered a couple of miles did Joel start to laugh. Great roars of it came rolling up from his belly and echoed round the bitter, stony hills. A gentle man at heart, he was amazed at the violence of his threats. He had felt like an actor playing a very strange role, but he fancied he had done it well.

The atmosphere at Torvallen did not improve thereafter, and the rancour between the brothers was felt at the timber yard, too. A feud was going on, and it was far from pleasant for the men.

'I've never known him as bad as this,' said Charlie Weekes, one morning.

'Can't speak to him nowadays without being cursed at.'

'Sore as a boil. Hardly a civil word for anybody.'

'Least of all his brother.'

'And that's the root of it, as ever.'

In the corner, heads together, Charlie, Eddie and Peter were eyeing Robert Lawrenson and frowning. They had always been slightly wary of him, never completely relaxed in his presence the way they were with Joel. However, he had lately grown so critical and surly that they all kept out of his way and said not a word to him if they could help it.

Down at the farmost end of the sawmill, Robert was working alone, feeding logs to the circular saw, splitting them down for planking. His back was turned to the men and the screech of the machinery was loud in his ears.

'I know what's biting him – Joel firing Alec like he did. Hell of a row they had over that.' Charlie nodded and pursed his mouth, thinking himself astute.

Chivers pulled a doubtful face. 'That was nearly a month ago. He must be over that by now.'

'Tell you what I think,' Eddie said. 'I reckon it's something to do with her.'

Charlie goggled at him. 'Who, Missis, you mean?'

'What are you saying?' demanded Peter.

'Well, snowed in together, weren't they, she and Joel? Nearly a week. And old Robert there stuck in Plymouth all that time.'

Chivers was indignant. 'She's not that type.'

'Joel's a good-looking man,' said Eddie, slyly.

'And you're a smutty one.'

'I know a bit about human nature,' countered Eddie. 'Just consider it, Peter. There she is, living in that house with those two brothers. Now, most of the time old Robert's about and there's not much opportunity for mischief. Then along comes a handy blizzard, shuts them in together and shuts the husband out.' He pushed his tongue in his cheek, a merry twinkle lighting his eyes.

Weekes did not like what he heard. 'Aw, no, she's a nice little maid. I don't care to think that of her.'

'Think it,' repeated Peter. 'I expect that's all there is to it. Pierce, you've a dirty mind.'

'So has Robert, then,' said Eddie, unabashed. 'Ten to one, it's all about her.'

'Mph! Well, he always was a suspicious man, half the time with no good cause.'

'Half the time,' agreed Eddie. 'That makes him right the other half. Who's to know what went on in that house while the snow was piling up outside? If it was my wife and brother, I'd wonder too.'

'Well, there's no love lost between you and your wife, is there?' Peter pointed out. 'I'd give mine the benefit of the doubt.'

'Course you would, being the easygoing soul you are. But Robert's not like you. And let's be honest, we all prefer to work with Joel when we can. Perhaps she's grown to prefer him, too.'

'You're making something out of nothing. I daresay they've fallen out over the business again. Might be he's worried. Perhaps the profits were poor last year – and who's to say what debts they've got? Wouldn't tell us, would they?'

'Aw, tripe! Robert paid cash for that new lorry. The order book is full. I don't believe they're in any trouble.'

The argument was cut off short as the whine of the saw abruptly ceased. His task completed, Robert looked around, spotted his three employees idling and sharply ordered them to various chores.

'Don't, for God's sake, talk any more about this,' Chivers growled, as he moved away from the other two. 'Robert'll have a fit if he learns what you've been saying, Pierce. If the notion's not already in his mind, then you might put it there. Just keep off the subject, both of you – especially in front of your wives.'

'Aw, yes, yes,' said Charlie, 'we're not stupid.'

Charitable Peter did not answer that. Trust Eddie Pierce, he reflected, to think up such a thing and voice it to Weekes and his runaway tongue. He feared it was too much to hope that Charlie could keep quiet, and he was right, though it was not the womenfolk who came to hear of it.

Alec Maunder did not care for Princetown, chiefly because of the gaol. A giant with radiating arms of cell blocks, it dwarfed everything around it, looming dismally above the little cottages. Maunder knew what prisons were like on the inside, and the sight of the place aroused bad memories. All the same, he had to buy supplies from somewhere, and Princetown was the nearest community to hand.

One Saturday morning he called in at the grocer's, and there he came across Charlie Weekes.

'Hello, Alec!'

'Charlie,' came the grunt.

'Found another job yet?'

'No.'

'Aw, I'm sorry to hear that.'

'Mph,' said Maunder, sourly.

'Like to go before me?' offered Charlie. 'Don't suppose you're buying much?'

'Can't afford it, can I?'

'Being a single man, I meant.'

Another grunt. Maunder turned to the grocer and asked for bread, a pound of tea and a slab of cheese.

'I thought Robert might stand up for me,' he said. 'He was the one who hired me, after all. Joel always wanted me out, I know that. Time was, though, when Robert used to take my part and go against him.'

'Perhaps it wasn't personal, Alec. They haven't replaced you with anyone else. I suppose they didn't need you any more.'

'Hah! Fat lot you know,' sneered Maunder. 'I know exactly why Joel fired me. Oh, I could tell you a thing or two about the Lawrensons – especially her.'

He could have, but he was not going to. Cryptic hints like that were all he dared. He had not forgotten Joel's threat.

Charlie, however, thought he knew what was meant.

'Oh,' he said, 'there's talk about that already.'

'What?'

'Rumours going round at the yard,' explained Weekes.

Maunder paused to pay the grocer for his goods. Then Charlie handed over his list and the man went looking for a carton big enough to hold the order.

Maunder dropped his voice. 'There's talk, you say?'

'Yes, yes, but I don't like to believe it, Alec. Eddie, it was, who started it, putting two and two together and making five.'

'How do you mean?' Maunder's forehead knitted. He had thought only he knew about Alice Davey.

'Well, saying Jess and Joel might be carrying on together, because Robert turned so nasty with his brother after that big fall of snow we had. See, they were in the house for days, while Robert was in town ...'

'Ah.' Maunder smiled as he listened. He had not known that, but it fitted his theory concerning Jess and Joel. 'Yes,' he nodded, 'oh yes, that was just before Joel sacked me.'

'Think there's something in it, do you?' Weekes asked, sadly. 'I've always liked all three of them, even if Robert is a bit snappy sometimes. I hate to see them at each other's throats.'

'I'm saying nothing, Charlie. I've never opened my mouth, despite the things I know, and I don't intend to start gabbing now, even though I was dismissed for no good reason. I'm not a vengeful man and I can hold my tongue. Not that it would make much difference now, with Eddie sounding off.'

Charlie received the message loud and clear, that Eddie was right.

'One thing I will tell you,' Maunder whispered. 'Joel sacked me mainly to please her.'

'Oh,' breathed Charlie. 'Now, I never guessed at that. But why ... ?'

'That's all I'm saying. I don't believe in raking up muck for spite. I'm only pointing out that I didn't deserve to be fired.'

The grocer returned from the store room with a carton, and so the conversation ended there. Alec Maunder took his leave of Charlie and stepped out into the spring sunshine with a smile lurking under his beard.

'Insidious', Jess had called him.

Maunder considered it one of his finer skills.

· Twenty-nine ·

July 29th, 1928, was Alice Davey's forty-sixth birthday, the second she had passed since Mr Honey moved in. He had made it his business to find out the date, and in the previous year had given her a musical box inlaid with mother-of-pearl. This year he had bought her what she wanted most of all.

He took her breakfast in bed that morning – tea, with

scrambled egg on toast, and a small dish of junket. Beside her plate lay a single red rose and a little jeweller's box.

It contained an engagement ring.

'I think it's time, don't you?' he whispered, sitting down on the edge of the bed as she opened it. 'After all, I've been here eighteen months.'

Alice was beside herself. 'Kenneth! Oh, how lovely! Oh, it's beautiful! When shall we ... ? I mean, how long shall we wait ... ?'

'That's up to you.'

'Not long, then. Just time enough for me to make a special frock.'

'All right. Engagements are really for youngsters, aren't they, not mature people like us?'

'Who've been living as man and wife in any case for over a year,' agreed Alice, quickly.

She tried on the ring, a band of three little diamonds. It fitted quite well. She held her hand away, admiring the stones, then flung her arms around Kenneth Honey's neck. He was very chubby and silky in his satin dressing gown.

'I'm so happy,' Alice told him, softly. 'Oh, I can't believe my luck, to have found someone like you.'

'It was my good fortune too.' After a short pause, he added, 'I knew you were lonely as soon as I met you. I could tell how sad you were, though of course I didn't know why, not then. What a rotten time you've had, Alice.'

She drew back a little. 'Yes,' she said, slowly, 'you've heard about me? You must have by now.'

'Hmm.' He smiled. 'Your neighbours made sure of that.'

'And you still want to marry me?'

'Alice, dear, I speak as I find, and I find you very lovable.' Just for a moment, a cloud crossed his face. 'Anyway, I've no right to judge. I have my weaknesses, too. When one has an affectionate soul, it's hard to be what the world calls well-behaved. I understand, Alice, believe me, I do.'

'Mrs Honey,' she murmured. 'Alice Honey. I shall feel reborn! Well, I already do, I have for a long time, but when

I have a new name, your name, then I'll feel completely transformed.'

'You don't mean respectable, do you?' he chaffed.

'Not exactly ... All right, perhaps a bit.'

'The very idea! We'll never be like them, Alice.' He waved an arm towards the window and the gesture embraced all the smug and self-righteous everywhere. 'Good thing, too!' he ended, merrily. 'That sort don't know how to enjoy life, really enjoy it to the hilt. They're too busy being proper or dutiful, and all too often their chief pleasure lies in sneering at those who aren't. You simply mustn't take any notice of them, Alice.'

'It's easy not to, now that I have you. When I was alone I was so afraid of them.' She picked up her knife and fork and started on her scrambled eggs. 'Kenneth,' she said, 'I've always wondered – did you truly look for other lodgings, or did you decide from the start that you wanted to stay with me?'

'After that first night I spent here ...' Sheepishly, he smiled. 'Well, I did make efforts to find somewhere else, but they were a bit half-hearted. I had a feeling about you, Alice, I guessed we were congenial spirits. And we've proved it, haven't we? I'm certain enough of that to make it official, now.'

'Jess will be so pleased,' said Alice. 'And Colin will have a grandad, too! I can't wait to tell them.'

Mr Honey had a bright idea. 'Isn't there a fun-fair coming to town next week? Why don't we take them both for a treat, and break the news that day?'

'Yes!' said Alice. 'Yes, why not? Let's make a lovely outing of it. I feel as if I'm on a merry-go-round already. You know, light-headed, things hardly seem real. We're going to be married! Oh, I'm so thrilled!'

It was a very big fair with every sort of ride and side-show. There were gondolas, red plush inside with shiny brass handles, swingboats brightly painted with patterns and flowers, a huge ferris wheel, a quivering cake-walk, prancing gilded hobby-horses, coconut shies and lucky numbers games, stalls selling hot meat pies and pasties, or jars of cockles and winkles. Everything was in whirling motion, the big wheel sedately turning, the chairoplanes whizzing their screaming occupants round in giddy circles, the merry-go-rounds revolving gently. The air was filled with the thumping, boisterous sound of a great fairground organ. A spectacle in itself, displaying banks of shining, silvery pipes flanked by little mechanical figures in regency dress, it pumped out favourites old and new, like 'Champagne Charlie', 'I'm forever blowing bubbles', and 'Daisy, Daisy, give me your answer, do.'

'Well?' asked Jess. 'What do you want to do next?'

Colin gazed around him, racked by indecision. He longed to go on the ferris wheel, but Jess said he was too small for that. Clutched beneath one arm was a big bouncy ball, striped red, white and green. In his other hand he held a half-demolished toffee-apple. Alice had won the ball at the hoop-la stand.

'Shall I take him down the helter-skelter?' asked Mr Honey. 'Don't worry, I'll hold on to him.'

'Go on, then,' said Jess. Colin passed her the ball and the toffee-apple, and went off hand in hand with the man he already called 'Gramps'.

'Kenneth's good with children, isn't he?' beamed Alice. 'Isn't it wonderful, Jess? Just think, this time next month we'll be on our honeymoon. Scotland – imagine that! I've never seen mountains before. I wouldn't have thought of making such a trip, but Kenneth's always full of these lovely ideas.'

She was almost girlish in her excitement, and youthfully dressed in a mauve cotton frock, plus a straw hat with a turned-back brim and a perky little posy of violets on one side. Beside her, Jess seemed the more mature, her clothing more plain and her manner more subdued. She was pleased – delighted – by Alice's news. But her mother's happiness and hopeful prospects made painful contrast with her own declining situation.

'Yes, that'll be an adventure, sure enough.' The words came with a smile, but a hint of strain showed through and Alice saw it.

'You do approve, don't you, Jess?' Her buoyancy ebbed just a little. 'You think I'm doing the right thing?'

'Lord, yes! He's made a new woman of you.'

'I fancied for a moment there was something troubling you.'

'Nothing to do with you and Kenneth, Mam. You have my blessing.'

Jess lifted her hand to wave as Colin and Mr Honey came shooting to the bottom of the slide on a rush mat. They tumbled off the end, picked themselves up and came over, both pink with the thrill of it all.

'What now?' puffed Kenneth. 'You haven't tried that one over there.' He pointed out a merry-go-round with model cars and boats and aeroplanes to sit in. 'Want a go? All right, then. Look, it's stopping. Are you going to drive a car or fly a plane?'

Colin decided to be a pilot. He scuttled across and jumped into the rear cockpit of a biplane, while 'Gramps' climbed into the front. The merry-go-round moved slowly off and soon it was cruising at a pleasant pace.

'I suspect your fiancé's a bit of a child himself,' observed Jess.

'Aren't they all?' said Alice, cheerfully. 'Mind you, there's childlike and there's childish. The one is endearing, the other is anything but.'

You don't have to tell me, thought Jess.

'Colin's having a lovely time,' said Alice, as the flying ace went gliding by. 'Never argues, does he, when you say no to him? Never throws a tantrum like some of them. You've raised him well, Jess. I used to be afraid that Robert would spoil him, but he's turning out a good child.'

'Robert doesn't – dote on him – the way he used to.'

Alice turned to look at her. Jess's profile was solemn as she watched the merry-go-round.

'Or me, either,' she added, quietly. 'I'm afraid I fell from favour quite some time ago.'

'Oh – my dear.' All gaiety drained from Alice's face and tone. 'I hadn't realised, Jess. You've never said much – I'd assumed all was well. Do you mean to say things have gone sour between you and Robert? Oh Jess, is it because of me?'

'You're a part of it, Mam, but only a part. It's more to do with the way he is. And the way he feels about his brother. He may have had an unpleasant surprise when he finally heard about you, but I've learned just as much about him that I don't like.'

'What does Joel have to do with it?'

'He's a widower, now, and there we all are at Torvallen together. Robert has a busy imagination.'

'Dear Lord!' exclaimed Alice. 'Oh, Jess, my poor love!' Her voice acquired an angry edge. 'Is Robert treating you badly, my dear? If he's ill-using you ...'

'You know I wouldn't tolerate that, and I'll give him his due, he isn't cruel in that way. But he's cold, very cold these days. Even in bed I know he's just serving his needs and taking his rights. There's no affection there at all. Oh, he can't prove anything, because there's nothing to prove. He can't call me an adultress in so many words, but that's what's in his mind, I'm sure.' A helpless, desperate look came into her eyes, so very untypical of Jess that Alice felt her throat tighten. 'What can I do, Mam? Walk out on him? Come back to the shop? What about my boy? I couldn't leave him behind at Torvallen – or raise him in that beastly street! What can I do, except endure it? Yet the atmosphere's becoming worse and worse out there. Rob and Joel own everything in common – the house, the business, all of it. We're all tied together like three angry cats in a sack, and I can't see any good way out of it.'

The merry-go-round was slowing down and the child was scrambling out of his aeroplane. Alice could offer no comfort or advice. She simply stroked Jess's face, while her own was abject with guilt and dismay. Here she was, revelling in good fortune, when she had helped to blight her daughter's life. Jess could say what she liked about Robert, but Alice still felt largely to blame.

'I wouldn't have believed it, Mam. I didn't dream when I married him that things could ever turn out like this. Robert was my rescuer, that was what I thought. I should have known it was all too good to be true.'

Colin came running up to them, arms outstretched like wings.

'Enjoy it?' Jess managed to smile. 'Like a pasty now, and a bottle of lemonade, before we go home?'

They joined the queue at a food stall, and Colin devoured the remains of his toffee-apple while they waited. The booth was not far from the foot of the ferris wheel, and anyone riding on it had a perfect view of those who were standing in line for drinks and snacks.

It was, in truth, a pity that they had not chosen another stall. Unhappily for Kenneth Honey, Nemesis was at the fair that day, while Alice, so perturbed by Jess's troubles, was about to receive a blow to make her forget them.

A compartment containing two women came down from the top of the wheel. It glided past the queue, backwards underneath the wheel, then up again. One of the women, spotting Mr Honey, jabbed her companion in the ribs and pointed, open-mouthed. Her friend, a dark, rosy person of perhaps forty, peered down through the girders and struts of the wheel, craning her neck to see. They were already halfway to the top again, and nothing could be seen of the queue below them except a row of hats.

But in no time they were coming down again. The first woman picked out Alice, then drew the other's attention to the man in the boater who stood beside her. The dark lady took a good, hard look as the wheel brought her level with him. Then rage suffused her face and a shriek broke out.

'Charlie! Charlie! You little worm!'

The cry was lost in the noise of the fair – shouting children, rumbling machinery, the strains of the big pipe organ as it played 'Little Brown Jug'. The wheel carried the women back and up again. They were gabbling furiously and when it brought them down once more, the dark one stood up in the carriage, yelling and shaking her fist in Mr Honey's direction. She nearly fell out and her friend hastily pulled her back into her seat.

'Stop the wheel!' she screamed to the attendant, who paid her no attention.

Unaware of all this, Alice and company came to the head of the queue. Mr Honey bought pasties all round, with bottles of fizz to wash them down.

'Let us out!' screeched the women, approaching the ground yet again.

The youth in charge of the wheel bestirred himself and gazed stupidly round.

'Eh?' he said.

Too late. They sailed past him and were borne aloft. The dark lady clenched her teeth and fists in frustration as she saw Kenneth Honey and his friends moving away from the food stall and into the crowd. She had to go around twice more before the attendant finally stopped the wheel.

Erupting from the carriage, the two women tore off in what they thought was the right direction. But Mr Honey could not be found. He and his party had gone straight back to the car and driven off. After searching for fifteen minutes among the throngs of people, the two women gave up, breathless and overwrought.

'It was him, wasn't it?' panted the first.

'No doubt about it,' confirmed the other. 'I'd know him anywhere, the little swine.'

'What are we going to do, then? Spend the rest of your holiday trying to find him?'

'Let's hope,' came the grim reply, 'that the law can do it for us.'

It took them less than forty-eight hours. On the Saturday morning, two constables walked into Alice Davey's shop, bid her a solemn 'Good morning, Madam', and asked:

'Is this the abode of a Mr Kenneth Honey?'

'Why, yes.' Alice stared from one to the other. 'It is.'

'And is he in?'

Bewildered, Alice nodded. 'Is anything wrong?'

'Would you ask him to come downstairs, please, Madam?'

'What's this about?'

'Immediately, please.'

'I just want to know ...'

'You shall, Mrs Davey, all in good time.'

Nervously, Alice began to wring her hands. The younger policeman's glance lit on the engagement ring she wore, then lifted to meet her eyes. Alice saw something frightening in his look – pity.

'I must ask you again to fetch him, Mrs Davey. If you don't call him down, we'll have to go up.'

Slowly, with many a backward glance at the constables, Alice went to the foot of the stairs.

'Kenneth? Come here a moment, will you?'

Unsuspecting, he appeared, bouncing down the staircase full of smiles. Alice saw his face fall at the sight of the police.

'These men ...' She clutched his arm and her voice was very low. '... they want to talk to you. Kenneth, what's the matter?'

He obviously knew what they had come for. Patting her hand, he gazed for a moment at the ring, then whispered, 'Oh, Alice! I ... Oh God, I should have known better.'

'Charles Kenneth Mead,' pronounced the older constable.

Alice's head jerked up. She opened her mouth to ask a question of Mr Honey, then closed it again. He did not deny the name. He did not seem in the least surprised. Forlorn, resigned, he simply looked at the officer and listened while he went on:

'... I'm arresting you, sir, on a charge of bigamy. We have a lady complainant down at the station now. She has given us a full statement.'

'No!' The sound was laden with disbelief. Alice started to babble. 'It's a mistake! It has to be! You wouldn't do anything like that, would you, Kenneth? The woman's lying. Perhaps she's deranged. Your wife died. You told me she died, ten years ago.'

'I'm sorry, Mrs Davey,' interrupted the younger constable, 'but we have also secured reports on this man from our branches in Bournemouth, Blackpool and Aberystwyth. It's quite a hobby with him, marrying his landladies.'

There was a long and terrible silence. Then:

'Alice, I'm afraid I've wronged you dreadfully.' Mr Honey's voice shook and his eyes were as anguished as hers. 'The officer makes me sound very callous and shallow. It has never been like that, but it's no use denying that I've been very foolish, very irresponsible. I – I can't help it, Alice. You see ...'

He broke off and begged of the constables, 'Might I have a few minutes alone with her before we go? I can't leave her like this, without explaining. Could we go in the store room, do you think?'

The men exchanged looks. Then the older one went to inspect the store room in case it had a back door.

'All right,' he said, emerging, 'there's no way out of there.'

The couple went inside and closed the door. Alice faced him, trembling. Her world was suddenly rocking like a logan stone.

'Are you saying it's true?' she breathed.

He gazed pathetically at her, a sinner utterly contrite. In her panic and horror, Alice was hard-pressed not to hit him.

'Kenneth, answer me!'

'I meant to stay with you, Alice, truly I did.'

A whimper came up from her throat.

Tears filled Mr Honey's eyes and trickled down his cheeks. 'But then, I meant to stay with the others, too.'

She saw her bright future receding, like a light going down a well.

'I do love you, Alice. I loved them all, at least at the start. That's the trouble, really. I just adore ladies, especially those who cook for me, look after me. In a way, you see,

I'm very much like you. I can't resist a nice woman, any more than you could resist men when you were young. That was why I understood about your past, why I couldn't condemn you, Alice. I'm the same. The only difference is that I'm apt to get carried away and marry my ladies.'

Everything was over, cancelled. Numbly, Alice stared at him.

'How many?' she croaked.

'You would have been the fifth.'

'And the other four are still alive?' Her voice went up to a squeak. 'You're not a widower at all?'

'Yes, yes. My first wife did die. But I've married three others since. My second wife, Myrtle, turned out far less sweet than I'd imagined. A harpy, to be blunt. I fled from her, I simply packed my bags and ran. To Aberystwyth, where I took lodgings with a lovely Welsh girl, and ...'

He hung his head.

'She became number three. And why, pray, did you abandon her?'

'Myrtle found me. I only just escaped in time.'

'To?'

'Bournemouth.' He blinked miserably. 'Where I met Sophie. She was lovely, at first, very gentle, very agreeable, but after we married she started nagging me to give up my music and find a more well-paid job. Something in an office – insurance, for instance. She wanted me to be a manager. I stood it for four months, then I left her.'

'Is that where you'd come from when you arrived here?'

A mumbled, 'Yes.'

'You told me Buckinghamshire.'

'That was where I was born and raised.'

'I see,' said Alice, dully. 'Well, well. I wonder which one it is down at the police station.'

He shrugged helplessly. 'Alice,' he ventured, 'you're the dearest of them all. I want to settle down, you know. I'm not a Casanova. I've just made rather a mess of things. You see, I had no real grounds for divorcing Myrtle, nothing acceptable to a court. So I just ignored the formalities and pretended she didn't exist. Then, once I'd married Bronwen, I knew I'd burnt my boats and I just went on and waded deeper into trouble.'

Alice started sobbing uncontrollably. 'How could you? Kenneth, how could you? You built my hopes so high. It's wicked, wicked! You must have known it couldn't succeed, that sooner or later you'd be found. You knew you were going to put me through this – after all I'd endured already!'

'No, no, I'm an optimist, Alice. I thought there was a chance that we'd be left in peace. Forgive me, my dear, for being so reckless and badly mistaken, but don't accuse me of deliberate cruelty. I wanted us both to be happy and so I took a risk.'

'With my feelings!' stormed Alice. 'Damn you, what will I do now? What will it be like when you're ... ?' She gasped at the realisation of what this would probably mean for him. '... locked away,' she ended, appalled.

Her mind's eye saw him in prison garb, shut up in a gloomy cell, eating tasteless food off a tin plate. Like a brilliant humming bird plucked of its feathers, confined to a cage. It would surely destroy the joyous spirit she had loved so much in him.

'Would they do that, Kenneth? Would they?' she whispered.

'I'm very much afraid they will.'

'How long?' asked Alice, faintly.

'Up to seven years, I believe.' He blanched at the thought. 'I don't know if that means seven years for each wife.'

'Oh, merciful God! My poor love!' Alice threw her arms around him. 'You mustn't tell them you were going to marry me! They'll add it to the charges! I'll swear it isn't so. No one else knows except Jess and the family.'

'I don't expect you to lie for me, Alice. I don't know how you can, after what I've done.'

'Once a fool, always a fool,' she sighed.

He had used a number of names, she later learned. Christened Charles Kenneth Mead, he was known by his Welsh wife as Charles Jolly, and by Sophie in Bournemouth as Kenneth William Sweet. In the past seven years he had worked in many theatres in various seaside towns, and thus the police had found him, through the Alhambra. It was indeed the fearsome Myrtle who had spotted him from the ferris wheel. Spending a fortnight with a cousin in Torquay, she had come to Plymouth that day especially for the fair.

Alice encountered her at the police station and hated her on sight. A pretty but waspish woman, she heaped abuse on Mr Honey as he was hustled past her and down to the cells. Such was her disposition that even the constables felt sorry for him.

A statement was taken from Alice, and now she flatly denied that Kenneth had ever proposed to her. The ring, she maintained, was from her first marriage. A bald lie and everyone knew it, but the officers did not make an issue of it. They were sorry for her, as well. In any case, they had evidence a-plenty to convict him. Myrtle was out for blood, and so, it transpired, was Sophie. They did not need any help from Alice Davey.

The case was tried at Exeter three months later, and Mr Honey was given a six-year sentence. It could have been a good deal worse, but the judge was favourably impressed by the pleasant little man in the dock, while the vengeful Myrtle and Sophie riled him from start to finish.

Charles Kenneth Mead was taken to London to serve his time. Alice went up to visit him once, and found herself face to face with Bronwen, down from Aberystwyth for the same purpose. It was all very embarrassing and depressing. Alice decided she would not go again. She returned to the shop and the taunts of her neighbours, who had read the account of the trial in the *Western Morning News*, and she started to drink as she had never drunk before.

· Thirty ·

When Alec Maunder drank too much, his behaviour was apt to take a reckless turn. One September day he made an early call at a pub in Princetown, where he sold a couple of rabbits to the landlord's wife. He stayed to drink away the money she paid him. When every penny had gone, he tried for credit.

'I'll have another.'

'Where's the money?'

'Put it on the slate.'

'For you? Think I'm simple? Pay now, or you get no more.'

Alec Maunder glowered at the landlord. His thirst was far from satisfied, but the publican was tough and not a man with whom to argue. He had once been a warder up at the gaol. Maunder's eyes were bloodshot after nine pints of beer. He wiped his mouth with the back of his hand and muttered something insulting, but not quite loudly enough for the landlord to hear, contenting himself instead with a lingering dirty look.

'Go on, get out of it.' The publican flicked his cloth at him, as if he were shooing off an insect, then snatched his empty glass off the counter and plunged it into the sink. Everybody knew that 'he from Liddy's Farm' never paid his debts.

Maunder saw the other customers watching. Some were grinning. Not one of them was going to stand him a drink. He sneered at them, then shambled outside and slammed the door behind him.

For a moment he stood in the middle of the road, looking this way and that, as if unsure which direction to take. His indecision did not last long. The only place he had to go was home.

Life was very austere again. He missed the money from his job, missed it very badly. In over three years with the Lawrensons, he had saved only thirty pounds, which had already dribbled away. No one else had offered him work. The truth of it was that no one liked him enough, but Maunder was more inclined to believe that the Lawrensons had given him a bad name.

In ugly mood, he tramped down the road. The acres of moorland fern had begun to wither, changing from brightest green to reddish-brown. Maunder kicked at a stone which lay in his path, booting it several yards. He followed and kicked it again and again, harder each time as his temper grew worse.

Of course, it was all on account of Jess. Joel had sacked him – for her. Threatened him with violence – for her. To please a woman whose mother was nothing short of a whore, to protect a sister-in-law with whom he had taken to fornicating.

'Hah!' A bark of laughter came from Maunder's throat. 'No better than me, any of them. Might have a bit of money between them, but that's all. Nice house, timber business, tobacco shop. Still, nothing so very grand. As for morals ... Hah!' he exclaimed again.

As he weaved along he consoled himself with a fantasy of burning down the sawmill one dark night. Gleefully picturing the blaze, he could almost hear the roar and smell the smoke. He could see the machinery melting and buckling inside, the flames shooting higher than the trees ...

His nasty little day-dream was dispelled by the sound of a motor vehicle coming up behind him. Maunder stopped and turned around, and saw the baker's van. He put up a hand in hopes of a ride and for once he was lucky. The driver took him three miles down the road and let him out at a fork not far from Torvallen. Maunder slurred his thanks and lurched on his way. This was not a route he would normally take, but today he had drunk enough to over-ride his usual caution and make him daring. Today he was going home through the woods that surrounded the Lawrenson place.

Autumn had brought a bumper crop of blackberries that year, fat and glossy, as big as marbles. And in a certain clearing in the woods there grew a vast clump of bramble, higher than a tall man's head. Casting monstrous, thorny runners in all directions, it was always laden with fruit from late summer onwards, and provided the Lawrenson family with many a pie and pot of jam.

Jess was there that morning, picking berries. Clad in a pullover, boots and trousers, she had come with her basket to take the first of the newly-ripened fruit. Colin had recently started at the infants' school in Princetown, and so she was free until four o'clock. Now it was just before twelve. For twenty minutes she had worked her way around the giant bush, stripping off the largest of the soft, sweet berries. Clusters of tiny green ones and others turning to red hung ready to take their place. Jess had scratched her hands once or twice, reaching into the prickly depths, and she drew her breath in sharply as blood was drawn again from the ball of her thumb.

The thumb went into her mouth to be soothed, and that was when she first became aware of something – watchful – in the quiet of the day.

The air was still, and the only sound was the humming of insects around the bramble. Two-thirds full, her basket lay nearby. She had just brought down a handful of berries from a sturdy runner above her head, but she did not drop them in with the others. For long, uneasy moments they stayed in her hand, forgotten. Something had distracted her – that old, unnerving sense of being observed.

Turning slowly, she looked around her. It was a large clearing, forty or fifty yards across, and the trees clustered thickly round its edge. Deep shadow lay beneath their lower branches, and not a whisper of wind disturbed the leaves. The bramble patch was close to them at one point, but it was not these nearby trees that seemed to conceal a presence. Her eyes had fixed on the belt of beeches at the far side of the clearing. Once or twice she scanned the woods full circle, but always her gaze returned to one place, the darkness under the beeches. Sunlight fell on the open ground, and on the upper canopies, but underneath were tunnels of gloom plunging into the woods. She stared for a long time at a certain spot and there grew in her the frightening feeling that someone was staring back, someone just out of sight.

Liquid was trickling through her fingers. Jess looked down, opened her hand and saw that she had crushed the blackberries to a pulp. Around her was still the drowsy buzz of wasps and flies. For a while she had cut out the sound, listening for she knew not what, but now she was conscious again of droning insects, and their busy movements seemed to counteract a spell. Flinging away the squashed berries, she wiped her palms on the seat of her pants, then took up her basket and started picking again.

But as she did so, her gaze kept flicking back towards the trees. She was moving steadily round to the opposite side of the bramble.

And then, for an instant, she saw him.

He had ventured a few feet forward to try and keep her in his sight, and a shaft of sunlight caught him as he darted from one tree trunk to another.

Maunder. It was Maunder. And his movements were those of a stalker, full of threatening intent.

Jess's heart seemed to drop to her stomach, but she gave no sign that she had spotted him. Controlling the urge to bolt, she went on slowly round the bush for a minute longer. Then, as soon as she was certain it was hiding her from view, she darted into the woods behind it.

There was no path here, but she knew which way the sawmill lay and struck a course towards it. The ground was rough and studded with rocks, thick with dock and shrubs, littered with fallen, rotting branches and stumps. A spicy smell of decay was in the air and all was dim, cool, motionless. Her tread was light and swift, disturbing the silence with only a gentle thump on springy earth, a swish among the leaves, an occasional crack as a stick broke underfoot. She hurried, diverted now and then by gullies, swathes of undergrowth too dense to let her pass, or slopes too steep to descend, but heading all the time towards the timber yard. After a while she could hear the sound of the river away to her left, faint but unmistakable. She had only to reach the track, and then she would feel safe.

Still clutching her basket, Jess carried on, her pace a steady trot. Every so often she paused to look behind her and listen.

No glimpse of him, no hint of following footsteps.

The feeling of menace started to leave her. She guessed she had covered a mile and a half since entering the woods, and the louder the rush of the river, the more confident she grew. Now there was a path again, and as the terrain became familiar she slowed her steps to a normal walk, for she was out of breath.

Within a few minutes the roof of the sawmill came in sight. Jess was on the ridge above it and had only to make her way down the wooded slope to the gate. She could hear the noise of the circular saw, and of someone hammering. Choosing what seemed the quickest way down, she started a careful descent.

She had gone no more than twenty feet when she froze at the sight of Alec Maunder's grinning face.

He was coming up towards her from the bottom, from the track. He had gone the easy way and caught her just as she thought herself safe. He was climbing the bank like a spider up a wall, on his hands and knees where the way was steep, scuttling forward, grasping hold of rocks and saplings and roots, climbing with awful speed, despite the slippery ground. Fired to recklessness by drink and rancour, Maunder was going to have his revenge on one Lawrenson at least.

Jess let out a scream, but even as she did she knew they would not hear it down below. The sound of the machinery was sure to drown it out. Dropping her basket, she scrambled back towards the top of the ridge, but slipped before she reached it and rolled some way back down. Maunder made a lunge, grabbing for her ankle. Jess kicked out at him and he ducked to avoid a blow from her boot. Panting, she pulled herself upwards again, clawing for handholds and scrabbling for footholds. She could hear him behind her with his wheezing chuckle, and once or twice she lashed out with a foot, half because she fancied his hand was about to close upon it, half in the hope of striking his face and sending him tumbling to the bottom. Maunder was too quick and canny to let her do that, dodging every time, but she managed to gain the top of the slope, where she stumbled to her feet and took off like a hare.

Seconds later, Maunder was after her, still laughing as he ran, enjoying a chase he felt sure to win. In her panic she had turned the wrong way and was now fleeing towards the house. But Torvallen was more than a mile away and her chances of reaching it were slim. She was not even halfway there when he caught her.

A hand closed on the back of her jumper, pulling her up with a jerk. She gave a gasping shriek, twisted round and flailed at him, but he whirled her off the path, dragged her some way into the woods and threw her down with a crash in the undergrowth. For a second or two she lay winded, face down among the ivy and the toadstools, then Maunder flipped her on to her back, knelt astride her and closed a hand about her throat. The pressure of his fingers was just enough to choke off any scream. Exertion and excitement had raised a sweat that shone on his forehead and trickled down his temples into his beard. He was giggling and his eyes were mad with glee.

'Oh, I hope you're going to be worth all this trouble,' he panted. 'What a chase! I'm half worn out before I've even started. Still, I think I can do you justice. I'll bet I'm a better man than that husband of yours.'

He tugged up her jersey, pulled at the buttons of the blouse underneath, then slid a quivering hand inside, grasping, kneading. The giggle went up to a higher pitch, almost hysterical now. She struck at him with both fists, clouting him, then tearing at his hair, frantically kicking and bucking in an effort to dislodge him.

'Go on, then, fight a bit, I like that.' Leering in her face, he whispered lewdly, 'Adds to the pleasure. Makes it feel better. I love to know I'm having a live one. I can't stand a woman who just lies there.'

She ceased all movement, allowing her arms to flop at her sides.

'Curse you,' she hissed. 'Damn you to hell, you filthy object! Let me up! Get your ugly carcass off me!'

'Ooh,' mocked Maunder, 'listen to this. How unladylike! To think you used to call me Mr Maunder! Still, this is no time to be formal, is it?'

He inflicted a noisome kiss, all spit and wriggling tongue, breathing a gale of beer and stale tobacco that made her retch. When he sat back, she saw that he had opened his fly and was squirming out of his trousers, freeing hips, backside, and apparatus gruesome in its size and eagerness.

'You wouldn't dare! Robert would kill you!'

'Hasn't killed his brother, has he?'

'What?' gasped Jess.

'Oh yes, I've heard about you and Joel. Amazing, eh, how things get around?'

'You're a liar! A liar! You slug!'

'Now, now, that's enough.' A threatening squeeze on her windpipe. Maunder's grin was filled with a sinister humour and sunlight spattered through the leaves far above, lending fiery glints to his beard. 'Don't presume on our intimacy, Jess.'

Her vision clouded, growing dim. Attempts to prise his fingers from her throat just made him grip all the harder. To gain some breath, she did the sensible thing, going limp again.

The hand relaxed and she gulped in air, but kept silent. It was not a good idea to call him names.

Maunder was fumbling with the fastenings of her

trousers. 'Don't know what you're making such a fuss about,' he remarked, scornfully. 'Nobody misses a slice off a cut loaf.'

Ungovernable rage came boiling up again. She gathered a mouthful of saliva, spat it fiercely up at him but missed, for Maunder sharply jerked his head aside. He shot out his free hand and clipped her smartly across the cheek.

'Aah, you little bitch! By the time I'm finished, you won't piss for a month without smarting.'

He ripped at her trousers and the panties underneath, trying to peel them down. But his own straddling weight was making it difficult, and so he had to raise himself a little. Her hands flashed up, the fingers curled, to claw at his eyes. She dug her nails in, drawing blood from the left lid.

By reflex, Maunder let go of her throat, distracted by the instinct to protect his sight. That one chance was enough and she knew how to make the best of it. From this position she could not kick him. Instead, she rammed a clenched fist up between his legs.

There came a roar of pain. He rocked backwards, toppled sideways and doubled over, clutching his testicles and bellowing his agony. Twisting free of him, she scrambled clear, then dived for a lump of fallen wood she spotted among the ivy. Maunder was rolled up into a ball, moaning and whining and swearing, when she brought the branch down over his head with all the strength she had.

He collapsed, flopping over on to his stomach, but still he was slowly stirring, his hands groping, his bare buttocks twitching. Something savage came snarling out in Jess. With lips drawn back over clenched teeth, she swung the wood up again, two-handed, slashed it down a second and a third time. Maunder, at last, lay perfectly still.

His head was a dark, sticky mess of blood and hair. For a moment Jess stood as though rooted, thinking half with joy and half with dread that she had killed him. The woods were completely silent, nothing moved. Everything seemed petrified. Even a red squirrel, clinging to the trunk of a tree, appeared to be frozen in shock. Then, abruptly, it scuttled up the bark and vanished among the branches.

Jess fled too, still clutching her makeshift club, and struggling to button her trousers as she ran. After a time she flung the branch away, hurling it far out into the undergrowth. She was weeping and gasping for breath. There were leaves and bits of twig caught up in her hair, and her clothing was smeared with earth and moss. She could still see his face and his foul equipment, his skinny backside and all that blood oozing out of his scalp. The wood had been rotten, not very heavy, but she fancied the force of the blows made up for that. Fears of prison and hanging mixed in her mind with a fierce exultation, hatred and gladness and terror clashing as she sprinted homewards.

She had not expected to find her husband in. Bursting into the kitchen, dishevelled and sobbing, Jess came face to face with a very startled Robert. He had caught his forearm on a rusty nail at the timber yard and was dabbing at the scratch with disinfectant.

Open-mouthed, he stared at her, taking in the state of her clothing, her ragged breathing and frantic face.

'Robert, Rob!' She flung herself against him and clung.

'Dear God, what's happened? Jess?'

He tried to prise her loose, but she would not let him go.

'Jess!' He forced her off and shook her. 'Tell me what's the matter.'

'Maunder,' she babbled. 'Maunder.'

'What about him?'

'He followed me, he caught me! Out in the woods. And once he had me down, he started pulling my clothes off ...'

'Jesus wept!' Understanding flooded in and bewilderment turned to wrath.

'He was reeking of ale. He nearly did it, he very nearly had me. But I beat him off. I hit him and hit him and he's still lying there. I hit him so hard, I must have pulped his brains. There was blood, a lot of blood. I think I've killed him.'

He held her by the shoulders, at arm's length. 'Slow down! There was blood, you say? In God's name, what did you hit him with?'

She made an effort to compose herself and answer clearly. 'A chunk of wood. Three times, and he didn't get up again. Robert, he scared me so! He was strong and he stank, there was no one to help, he half-stripped me, half-choked me ...'

'God in heaven.' Shock had brought his voice down almost to a whisper, but it held a tremor of fury. 'Where did it happen? Where did you leave him?'

'Up on the ridge. He pulled me some way off the path.'

'More or less than a mile from here?'

'Less, I'd say. Robert, what am I to do? I'm sure I've killed him. I'm afraid.'

He lifted her chin with his hand, turning her face from side to side. Maunder's slap had left a red weal on her cheek and his fingers had bruised her throat. Robert noted every mark and his face was thunderous. His gaze locked intently with hers.

'He didn't have his way? You're sure of that?'

'Of course I'm sure, and it wasn't my fault ...'

'I know that.' He might distrust her with other men, but he did not doubt her contempt for Maunder.

'He was out to get his own back.'

'Yes, and he wouldn't have the guts to tackle Joel or me.' Robert's gaze flickered over his wife. 'Do you need a doctor?' The question had an absent ring to it, devoid of genuine concern.

'No, I need you.'

She wanted to be cuddled, comforted, but instead he thrust her aside. An odd, fevered look had come into his eyes. They were hot and bright and distracted.

'You'd better heat some water and have a bath,' he said, brusquely. 'Then take some brandy and go to bed.' He stepped away from her, his expression set and purposeful. 'I'm going up there to have a look.'

'If he's dead ...' quavered Jess.

'I'll decide what to do.'

'And if he's not?'

'Then he'll be dealt with.'

'Rob ...' She caught him by the arm. '... please stay with me for a while. I don't feel well. Don't leave me alone after what I've just been through.'

He took her hand away and put on his cap.

'You'll feel better if you just do as I say. Have a bath and a sleep and something to drink. I'll be back as soon as I can.'

'Rob, not yet. Please sit with me for an hour.'

'Later. This can't wait.'

With that he was gone. She heard him striding down the passage, heard the front door close behind him. He had not offered so much as a kiss or one consoling word. No sympathy, no affection. Robert could think of nothing but the loathsome man who had dared to handle his wife. He took it first and foremost as an insult to himself.

From the depths of the undergrowth there came a grunt and then a moan. The bushes crackled, the creepers quivered, and Alec Maunder slowly sat up. He looked, and felt, horrible. Hung over from the beer, he had an earful of blood from the cut on the right side of his head, and more had run down the back of his neck from the two gashes up on his crown. None of them was deep enough to cause any serious damage. They had merely stunned him and bled a lot, as scalp wounds usually do. Nevertheless, they stung, and his skull was full of a heavy, pounding pain. His loins were still aching as well, but worst of all, sobriety brought the awful realisation of what he had done. The drink had given him nerve, which was now replaced by stark fear. One of the Lawrenson brothers was sure to be coming after him – perhaps the both of them.

Maunder lurched to his feet, pulling up his trousers. The blood had congealed at the cuts and was stiffening in his hair, so he feared he might have lain there for quite some space of time. The brothers would be sure to know by now.

They were probably on their way. He had to get home as fast as he could. He would shut himself in with his gun. Or perhaps he would pick up a few belongings and flee the district. Such was his fright at that moment, he could contemplate abandoning Liddy's Farm.

Urgency also impelled him to take a shorter route than the one he normally followed, a route he would otherwise choose to avoid because it took him across the railway viaduct. Alec Maunder had a dread of heights.

Robert searched the ridge for half an hour before deciding that Maunder must be very much alive. He beat back and forth through the bushes in the area Jess had described, but discovered no corpse. So the brute had come round and taken to his heels. Robert stood still for a moment or two, listening, scanning the woods with baleful eyes, debating what Maunder was likely to do. The conclusion he reached was perfectly accurate. In the crook of his arm he nursed the shotgun, and he gave a mirthless grin as he fingered the cartridges in his hip pocket. Then he set off in pursuit. He, too, knew the short-cut to Liddy's Farm.

For fifteen minutes, Maunder had been following a railway track built for the transport of granite from the moorland quarries. Stepping from sleeper to sleeper, he had come within sight of the deep ravine and the lofty bridge that ran across it, the long, long span of the viaduct. The country hereabouts was rough and very lonely, a treeless valley between stony hills, with a shallow stream at the bottom.

Maunder hated this place. Only once before had he crossed this bridge and the walk had not been pleasant. He had done it by keeping to the middle of the track, eyes downwards, counting the sleepers to distract himself. Nothing could have induced him to look over the guard rail into the gulf below. He knew it was there, and that was horror enough.

Maunder quailed at the prospect of tackling the viaduct again, but he was even less keen to face Jess's menfolk. He stood for a moment and stared down the narrow length of the bridge, trying to scrape up some courage. His head was hurting badly and he felt sick.

Then he saw a train approaching from the other end, so he moved to the side of the track, sat down on the grass and fumbled in his pocket for his matches and tobacco tin. He would roll and smoke a cigarette to calm him while he waited.

The engine and trucks went slowly past, twenty clanking freight wagons, loaded with granite blocks. Maunder puffed on his cigarette, watching the rusty wheels roll by. The train moved on, its rattle and thunder fading in the distance, and silence closed in behind it. Maunder lingered to smoke his cigarette down to the last half inch.

Tossing the butt away, he finally stood up and stepped out, doggedly treading the sleepers and counting as he went.

At thirty-eight, he was interrupted.

'Maunder!'

He gasped and his head snapped round.

There, no more than twenty yards behind him, was Robert Lawrenson. He had been running and was sorely out of breath. Maunder was relieved to see no sign of Joel, but the sight of the shotgun set him trembling, and for Robert to catch him here, of all places, was cause for dread indeed.

Maunder did not know quite what to do. He thought about fleeing, but the shotgun was already levelled at his knees, as if in readiness to bring him down. So he stood and he waited, there between the railway lines.

'Here, look ...' He spread his hands, placating, as Lawrenson approached. '... I was only fooling about a bit. I didn't mean no harm. She took it all wrong and got upset. Honest to God, I was only larking around. She took fright and became hysterical, see. Hit out at me and started running. I was scared she might hurt herself, so I ran after her. Come on now, you know I wouldn't be daft enough to try it on with your wife. I respect her too much.'

Robert had caught his breath by now and had come within a dozen feet of him. Maunder had seen a similar glare in the eyes of a tom cat battling over a she. His own eyes blinked and wavered in submission.

'I swear it was all about nothing. I'd had a few pints and perhaps I was a bit frisky, but it was all in fun and she misunderstood.'

Blood had caked around Maunder's right ear and on his cheek. Robert noted that two of his trouser buttons were undone.

'Let's see the back of your head.' The order was curt and emphasised by a jerk of the shotgun barrel.

'Why would you want ... ?'

'Show me!'

'I'm not turning my back on you! You're as mad as she is!' Maunder started edging away.

'Humour me,' smiled Robert, and cocked the gun. He made a turning motion with his hand. Maunder scowled at him, defiant for several seconds more, then did as he was told.

A second later, an arm closed around his throat, stopping his wind. He was bundled off the track and up against the guard rail. Robert had thrown the shotgun aside, and with his free hand forced Maunder's head downwards. Two gashes, almost vertical, could clearly be seen through the greasy locks. 'See what she did!' babbled Maunder. 'She might have killed me!'

Robert's weight was pinning him against the rail and Maunder could not throw him off. He struggled, but vertigo had seized him and drained his muscles of power. A hideous dissolving sensation, spreading up from the soles of his feet, was sapping the strength from his legs. Below him lay a drop of a hundred and eighty feet. He could hear the guard rail creaking under him.

And then, to his utter terror, he felt himself being lifted, hauled up and thrust out over it. Robert had him by his belt and collar, bent double over the barrier, head down towards the valley floor, where the rocks and the river looked very tiny, very far away. Maunder felt as if he were completely upside down, and he fancied that the rail was starting to give way. Any second it would crack and sag, and down he would go. His eyes bulged and his arms flailed. First he blubbered, then he screamed, as Robert hoisted him a little further, raising his feet just off the ground.

'Pull me back! Pull me up! Oh, Sweet Jesus! Please!'

This last was a shriek that rang down the valley. Maunder was snivelling, afraid now even to wriggle, for Robert's hands were all that held him. The ground below appeared to swing, up and down like a see-saw, so he squeezed his eyes shut, only to experience an even worse sensation, as if he were somersaulting tumbling over and over in endless empty space. He whimpered, he wept, his mouth wide open and his fingers clawing at the air.

'You laid hands on my wife,' came the growling reply. 'A bloody thing like you, mauling and pawing her, half choking her, scaring the wits out of her. My wife? You were going to strip her off, get into her, use what's mine? Well, it's going to cost you very dear.' Robert's voice grew smooth, almost cooing. 'I'm about to drop you, Maunder. I'm just going to loosen my fingers and let you fall.'

An anguished howl and a gobbling sound came up from Maunder's throat. A smile appeared on Robert's face, a grin of savage satisfaction. He was sweating and the muscles of his shoulders, arms and trunk were knotted with the strain of holding Maunder's weight. Beneath the peak of his cap, his eyes were alight with the joy of revenge and he meant to spin out the torment for as long as he could.

'When I was a boy,' he said conversationally, 'I used to throw stones off this bridge and count to see how long they took to hit bottom. About six seconds, as I recall. Now, if we were ten yards further on, you'd probably land in the water – not that it would help you, being only one foot deep. But from where we are now, you're certain to come to earth among the boulders there, just at the foot of the trestle. Picture it, Alec. You'll see them coming up to meet you, and then your head'll shatter like an old cider jar. I daresay you'll die instantly,' he added, cheerfully.

Maunder started to vomit. Then he sobbed and then he begged.

Robert listened attentively. Promises, pleas and grovelling apologies spilled from Maunder's mouth. His voice had risen as high as a woman's, hysterical with fear. When at last he ceased, there followed a long, long silence. Lawrenson looked down at him with loathing. His fingers itched to release their grip. It would trouble his conscience not at all to do away with a creature like Maunder. Unlike his brother, Robert was capable of it.

For nearly half a minute neither spoke or moved. Maunder thought he might be reconsidering. A timid hope was born in him. Then Robert said, briskly:

'Aah, let's get it over with. I've had enough of this.'

Maunder gave one more despairing scream and lost control of his bladder.

And then he was jerked up and back, sent reeling to the ground beside the railway line.

Robert picked up the shotgun and stood watching him. Maunder was wild-eyed and panting, his beard fouled with vomit. The fly and left leg of his trousers showed a dark, spreading patch of wetness. Lawrenson's lip curled with contempt.

Maunder shuffled away on his backside, amazed to find himself alive. Shaken to his very soul, he eyed the other man with a fear-filled respect.

Only the thought of the hangman had prevented Robert from letting him drop. In this high, open place, he could not, after all, be sure that no one was watching. But he meant it when he said, 'If there's a next time, Maunder, if ever you give me cause to seek you out again, I'll make an end of you, no matter what the consequences. Is that understood?'

A breathless nod.

'I hope so, because I tell you truly, I was very close to flinging you off.'

Slowly Maunder stood up, on legs that felt like melting toffee. Wiping some muck from his beard, he started backing away. Robert remained where he stood, the shotgun cradled in his arms. Maunder turned and scuttled off along the bridge, with many a nervous glance across his shoulder.

When, finally, he reached the end, he spun around and saw that Robert had not moved.

'You sod,' he breathed, 'you sod!'

There was something about what Robert had done, something Maunder deemed to be sadistic. He would truly have preferred it if Lawrenson had used his fists. He realised, as well, that Robert's motives had less to do with avenging Jess than punishing another male who had tried to poach on his preserve.

'... use what's mine.'

Robert's words came floating back. Oh yes, it was all to do with ownership, pride and rights. Maunder's bloodshot eyes glared out from under his brows and a gleam of evil humour kindled in them. He felt stronger now he was off the bridge. His legs had steadied and he had put two hundred feet between himself and Robert. Battered and humiliated, he found enough boldness left in him to fire a spiteful, parting salvo.

'She put up a good fight,' he yelled, 'I have to give her that, she made it rough for me. But then, my name's not Joel, is it? I'll bet he's never had to hold her down. And another thing – take a good, hard look at the boy, Robert, see how dark he is and how your brother loves him. He isn't yours, I'd stake my life on it! You're blind if you can't see it. God, how they must laugh at you, just as the men laugh down at the yard. They all know, Robert. Quietly, they know – and not from me. They've eyes and ears and wits of their own. They know as well as you do what happened last winter when it snowed.'

He was laughing himself by now, but the grin vanished when he saw Robert start rapidly towards him. Scrambling down the embankment, Maunder made off as fast as he could go.

Robert did not bother to follow him far. He had too much else to think about, now.

Jess washed as she had never washed before, scrubbing her skin with a loofah and a pumice stone until it stung. She went through a whole bar of soap, a bottle of disinfectant, twelve kettles of boiling water and three fresh towels before she could think herself clean. Not even Alice had felt as soiled and frightened as Jess did now. At least the men in the dockyard had not tried to rape Mam, nor had she left one of them lying on the ground with a battered head.

Moving stiffly, Jess put on her nightshirt and her purple dressing gown. Her right hip and shoulder had been jarred when Maunder threw her down, and only now had the ache set in. A little mirror hung on the wash-house wall. She wiped the condensation off it and stared at her reflection. Uncombed, the fair hair hung in wet clumps around her face, which was blotchy from fierce rubbing with a flannel. Red-rimmed, with swollen lids, her eyes took in the ugly welt on her cheek. The imprints of Maunder's fingers and thumb showed black on either side of her neck. She was not at all pretty just at this moment.

'Go to bed,' Robert had said. But she knew she would not sleep, too much in dread of what he would find out there in the woods, what she would hear when she woke, especially since she knew he had taken the shotgun. No, she could not go to bed, much as she craved a few hours' oblivion.

The brandy, however, had been an excellent suggestion. She fetched the bottle from the sitting room, went into the kitchen, slumped down at the table and poured some out into a teacup.

Good – oh yes, it was very good, hot and strengthening. A bracing warmth expanded in her stomach, and soon the day's events began to seem a little unreal. A pleasant calm descended on her and fear retreated to a distance. She drained the teacup, then filled it once more to the brim. It was easier now to understand Mam and her need for spirits.

Jess had never been much of a drinker, sticking to small amounts of cider and wine. But now, sipping slowly, steadily, she put paid to the second cupful of brandy and poured herself a third.

She was halfway through the fourth, dozing and swaying at the table, her head on her hand, when Joel came in at half past three and found her.

'Jess?' He squatted down beside her chair, took the cup away and grasped her hands. Her head lolled forward, then pulled back. She blinked at him, half-stupefied.

'What's this? What's happened, eh?' His fingers traced the marks on her neck and cheek, and fury distorted his face. 'Where's Rob? Did he do this?'

Emphatically she shook her head, and then got out the name.

'Maunder.'

'What?' snarled Joel. 'Where? And how?'

'In the woods. He tried to rape me.' Her speech was clumsy, her tongue feeling huge in her mouth. 'I got away from him. I brained him and ...' She paused, collecting spittle, for her mouth felt very dry. '... I think he might be dead.'

This final statement came out in a manner quite matter-of-fact. Brandy and exhaustion had taken all agitation away. Her eyes focused wearily on Joel. 'And if I haven't killed him, I'm afraid that Robert will. He's gone out to find him. He's taken the gun.'

Joel closed his eyes. 'How long ago?'

Jess had lost her sense of time. She thought perhaps two hours.

'He wouldn't stay with me,' she explained. 'I didn't want him to go, but his temper was up.'

'I wondered why he hadn't come back to work.' Joel was talking more to himself than to her. 'Well, whatever's happened, it's done by now.'

Suddenly Jess felt queasy. The lightness in her head was no longer a comfort and a gimlet pain was growing in her left temple.

'Joel ...' She put out a hand and clutched at his shoulder. '... I've drunk too much, I'm feeling sick. I can't hold my head up. I want to lie down.'

'All right, come on.' He stood up with her as she hauled herself to her feet. The movement was too much for her stomach. Abruptly she spun away from him and doubled, retching, over the sink. Joel supported her forehead with his palm, stroking her back until the urging ceased, then turned her round and hugged her tight against him. He was warm and the good smell of fresh-sawn wood was on his clothes.

This is what Rob should have done, she thought. This is what a husband would do for a wife he loved. But he scarcely even touched me. He didn't care how I was feeling. I needed this and he didn't give it to me, not even a minute or two.

'Let's take you upstairs,' said Joel, at last. 'You'd better stay there the rest of the day.'

'I won't be able to sleep ...'

'Oh yes, you will, after what you've drunk.'

He took her up to the bedroom and tucked her in. She thought, as he punched up the pillows and straightened the quilt, that he would have made the best of fathers.

And then she remembered her son.

'Colin! Dear God, I forgot him! He has to be fetched from school. It must be nearly five!'

'No, it isn't four yet.' Joel pressed her down in the bed. 'Don't worry, I'll go and collect him.'

'Straight away?'

'Yes, straight away.'

Jess subsided, closing her eyes. Shock and drink and rough treatment had made a mess of her. Joel had never seen her look so awful. Once he had only admired and wanted her in the way any healthy man would. There was more to it now, a great deal more, if he could love her when she looked like that.

As soon as she dropped off to sleep he went downstairs. He was halfway to the front door when Robert came in.

Joel stopped in his tracks. Robert's face was stony and his gaze moved over his brother, hard and cold. Joel eyed the shotgun, then asked softly, 'Well?'

'Well what?'

'Keep your voice down, don't wake her.' A nod towards the stairs.

Robert brushed past him and went into the kitchen. Joel followed and shut the door. His brother laid the weapon on the table.

'Told you all about it, has she?'

'Yes. So did you find ... ?'

'She needn't worry, she didn't kill the sod. Nor did I.' Robert swigged some brandy from the bottle.

'Thank God for that,' breathed Joel.

'Mind you, it was touch and go.'

'What did you do?'

'Gave him a nasty experience.' Robert sniggered. 'He'll be the one having nightmares, now.' His gaze swivelled towards his brother and his voice acquired a gently sneering tone. 'Been comforting her, have you?'

'I understand you didn't bother ...'

'She wasn't hurt.'

'Of course she was, and you did nothing to help matters.'

'I did what was most important.'

'To you.'

'Don't you lecture me,' roared Robert. 'Like it or not, she's still my wife.' His right fist was slowly closing and unclosing at his side.

'When you treat her this way, I admit I don't like it at all.'

'Wish she was yours, don't you? Wish she was free?'

'Perhaps I do.'

'Well, there's an admission at last! How about Colin, hmm? Would you like him, too? Perhaps you've a right to him. I'm not sure any more.'

Joel stared at his brother. 'What the hell does that mean?'

Robert considered him, gulping again at the brandy. Some remnant of sense reminded him that Maunder would say anything to wound him. But he would never be certain, now, would he? Now that the notion was in his mind, he would never be positive that Colin was his, and so he could never really love the child or be a proud father again, in case that pride and affection should make him a dupe. Condemned to wonder, Robert could neither quite accept or disown the boy, and so his answer was shaped to evade the issue.

'He seems to enjoy your company better than mine.'

'If so, it's your own doing,' retorted Joel. 'Now, will you go and fetch him from school, or shall I? It's time and I promised Jess.'

'Be my guest. We share almost everything else, so why not him?'

· Thirty-one ·

Robert never wanted his wife again after that, not even in the most impersonal way. There was always space between them in the bed. He seemed to have a physical aversion to her, now, as if repelled by her contact with Maunder, as if the smell of the man were on her still. That, at least, was what she thought. In truth, he was just as much repulsed by what he believed of Jess and Joel, and what he feared concerning Colin. Jess said nothing about the sudden ceasing of sex. She did not feel she was missing much with Robert. There had been no love in it for a very long time. She suspected that he slept with her now for one purpose only – so that she could not go to Joel at night.

Lately she wished more and more to do just that. How hard it was to lie beside a coldly hostile Robert and know there was affection out of reach across the landing.

Colin, too, had felt the chill become an Arctic frost.

Robert could not look at the child any more without seeing his brother in him. His colouring, his stature, his wavy hair, his easy temperament – it was all Joel. Not that there was anything in Colin's features resembling Joel – but then, there was nothing of Robert, either. Facially, the boy was much like Jess. He was going to be a beautiful youth and probably a handsome man. Robert's suspicions fed on subtler signs. Colin's laugh, his walk, even his childish handwriting came under his father's scrutiny, and in all of it he fancied he saw Joel. They were things that might simply be copied, but Robert feared they were inherited. What was more, the boy now openly displayed a preference for Joel. It was Uncle Joel this, Uncle Joel that – which was hardly to be wondered at, as Robert became increasingly strict and intolerant. Colin did not know what he had done to deserve it. He only knew there was something more than parental annoyance these days when his dad told him off, something harsher by far.

Almost everything he did seemed to displease Robert in one way or another. For instance, his pet collection didn't meet with Dad's approval.

It started with a small green lizard. Then he found a hedgehog. Then a fieldmouse, and a newt, and a slow-worm. Soon there were all kinds of things – beetles, caterpillars, moths, sticklebacks, a pygmy shrew, a toad, a grass-snake – which Colin kept in jam jars, cardboard boxes, an old fish tank, even a porcelain chamber pot, so that his bedroom was crowded out with little creeping, scurrying, slithering guests. In addition, a local farmer made him a gift of two tabby kittens, and one day Colin brought home an injured skylark to nurse and was tearful when it died.

Colin loved his pets, but Dad didn't seem to think much of them. He had offered to get his son a puppy – a sheltie, perhaps, or a spaniel, nothing big or frightening. But Colin wouldn't have a dog. He would never like the sound of barking or the sight of canine teeth.

His dad was impatient. 'I'm quite willing for him to have

a pet,' he said to Jess, 'but if a boy's going to keep an animal, it ought to be a dog. What does he want with all those rodents and creepy-crawlies? As for the kittens, they're good fun now, I know, but it'll be different when they're grown. Cats lead their own secret lives, they're not the best companions for a child. Any other boy would love a dog. I don't know why he has to be different.'

It seemed that nothing Colin did was right with Robert, therefore he turned for kindness to Joel. And so, too, did his mother. Indeed, were it not for her brother-in-law, Jess thought she might have taken to drink like poor Mam.

Davey's shop was closed a lot these days. Alice opened only if and when she felt like it. As long as there were takings enough to keep her supplied with spirits, she cared about nothing else. Drink for today. She rarely gave thought to tomorrow. In time she would probably lose all her trade, but she did not dwell on that, any more than she stopped to consider what the gin was doing to her body.

Then, one day, she was very bluntly told.

It was April and the streets of Devonport were splashed with sunlight. Two children, sitting on a doorstep, were playing fivestones. One was a girl, plain of face and aged about twelve. The other was her brother, two years younger, a mean-featured little boy with lank brown hair. He was losing the game to his sister, and bad-tempered about it. It was just after four in the afternoon and the street was quiet.

The girl won another throw and nudged the boy to take his turn. But as she passed him the stones, his attention was caught by the sight of a woman coming along the pavement.

No one could have said she was walking. She tottered, she staggered, she reeled, stopping every so often to steady herself against a wall or a lamppost. The boy jabbed his sister in the ribs and then pointed at the woman.

Sombrely, the girl watched Alice Davey's halting progress.

Alice could not remember why she had left the house.

She had been resolved on something when she went out, some purpose or errand, but had quite forgotten what it was by the time she reached the corner of the street. For a while she had kept on going, trying to recall what she meant to do, but whatever it was had gone from her mind. Now she wanted to go home again, but seemed to have turned in the wrong direction. It was, in fact, remarkable that she was on her feet at all, having downed a pint of gin in little more than an hour.

The boy eyed her scornfully as she drew nearer. He jiggled the stones in his hand, glanced slyly from his sister to the drunken woman and then back again. Temptation was stealing over him. Grinning, he stood up, looked down at the pebbles and selected the largest, taking it between finger and thumb.

His sister, glancing up suddenly, tried to grab it from him. 'Don't you dare! I'll ...'

Too late. His arm went back and then snapped forward, his wrist flicked with the expertise of one who was used to pelting dogs and cats.

The stone struck Alice high up on the right cheek. She gave a cry and lurched against a lamppost, one hand clinging for support, the other pressed to her face. Whimpering, she leaned for several seconds, head bent and shoulders hunched. Then, hearing the boy's laughter, she looked up.

Hands on hips, proud of his aim, he poked his tongue out at her. But the girl, meeting Alice's stricken and bewildered eyes, flushed red with shame and anger. She jumped to her feet and swung her arm, clouting her brother soundly across the ear, then grasped him by his collar and hauled him, yelping, into the house. The door banged shut behind them.

Alice felt the wetness of running blood, took her hand away from her face and blinked stupidly at the red-smeared fingers. Her cheek was stinging, she felt dizzy, sick – and frightened, too, because she could not remember how to get home. She bent her head again and started to sob.

It was only a minute later, though it seemed much longer to Alice, that help came along in the form of a grocer's boy. He had made a few late deliveries and he sailed past on his bike with an empty basket. His head turned sharply when he spotted Alice. He circled round in the road and came back, halting at the kerb beside her. He was fifteen years old, with a fresh complexion, and to him she seemed almost elderly.

'Here, what's the matter, old dear?' He laid a hand on her shoulder and she started with fright. 'Now, now, it's all right.' He lifted her head and peered at her. His nostrils twitched and he flinched from the reek of spirits. Then he murmured, 'Oh, I know who you are. From the tobacco shop. What's happened to your face, eh? Fell over, did you?'

She shook her head, but made no attempt to explain.

'Tsk,' said the lad, 'looks nasty, that. Come on, I'll walk you home, shall I?'

'Yes, please,' came the whispered response.

'All right, then let go of the lamppost, that's it.'

He took a firm grip on her arm, supporting her with one hand and wheeling his bike along the gutter with the other.

'You shouldn't be on your own,' he said, when they finally reached her door. 'Is there somebody I can fetch?'

'No one,' came the slurred reply.

'That's a bad cut, very near your eye. Shall I call the doctor for you?'

Alice nodded. Her face was still bleeding, and blood had always distressed her.

'Go on indoors, then. I'll tell him to hurry.'

She watched him ride off, his backside up like a jockey.

It was nearly an hour before the doctor came, by which time the cut was sealing itself and Alice was somewhat more sober. He cleaned the wound and put a dressing on it, and said it presented no danger to her sight. On her general health, however, his verdict was dismal, for the smell on her breath and the yellowish colour of her skin prompted him to make a full examination. He found her emaciated, her feet and legs bloated, her chest covered with spidery red veins.

Alice, in her underclothes, had slipped beneath the eiderdown, and she lay half-dozing against her pillow as he silently packed his bag. He had sighed and tutted and shaken his head while he examined her, but not until he was ready to leave did he issue a sombre warning. He sat down on the edge of her bed, and Alice's eyelids lifted.

'Do you live alone, Mrs Davey?'

'Yes,' came the cracked reply.

'Is that why you drink so much?'

'It's one reason,' muttered Alice. She closed her eyes again. 'I need my gin.'

'It's a false friend,' she heard him say. 'I'll go further, Mrs Davey, it's a very dangerous enemy for you.'

Alice made no response, so he took her hand and urged: 'Please look at me.'

She rolled her head towards him, opening weary eyes, uninterested.

'Perhaps your life has not been very happy, Mrs Davey. I suspect you have been through trials and disappointments. I find that such is frequently the case when solitary ladies "need" their gin. But I have to tell you this: if you carry on drinking much longer, you will have no life at all. You show the signs of cirrhosis, my dear. Your liver is damaged, diseased, and unless you forgo this treacherous prop called alcohol, you will not last eighteen months. You must stop, Mrs Davey, completely and at once. The alternative is stark and certain. You will die.'

Her expression did not change by so much as a flicker. Die? Well, well. Really? Was she supposed to care?

'Do you understand me?' pressed the doctor. 'I am giving you the sternest ultimatum.'

For a brief space there was still no reaction. Then the faintest of smiles appeared, and the haggard features seemed to relax.

'Yes, thank you, that's quite clear.'

'And you're going to take my advice? Give it up?'

'Give up,' repeated Alice. 'Yes, that's the best thing, isn't it? Put a stop to it all.'

The doctor misunderstood her. 'Bravo, Mrs Davey, that's the spirit! Of course, it won't be easy. A very great effort of will is required. But with determination you can vanquish this foe and live out your normal span.'

He was beaming now. Youthful, newly-qualified, he was all optimism and ideals. A fervent preserver of life, he could not yet imagine what it was to be sick of it.

'Do you have any family?' he went on.

'A daughter, and a grandson.'

'Well! I'm sure they'll be delighted to hear of your resolve. They must worry about you. Think what a weight it will take from their minds.'

'Yes,' agreed Alice, gently, 'I must take the burden off Jess. Poor Jess, I've caused her so much trouble.'

'Nevertheless, I'm sure she wouldn't want to lose you. Does she often visit?'

'Every week.'

'And you have a nice little business here, I daresay? No financial problems?'

'No – not yet.'

'In short, you have a lot to live for! Yours is a better situation than many. Far from hopeless!' He patted her hand, his face cherubic behind his spectacles. 'Now then, I'll leave you a powder to make you sleep the clock around. I wish I could also prescribe you something to guarantee self-control, but that, I fear, can only come from you. I'm confident that you can do it, Mrs Davey.'

Give it up, her luckless existence.

After he had gone, Alice dwelt for a long time on the prospect. She was only forty-six. She had a daughter and a grandchild, and money enough still to pay her way. People far worse off would cling to life, do anything to keep it, no matter how wretched it was. Yet Alice was willing to let it go, quite relieved to have this convenient option to die of doing the thing she enjoyed. She was not the sort to gas herself or swallow a bottle of pills, jump from a window or open her veins. She did not have the nerve to make that kind of exit. Here was something more agreeable, neither dramatic nor frightening, but cosily familiar.

Serenely, she stirred the doctor's powder into a glass of water and drank it down. She thought about him with amusement. A nice young man, but naïve. He was going to be disappointed in her, she supposed. Immediate, total and permanent abstinence. Ridiculous, of course. How unbearable life would be without her drop of drink, her anaesthetic. Without Mr Honey. Without anything in prospect except old age and infirmity. Live out her normal span? Lord, the very thought of it! Another twenty years or more. Alice did not expect them to be any better than those she had already lived. The show was already a wash-out and she did not care to stay for the end.

As for her daughter and grandson, Alice felt that she could do them good service by fading away. Jess should have security, money of her own. That was one good thing that Alice could arrange. Her debts were small and few, and she knew the shop and house would fetch a tidy sum. If the worst befell and her marriage ended, then Jess would at least have some cash behind her. With Alice gone, she could sell the place, take the boy and move somewhere new. Somewhere a long, long way from here.

Settling back, awaiting sleep, Alice shifted her thoughts from those she loved to those she hated – and something very strange came over her. A fierce, exciting feeling, a sense of something punchy loose inside her. She would not have to live with them much longer. In a couple of years she would be out of their reach. And if she could face up to death with so much equanimity, what was there to fear from a few loud-mouthed women?

'Give as good as you get,' Jess had told her, over and over.

Alice vowed to do precisely that in the time that remained.

· Thirty-two ·

High up on Leather Tor among the boulders was a place where Joel often went to sit and think. He had come here all through his boyhood and his youth when plagued by small dilemmas that seemed very great at the time. He had come here every time he was on leave throughout the war, to rid his mind of horror for a while. He had come here three days after he met Pauline, debating whether he should propose to a girl he hardly knew and whom he might leave a widow if his luck ran out. He had come here after her death and sat in the rain and bitter wind, and wept until his throat and chest and head were aching. All the milestones of his life had been marked by expeditions to Leather Tor, and lately he had been coming here again, because he felt he had a decision to make.

Today there was no wind or rain, only a gentle breeze, and the sky was a delicate blue. He was sitting in his usual place, absently turning his cap round and round in his hands. Below, and something like a mile away, lay the glittering sheet of water that was Burrator reservoir. It had a fringe of trees around it, like a setting round a jewel.

The atmosphere at Torvallen was going from bad to worse. They were miserable all of them, Robert no less than his wife and son and brother. Jess was sullen towards her husband, while the boy was edgy, hesitant, never sure of what to say or do in front of his father. And Robert, like a watchful cat, kept vigilant eyes on all three of them, and let them know it, too. He was racked with pain at what he imagined, and nasty in his suffering, irascible like a wasp at summer's end. He felt he was a man betrayed, a man who was in the way. He fancied that Jess and Joel would like to see him gone, but he was not going to oblige them. He was going to be there, at the house, at the sawmill, come hell or high water, and have the satisfaction of knowing he stood in their way. Robert was sure they would like him to leave, so he was determined to stay.

Joel's thoughts, in truth, had never worked along those lines. It was not in his mind to oust his brother and have everything for himself. At first the situation had confounded him. Torvallen was his home and the sawmill his business, but he was trapped in partnership with a brother who openly hated him now. He loved that brother's wife, but he could not have her – or, out of decency, would not move to take her away from Robert. She was always before him, an object of yearning, but principle held him back. He did not feel to blame for what had happened to their marriage, and yet he knew he was a large part of the problem. Robert had always made every aspect of life into a competition with Joel, so perhaps it was inevitable that rivalry would arise in the end over Jess. In a way, the die was cast from the day Pauline was killed.

The breeze swept a ruffled pattern across the reservoir from bank to bank and then the water was smooth again. Joel drew his knees up, resting his forearms on them.

He could not live in such an atmosphere of suspicion and strife. Robert could, he seemed to draw a grim energy from it, but Joel was wearied by it and depressed. He wondered if it would help if he went away. Perhaps if he were gone, Robert would come to his senses, perhaps some peace and harmony, some kindness, would return.

You have to take the thorn out, Joel thought, before the wound can heal. If I leave it might be best for all of us. She's still his wife, and Colin's his son. I'm the one who's alone. It would be simple enough for me to go.

His mind turned to practicalities. Robert could not buy him out, but Joel could sell his share in the property to some third party. He would come out with a goodly sum, sufficient to set himself up elsewhere.

Joel picked up a pebble, tossing it thoughtfully in his

hand. A fresh start, new horizons. He might travel for a while before settling down to business. He might embark on a new trade entirely. He might become rich. Eventually he would forget about Jess, and then he might find a nice woman and marry again. He was still only thirty-two. Perhaps a great adventure lay before him.

No, it wasn't, it was exile. Fury surged within him and he hurled the stone away so hard that it shattered against a rock far down the slope. Was it not enough that he had lost Pauline? Did he have to be driven out of Torvallen as well? It was his home. He had meant to stay there all his life. And he was not ambitious. He liked the business he was in and he did not wish to be rich. Joel had always been a contented man and he did not want to be uprooted.

And yet the prospect had to be faced. He could see no pleasant future at Torvallen, no hope for any of them, if he remained.

In the end the choice was made for him, as events took their own, decisive turn.

Trouble started one morning over breakfast and a soft-boiled egg. Joel, as it happened, had gone out early, taking flowers over to Pauline's grave in Widecombe churchyard, so he missed the little domestic rumpus that brought about the final rift.

Colin sat at the table, toying with his spoon. He had no appetite to an egg that day. He looked down into the glutinous yolk and pulled a face. The white had not set as firmly as he liked it, and he knew that when he dug down inside, up would come a nasty, runny mucus. He ate the bit that was lodged in the top of the shell, then dipped a finger of bread in the yolk and nibbled it without enjoyment. After a couple of minutes, he pushed the egg aside, half-finished, and moved to get down from his chair.

Robert shot him a glance and ordered, 'Eat your food.'

'I'm not hungry.'

'Do as I say.' The words were clipped.

'I feel sick, I don't want it.'

'Sick, my foot.' Robert waved his knife at the egg. 'Go on, finish your breakfast.'

The child slid back in his seat, but did not touch the egg. Jess was at the stove, frying sausages, bacon and tomatoes.

'Never mind,' she said. 'He can have some of this when it's ready.'

'He'll eat what's in front of him first. Go on,' Robert instructed, 'do as you're told.'

Under his father's warning stare, Colin tried to tackle the egg. It was fast going cold and his stomach rebelled, but he did his best to force it down.

Robert nodded, satisfied. 'That's better. Don't you start being fussy about your food, my lad. I was never faddy when I was a boy. And another thing, while I think of it – I'm altogether fed up with finding wildlife all over the house. You've turned the place into a zoo. The damned things are everywhere and they make a lot of mess.'

Jess flipped over a sizzling rasher in the frying pan. 'His pets don't do any harm,' she said, spearing half a tomato and shaking it on to a plate. 'I don't know what you're carrying on about. Torvallen's never been immaculate, has it? You wouldn't want it that way.'

'Clutter's one thing, animals are another. Rodents, insects – it's unhealthy. He'll have to get rid of them. I've decided. I want them all cleared out today.'

She snapped a look at him. 'Robert, that's mean.'

'Call it what you like. Take them out and let them go,' he flung at the boy.

Colin's eyes filled, but he dared not argue.

'No business keeping wild things cooped up,' muttered Robert.

Joel, he was thinking, had been the same when he was a child, filling the place with creepy-crawlies and scuttling, slithering creatures. Yet another thing he had in common with Colin. The more he studied his son, the more similarities Robert detected. In so many ways, the boy took after Joel.

Jess banged Robert's plate of bacon down in front of

him. 'Don't pretend you care about the animals. You're just being spiteful.'

Unmoved, her husband repeated, 'As soon as you've finished your breakfast, Colin. You're to let them loose before you go to school.'

'What about the cats?'

'They can stay – but nothing else.'

'My hedgehog ...'

'Out.'

'Please, can't I just ... ?'

'That's final.'

His pets, his friends, to be evicted, one and all. And Mam was right, his dad was just being spiteful. Weeping angrily, Colin knocked over his eggcup and pushed back his chair.

'No temper now!' commanded Robert.

'I can't say I blame him,' Jess began, hotly.

'Don't interfere!'

Colin was walking away from the table.

'Come back here!' Robert roared.

The child paused at the door, eyeing him fearfully, but still defiant.

'I don't work to put food on the table for you to waste.' Robert was rapping his forefinger on the wood. 'Sit down and finish your egg.'

'No! And I don't care what you do!'

Robert stood up. In two strides he was across the room and had Colin by the collar. He bundled him back to the table and plonked him roughly down in his chair. The child immediately wriggled off it and made a dash for the door. Robert caught him again. This time he cuffed him hard across the ear, a swipe that was harder, in truth, than he intended. When angry, he always forgot his own strength.

'I hate you!' Colin shouted, beating back with his small fists. 'You're nasty, nasty, nasty! I love Uncle Joel, not you!'

Whereupon, Robert slapped him again.

'Damn you, leave him alone,' flared Jess. 'If you do that once more ...'

'Yes?' yelled Robert. 'Yes? You'll do what?'

He released the child and Colin fled, sobbing, upstairs.

'What will you do, Jess? Go to his other father? Go to Joel, eh, complain to him? Does he have some special say in the matter? Does he have some right to object if I discipline my son?'

She fell silent, her hands twisting at the fabric of her apron. His other father? A sick apprehension rose in her. She had never thought that Robert could have any doubts about the boy. Yet lately he had been so hard on him ...

A second later, he confirmed his meaning.

'Assuming he is my son.'

There, it was out at last.

Her words, when she found her voice, were incredulous. 'You must be mad.'

'No, I don't think so. I've good grounds to wonder.'

'You've no grounds whatever! Nothing but the wild ideas you hatch out of lunatic jealousy! For God's sake, Colin is six years old. We'd been married less than a year when I conceived him. How can you imagine Joel and I ...? It's crazy! What about Pauline? Oh, I know how you've been fretting since she died. I know what's been going through your mind, you stupid man. That's bad enough, by God, but to think he betrayed her while she was alive – that's unworthy even of you. Robert, I've never been unfaithful to you, never, not with your brother or anyone else. You're being ridiculous! Just as you were that day in Mevagissey.'

'Mevagissey?' He had to think for a moment.

'Our honeymoon, Robert, remember? Yes, it started as early as that, didn't it? We hadn't been married a month before your true colours began to show.'

'My true colours? What does that mean?'

With an effort she controlled her voice, keeping it low and the words deliberate. 'Just this – a scaly green demon sits on your shoulder, Robert. He's always been there. He was there long before you met me. And it wasn't Vanessa Crane who put him there, either. I know, I've met her.'

'What?'

'That's right. A couple of years ago. We had an interesting chat.'

'You bitch! You bitch, to believe her ...'

'Why should I not think ill of you, when you suspect the worst of me?'

A plea came into her eyes and her voice. 'Why do you have these idiotic notions, Rob? Of course Colin is your son. I don't know why he's the only one we've had, but I promise you he's yours. Why are you always imagining slights and plots and deceptions, always inventing trouble?'

For a moment she thought she had reached him. A lost, bewildered look passed over his face, a great uncertainty. She moistened her lips, then ventured a suggestion.

'Perhaps you ought to see a doctor, one who understands the mind ...'

That was a mistake. Robert, enraged, gave her no chance to finish.

'Oh yes, that would suit you, I'm sure. Lunatic, crazy, mad – you've used all those words to me in the last five minutes! Perhaps you'd like me shut away?'

'No, Rob! I'm only trying ...'

'Well, the obstacle's not going to be so easily removed. You'd like to have Joel and this house to yourself, but I'm here spoiling things, aren't I? Learn to live with it, Jess, because that's not going to change.'

He pulled his cap and jacket from the peg behind the door, and slammed it as he left.

For some time after he had gone to work, she stood at the sink, staring down. A spider had found its way in there and was desperately trying to scale the porcelain wall, first here, then there, forever falling back. Jess's eyes followed its movements without really seeing it. She was shaken by the enormity of her husband's doubts about Colin. And yet, she supposed, she should not be surprised. Perhaps it was inevitable, the logical next step. He did need a doctor, she felt sure. But he would not be persuaded to see one, of that she was equally certain. Robert bore scant resemblance now to the pleasant young man she had married. In those days he had had the green demon under control, and he had been a lovable husband before it gained the upper hand.

Tears flowed freely down her face, though she made no sobbing sound. Tears for him, for her, for Mam, for Joel, for all their blighted lives.

Eventually she rescued the spider and put it out the window. Then she made herself a cup of tea, put in a lot of sugar and sat down to drink it. The warmth from the stove was comforting upon her back and the house was very quiet. Moving round the room, her weary gaze took in the familiar details, all the things she had always loved so much – the colourful plates and mugs on the dresser, Pauline's dried flowers and corn dollies, the wheelback chairs and the copper saucepans. This whole house, this charismatic house, Jess had adored it from the very start.

Every bit as much as she had cared for Robert.

Her gaze froze at a point in mid-air. Yes, she supposed it was true. Jess closed her eyes, fighting down jabs of conscience.

But she had loved him, in the early years. And tolerated much from him since the day he learned about Alice. In every way she had been a good wife, and a good mother to their son – his son. Well, what indeed if the house had been part of his attraction? Romantics might not like to hear it, but if the truth were told, a spouse was often chosen for something more than himself. There were usually practical considerations too. The promise of entry to a certain class, a certain way of life, were frequently part of a lover's charm. That was not so very dreadful, was it, as long as there was kindness and affection in the marriage, as long as faith was kept? And how much genuine love, she wondered, had he felt for her? Had she not been a trophy to parade before his brother and outshine Vanessa Crane? Jess had no doubt that such motives had formed a goodly part of Robert's passion for her.

'Mam?'

Jess looked up and there was her boy in the doorway.

'I've done what he told me. I've let the animals go.'

She nodded, then stretched out an arm. Colin came and stood by her chair for a sympathetic squeeze. 'Well,' she said, wiping her cheeks, 'he may be right. Perhaps it's kinder to set them free.'

'He isn't kind to us any more,' said Colin, starkly. 'Is he?'

Jess kissed his forehead. 'Come on, I must take you to school.'

Joel returned from Widecombe at ten. He stabled the horse and went indoors, upstairs, where he sat for a time on the edge of his bed, still thinking about Pauline. It always affected him badly, visiting her grave. It was still somehow shocking to see her name on a headstone, and more shocking yet to see moss and lichen gaining a foothold already and the grass growing up around it. Joel had tidied it up, put on it the daffodils he had brought, and sat for an hour beside it. Not a religious man, he had no beliefs or notions about where she was and in what state of being.

The clock said half past ten when he heard the Humber pull up outside. The engine stopped and a moment later the front door opened and closed downstairs. He realised it was late for Jess to be returning. She was usually back by half past nine when she took the boy to school, even if she stopped to buy a few groceries in Princetown. Joel supposed she might have gone for a drive, seeing the morning was fine.

He was right, she had, cruising round the moorland roads, trying to sort things out in her head. She had found no solutions, ending up with nothing but an overwhelming urge to flee from Robert. Home to Alice. What a turnabout! She had come out here to escape the shop and the street. Yet now, for a time at least, she would be thankful to go back. There, if nothing else, she could shut the world outside at the end of the day. She could lock the doors, pull the curtains and be at peace within the house, without a watchful husband to criticise and accuse her, study her every move and pounce on any careless remark she made.

She had to leave him, take her boy and go. She would tell him when he came in for his lunch – not that there would be any lunch. Jess was going to spend the morning packing.

Joel heard quick, light footsteps coming upstairs, going into her bedroom. Shortly afterwards there were thumps, and the sound of something being dragged across the floor. Then cupboards and drawers were opening, closing, and all the time she was back and forth, in and out of Colin's room.

All the child's clothes were in a suitcase and all his favourite toys in a trunk by the time curiosity drew Joel out on to the landing. He went across to Jess's room and stood in the doorway, silently watching her cramming armfuls of garments into a valise. She was in no mood for orderly folding and arranging. Her possessions were flung and pumelled and forced into cases and carrier bags. Most of them were things that Robert had given her. They had little sentimental value now. She would have left them all behind, but she had to have clothes on her back. Jewellery, though, was another matter. She was leaving all but her wedding ring. The street gossips would not be seeing her without that.

'Jess?'

She whirled at the sound of Joel's voice.

'What's this? What's going on?'

'I'm leaving. I can't bear it any longer.' She went on packing, but paused to fling him a look across her shoulder. 'Oh, you should have been here at breakfast! You should have heard what went on!'

He stepped inside. 'Tell me.'

'Robert started bullying Colin. He's made him get rid of his pets. They're all gone, except the cats. Robert's orders.'

'Oh,' grunted Joel. 'Yes, he's been grumbling about them lately.'

'Well, that was just the start of it. Wait till you hear the rest. Robert's been rough on the child for months ...' She straightened up and turned around. '... and this morning I found out why. Know what he suggested? Something so shameful, so ridiculous ...' Her gaze locked with Joel's and she gave a mirthless chuckle. 'Do you know what Robert thinks? Can you guess why he's so harsh with Colin these days?'

Joel was silent, waiting.

'He has the notion the boy may be yours.'

Joel blinked. 'What?'

'Because Colin is so dark, because you're so very fond of him ...'

'Well, of course I'm fond of him! He's my nephew and I haven't a son of my own!'

'That's far too simple and innocent for Robert. He chooses to read more into it.'

'Oh, ye Gods! The idiot!'

'I can't stand any more of it, Joel, and I won't see my son persecuted because Robert's formed some cracked idea that Colin's not his own. He doesn't want us any more, either one of us. He's turned against me and against his son. I would have endured it, I would have stayed if Robert still loved the boy, because I can't offer Colin anything like Torvallen. But even the child is unhappy here now, and I'm afraid Robert will be more and more unkind to him as time goes on.'

'And if I step in to defend him, Rob will take it as yet more proof that the boy is mine,' said Joel, wearily.

'Yes. You understand.' She threw a few more items in the suitcase lying open on the bed. 'There's no way out of it, Joel, except for us to go. It's hopeless trying to talk to Robert. He distorts everything he hears and sees.' Pausing again in her chaotic packing, she looked at him, resigned and wretched. 'I suppose the seeds of trouble were there from the very start, like the first spores of dry rot in a building. Well, they've sprouted and spread and now it's all beyond repair.'

Turning, she went to the window and looked out. The moor was looking its best this April day.

'Everything's bright and new out there,' she murmured, 'just as it was when I came here first, just as I thought my life was going to be. Yet it's all gone rotten and fallen to pieces in the space of seven years. Do you know, he hasn't touched me since that horrible business with Maunder. It's as if he feels I'm unclean. I'm surprised he doesn't put the bolster between us. I believe he only sleeps in the same bed with me to be sure that I don't come to you at night.'

'Have you wanted to do that, Jess?'

She had not heard him cross the room, but his voice now came from very close behind her. She could hear every nuance in it, she could hear his tension and his hope.

'Time and again,' she admitted, quietly. 'There's nothing more lonely than lying with someone who keeps his back turned.' Bitterly, she asked,'You don't think I'm soiled, do you, Joel? You wouldn't be too fussy to touch me, would you?'

'You know the answer to that.'

'Yes, I do. And how I've been tempted. There were nights when he was so fast asleep he would never have known if I'd slipped out of bed and crept across to you. But like a fool, I opted to keep my conscience clear.' Snorting softly, she observed, 'Damned cold comfort, that is.'

Turning around, she scanned his face. There was longing in it, plain to see.

'We're both too honourable, aren't we, Joel? I didn't betray my husband, nor you your brother, and see how we're repaid for it.'

Wryly, he smiled in agreement.

'Well ...' she lifted the fall of hair from her neck and turned, presenting the row of buttons down the back of her dress, '... I think we've been honourable far too long.'

Through the haze of slumber, there filtered the sound of a door opening and closing. Jess stirred uneasily, but Joel did not wake. She opened her eyes and looked around her, briefly startled to find herself in Joel's room. She thought she had heard someone out on the landing, someone who had gone into one of the other bedrooms and then come straight out again.

Her bedroom – hers and Robert's.

He was home and he was looking for her.

He had come for his lunch and had been surprised to find she was not in the kitchen, that nothing was in the oven or bubbling on the stove.

Her glance flew to the clock – twenty past one. They had only meant to sleep for an hour! Her eyes turned sharply to the door, to the small brass bolt they had not bothered to shoot.

A floorboard creaked outside. She tried to sit up, shaking Joel by the shoulder. His cheek was pillowed on her breast and at first she could not rouse him.

'Joel, please ...' she whispered, trying to shift his weight. '... he's back, we slept too long.'

Joel's eyes were flickering open when his brother threw wide the door.

Robert knew the scene. He had pictured it a thousand times in his mind. The reality differed hardly at all from what he had imagined, and the words he uttered now were those he had rehearsed in many a grim fantasy.

'Just like a bitch on heat.'

His voice was hoarse and his face was the colour of lard.

Joel sat up. 'That's enough, Rob. She's here because you drove her to it. We've no excuses to make, we don't need them. You've made her miserable time and again, and today was once too often.'

'So today's the first time, is it?' came the mocking response. 'What do you take me for?'

Robert leaned in the doorway, pushing his hands deep in his pockets. An ugly grin distorted his features and within him there churned a peculiar stew of emotions. There was undeniably pain and anger – but also a strange satisfaction in thinking he had been correct about his wife and brother all along. He had not been unreasonable after all, he had been shrewd, perceptive. He felt oddly powerful, too, confronting this naked, guilty pair, for he had clothes on his back and, he believed, right on his side.

Jess's mouth had gone completely dry and her tongue seemed glued to her palate. But at last she managed to tell him, 'Go away, Robert, let me dress. I'll talk to you downstairs.'

'We'll talk,' corrected Joel.

'No. I want to see Robert alone.'

'Very brave of you,' sneered her husband.

'Please go,' repeated Jess, levelly. 'I'll be down in a few minutes.'

'If he hits you, I'll pulverise him,' Joel said, when his brother had gone.

'I don't think he will. He'd rather injure with words and I'm used to that. Anyway, nothing he says can hurt me much, now that I'm guilty.'

Nuzzling her ear, he murmured, 'Caught in the act, eh, Jess? Or very nearly, anyway.'

'An adultress,' she sighed, half-smiling. 'That much is true now. And I don't care. Virtue never gave me any protection from nasty minds.' Tousled and tired, she kissed him. 'Will you drive me into town when I'm ready? We'll pick up Colin on the way.'

'Of course,' said Joel, softly.

Her forehead puckered and she pressed a hand to his cheek. 'I have my escape, but there's none for you, is there? How are you going to live with him, Joel, and work with him and run your business?'

'I'm not.'

'But ...'

'You're not the only one who has to go. I've felt for a long time that I couldn't carry on. I've hesitated, because Torvallen is my home, but after this there can't be any question of staying here. He'd make it hell on earth. I'm going to sell out.'

'Oh God,' she whispered, 'see what I've done.'

'No,' said Joel, firmly, 'don't go thinking that. With or without you, it might still have come to this in the end. Even if Pauline had lived, even if Robert had married someone else. We don't get on, my brother and I, we never did. It's best for us to go our separate ways and I don't want to hear you blaming yourself.'

To please him, she nodded and said no more. But as she slipped out of bed and gathered her clothes, some words from years ago came floating back to her. In Mrs Rogers' corncrake voice, they echoed triumphantly:

'You'll cause more trouble than your mother ever did ...'

Robert was waiting in the sitting room, hands clasped behind him, nose and chin lifted in righteous umbrage, looking for all the world like a wrathful headmaster. Jess went inside, closed the door and faced him calmly.

She had no repentant speech to make and simply stood before him, ready to hear the tirade that was bound to follow. He was, she supposed, entitled for once to an outburst. Past injustice had moved her to fury and helpless outrage. No longer the innocent accused, she was almost placid now. It was all over, all lost – her marriage and her life here. He would not forgive, he would never forget, or allow her to forget it, either. Nothing could be mended after this.

'I wish,' said Robert, silkily, 'I wish I had a bucket of tar for you. Tar and feathers for a whore.'

Mildly, she parried that, saying, 'If it will make you feel better, I'll wait while you go and fetch some. Would you like to do it here privately, or down at the yard where everyone can see?'

Robert snorted. He went and sat down in an armchair, crossing his legs and steepling his fingers as if he were chairing a meeting. 'What's he like, then?' he enquired, tensely. 'Good? Better than me, I suppose? More exciting? More – skilled?'

Jess disdained to answer that.

'He always had a healthy rutting instinct. I daresay that's what you like. Plain, straightforward copulation, like a couple of dogs on a street corner. Still, I suppose you just can't help your inclinations or your upbringing.'

Her anger rose on Joel's behalf, the memory of peaceful, soothing sex still fresh in her mind. And yes, he was good, with his understanding and his patience, relaxed in that as in everything else.

'You may say what you like about me. Now that I've done the deed I couldn't care less. But don't talk as if Joel's an animal and you're something higher. Believe me, Robert, it hasn't been any uplifting experience with you these past few years. Many's the time you've made a coarse job of it. You can be a good lover when it suits you, but on the whole you're a lot less sensitive than he is.'

'That's a hasty judgement, if you've only had him once.'

Careless, thought Jess, to leave herself open to that. She sighed, then stated firmly, 'I'm going to say this, even though I know it's futile. Today was the only time. In all the years we've been together, I've never had another man until this morning. I loved you when I married you, Robert, and I've tried to be a good wife ever since. I'm saddened, so saddened, by what's become of us, but it isn't my fault. I daresay you hate me. I don't hate you. But I fear for you, Rob ...'

'There's nothing wrong with me,' he snarled. 'I live with a pair of alley cats, that's my only affliction.'

Her tone hardened. 'All right. You don't want to listen, so I'll waste no more time. I wish I had gone to Joel before, I truly do. As you no doubt saw, my things are packed and so are Colin's. You won't have the pleasure of throwing me out, because I'm going gladly. I'll miss this house, but I shan't miss you.'

Robert had taken hold of the arms of his chair, his fingers digging into the upholstery.

'Finished?'

'I think so.'

'Just as well, because nothing you say will justify your conduct, and no faults of mine will excuse it. No wonder you kept quiet about your background, Jess. A bad name and bad blood. Naturally, I'll be wanting a divorce.'

'I shan't fight it.'

'And I won't support a child that isn't mine. Let Joel pay for his bastard. I don't suppose he'll mind.'

Jess's look became pitying. 'Oh Robert, what a fool you are.'

He stood up and turned his back on her. 'Go home to your mother, Jess. Birds of a feather should roost together. That's where you belong, not here. Her place is more convenient for Union Street.'

Robert sat with his back to the window. He could hear them loading the luggage into the car but he would not look. Let her go, good riddance, her and her misbegotten brat. He hated her, hated all three of them, but Jess in particular for making a fool of him, using him. She had clearly admitted it, hadn't she?

'I'll miss this house, but I shan't miss you.'

She had never loved him. Robert was sure of that, now. She had simply wanted a better place to live, and perhaps from the very start she had felt an attraction to Joel. Most women did, after all. She might have been secretly glad when Pauline died. In his fury, Robert was willing, now, to believe any evil of Jess.

As for his brother ...

Robert heard the car drive away.

As for Joel, well, there could never be even a truce between them after this. It was not merely the end of his marriage, but the end of the Lawrenson partnership too.

Hours went by and still he sat in his chair, thinking back on the past seven years, distorting every memory and dismissing as pretence every little act of fondness Jess had shown him. As evening drew in, he stirred himself to light a single lamp and the lines of his face were dark and ugly in its yellow glow. When Joel at last returned, he found him still sitting there, grimly waiting.

'You've been a long time,' said Robert, coldly.

'I helped her unpack. And I went up to Burrator on the way home to sit for a while and think.'

'Reliving the passion, Joel? Savouring it again?'

'Partly that.'

'You ... !' Robert made a spitting sound. 'My God, you'd only just come back from visiting Pauline's grave.'

'She'd understand. She wasn't like you. You don't

understand anything. You think you do. You think you're sharp. Truth is, your impressions are warped half the time. Jess told me she asked you to see a doctor. I reckon that was good advice.'

'Oh yes, she said I imagined things.' He stabbed a thumb towards the ceiling. 'Did I imagine that up there this morning?' Then, almost gloating, he bent forward in his chair and grinned. 'How much do you know about her, Joel? I could tell you something very dirty, but you might not want to take my word, so ask around her neighbourhood next time you're there, see what they think of the Daveys.'

'If you're talking about poor Alice, I've known for quite some time.'

Robert's grin sagged, his bombshell defused. This meant, as well, that Jess had confided in Joel, as she never had in her husband.

'And that doesn't bother you?' he demanded.

'No. Alice is just a weak, unlucky soul. It always rains on people like her. You could have a bit more charity, Rob. Jess is made of stronger stuff. She'd never go the same way. Dear God, you were so fortunate to have her, and look what you've made of it all.'

'Oh, drop the pretence, for pity's sake! You're only too ready to step in, aren't you? Of course, that's why you haven't looked elsewhere for another wife. You had your sights set on mine all along.'

'All right!' snapped Joel. 'Have it your own way. I can't be bothered to argue with you. Look, I said I did some thinking earlier on. It's plain to me that you and I are going to have to split the property, Rob. There's no other course of action.'

'For once we agree. But I'm not leaving Torvallen. You're the one who'll have to go.' Spitefully, Robert added, 'I know she loved it here. Well, she'll never live under this roof again. I'm not going to move out so that you can bring her here. Who knows? She may not want you quite so much when she realises that. Jess married me for Torvallen.'

'We'll see. I guessed you'd probably dig in. All right, then, I know you can't buy me out, so I'll just have to sell my share to somebody else. It'll mean some stranger coming in, but that's your lookout. I wonder if you'll get on better with him than you did with me. Somehow I doubt it. I always made allowances for my own flesh and blood. But it's been hard, Rob, hasn't it? We should have been close, we should have been friends, but you would never have it so.'

In the lamplight it was difficult to tell, but he thought he saw a tremor of uncertainty flit over his brother's face, a fleeting glimpse of something akin to fear, or perhaps regret. Then it vanished and Robert asked:

'What will you do? Set up in opposition?'

'Nowhere near here. Dorset, perhaps. I like Dorset, and Jess would like it, too.'

Again his brother's feelings briefly surfaced in a look of pain.

'Rob,' said Joel, gently, 'I didn't take her from you. You threw her away.'

Robert's face hardened. 'That's what you do with rubbish,' he snarled. 'I'll be seeing a solicitor in the morning.'

· Thirty-three ·

Mrs Fitch was cleaning her windows. A trio of passing youths kicked her bucket over and booted it into the gutter, and she let fly some colourful words. A stray dog cocked its leg against a lamppost, and the dockyard hooter signalled the end of another shift.

The street never changed, and here she was again, back where she started, at least for the time being. Looking out through the shop window, Jess absently took the lid from a jar of gob-stoppers and let her son help himself. Three weeks had passed since she left Torvallen, with no direct word from Robert. There had, however, been a letter and papers from his solicitor. The wheels were already in motion. She dared not even contemplate the court proceedings, guessing the sort of things Robert would say, knowing he would contrive to bring up all the dirt about Alice. If only the law were not involved, if only the whole sorry business could end quietly. She wanted nothing from him but her freedom.

Freedom to go away with Joel. She had heard that Dorset was lovely. He came to see her almost every day, and was urgently seeking a buyer for his share in the house and business. The lives they had known were unravelling fast. The whole which had once been Torvallen and the Lawrenson family was sundered, like a tapestry slashed down the middle. Jess and Joel and Colin were left on one side, Robert and Torvallen on the other. Such destruction, enough to break her heart if she dwelt on it too much. Jess tried hard to think about the future now, since the past and the present were so disagreeable. Beyond the divorce there would be a fresh start and she made herself focus on that.

Across the road, Mrs Fitch was bending to pick up her bucket, buttocks straining at the fabric of her overall. The neighbours all knew something was up. Jess Davey was home, with her kid. A man came calling, a man who sometimes stayed the night, a man who was not her husband. He entered and left by the front door, bold as brass. They had even seen her kiss him in the doorway.

Straightening up, bucket in hand, the Fitch woman went stamping indoors for more water. Jess caught Colin cramming a handful of gob-stoppers into his pocket and took the jar away from him. He had settled into the local infants' school quite well, for which she was thankful. And he liked having Nan around every day, so the move from Torvallen had not upset him.

Jess's thoughts turned to linger on her mother. There was

something strange about Alice these days, something new in her. Physically, she was frail, and she made no effort, now, to hide the extent of her drinking. Jess no longer tried to stop her. She knew Mr Honey had been the final straw. But in Alice's temperament Jess had seen a change. A certain strength had grown in her, accompanied by a sharper tongue. Gone were the days when Mam would tolerate any imposition. Jess had heard her shout at the man next door to turn his gramophone down. The old Alice would never have dared, no matter how much it annoyed her. She had actually sworn at him, and he, from pure shock, had obeyed her. Lately, Mam was apt to chivvy awkward customers too, and tell them not to waste her time. More startling still, she had kicked up merry hell at the greengrocer's when he tried to sell her rotten apples and a slimy lettuce. Nowadays she had a gleam of challenge in her eye, and people who had always ridden roughshod over gentle Alice Davey were finding she had both bark and bite after all. They did not know she expected only a year in which to repay a lifetime of insults and scorn.

Jess did not know it, either. Alice had never seen fit to tell her of the doctor's warning, feeling that her daughter had worries enough without that. Jess only knew that Mam had been a fount of sympathy and support through these painful weeks, and was proud of the tougher woman inside the wasted body.

Alice was proud of herself as well – and that was how a splendid thing came about. If ever a symptom became a cure, that was what happened to Alice Davey. She was braver because she believed her days were numbered, and out of that bravery finally came a new outlook and, with it, determination to save herself.

To the end of her life she would always remember a certain sunny Tuesday, for that was when the turning point arrived. She was going into Plymouth that morning, and on her way to catch the tram she encountered the dragons outside the bread shop. There they were, Rogers, Fitch and

Bonnet, gabbing and cackling like three old fowls in a coop. She could hear them from thirty yards away, but the prattle abruptly ceased when they spotted her. They bridled as Alice drew near. They stared hard and she stared back. It pleased her to know she was looking smart in her best fawn frock and a brown cloche hat. As usual, they were all in aprons. For the first time, Alice truly noticed how squat her three enemies were, and she drew herself up a little to emphasise her height. Although she was terribly thin, she could still carry herself with grace when sober.

'Hmph!' said Gwennie Bonnet, as she passed.

Ignoring her, Alice went walking on. But then a raucous voice stopped her in her tracks. It was that of Mrs Fitch. She had to have something to say about Jess.

'What's your daughter doing home so long? Gone wrong, has it? What happened? Did he send her packing, or did she just get bored out there in the country? Bit of a comedown, whichever it is. At least my Brenda and her husband have stuck together.'

Alice halted. She thought. She walked back.

The women looked surprised.

'It's none of your business,' Alice told them, levelly, 'though I suppose that's guaranteed to whet your appetites, being the prying, impertinent things you are. Whatever I say, you'll think what you please, and what pleases you best is usually foul, because you feed on dirt, don't you, like flies on dog's mess? Only there's nothing on the pavements half so filthy as your minds.'

This from Alice Davey! Fitch and Bonnet were dumbstruck.

Not so Mrs Rogers. 'Hah! Listen to you! They do say attack's the best form of defence, but you can't sidetrack me like that. Come on, let's have an answer. Why's she here all this time? And where's her husband, eh? That's not him, that one who's been calling. Been up to mischief, has she? Oh, I wouldn't be surprised. I knew how she'd turn out.'

Alice considered her briefly, then she smiled. 'You know, Mrs Rogers, it's not only women who talk. Men do, too, especially in bed.'

'What?' Mrs Rogers looked puzzled, uncertain.

'They give away family secrets,' said Alice, softly.

Rogers took her meaning then, and her face began to register alarm. She had always suspected her late husband of a fling with Alice in their younger days. It had never before occurred to her that he might have told the Davey woman of certain things that went on in his home.

'How would it be,' continued Alice, 'if I were to go around gossiping about the way you treated your poor old father in his last years, when his mind started to go?'

'You ... !' Saliva spattered round the corners of Mrs Rogers' mouth. 'Slander! I'll have you up in court!'

What did Alice care, she who had little time left?

'You can try, if you like. But I'm willing to bet the doctor's records would stand me in good stead. I gather he had harsh words for you the night the old boy died.'

'Father had a stroke!'

'I'm not denying that. I'm saying it was a happy release after years of neglect and abuse.'

Alice turned to Mrs Fitch. 'Now you – I didn't need your man to tell me you're a thief. Every trader in this town knows it. Money, goods, anything you can pocket or stuff inside your coat. Caught once, weren't you, pinching pillowcases down at Jimmy Love's? Lucky you were pregnant and they let you off with a fine. If you were properly punished for everything you've ever stolen, you'd spend fifteen years in a cell.'

Mrs Fitch's court appearance was certainly no secret, but she had always passed off the incident as an emotional side effect of pregnancy, a single aberration. The local shopkeepers knew better.

Gwennie Bonnet smirked a little. In the way of their kind, the three cronies did not actually like one another. They simply shared certain antipathies and a relish of gossip. They would just as soon dissect each other as anyone else.

'You needn't laugh,' said Alice. 'Joe Bonnet was a happy

man before he married you. Took the bounce out of his walk and the joy out of his soul, didn't you, Gwennie? Let him have his way one night, then told him there was a baby coming and he'd have to marry you. Only there never was any baby, was there? No child then – or ever afterwards. You made sure of that, one way and another. Joe wanted children, didn't he, Gwennie? But you don't like them, do you?'

Mrs Bonnet blushed to the roots of her hair. She did not feel guilty for catching Joe under false pretences, or leading him a cheerless life and cheating him of children. But she had always boasted of going to the altar unsullied, and was stung to be revealed as a hypocrite.

'Well, well,' breathed Mrs Fitch, 'so it does have teeth and claws after all.' Alice heard a grudging admiration in her voice and wished she had bared those teeth and spread those claws long ago.

'I could go on,' she said, 'I could go into details. As I said before, some men are apt to talk a lot in bed. Of course, I've never been one to repeat things. Still, anyone can change. You think about that, all of you, before you say anything more about Jess.'

'Found a mite of courage, it would seem,' observed Gwennie, dazedly, as Alice marched off.

Of the three, only Mrs Fitch remained unshaken. She had never been ashamed of her sticky fingers. Pilfering, to her, was something of a sport, and she quite appreciated Alice Davey for returning fire.

The Rogers woman, however, was looking very uncomfortable, and the other two exchanged knowing glances. They, too, remembered her poor old father and his bruises. She had always claimed he was clumsy, forever falling about.

'Funny, isn't it?' mused Mrs Fitch. 'When Alice was young and bonny, she wouldn't say boo to a goose. Now she looks ready for the embalmers, she's found a bit of backbone.'

*

Alice rode into town on the tram, triumphant. Sitting upstairs in the open air, she surveyed the city and felt like an empress making a glorious entry into Rome. She could almost imagine the pavements lined with cheering, petal-throwing crowds. Alice could hardly believe what she had said. She had doled it out, and they had taken it. How easy it had been in the end, this thing she had so often dreamed of doing but never dared. Her nerve had held, the right words had come, and she had emerged the winner! Alice would never fear them again. Like bullies everywhere, they only had to be beaten once.

Arriving in the city centre, Alice walked up Bedford Street to Popham's department store. A smart shop, Popham's, with wood-panelled walls and lofty assistants. There, she spent an hour poring over the pattern books. She was going to make some new summer frocks for Jess. There were memories attached to almost every garment Robert had bought his wife – uncomfortable memories, or ones that filled her with a tearing sense of loss and grief for the briefly happy marriage which had gone so terribly wrong. Alice had decided that Jess should have some fresh, bright clothes to help revive her spirits. She knew her daughter was dreading going to court.

Eventually she left the shop with patterns, fabrics and buttons for three dresses. Expensive materials they were, too – she had spent nearly five pounds altogether. It did not matter. Jess was to have the best. How much longer would Alice be around to sew for her?

Having no other errand in the city centre, Alice headed straight back towards the stop to catch the tram. She was taking more than dress materials home to cheer her daughter. How Jess would laugh when she heard of the confrontation outside the bread shop. How delighted she would be. Alice could scarcely wait to tell her.

Had she taken the next tram, Alice would have been home by half past two. Halfway to the stop, however, something occurred to delay her. Passing by a restaurant, she was halted by the sight of a sumptuous window display.

Alice had thought she had lost all interest in food, but this was a spread that caught and held her attention by its sheer gorgeousness. In the centre was an arrangement of shellfish on a bed of crushed ice – oysters, scallops, mussels, king prawns. There were platters of roasted game birds ornamented with their own striped and speckled feathers. A lobster, glazed and shiny. A great roll of gammon stuck full of skewers, on which were impaled cherries and honeydew melon and chunks of fresh pineapple. There were carrots, courgettes and aubergines, sliced and set in aspic with chicken and ham; then a basket of cheeses and bread sticks, and a great round venison pie. Chocolate, whipped cream and nut desserts, frothy mousses with raspberry purée, syllabub flavoured with sherry, a golden apricot flan ... Such a show – enough to awaken appetite even in the lean and haggard woman reflected in the restaurant window.

It all looked so beautiful – and suddenly she seemed to see it through Kenneth Honey's eyes. She could almost hear him saying:

'Look, Alice, how pretty! The chef in there is an artist, he loves his work. What colour, what design! See the trouble he's taken! My dear, it's calling to us, we must go in.'

Yes, it did appear to beckon. The fruits were like jewels, the shellfish plump and moist and glistening, the meats delicately pink or richly brown, all the garnishes crisp and the puddings fluffy. A scent of mingled sauces drifted out through the doorway and hung around seductively. Alice looked at the menu and the prices, while the traffic of Bedford Street roared by. She still had quite a lot of money in her purse – over four pounds – and could well afford a meal.

A short curtain was drawn across at the back of the window. Alice peered over the top of it, pressing close to the glass. There were not many people inside. It was ten to two and the lunchtime rush was over.

'Last Orders for Luncheon at Two,' said a note at the foot of the menu.

She was tempted. Very tempted. It was something she had never done, to go into a restaurant by herself, and in her newfound boldness Alice felt inclined to take the plunge. She had fought and vanquished three foes that morning and deserved a treat in celebration. She was perfectly presentable today, and after all, there was really nothing to fear. What was the worst they could do – ask her to leave because she was a woman on her own? Laugh and sneer because she was a working-class person, out of her depth? Sentence of death had taught Alice that scorn and ridicule were unimportant in the scheme of things. Anyway, her money was as good as anyone else's, and she was ready to say so, if she had to.

Resolved, she went inside. A grey-haired waiter saw her hovering, looking all around her. He hurried forward, smiling.

Yes, he assured her, of course Madam was in time to order. Where would Madam like to sit? He indicated all the tables free and ready laid.

Alice chose and was ushered to her seat. The waiter fussed around, bustling back and forth, fetching a menu, a bread roll, and then a single half-open rose in a narrow vase to ornament the table.

Alice stared at the menu. At first it all jumped up at her at once, so she made herself read slowly, item by item. The waiter stood by, a tall, lean figure in his black trousers, white jacket and bow tie. Alice ventured to ask him about some unfamiliar dishes and he was more than happy to explain. She pondered a little, then opted for onion soup with parmesan cheese, followed by scallops baked in white sauce with juicy little mushrooms, then the venison pie with broccoli and new potatoes.

Something to drink? enquired the waiter.

Alice asked if they served gin. Alas, no, the waiter was gravely sorry. So she ordered a carafe of table wine instead. Wine was all the same to Alice, as long as it was not too sweet. Not her favourite tipple at all, and she would not waste her money on anything with a fancy name.

The food arrived quickly. It was good – extremely good. Alice ate slowly, savouring it. She had felt conspicuous at first, sitting here alone. But no one took any notice of her, except her own attentive waiter. Around her the other patrons concentrated on their meals, their companions. The staff cleared tables, relaid them, pottered about at the sideboard or the cash desk. She was not, after all, a focus of mocking or critical eyes. A sense of peace and pleasure settled on Alice. It was all right, all smooth. Again she had dared, and everything was well.

Now then, dessert? Oh yes, she certainly would like something from the trolley. Lemon soufflé? Good idea. Followed by a little cheese? prompted the waiter. No, Alice could not manage that.

Coffee, then? He had noticed that the carafe was nearly empty. He rarely saw a woman drink like that and remain unaffected. Alice divined his thoughts and assured him she needed no coffee.

I could do this every week, she thought while eating the soufflé. I could have done it half my life, just as I could have faced down those three harpies long ago. All it takes is a bit of nerve. Why did I have to find mine so late, now, when there's little time left? Why did it take terminal illness to bring it out?

She laid down her spoon beside the empty soufflé dish and reached for the carafe. There was about a glassful left in it. Alice had never been one to leave a drop of drink. She always drained it all, unable to throw away even the tiniest trickle.

But her hand wavered now; her fingers hovered about the neck of the carafe and many seconds passed before she finally grasped it and poured the wine. It was greenish-gold in the glass, and pleasantly scented.

Alice wanted it. She lifted it to drink – then put it down again. It gleamed, reflecting the restaurant lights, waiting to be swallowed.

For Alice Davey, a draught of poison. There it stood, alluring, fragrant – and suddenly sinister. Alice stared at it and felt a chill. Too late? Was it too late now? Several months had passed since the doctor's warning. She had not even tried to stop.

Alice looked through the window, out at the street, all the people and traffic. Life. Noisy, hurried life, full of toil and problems, hurts and let-downs. Still, the sky was blue today, and across the road outside the florist's shop were baskets and pots and tubs of brilliant flowers beneath a red and white striped canvas awning.

Kenneth had lived for such things. Again she could almost hear him speak. What was it he had said the first time they met?

'I firmly believe it's the secret of happiness.'

What had she lived for, apart from Jess? Men, she supposed. They had been her delight and her downfall. She had never felt there was any life without one. For the loss of Kenneth Honey she was drinking herself to death. He would be appalled if he knew.

'But Alice,' he would say, 'there's so much else. Food tastes just as good when you're on your own. Sunshine's just as warm, birdsong sounds the same. You could still see Scotland by yourself, if you wanted to. And you don't need me to take you into a restaurant now, do you? Or to a theatre. Good company is lovely, but it isn't everything. Fancy making yourself so ill, all on account of me. Do as the doctor tells you, my dear. See how strong you've been today. You don't need anyone or anything to prop you up.'

Alice looked again at the wine. Was it really impossible to do without her drink? Did Jess really need the shop, if she had Joel? Was there still a choice, though? Perhaps she had left it too long to recover.

Or perhaps she was tougher than the doctor had imagined.

Pushing the glass away, Alice called for her bill, paid it and left the waiter a generous tip. She stepped out into the sunshine, charged with a heady feeling of strength. She could live to be eighty. Yes, she could. Her body could rally, even now. She sensed it. The reserves were there, and her mind was set to summon them. She would stop the drink, return to health, and see her grandson grow up. She would not disappoint that nice young doctor after all.

Alice's gaze returned to the baskets of blossom outside the florist's. Sweet peas, pink and mauve. She loved sweet peas. She would buy a big bunch and take them home. That, too, was something Alice had never done before. She had always loved to receive flowers from men, but buying for herself had seemed extravagant. Kenneth had never thought so. He had bought himself a fresh buttonhole every day.

Alice crossed the road, selected a bunch from the tub and went in to pay for them. Coming out again, she started off towards the tram stop. But after a few yards she paused, considered, and turned in another direction. To complete this very special day, Alice was going home in a taxi.

· Thirty-four ·

Torvallen was a lonely house these days. The brothers took their meals at different times and avoided one another as much as they could. They spoke very little and would not sit in the same room together. When both were at home, each was tensely aware of the other's presence and movements about the house, of doors opening and closing, footsteps on the stairs or clatter from the kitchen, and each was always glad to hear the other go out.

At work it was not so easy to ignore one's partner. Joint decisions had to be taken, discussion was sometimes required. And so there were curt consultations, grudging compromises, and all the time a general air of impending conflict. The employees had a fair idea of what had happened. They knew that Jess had gone, and that Joel was selling out. It made them all feel worried and insecure.

Small wonder, then, that Joel soon felt the need for a break from the situation. His only happy hours were those he spent with Jess, and so, one evening in August, he suggested a holiday.

'We could have a week down in Cornwall,' he said. 'God knows, I need to escape for a while, and it wouldn't hurt you, either. You've been looking peaky these last few weeks. We should go away for a change of scene before the summer ends.'

'Am I – looking peaky?' She glanced at him from under her brows.

'Perhaps that's not the right word, but there's something, Jess. You're not entirely yourself.'

An odd smile crossed her face. 'That's very true.'

Joel went on eagerly, 'A few days on the beach would do you good. And Colin would enjoy it. What do you say?'

'I don't need a rest cure, Joel.' She sounded amused.

'I know you're apprehensive about the divorce. I suppose you're thinking it'll just give Rob more ammunition, but ...'

Jess laughed at that. 'Oh, he has quite enough already.'

More than he knows as yet, she thought. More than you know, either. Oh my, we're going to have a spectacle in court.

'Well, then?' pressed Joel. 'Shall we? How about Perranporth?'

'All right, perhaps it would be nice. It certainly can't make matters any worse.'

They went down by train the following week, and stayed in a hotel up on the cliffs.

The first few days were beautiful and they soon felt the good effects. The beach was a great golden plain beneath a royal-blue sky and pure white horse-tail clouds. Sharp winds flicked spray off the big Atlantic breakers as they reared and curled over, the sunlight darting through them.

The Lawrensons set out early every morning, equipped with bucket and spade, bat and ball, stripey towels, sandwiches and bottles of lemonade, and remained on the sands till the incoming tide drove them off.

Joel bought Colin a little wooden yacht with a cotton sail, and hours were spent propelling it back and forth across the rock pools, prowling with a net in search of tiny fish among the green weed, or picking up shells, pebbles and bits of mother-of-pearl. They busied themselves with little engineering projects, building castles, then jumping on them, burying each other up to the neck in sand, or digging connecting channels between one pool and the next, while Jess reclined in a deckchair, reading a novel, or dozed away the hours with a straw hat over her eyes.

'Your colour's come back,' said Joel, one morning.

'I think I've caught the sun.'

Jess reached for the holdall they had brought, pulling out the three packed lunches the hotel had provided. She was in a blue swimsuit today, and Joel in shorts. His upper body was perfectly smooth, but his legs were darkly furred. They were spending the day in the dunes, in a hollow of hot, dry sand surrounded by marram grass. The tide was a long way out, the sea a distant stripe of blue. Colin, tireless, had spent all morning charging up and down the banks of sand. Fine and silky, it poured down after him, filling his footprints as fast as he made them.

Joel stood up and stretched, facing out to sea.

'Where's that boy?' he wondered, aloud. 'He must be ready for something to eat.'

Jess paused in what she was doing, looked a moment at his back, then hesitantly said, 'Joel – don't call him yet.'

'I thought it was time for some food.'

'It is. But I have to talk to you about something, and I feel like doing it now.'

He turned. She had laid the bag aside and her gaze was on him, intent and slightly nervous.

'Something wrong?'

'No, I wouldn't say that.'

'Well, then?'

'Do you really plan to stay with me, Joel?'

'God's truth, you know I do!'

'Will you never feel bitter about Torvallen? Never blame me in years to come?'

'I've told you often enough that it isn't your fault.' He came round behind her, sat down and pulled her back against his chest, long legs outstretched on either side of hers. 'It'll be a wrench, because it was my home and I loved it. But I'll love it less and less if staying there means living in a state of war with Rob. Anyway, it's only bricks and mortar. I wouldn't trade you for that.' He folded his hands together over her belly, kneading and stroking as he spoke. 'I didn't mention it before because I wasn't certain, but I think I've probably found a buyer who'll give a good price for my share. He'd only be a financial partner and that would suit Rob very well. He likes to have the running of the place.'

'All on his own,' murmured Jess. 'Alone in that house, with all of us gone.'

Joel heard a tinge of sadness in her voice. He turned her face towards him.

'Jess, do you still feel for him?'

'I'm sorry for him, Joel. And I remember how he made me happy at the start, and lots of dear, nice things he said and did, before his demon got the better of him.'

For a moment Joel was uneasily silent. The wind went rustling through the marram grass and the sound of Colin's yodelling voice came faintly from the foot of the dunes.

'If he had a change of heart, would you go back?'

'No,' said Jess, 'because it wouldn't last. I don't think he could genuinely forgive me. And I couldn't live there, knowing you'd had to leave. I tried my best to come to terms with him, and I've had enough.' Drawing a deep breath, she added, 'Anyway, it's impossible now. There can't be any reconciliation. There's an extra complication, you see. That's what I have to tell you. I've known for over a week, but ...'

'Known what?'

'I'm pregnant, Joel. You're going to have your own child, after all.'

His hands were still for a second or two, then he pressed his fingers flat against her belly.

'Are you sure?' he whispered.

'I've seen the doctor. It won't show yet, not for a month or so, but it's there.'

'Jess!' Joel threw back his head and whooped for delight. His own, this time truly his own! It was much, much more than he had hoped for. He would have been content with Jess and Colin, but to have his own child as well ... ! 'Lord! Oh, Jess, that's grand! That's wonderful! I never thought to see the day!'

'I'm glad you're pleased. What do you want it to be?'

'A girl would be nice. Whatever it is, I'll be daft about it.' His arms went tightly round her waist and he playfully bit her shoulder. 'When will you start to have cravings? I'll fetch you anything you fancy, no matter when you want it.'

'No matter how horrid.'

'No matter the cost,' finished Joel.

'It was sour cream and sardines while I was carrying Colin.' Her smile faded, she looked down, running her nails through the hair of his forearms. 'Of course, this is going to make the divorce uglier than ever. I don't suppose the child will be born before the case is heard, so I'll have to waddle into court with the evidence filling out my frock. Nobody's going to understand what I went through with Robert. I don't expect much sympathy from the judge.'

'It'll be just another case to him. I'm certain he'll have heard far worse. Whatever he says, you needn't take it to heart.'

'And I'm used to condemnation, aren't I? What's a little more?' She leaned her head back, looking up at him. 'Are you going to tell Robert about this child when you go home?'

'He'll have to hear sooner or later.'

'Yes,' she sighed. 'If only he didn't. I'm afraid it's going to hurt him badly, after all those years of trying for another one himself. Lord, I wish he didn't have to know.'

The fine weather lasted one more day and then it broke. Rain clouds came in from the west on the Friday evening, carrying a soaking drizzle. Jess and Joel and Colin wandered round the town in mackintoshes, whiled away an hour in the little shops, had fish and chips for lunch at a café, then took the branch line train into Truro to see a cowboy film.

That night, rolls of thunder slowly approached and passed overhead, and sheet lightning glared through the curtains a dozen times over. Jess lay awake beside Joel, listening to gushing rain. She could hear it streaming from a broken downpipe and gurgling into a drain somewhere. She had always hated heavy rain, the feel of it pounding on her head and skin like a million tiny blows. It had rained like this on the day she met Robert.

Jess turned over, seeking Joel's warmth. She had been feeling so much better before the weather changed, cheered by the sun and Joel's welcome for the child inside her. But the sound of the rain disturbed her tonight, and she found herself filled with a vague apprehension. She was still nervous about the divorce, she supposed. What else could be playing on her mind? Perhaps it was just that the holiday was nearly over. Naturally the thought of going back to the street made her feel despondent. Yet, there was something else as well, a kind of low-keyed fear for which she could not pin-point any precise reason.

If only there were silence, if only that pattering and trickling would stop. She tried to sleep, but could not, and the rain went on and on.

The downpour continued all the next day and the three stayed inside the hotel. Jess had brought a few of her son's favourite toys in case of bad weather, while Joel had shown the foresight to order magazines and comics at the reception desk. They came with the morning papers, and kept Colin quiet through the hours between meals. The

Lawrensons read the newspapers, plus the *Sketch*, the *Bystander* and the *Windsor Magazine* from cover to cover. Beyond the window of the lounge, beyond the cliff edge, the sea and sky were grey and violent. Three miles of empty beach stretched into the distance.

When Sunday dawned, however, the sky was clear again. Colour and warmth and the sense of well-being returned. The Lawrensons sallied forth after breakfast to spend their final day among the pools and dunes.

· Thirty-five ·

On Dartmoor the mires were glutted with rain. The streams that drained them were all in spate, gushing down from the high ground to feed the rivers and send them storming through the valleys. Water, deep and turbulent, chewed away the banks on either side, ripping up bushes and saplings. The debris rode away on the flood, and reinforced its power. At Torvallen, the river's flow became a raving, headlong charge, and its voice was no longer a chuckle, but a roaring and hissing that echoed far into the woods. Here and there a tree toppled, as churning water cut the soil from under it. Sometimes the river took it away, sometimes it lay to rot among the ivy on the bank. And sometimes it came to rest across the torrent like a bridge.

Late on the Saturday evening, such a thing occurred four miles upstream from the sawmill. With a despairing groan, a young oak tree fell. Its roots gave up, tearing free of the mushy ground, and its head came down on the opposite bank. Very soon, the flotsam borne on the river began to build up around it – twigs, shrubs, dead stumps, even a sack, half a barrel and a cart-wheel collected by the marauding river, came to a halt, snagged among the oak tree's branches. By Sunday morning, when at last the rain stopped, nature had constructed quite a dam.

Robert had worked on Sundays ever since Jess left. He did not know how else to pass the time and keep his mind off her and his brother. Joel always went into Devonport early on Sunday mornings, to spend the whole day with Jess and Colin. The fact that they were all in Cornwall this week made no difference. Robert would spend his solitary Sunday at the yard as usual. It was better than moping about the house, gnawing at his wounds. He always saved himself a job for Sunday, something strenuous to tire him out.

The woodland track was very muddy and the leaves still dripped as he made his way to work that morning. With his eyes on the slippery ground and his mind on what he meant to do, he did not notice then that the thunder of the river had died away. Reaching the timber yard, he opened wide the sawmill doors, stepped inside and went straight to the switch to turn on the circular blade.

The generator stuttered feebly, the saw made a sluggish half-turn, then stopped.

Robert pushed the button again, and then a third time, with the same result. He went outside. The waterwheel was revolving only slowly. The river's force was less than normal, even after all that rain. Robert guessed the reason straight away. It was not the first time this had happened.

The only course was to go upstream and try to find the obstruction. Even then, there might be no way to shift it without other men to aid him, but Robert had nothing else to do except try. He tramped back along the soggy path to Torvallen to fetch the mare.

For half an hour he rode along by the river, where tons of earth had been gouged from the banks, leaving dark brown scars. As he travelled, his thoughts pulled uncontrollably towards Jess. They were vengeful thoughts at first. He rehearsed what he would say in court, the tone he would use, even his facial expressions. He pictured the judge listening with sympathy, imagined the way that everyone present would turn censorious eyes on Jess and Joel. He could see her hang her head, ashamed at last. Even his brother would fidget and stare at the floor, for once embarrassed, for a change the target of disapproval. Both would be soundly lectured from the bench and everyone's heart would go out to Robert. They would say he had married a Jezebel, poor man, that he was too good for her.

By now, Robert was well beyond the boundaries of Lawrenson land. He had passed the spur of track which led up on to the Postbridge road, and the path beside the river was very narrow here. Before long it would dwindle away to nothing and the valley would become a steep-sided rocky cleft.

The track lasted long enough to bring him just within sight of the dam. Robert climbed down from the mare's back and walked the rest of the way, pushing through thick undergrowth until he reached the tree.

Around the oak had accumulated a mass of vegetation, a hopeless tangle of branches and logs and shrubs, mats of grass and roots torn away from the banks, a barrier beyond his power to break. The river was spilling through it in a shallow waterfall, and the surplus was flooding out on either side, swamping the ground for yards around.

Robert paddled up to the base of the fallen tree. It was nearly submerged by now, and water was pouring over the trunk. He uttered a few strong words. Not only would he lose today, but it could take all of Monday, too, to deal with this. No vehicle could be brought up here to pull it free with chains. It was going to be a difficult task and this was not his property. He knew the landowner – a tardy, awkward man more likely to hinder than help.

Again his thoughts swung towards the divorce. His solicitor, too, was somewhat unhelpful, in Robert's opinion. The wretched man seemed to have doubts about his petition, especially where Colin was concerned.

'What if the boy is yours, Mr Lawrenson?' he had asked. 'Don't you feel you're being hasty, casting him aside? Your wife maintains even now that he is your son. Why should she do that, if it's untrue?'

'To make me pay for his upkeep,' Robert had snapped. The solicitor had admitted the possibility, but without much conviction.

'She admits her adultery freely enough, does she not?' he had pressed. 'She doesn't seem a devious type. Think about it, Mr Lawrenson. I say again, what if he is your child? Surely you'll want rights, if not custody? Even if you are uncertain about him, would it not be rash to reject him altogether? I have to warn you that the court may consider your attitude and reasoning rather odd, not entirely rational ...'

Irrational. Robert felt a shaft of fear go through him. What if he was wrong about it all? What if he had been wrong all the time? Which was worse, he wondered, that or being right?

Had he driven her to it? Had he? Joel's words came back to spear him.

'I didn't take her from you, you threw her away.'

Anguish welled up in his soul. Whatever the truth, it meant suffering for him. Pain if she had deceived and betrayed him, pain if he had wrecked and ruined things himself. In truth it hurt less to believe her guilty than to entertain the thought that he had created this mess. He had caught her in bed with Joel, and he clung to that fact very fiercely. It armoured him against the fear that he might, as the solicitor had gently suggested, be 'not entirely rational.'

Frustrated, Robert whipped off his cap and kicked out at the roots of the tree. Nothing went right for him, did it? Even natural mishaps seemed calculated to annoy him.

He had a good mind to drop that solicitor, go to another – one who would agree with him, one who would not make the upsetting suggestion that he might have discarded his own child. Robert could not visualise his future at all. He could see Joel's, all right, but not his own. Remarriage, more children, he could not envisage those things. He would have his vindictive day in court and then there would be nothing.

He stared at the dam. It looked so solid. And yet it was largely made of little flimsy things – sticks and leaves and knots of root. Without the tree, it would never have been.

Without his jealousy ...

Robert recoiled, but still the comparison forced its way to the forefront of his mind. What a structure he had built – and with what? Little flimsy things. Suspicions, imaginings, misinterpretations, then gossip, then hints, then lies ...

But he had caught them together. He had!

Still, it was the only sturdy, significant item in the whole case he had constructed against his wife.

'Perhaps you ought to see a doctor, one who understands the mind ...'

Robert's eyes filled up and overflowed. Water went on frothing, white and swirly, through the latticework of wood and foliage choking the river. It fell in bubbling cascades, and through the blur of tears reminded him of Jess's hair.

That beautiful, beautiful hair.

In his mind's eye, the woods and the river faded away. Instead he saw, outlined in the flickering light of the cinema screen, a girl in a tam, eating pear drops, a girl who didn't want to talk to him at first. And then, outside in the rainy street, a girl who was not at all keen to get into his car. Images followed in quick succession, memories of things she had worn and said and done, meals and clothes she had made for him. The blue frock she wore to the Gilbert and Sullivan concert. Her face that day in Mevagissey at his first accusing outburst. Colin's birth, the Fair Isle sweater, all her smiles, her pleasure in his presents. Then the wary looks, the fights, the pleadings, the smiles growing fewer and fewer. Her glow had gradually died down, until she was resigned and joyless. Where was the sparkle to hint of a secret, lustful affair? A jumble of impressions, in no particular order, went clicking through Robert's mind like lantern slides, and out of them emerged at last the dreadful, certain knowledge that he had indeed driven her – and his son – straight into the arms of his brother.

What have I done?

His mouth formed the words, but no sound came out. His eyes, unseeing, were very blue and childlike.

God help me, what have I done?

It was awful, too awful, he could not bear it. He seemed to hear Joel's voice again, calling him a fool. His wife, his son, his brother – his good brother – he had cast off every one of them. Robert wanted to halt the destruction and set all the wheels in reverse, but he feared it was already far too late. He could stop the legal proceedings, but that would not be enough. He could not imagine being forgiven. Nor could the feelings between Jess and Joel be made to evaporate now.

The silent tears became racking, shuddering sobs. He dropped to his knees on the flooded ground and rocked with the anguish of remorse. Had he brought the shotgun with him, Robert might have used it on himself just then, such was his misery.

After a time, however, he grew calmer. Slowly he stood up and walked back to where he had left the mare. He did not care about the fallen oak any more. In a day or two he would see to it, after he had dealt with matters more important. Jess would be back from Cornwall tomorrow. Robert would go to visit her and offer her a choice. She could return to him if she so desired. If not, he would give her a quiet divorce when the time required by law had passed. Robert held out no great hope that she would choose to come back. She would not want to leave Joel out in the cold, and never again could they all share the same house together. Jess would doubtless opt for the dignified divorce. Robert hoped they could come to some arrangement over Colin. Holidays, perhaps, at Torvallen with his father.

Crumbs from the table. The scraps from his own banquet. Robert rode slowly homewards. With the energy of hatred gone, he felt terribly tired and empty now. His fault, it had all been entirely his fault and now he was resigned to paying the price.

He had covered perhaps a mile and a half when a movement across the river caught his eye. Among the trees on the opposite bank, he saw a figure searching here and there, then crouching down, apparently digging at the ground. The man's back was turned, but Robert recognised the clothing, the unkempt hair, the bony haunches and gangly legs.

All his fault? No, not quite all.

'A green demon,' Jess had said. 'He's always been there.'

Perhaps. But it was a bearded demon who had really started the rot, a grinning, fawning man who turned spiteful when thwarted. Dartmoor had its devil, all right, and there he was, across the river. Not a spectacular, sulphurous devil with horse and hounds, but a base and sneaky devil who smelt of mould.

Robert brought the mare to a halt and watched him for a moment. He could see now what Maunder was doing – setting a snare. Robert hated gin traps, and people who used them. He would have liked to wrap that wire round Maunder's neck and pull it very, very tight.

The heat and force of hatred came surging back and it felt good. Over there was a truly deserving target for it, and Robert was all too glad to shift some of the blame. There he was, the teller of tales, dropper of hints, attacker of women, taunter, all-round mischief-maker. Robert's sorrow became red rage and he gave it free rein.

Maunder heard a rattle of hooves, then a wild splashing as Robert urged the mare across the river. The green eyes bulged in the bearded face when Maunder saw the horse and who was on her back. He dropped the snare and sprang to his feet as the mare came bounding up the bank towards him. He saw murder in Robert's eyes and he took to his heels.

He dodged among the trees, scurrying madly from one to the next. Lawrenson plunged after him, weaving the mare between the trunks with a speed and skill that amazed and horrified Maunder. He tried to run this way, that way, but was always headed off. All he could hear was his own panicky breathing and the thump of hooves ever beside or close behind him. Robert had not spoken a word. He had nothing to say to Maunder, he simply meant to beat him to a pulp. For Jess. The viaduct had not been for her. Robert had done that for himself. Belatedly, this was for Jess.

After a couple of minutes, Maunder tripped. Robert was off the mare in a trice, and hauling him to his feet. Alec Maunder had never been good with his fists. He doubled over, shielding his body and face with his forearms, just taking the blows and making no attempt to strike back. His balled fists were pressed protectively over his eyes and forehead.

It further infuriated Robert. He wanted Maunder to fight, but this was like punching a dummy.

'Stand up!' he bawled. 'Come on, hit me back, you cringing thing!'

In answer, Maunder sank down to a squatting position, still folded up like an armadillo.

'God damn you!' Robert exclaimed.

In pure frustration, he raised a foot and shoved Maunder over. The man rolled on to his side, still tightly curled.

Robert was above kicking him. Defeated by passive tactics, he stood panting, glaring down at his enemy. Yes, the only real enemy he had ever had, apart from himself. He had sought a proper fight, like the one in Ottery that night. He had been prepared to take as much as he gave, almost by way of penance. But Maunder would not co-operate. He was not going to serve out punishment to Robert, or give Lawrenson any honourable means of punishing him. He was just going to lie there and cower, giving no satisfaction at all.

'Oh, you're not worth the effort, are you?' growled Robert. 'I might as well be whipping a dog, and I'm ashamed enough already.'

For a moment he stood watching the man on the ground,

then suddenly he lashed out with a foot. It ploughed through the leaves and earth an inch from Maunder's face. Maunder gasped and shrank, but made no other move.

Robert turned and stalked off, contempt in every line of him.

One of Alec Maunder's fists uncurled. A finger moved aside and a green eye peeped out. There was Robert a few feet away, about to mount the horse. He had his back turned.

A hand slid stealthily into Maunder's trouser pocket and closed on a knife. Drawing it out, he unfolded a blade five inches long. He moved very swiftly then, and his footsteps were just a light patter over the earth. Robert had one foot in the stirrup when the blade went into his back. His only thought as he died was that he had been a fool again. His body thudded to the ground. The mare rolled her eyes with a nervous snort and backed a few paces.

Now it was Maunder's turn to stand over Robert. It had been an impulse. He did not regret it. He smiled to himself, remembering the viaduct, and tucked the knife back in his pocket. Then he bent down, grasped the body under the arms and dragged it to the river bank. There, with a nudge of his foot, he sent it rolling down into the water and watched it drifting away.

The mare still waited among the trees, but she shied away when Maunder went towards her, and galloped off. Coolly, the man returned to finish setting his snare.

A little later, however, it occurred to him that he might profitably have gone through Lawrenson's pockets before pushing him in the water. Perhaps he had a watch on him, perhaps a note or two. Cursing his oversight, Maunder scurried after the corpse.

While he followed it, something happened upstream at the dam. There came a splosh and a sudden cracking noise. Where the current was washing the earth away from under the head of the oak, a section of bank had collapsed. The tree moved slightly sideways, and now lay at a slant across the river. Some of the debris floated free and bigger gaps appeared. The tinkle and splash of the waterfall became a stronger rush.

Maunder knew nothing of that as he scuttled along by the water's edge in pursuit of Robert's body. Soon he could see it ahead of him and he started gaining on it. The current took Robert nearly a mile downstream before his clothing snagged on something in the water, which anchored him a few feet out from the bank. Maunder waded in. A pity it meant getting wet, but he thought it might be worthwhile.

Robert's pockets yielded only half a crown. Around his neck, however, Maunder saw the St Christopher medal Lawrenson had always worn. Real gold, with a good, thick chain. That would fetch a pound or two, all right.

Upstream, where the river had eaten away another portion of the bank, the oak tree moved again. It rolled as support dissolved beneath it – then the whole structure subsided with a groan and began to come apart. In a wave like the Severn bore, the water heaved forward, carrying on its crest a ton of logs and branches.

Not until it was almost upon him did Maunder hear it coming. He was too absorbed with the clasp of that gold chain. He did not want to break it, the jeweller might pay less. By the time he noticed the added force in the current, and the whoosh of the oncoming wave filtered through to his greedy brain, the surge was in sight and moving so fast that he had not a hope of escape.

His mouth dropped open when he saw it. His expression was more of stupid surprise than terror.

It hit him like a speeding train, battered and crushed him among its wreckage, tumbled him over and over and beat him under. The corpse was carried many miles, as if the river wished to spit him out to sea.

The flood took Robert's body as well, but not very far. It left him among a clump of reeds, quite near the spot where he had always loved to fish.

· Thirty-six ·

On Plymouth Hoe there was a shelter, facing out to sea. The seat was of slatted wood with wrought-iron arm-rests, and a fancy ironwork crest ran along the ridge of the roof. Two women, very much alike, sat there one Easter day. The younger held a month-old baby in her arms. Everything was sharply blue and green, and daisies dotted the grass. Not far away, by the statue of Drake, a man and a small boy were kicking a ball back and forth. Further over towards the bandstand, an elderly couple and their three grandchildren were flying kites, red, yellow and white.

The baby began to whimper and the older woman said:

'She's hungry. You'd better feed her soon.'

'I know,' replied Jess. 'We'll go in a while, when those two have finished their game.'

She shook her head and laughed a little to see Joel slip and land on his backside while running for the ball. Colin's peal of mirth came ringing across the grass.

'So he's delighted it's a girl?' asked Alice.

'Yes. He wanted a daughter.'

'Dorothy,' murmured her mother. 'It's a nice name.'

Jess grew pensive for a moment, then she said, 'I can't imagine how Robert would have taken this. I remember saying that I wished he didn't have to know. After what happened, it sometimes makes me feel I wished him dead.'

'No, Jess, that's being silly.'

'I suppose so,' came the sigh. 'If only I knew exactly what occurred that day, how it came about. I imagine all sorts of things and I know that Joel does, too.'

'The police have little doubt about who did it.'

'Nor do we. The brute still had the knife on him when they fished him out at Dartmouth. Joel thinks there must have been a fight, which was how they both ended up in the river, but Lord knows who started it or why. What preys on my mind is the fear that it might have been to do with me.'

'You can never know, Jess. Nor can you do poor Robert any good by worrying about it. He's gone and that's that.'

'That's that? Well, yes and no. In one way it's made things oh, so simple for Joel and me. And yet, because Robert's dead, and because of the way he died, his shadow falls across us still. We no longer think of him angry, difficult, unkind. What haunts us is the way he was when Joel finally found him there against the river bank. He said he looked so pitiful.'

Alice turned her daughter's face towards her. 'Jess, that shadow will disappear in time. Life will give you new concerns and joys to drive it away. In the end, I believe, you'll remember instead the good years you had with Robert. That was how it was for me after Kenneth went to gaol.' Her brows drew together. 'At first I kept on seeing him in that awful prison garb, with those dreary brick walls around him. Bars and echoing passages and the crash of slamming doors – it grieved me to know he was in that terrible place. I was always thinking of him there, day in, day out.' She paused and her expression lightened. 'But eventually I started to see him in his own lovely clothes again, laughing and playing his violin, or enjoying something I'd cooked for him. Those are the sorts of things that I choose to recall these days. You must do the same with Robert.'

Jess contemplated her mother and smiled. Mam was the wise one nowadays. Alice was still thin and her face was lined. But she was also well-groomed, and her leanness now suggested not frailty but a kind of emotional sinew. There was certainty and calm, the air of a woman who had won through. She was, in truth, grateful to be alive and was making the most of it. Had she not stopped drinking when she did, Alice might have been dead by now, as she was keenly aware.

The baby cried softly and Jess quieted her with gentle joggling.

'There was a period after the funeral when I felt like a trespasser at Torvallen,' she said. 'I felt almost as if I had no right to return, as if Robert knew and resented me, that he would say I was taking advantage of his death.'

'Joel's home is your home,' said Alice, firmly.

'Yes, well I'm glad to say that feeling's passed, but it was so strange for a while. I've settled in again, now, and Joel is relieved that he doesn't have to go away. The men are certainly glad he's carrying on.'

She heard a shout of 'Foul!', glanced up and saw that Colin had seized the ball and was dashing off with it under his arm. Joel went loping after him. As it followed the two running figures, Jess's gaze was led towards the pier, and her memory called up that day nearly twelve years ago when she had sat there alone and longed for somewhere to escape. And – Hey Presto! – the wish had been granted, or so she had thought. So much for trying to run away, so much for easy solutions. She had probably now found peace at last, but it had taken far longer than she expected, and the road had been a rough one.

Alice broke in on her thoughts.

'Didn't tell you, did I? Gwennie Bonnet stopped me last week when I was out wheeling the baby in her carriage. She noticed the pink layette and said to me "A girl this time, I see." Yes, I told her, a lovely child. We're very proud of her. She just nodded and she said, "Hmm, looks like a Davey, all right." Then she walked on and I heard her mutter, "Another bad penny." '

'Tch,' snorted Jess, softly. 'Did you take her up on it?'

'No,' scoffed Alice, 'I ignored it. I wouldn't waste my breath. They don't upset me any more – and anyway, what's the use?'

'True, it wouldn't change a thing. That's how they'll always regard us – a couple of bad pennies.'

'Two wanton women,' agreed Alice.

'A pair of strumpets!' declared Jess, mimicking Mrs Rogers.

Both of them laughed aloud. Then Jess said, 'Mam, you could come and live at Torvallen, you know, and never see them again. Joel mentioned it to me the other day. We'd both be happy to have you there.'

Alice looked out over the Sound, to the thin line of foam where the sea washed against the breakwater.

'Perhaps when I'm older I shall. But who knows how many children you're going to have? You never can tell, you may need all the rooms.'

Colin was scampering round and round the base of the statue now. Joel, exhausted, had had enough and subsided on to the grass. The boy went and flopped down beside him and together they watched the dipping, soaring kites.

'What would they all find to gossip about if ever you went away?' mused Jess. 'I reckon they'd miss you, Mam.'

'Lord, no. They'd talk about somebody else, that's all.'

'Oh, they do that anyway, they always have. It's just that you're their favourite, the choicest topic in town.'

And again they laughed, because they did not care any more – which, as Joel had once said, was the only way.